Exalted Father
THE BOOKS OF MARDUK

Anthony M. Alioto

This is a work of fiction. Names, characters, places, and incidents either are the product of the author's imagination or are used fictitiously. Any resemblance to actual persons, living or dead, events, or locales is entirely coincidental.

Copyright © 2018 Anthony M. Alioto
All rights reserved.
ISBN-13: 978-1975747749
ISBN-10: 1975747747

Illustrations © 2018 Luciano Alioto

To John Yonker

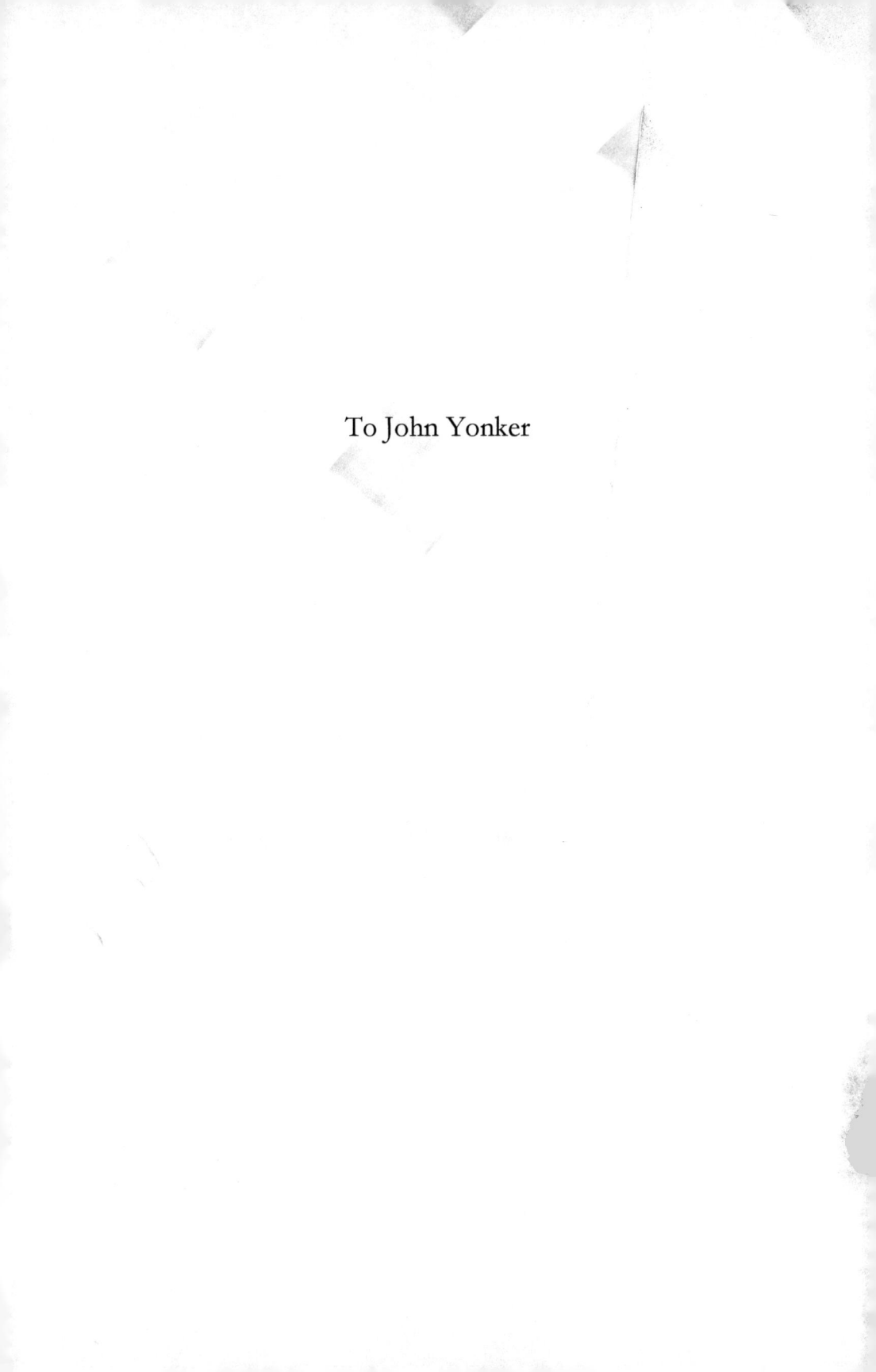

THE RECOVERED BOOKS OF MARDUK
(presented in accepted scholarly order)

The Book of Silence pg. 8

The Book of Winds pg. 140

The Book of Plagues pg. 214

The Book of Confessions pg. 337

The Book of Runes pg. 447

Supplemental 1 pg. 619

Supplemental 2 pg. 621

A Modern Commentary pg. 625

Exalted Father

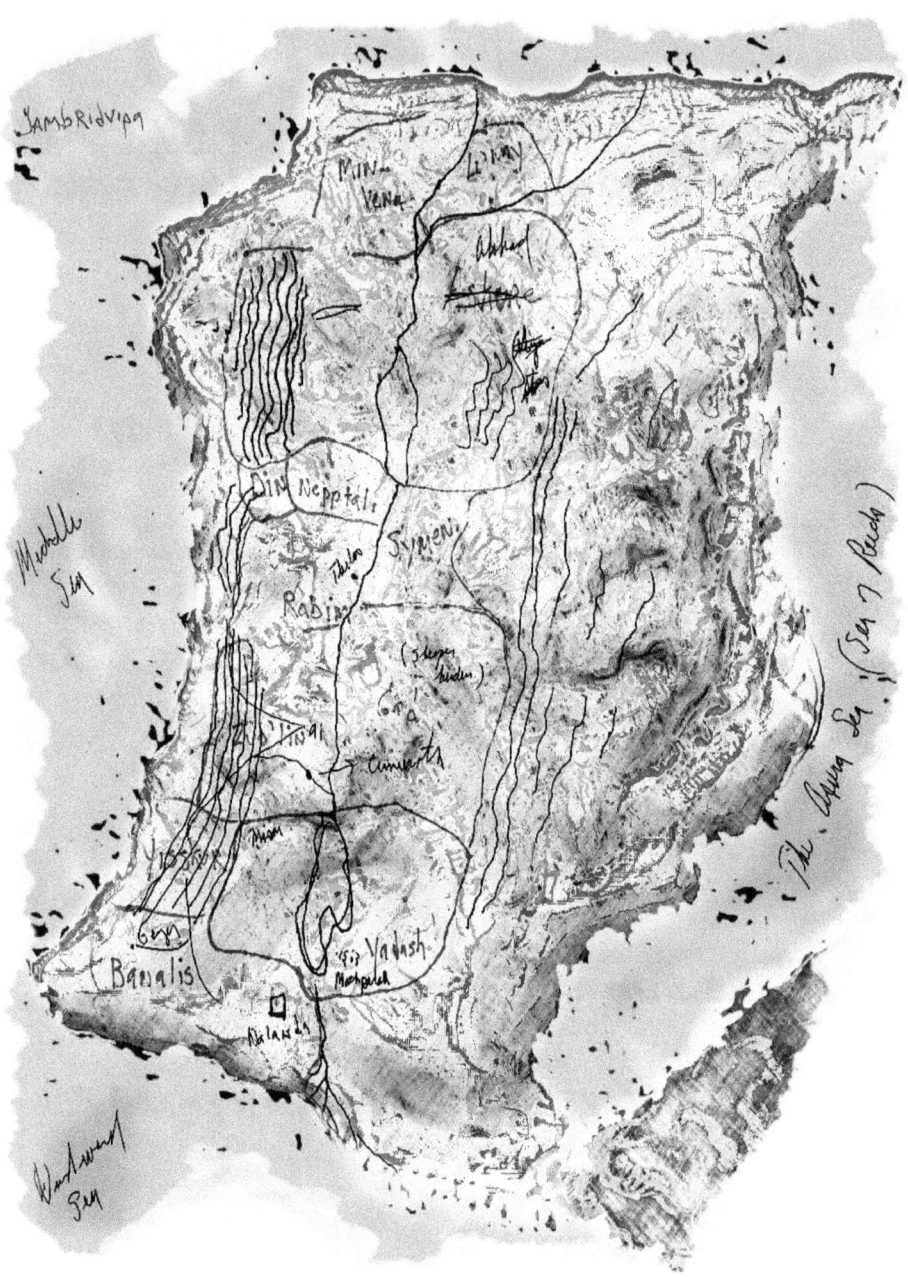

THE BOOKS OF MARDUK

EXALTED FATHER

THE BOOK OF
SILENCE

THE BOOKS OF MARDUK

PASSAGES FROM THE
RUNEHAYANA

Katha, Book II of Part One. *The Books of Elsseleron* (The Lord's Holy Mountain).

The following is re-calculated, transliterated and translated into Sandi by the *sramana* Marduk, former priest of Nalanda.

Verses from the First Chapter:
1. When the Lord fell from The Kingdoms of the Heavens and came to rest on the Holy Mountain [....] Our world was (without) the sacred order of the Kingdoms.
2. The Light of the Lord banished the darkness. Even the daystar (as it is named by the most ancient Runes: *proxima centauri*) became dim in the Lord's brilliance.
3. The Lord's fire melted stone and earth [....] Elemental matter became fluid and yielding (like hot wax).
4. The Divine One caused it to rain acid (forty days and nights).
5. What of the world primordial before the appearance of the One Lord? Priests and Seers searching their hearts say they know. Perhaps they (do not).

Verses from the Second Chapter:
1. And the Lord scooped up the fiery soil as a potter scoops mud from the bottom of the River Pearldew.
2. And the Lord exhaled His divine breath into molten mud. Behold, the Lord's breath bore words (of design) or [....] (syllables of creation). And the Lord said: "Let there be Kingdoms of the Heavens reborn on this world."

6. The Lord's words soaked into the sizzling dirt like water into the heat-cracked surface of Edom Desert. (A cool spring in the desert waste and welter). The Lord's breath brought forth life.
7. Who heard the words of the Lord? (Who observed and preserved?) Was there another?
8. Priests (and *Seers*) seeking in their hearts ask: Were (Where are) there others?

Verses from the Fifth Chapter:

9. Why now this silence? Some priests (oh, blasphemy!) said that the Lord became old. Had a stroke. Emigrated. Went home. Abandoned Elsseleron (and returned to the Kingdoms of the Heavens).
11. Cursed is the Third Kalpa (called the Kalpa of Silence). Divine silence, oh brothers (and sisters), is deafening.

THE BOOK OF SILENCE

CHAPTER ONE - The Yakashas Steppe

VERSE 1.1.1

In the beginning of spring Grand Duke Rudra met the Lord.

More precisely, Grand Duke Rudra came to the conclusion he met the Lord. The journey to this conclusion took some time and cost him not a small amount of effort.

Their meeting was quite unexpected, at least for the Grand Duke. Who can say what the Lord expects, if He expects anything?

The propitious event occurred east of the ancient Yadish Bridge where the Pearldew River once flowed into Red Lake.

(Let us perverse the memory of ancient days and speak of those times as though time itself did not flow. Come, fellow travelers…)

…and having crossed the stone bridge, the traveler discovers an irregular series of shattered rock steps that climb out of the river valley. The stairs are actually an ascending series of outcroppings. The old priests claimed that the series was a ladder built by an ancient race of giant beings. Giants once inhabited the valley, but that ancient race had vanished with the coming of the Yadish Tribe. Destroyed by the Lord, priests wrote, adding to hoary legend as they are prone to do.

Exalted Father

Contrary to the lying pens of priests, the Yadish claim the victory.

During the time of the Grand Dukes, before the coming of the Yadish Unified Kingdom, the massive rock stairs were dubbed Joseph's Ladder after Joseph one of the first Grand Dukes, not Joseph I the first King, although these two, nearly a Kalpa apart, are easily confused.

Mounting the ladder (not an easy task for a man of Grand Duke Rudra's years) brings the intrepid traveler to a great plateau that priests say stretches all the way to the Sea of Reeds.

Long ago, perhaps in the First Kalpa, priests named these grasslands the *Yakashas' Steppe*. And having named the steppe, they immediately cursed it and declared it evil, as priests are in the habit of doing.

Blessed (or cursed) with fertile minds (the only fertile thing about them), the ancient priests imagined a grassland world of wicked monsters they dubbed *Yakashas*. These creatures haunted the steppe and preyed upon the Tribes of Men.

Grand Duke Rudra scoffed at such stories. He often remarked that all sorts of monsters lived within those thick volumes of papyrus books that filled the library of Nalanda—and only there. Things being what they are, it turned out he was gravely mistaken.

The word "Yakashas" means *imp* or *wisp* of the desert. Some priests said it could also mean *red devil*. Other priests laughed at this translation. Red devil, they said, better fit a certain kind of Banalis brandy, much favored these days by the archbishop himself. The popular word was *Redfolk*.

"Nightmarish denizens of feverish dreams" (one of of Grand Duke Rudra's sarcastic witicisms), such creatures lured unsuspecting travelers to a grisly end. They dined upon human males, a real delicacy. What they did with human females was so shocking the priests dared not commit such lurid tales to writing. But many priests dreamed the stories in vivid detail, and their dreams were far from delicate.

In his old age—he was seventy-five—the Grand Duke ridiculed just about everything priests said. Had he known, it might have surprised him that the current archbishop shared his cynicism.

The Grand Duke had given up all *belief*. Over the years he'd discovered that belief was bad for sleep. Meeting the Lord changed all that, he said. But much later.

In those days the Tribes of Men believed very little of what the priests taught.[1] What sane person was able, or possessed the patience, to decipher their convoluted writings? Their words were as thick and knotted as Banalis vines in midsummer. When someone like the wandering *sramana* Marduk did try to explain the *Runehayana* to the Tribes, the ideas ended up sounding quite infantile when they made sense, and quite mad when they feigned profundity. Most people laughed and shook their heads, and went about their business. Everyone knew *sramanas* were cracked, or cracking.

Nonetheless, common sense, which Rudra called common prejudice, warned that venturing into the steppe was bad for one's health. Golden grasses, tall yellow-flowered daisies, thick colonies of wild lilies growing to the top of a person's head—pollens, spores, dust and who knew what else—made the steppe into a cesspool, not unlike the polluted Grand Canal of the disgusting Ra'bim Tribe. The Lord had not created the Tribes of Men for life in the wild. The steppe was mysterious and mystery was always dangerous, priests warned, and in this case most people believed.

What stands at the beginning of received wisdom, the Grand Duke often asked? One day the youngest noble of the Tribe,

---

[1] According to ancient queeti poet-historians, the disjunction of "these days" and "those days" indicate the existence of two sources sown together by some unknown redactor. The source hypothesis is ridiculed by some, but we will generally adopt it here as it does seem to explain problems within the text.

Exalted Father

Viscount Vladimir, a man in his sixties, told the Grand Duke to his face that all wisdom came from the Lord of Lords. Duke Rudra roared with laughter, reminding many of his father, the Laughing Duke. He shook his overlarge head from side to side as though to avoid a buzzing insect. He snorted and repeated his admonition about common sense, which he thought of as common nonsense.

"And the most common, and therefore the most empty, is the Lord," he added, which became another wisdom saying of his, which he uttered often in the hope that some scribe would record his words since it was beneath his dignity to write his own wisdom book like some self-inflated priest; although, if he couldn't be King he dearly wanted to be remembered as Duke Rudra the Wise. Of course, since he'd given up all belief, he shouldn't have believed his own wisdom. At times, however, belief was useful, especially when it came to his own person.

That one of those dangerous mysteries of the steppe might be the Lord of the Mountain made little sense, common or otherwise. That the Lord Almighty would suddenly and unannounced appear to such a one as Grand Duke Rudra (why not a priest?) … Well?

THE BOOKS OF MARDUK

BOOK OF SILENCE
VERSE 1.1.2

Yesterday he'd come to the fortified citadel town of Machpelah, the southern-most Yadish outpost east of the river. Nearly a century ago during the time of his father, the Laughing Duke, a terrible disaster had befallen Machpelah. It is written that an army of Yakashas sacked the looming citadel of cut stone, twenty-foot walls, soaring towers, and magnificent mansions. The fortress's entire population had been slaughtered and, according to not a few hysterical priests, *eaten*. Despite the fact there had been no survivors, and therefore no eye witnesses, priests knew every detail and wrote the story in many, many volumes.

The legend (now history) goes on to say that Rudra's father had laughed at the news, living up to the appellation "Laughing Duke." He'd done nothing about it. Much of his reign had been dedicated to the arduous task of doing nothing. Nothing is best, he often said. The best ruler does nothing and when nothing is done things happen of themselves. He did do one thing—he laughed. He even laughed when the title was taken from him in the uprising. The son saw nothing humorous in *his* wisdom. The son seldom laughed.

Grand Duke Rudra devoted his life to atoning for his father's sins, as he defined them. And, as it turns out, he is judged in these latter days as having been generally unsuccessful. He never rebuilt Yadish power. He never regained the title of King. It is whispered among the Tribes, especially the hated Akkadeans, that he sired only one son who disappeared, or died, or went into the priesthood, or became a Yakashas meal, no one knew what. Some whispered that the boy was not his. He denied these rumors and blamed them on the envious Akkadeans. He sired thousands, he claimed—apparently, he wasn't joking. Many of his own Tribesmen called him Grand Duke Delusion.

So, a bitter Grand Duke Rudra stubbornly refused to believe in the existence of devils or divine beings who called themselves Lord, even after he met one. Normally, a divine encounter ought to have shaken any person's unbelief in divine things. If the sudden appearance of the Lord forced Rudra to believe, he refused to admit to himself *at the moment of the encounter* that he believed. Of course it might benefit him to believe, but that was another matter.

The Lord, after all, never called His divine self the One Lord, the Lord on High, the Lord of the Mountain, the Almighty, or any of the numerous titles priests bestowed upon His august-but-mythical character. For all Rudra knew there may have been other Lords, other Mountains, other on-Highs—perhaps this Lord was not the *One* he should worship, if he were capable of worship in the first place, which he was not.

Rudra knew that the priests could not even agree on the origin of the word *Lord*. The two Runes whose probability combinations yielded *Lord* in plain Sandi could just as easily give the word *ma-quah*, which Rudra understood to mean literally *mouth*. Naturally when priests babbled about the One Lord of Elsseleron they lied. More precisely they lied more than usual.

Grand Duke Rudra held onto his unbelief like a child who covers pages and pages with its written name, forming the letters in a ritual of self-assertion. In his seventy-fifth year a strange being appeared to him and tried very hard to change his mind.

THE BOOKS OF MARDUK

BOOK OF SILENCE
VERSE 1.1.3

Grand Duke Rudra savored the solitude of the steppe. In years past, he traveled about his duchy with an army of nobles and a large routine of peasants armed with bows and pikes, and over a dozen L-guns. He did this mostly to enforce taxes, but he also liked the feeling of power, fancying himself King of the Unified Kingdom.

Nowadays L-guns fizzled and went dead. Nepptali technological expertise had precipitously declined in the last century. No Nepptali craftsman knew how to repair an L-gun. No Nepptali had the faintest idea how one was constructed, or so a wandering *sramana* had told him. The same held for almost all other types of technology, except basic simple machinery—and, of course, the still.

He never believed anything he'd heard about the Nepptali. They were a secretive Tribe. While they provided weapons to all sides, they never took one side or the other in the Great Akkadian War. They possessed their own version of the *Runehayana* it was rumored. Their lands were poor and desolate. No one had visited them, no one had even spied a Nepptali in nearly half a Kalpa—except the *sramanas*, and being priests they were liars, the two words being synonymous.

Nowadays no Yadish Lord cared to venture beyond the Pearldew. None of the great nobility felt an overwhelming need to expand their fiefs eastward. No one paid taxes, and the Grand Duke had given up trying to enforce the laws. He might as well be ruler of the green-skinned Minvena Tribe where people lived in slimy, moss-decorated wells like frogs.

Rudra preferred the bleak emptiness of the grasslands. For brief moments he shed the burden of his years. He walked less stooped, a bit more erect and dignified, as in the days of his youth. Rudra of a thousand sons. Of a full head of hair.

Exalted Father

Like a leaky wine-barrel the Yadash Tribe slowly bled people without hope of refill. No more births. No woman had conceived in a generation. Rule over such steady decay was about as satisfying as commanding an army of corpses. The Tribe had become as dry and barren as the land itself. He had heard it said from a wandering *sramana* that all the Tribes suffered the curse of barrenness—which included the Tribe of Akkad, to his great satisfaction.

This particular morning the northern gusts of Greater Wind felt a bit warmer. Pale yellow and flawlessly empty, the sky appeared as a washed crystal dome, free from the smudge of clouds and the poisonous smog of *kittim*. At dawn the steppe glowed like an ocean of gold. Greater Wind stroked it like the hand of the One Lord stirring a tranquil sea. At dusk, with the coming of Lesser Wind, a new fire touched the golden waves, igniting the world into flames of color, into red and orange and gold and silver.

In recent years—and this was strange—bird and insect songs filled the silent air. Rudra thought he heard the muffled sounds of scurrying life in the high grasses as spotted mosscats hunted brown marmots. Maybe he would see a farvel.

In the Book of *Surya*, the Lord on High ordered the destruction of these creatures, and many, many more. The Tribes of Men had done their best to obey. In *those days* the Yadash Tribe had taken the lead. They held the record in the divine exercise of extermination. Naturally the Akkadeans challenged this claim. The Grand Dukes, they sang, killed thousands, but the Akkadean Khans killed tens of thousands, and tens of thousands beyond that.

In *these days* of divine silence, the annihilated came back to life and sang to the Grand Duke. He inhaled the perfumed air and felt young again. He wondered if he might be able to sire another child. He'd need to consult with Miriam of course, if the child was to be legitimate. Instantly his mood soured. He checked himself and decided not to pursue *that* thought.

He sighed and pulled a few more white hairs from his beard. In recent years he found himself becoming prone to what he thought of as *moments of distraction*. His mind simply slipped out of gear. Spinning freely, his brain churned out visions, illusions that took shape and danced before him like scantily-clad Tribal girls of many a priestly dream. His aged mind created sounds, manufactured odors, and generally behaved quite badly. It skipped too, from one thought to another, in no logical sequence, as a bird from branch to branch.

He was starting to behave like a priest, he thought ruefully. All priests were really old men at heart, even the youngest of them--who were actual old men anyhow. Rudra was determined to resist the great temptation to give in to his visions and treat them like revelations. The place most suited to resist temptations was the wilderness—which was another of his proverbs.

Stubbornly, he wandered the steppe in the season of rebirth. Stubbornly, he clung to the *will not to believe*. Stubbornly, the world refused to cooperate.

Then, like the steppe, the Lord surprised him.

EXALTED FATHER

BOOK OF SILENCE
VERSE 1.1.4

Early spring and already the daystar baked the steppe in colors of gold, yellow, brown, and here and there a hint of green. A gentle breeze brought the sweet aroma of newborn morning grass to his nostrils. He inhaled deeply.

He mounted a gentle slope which was the final rung of Giant's Ladder. From this rim-like bluff running north and south, the ground leveled off to a vast flatland. Rudra shrugged off his ducal great-coat and let the warmth of the daystar penetrate his silk shirt. The shirt was embroidered with Runes representing the Yadash Tribe. It was dingy yellow. Gold had been the color of the Yadish Tribe. In the Third Kalpa gold faded to yellow.

The heat messaged the pain from his old joints. The moist air seemed to oil his weathered skin, smoothing the wrinkles and healing the cracks. Once a stocky, muscular man, the years had melted his flesh away until he was a collection of loose bones within a bag of leathery skin held together by tendons and muscles that were little more than memories. Memories came filled with wide gaps, which the Grand Duke had little trouble filling. When memory clashed with imagination, pride took the lead— He had been a man of immense power, restless energy, immense appetites and virility, exalted above others, the father of a thousand sons. His name was well known, even to the humblest peasant of the smallest Tribe in the smallest corner of Greenbottom, though the river valley lacked *corners*. The Two Winds bore his name to all the lands, he said.

He stood and inhaled the aromas of life. He drifted in the soothing warmth, frail old age draining from his body, the gaps in his mind filling, his memory strong. Rudra, Duke of Proverbs, the Winds sang, father of multitudes.

And up popped the Lord.

At first, the Lord appeared to be a pillar of fire striding through the grasses—a torch so bright that in its brilliance the daystar disappeared, as the verses supposedly sang. The Grand Duke of the mighty Yadash Tribe lowered his eyes as though he were bowing.

The Lord mounted the slope, *ponderously* a priest might have added—they were certainly fertile in useless words. The Lord's size was ponderously impressive. He—or it—towered over the Grand Duke who was himself—more truthfully *had been*—one of tallest men in all Greenbottom. This fact is impossible to verify: by ancient tradition Yadish Grand Dukes were the tallest men among the Tribes of Men, therefore Rudra had to be the tallest man[2]. Proportionately massive, although somewhat stiff-legged—if not oddly inflexible—the divine-Lord-torch walked, or rather lurched, like a marble statue temporarily granted life.

As the statue of stone came closer, Rudra saw that the Lord possessed the blazing fire on loan. The Lord-pillar was a thief stealing its flame from the daystar. Dressed in a full length white robe that looked as if it had been chiseled from flawless marble, the Lord did not shine blinding light of his own. He reflected.

The Lord's eyes were featureless black. Everything else about *him*—the Lord, Rudra decided, was male—his shoulder-length hair, his skin, was pure white and seemed to be made of the same marble as his robe. Rudra found it difficult to say where exactly the Lord's flesh ended and the Lord's robe began.

The Lord's face was without distinguishing feature. Smooth as glass, it apparently lacked those fine facial muscles that mean so much in human exchanges. Nothing the Lord on High subsequently did or said disturbed the uncanny tranquility of His face. If the Lord

---

[2] A queeti scribal interpolation according to many modern scholars. We will indicate such interpolations only when there is a scholarly consensus.

was perfect as the priests taught, which seemed to be the case, perfection was surely boring.

Rudra inhaled and repressed a laugh. The Lord suddenly became interesting.

The Lord had a tail.

The Lord's tail was His only body part that did not seem chiseled from marble. Extending beyond the hem of his stony robes, scaly and reptilian, His tail swayed and jerked in agitation as though it were subject to continual and uncontrollable spasms.

Wait until the priests hear about this, Rudra thought with pleasure. He anticipated a deep satisfaction in mocking the old drunken archbishop with this bit of news. Later, when he had the time to ruminate over his encounter, he decided that the opportunity to mock the priesthood was one of the reasons he decided to believe that this *thing* was the Lord.

"We are the Master of Starmirror," the living block of milky stone declared in a deep stony voice. "We rule the continent south of Jambridvipa, which is home to the Holy Mountain Elsseleron. It is named Starmirror."

Rudra decided that the Lord must be speaking in the third person. For reasons priests were never able to explain, the third person happened to be the normal speech pattern of divine beings. The thought came to him that this creature might just as well be a Yakashas. This idea he dismissed as suddenly as it had formed. It was hard to confuse red with white, even for priests.

This was the Lord, at least for the time being. At age seventy-five Rudra no longer cared about self-contradiction. He decided long ago that the world was insane, so why worry about triviality such as logic? This walking slab of stone may well be the Lord even if the Lord did not exist. He had a proverb that covered such cases: *What does not exist does so, and it can really fuck with you.*

Naturally, words assumed logic in the first place. Otherwise, how could he express such trivialities? But this was another triviality, and so another of his proverbs.

"Say what you have to say, Lord. I don't need a geography lesson. By the way, if you're the Almighty shouldn't you be ruler of *everything*? And you're blocking my light. And don't play games. I'm not one of those damned superstitious Gads who think they hear the voice of the Almighty in the screech of an owl. And be quick about it—"

Rudra mustered his deepest ducal voice. This ought to do for openers, he allowed.

Not a twitch of anger marred the perfect face. The monotone voice betrayed no emotion. It sounded mechanical, like a recording.

"Come forth from this land, you and your Tribe.

"Bring your women. Bring all the women of all the Tribes—

"Come forth and cross the Windward Straits.

"To Starmirror will you journey.

"The way will be revealed to you—

"Those who refuse, We will destroy—

"Those who oppose, We will blot out, as a flood cleanses the world—

"Even their names will be no more, their memory vanished forever.

"As the farvels, as the whittlings, as the queeti, as the guam, as all the others who were not…

"Of the Kingdoms of the Heavens—

"And you We will make great."

Rudra gave an exaggerated yawn. "I'm already *great*."

"Are you great in offspring?"

The question, if a question is what it was—and how could he tell with such a flat voice—startled him.

"I am the father of many." He tried to sound convincing. It struck him that the Lord ought to able to detect lies. Well, he could always say he was speaking symbolically like a damned priest. But the Lord on High apparently accepted what he said at face value. It amused him to think that the Lord was a literalist

The tail flicked as if swatting an insect. The mask of a face remained impenetrable.

"How many?"

"Very, very many. Like the sands of Edom. I have many wives, you know, as befitting the Grand Duke of the most powerful Tribe in all Greenbottom. My sacks are overflowing. My women are young and fertile. They keep me quite busy. Many other Tribal princes wish to marry their daughters to me. But I am forced to refuse. Who'd have time to govern?"

And the Lord said to Rudra: "Bring these wives to us, to our fortress-city, so we may know them.

"And We will bless you.

"And ten thousand tribes shall issue from *Our loins*,

"Like the stars of the Kingdoms of the Heavens.

"If you could count the stars, Our offspring would still outnumber them.

"And We will make you Exalted Father,

"Holy Father.

"Like a son to Us will you be."

Thus said the Lord.

The *Lord* seemed a bit confused, Rudra thought. Surely he meant *your* instead of *our*. The offspring he promised had to belong to Rudra. Stone did not give birth to flesh. And how could the Lord, who priests claimed was a spiritual being, have *loins*? But then, spiritual beings and living stones seemed infinitely far apart.

"I will consider your generous offer, O Lord."

The tail snapped like a whip. "Do not tarry."

"I have questions." He was feeling more confident. Apparently he was able to deceive the Lord with impunity.

"Do not tarry."

"I have questions. Exactly what does it mean to be Holy Father?"

"Do not tarry."

Either the Lord was unaccustomed to having his divine words questioned or he'd become like one of those old Nepptali gramophones that stuck in a single grove and played the same song over and over.

"Do not tarry."

Rudra yawned. He turned his back to the Lord (a deadly insult among the Yadish). "I cannot, uh, *tarry* here any longer and bandy words with, uh, a stranger, Lord or no. Tribal business urgently requires my attention—"

He paused, yawned again, and then ventured a backward glance to see if this brought a crack in the stone.

Empty space had cracked instead. *The massive white Lord had vanished.* The strange being left behind no trail of light or crushed grass. Neither a grinding of stone nor swish of tail.

Rudra rubbed his eyes. He perceived a faint flash of light slicing through the grasses. For a weighty piece of stone, the Lord moved quite fast. Maybe the priests were correct. Stone was spirit. But then he considered that the stone might be nothing more than the play of daylight on ancient eyes.

He did like the idea of being chosen by the Almighty. He liked the sound of *Holy Father* too. Even at his advanced age he still might have the opportunity of becoming the greatest Grand Duke of the Third Kalpa. He'd become King.

It would take a considerable effort, but he just might be able to convince himself that the encounter was real. That this was the Lord on the Mountain—come down, of course.

EXALTED FATHER

BOOK OF SILENCE
VERSE 1.1.5

On the first evening of his journey back to the ducal castle at Haran, capital city of the Yadish, Lesser Wind arose unexpectedly and swept down from the north. Neither Lesser Wind nor Greater Wind blew in the spring and summer. And not only that, but the Grand Duke spied a flock of *kittim* spreading like a black cloud on the northern horizon. He immediately sought cover, looking for an outcropping of rock. But the steppe was an open sea and he was caught.

The black cloud swirled over his head. A single silken-winged *kittim* would be fatal. He held his breath and waited. Lesser Wind stirred the cloud like an air-born pond of black water. Then, in the next breath, the *kittim* passed over his head and sped south into Edom.

The priests said *kittim* were creatures on the edge of animal life, half-leaf, half-insect. One clever priest—probably Marduk—called them "vegetation with a purpose." The Grand Duke thought of them as those old style paper kites some of the Tribes used to make for their children, when there were still children among the Tribes. *Kittim* usually dissolved in the warm daystar of summer, or in the arid heat of the desert.

Rudra shrugged and continued on his way. First the Lord and now *kittim*. He didn't want to acknowledge the fact, but the steppe did indeed give birth to delusions. Delusions, however, might prove useful.

Grand Duke Rudra ruminated on his experience in the steppe for several weeks. He reached several conclusions. To be convincing, he had to make himself believe that the One Lord, the Almighty, the

Lord on the Mountain, Maker of Earth and Heaven, and so forth and so on, had chosen him. So, first he had to actually *believe* in the Lord. This shouldn't be too difficult, certainly not beyond his formidable will.

Naturally, whatever he met in the steppe had to come from some *natural* source. The most likely explanation was mistaken perception caused by intoxication. He recalled the pungent aromas of the wildflowers, the sweetness of the fresh pollens that had filled his lungs. He had seen *something* and his drunken imagination gave it life. A vision of the One Lord had oozed from his toxic brain as does pus from an infected wound. Well, pus is natural, is it not?

He smiled. Today his own brilliance amazed him.

He worked it out: His brain was a natural object. If his brain was part of nature, its illusions were natural too. A natural cause could not produce a supernatural effect. What was natural was real. Rudra believed that *only* the natural was real. So, the Lord, an illusion caused by his natural brain, was real. Therefore, the Lord's words were real too.

Although he'd abandoned logic, he had to admit that sometimes it was useful, especially when it served his needs.

He liked the sound of *Exalted Father* more than "holy". He especially liked its literal meaning. Therefore, the conclusion: The Almighty had appeared to the Grand Duke and ordered him to bring the women of the Tribe—and other Tribes—to the Lord's Holy Mountain on Starmirror. For this service the One (and *only*, he added) would reward him with the titles Exalted Father and Holy Father. Exalted Father could be translated into *King*. For this task of translaton he required a priest smart enough to recalculate the Runes. A priest who was a trifle dishonest.

Fortunately, he knew a priest perfectly suited for the task.

Rudra grinned. It was turning into a spring of fortune.

BOOK OF SILENCE
VERSE 1.1.6

And so the Almighty appeared to Grand Duke Rudra in the spring of his seventy-fifth year.

On the evening of the fourteenth day after his calling, the Grand Duke sat upon his cushioned throne staring into the creeping darkness of the ancient throne room, which was called the *Great Hall of Splendorous Beauty and Beneficence of the Golden Tribe of the Daystar*, or the *Great Hall of the Daystar*, for short—or shorter yet, the *Great Hall*. The throne room, and the necropolis beneath it, comprised the Ducal Castle of Haran overlooking Red Lake. The proper name of the Ducal Castle is far too long to be recorded here, and besides, it has been forgotten, except by the priesthood, and the consensus among the Tribes holds that even they have forgotten.

The Grand Duchess approached the throne like a shadow emerging from the dark. She hardly ever set foot in the cavernous castle. It stank of death, she complained. Its finely-crafted cedar beams, carved to resemble bolts of lightning, were rotted and decayed. Any day, she declared, the ceiling would collapse. The brick walls were not much better. With large cracks and greenish-yellow friff vines pushing through these fissures, the walls appeared ready to crumble. Colorful frescos depicted ancient times of glory when Yadish Kings ruled Greenbottom. Their scenes of Yadish victories were fragments of dirt-covered memories, distorted by the years.

Long wild hair white with age, bloated body hidden beneath the soiled golden gown of the Yadish Grand Duchess, bulging fish-eyes, hook nose, black, fang-like teeth—those few that remained in her head—Rudra imagined that if the Yakashas actually existed they must look like the Grand Duchess. Except for her yellowish skin.

"What's this nonsense you've been telling the nobility, old fool?"

"My dear Miriam, I am still your Duke and shall be addressed in a dignified manner." He tried to sound strict and formal, but it came out in a long-exhaled whine.

"Pardon me, my *dear* husband. How surly you are these days. You share so little. Do you know how much it pains me to hear odd bits of news floating about Haran? I should be hearing such bits directly from my dear, dear husband."

Miriam had a way of sounding hurt even when she mocked him.

"And these bits are?"

"There you go again. Such bad temper. Well, didn't you encounter something strange in the steppe? Viscount Vladimir says you met a strange creature that ought to be extinct. Well, you know how *he* exaggerates. I explained to him that you've been suffering mental lapses. You see things that aren't there. Why, the other evening I heard you talking to old King Joseph who's been dead for over two hundred years—"

He sat up straight and gathered his faded yellow robes. "I am chosen, called by the Lord on High," he declared.

She sighed and then gave a soft laugh. "Old fools, even Grand Dukes, hear all kinds of calls. At last they hear the call of death. Death's voice and nothing else does the choosing."

"We are *both* old, if you've not forgotten. I'll live on. The Lord is Lord of life. He will make of me a great people. I'm to bring our Tribe to Starmirror. He will enthrone me upon His Holy Mountain and there'll once again be a Yadish King. *My* progeny will be like the stars in the heavens."

She snorted. "I name you Joking Duke, son of the Laughing Duke." She raised her arms in blessing.

"The Lord has finally broken His silence," Rudra said, his determination to believe growing.

"He spoke to *you*? And promised you many children? Congratulations, father of thousands." She laughed. "So the Lord called a withered old thing like you. How many children have you sired, my virile Duke Rudra the Strong? Did you tell your Lord how many? Oh yes, did you tell him the fate of our only son? What you did with the boy?" Here her voice began to sizzle. She spit the words at him.

"Did you explain to the One Lord why you don't believe in His divine existence?"

"The Lord called me," he insisted in a small voice. Miriam was the only person who could drain his strength with mere words. She detected falsehoods as easily as the priests created them. In her presence he reverted back to a naughty child foolishly concocting stories and changing them at every adult challenge.

She turned away and noticed the stone sarcophagus of King Joseph I at the far north wall. Joseph I was known for his physical strength, and for his dreams—he was named Joseph the Dreamer.

"King indeed. Father of thousands."

How easily she saw it. Yet she did him a favor. She helped him overcome his doubts. In her presence he believed.

"I have decided," he announced. "The Lord has spoken. The Third Kalpa shall no longer be called the Kalpa of Silence. It will be the Kalpa of Rudra the Great. The One Lord chose to speak...not to the drunken old archbishop...not to the priesthood. He has revealed His Will to the Grand Duke of the Yadish Tribe. And the Grand Duke will do His work. *Tomorrow* the Grand Duke will summon the glorious feudal host of the Yadish Tribe. He will demand allegiance from the other Tribes. If they refuse, we will destroy them. We go to war in the name of the Almighty."

"That name being Rudra?" she snickered.

"I am the mouth of the Lord among men. My words are His. To hear me is to hear Him."

"Does this Lord of yours cure the infertile? Bring back the dead?"

"He has promised me offspring like the stars of heaven. He is Lord of the living, not the dead."

"What a promise. What a miracle it would be. Did you tell this Lord of yours that you are a withered twig and have been so since both of us can remember? Did you explain that I am old and dry, as wasted as the barren sands of Edom?"

She waved her hand in a gesture of dismissal.

"Nothing is too wondrous for the Lord," he called after her. His voice carried little conviction.

Miriam laughed.

BOOK OF SILENCE
VERSE 1.1.7

Women worked the fields. Alone, unguarded, not a male in sight. Scouts reported that a few males lingered in the mostly deserted hamlet. They were old and frail. Not warriors. They were drinking the juice of fermented berries.

Captain Mose ordered a company north. "You flank them," he directed Subaltern Osses. "Go north, turn west. Do not stop 'til shining river. Attack midday, when shadows are nothing."

Subaltern Osses looked doubtful. He barred his fangs and emitted a low growl. "Scouts are uncertain of numbers in village. What if they wield thunderbolt?"

"Then you die gloriously."

A few troops heard him. They moaned and whined.

This early in spring, steppe grasses were not tall enough to conceal Redfolk. They dug holes in the soft soil like steppe mice.

Their fear quickly evaporated in the heat of anticipation.

They drooled over the tailless females. Overly large and plump, these particular women were not as enticing as the last Tribe. They appeared sickly. The scouts described quite graphically (as much as Redfolk language would allow), their dense flesh, their round thighs, their heavy breasts swinging out as they bent over to work the fields. They had to be fertile. Listening to these words, many Redfolk experienced tiny erections.

But Osses objected: "Are such worth the effort?"

"Orders, Subaltern. From White Lord of Starmirror. I'll water red clay with your blood."

Osses studied the Captain. He saw by stiff ears and thrashing tail Mose was not in the mood to be challenged. Osses was not yet ready for a duel. The Subaltern slunk off on all fours. Soon a hundred troops departed and followed him north.

The daystar reached its zenith. Captain Mose rose up on two legs and let out a shrill bark. The assault began.

Poor Redfolk usually fight naked. Only Captain Mose wore the silver livery of the Lord of Tharas Major, which was a silver-threaded linen tunic designed to resemble plate armor. Nomadic *redimps* (as Redfolk are named by the White Lords) of the desert are hardly civilized.

They darted forward like a school of maddened fish. In seconds, the formation disintegrated. Attacking in a zigzag maneuver, they hoped to evade linear bolts of fire that might come from the tailless. After twenty yards the formation disintegrated and they ran headlong. A hundred yards remained to be crossed.

These females did not command the thunderbolt. Once this fact became apparent, the last shreds of discipline vanished and they began to collide with one another. Biting, scratching, pounding one another with their fists, they did severe damage to their own army long before they encountered the foe.

Despite the self-destructive melee, they took the females by surprise. A few screamed for help. A few screamed in fear. Others tried to fight them off with scythes and hoes and picks. Armed with fangs and claws—only officers like Mose bore dull swords of bronze—the Redfolk were too quick for clumsy blows and wild cuts. They fell upon the plump females, tearing and biting.

High pitched barks and whines mingled with screams and shouts. Overeager troops ripped the peasant smocks away and swarmed on the naked women like locusts. They bit breasts and frantically clawed legs apart. Turning upon one another, many fought their companions for the privilege of being the first to penetrate the thick folds of pink and brown flesh.

Exalted Father

Captain Mose killed five with his sword. Subalterns killed three times that number. At last the officers restored discipline.

"Prisoners!" Mose roared, slashing the throat of an offending soldier. Stupid sprite. Damned imps. All of 'em were behaving like immature sprites!

"Bind prisoners. Back to caves."

A few women fought like enraged mosscats. These they killed, for they knew from experience that mating with such beasts was impossible. On the other hand, usually the most vigorous were the most fertile. It was a terrible dilemma.

Captain Mose wiped the black blood of his blade on his leathery thigh. The blood blended easily with his natural rust color. He stood on two legs and gazed west towards the river. Smoke was rising from the hamlet. Either the males still wielded the thunderbolt and destroyed Osses—good riddance—or the Subaltern had been successful.

In the late afternoon Osses returned to the main body of the army. He had not lost a soldier. Captain Mose congratulated him without enthusiasm.

"To caves," the Captain barked, "before evil night wind bring blowflies."

Dragging about a dozen tailless female captives, the army retreated from the eastern border of Greenbottom towards the deep steppe.

It was too late. As the Captain feared, dusk wind brought blowflies. He had counted on the spring heat to dissolve the flies before they could alight. The White Lord had promised him this.

Alas, the White Lord was mistaken. Fiery blowflies fell among the troops. The mayhem was sickening to behold. The cries of the poisoned froze his blood. Some troops reverted to beasts and succumbed to a frenzy of madness, biting and clawing anything in reach. He killed three lest the females come to harm.

The blowflies ignored the tailless.

Just when it seemed that the deadly shower had subsided, a large blue and green bug swooped down and took Captain Mose. It embraced him like a lover. He emitted a single shrill scream and died in withering agony as his tough skin and treasured livery melted away. Osses retrieved the Captain's short sword, gingerly extracting it from the dark pool of viscous fluid that had once been a Redfolk Captain.

Osses snarled that he was now Captain. No one challenged him.

Later that night they came to rocky outcroppings that rose from the steppe like small volcanic islands in middle of an ocean. They filed into crevices leading down into caves. To anyone watching, it appeared that the land itself swallowed the army.

Captain Osses chose the largest female for himself. Two of the other Subalterns warned him that the Lord of Tharas Major had instructed Captain Mose to spare the women for His divine pleasure. Osses killed these two with the short sword. No one else protested.

With eager claws he tore away her peasant rags. She fought him and he cut her with his sword, which was no more than a small dagger to her.

He held the blade to her throat. She smelled of vegetation and moist soil. Her curses were unintelligible. She spoke a language taught to her by plants. Her very flesh was of the mud and river muck, dirty dirt.

His tail wiped back and forth in passion-driven frenzy. Alas, he was too small. His best efforts proved fruitless. He could not penetrate her. She laughed at him. He did not understand the words. He thought that she mocked him and his diminutive member, which because of her mockery had begun to soften. He howled in frustration.

Suddenly her passion rose to the surface. It erupted like a monstrous beast that had hibernated for many years. She pressed him to her. Her massive legs encircled his torso and crushed him in an unforgiving vise. Her fists the size of boulders beat upon his back, pounding at his frail body in her frustration.

EXALTED FATHER

His bones snapped like dry twigs. His lungs collapsed beneath the terrible pressure and he couldn't breathe. In a moment she reduced him to red pulp.

The other Redfolk howled like desert jackals and threw themselves upon the rest of the tailless females.

Their efforts proved as fruitless. Many died. In mindless fury they killed the prisoners. All of them. The White Lords would not be pleased.

THE BOOKS OF MARDUK

THE BOOK OF SILENCE

CHAPTER TWO - Akkad

VERSE 1.2.1

The Khan stood on the balcony of the tallest tower in Emerald, City of Towers. He gazed east, across the dark brackish waters of Lake Emerald to a layered series of blue and white hills that formed the famous Akkadean Stairs. At his back, the sinking daystar brought the craggy slopes to life in a dance of shadows and light. They shimmered and undulated like the glistening backs of serpents slithering through Edom at dusk. The Khan imagined a red flood of desert imps spilling down from the hills and threatening to overrun his beloved land. In this recurring nightmare his mortal enemy Grand Duke Rudra led the imp army.

With a grunt the Khan gingerly stepped down from the balcony and lumbered across the tower's upper room to his iron tub. He peeled off his dark blue uniform, heavy with rows of medals, shed his gold stripped trousers, and lowered his considerable bulk into the soothing water. The bath water was treated with a special salt gathered on the shores of Emerald Lake. He sighed as the warmth penetrated his body. It felt like thousands of tiny needles. The water softened the scar tissue of old wounds. It had no effect on the blue-black stain that covered his upper right arm. *Nothing* eased *that* pain.

EXALTED FATHER

A floating barrel of ancient flesh, he lolled in the tub and called for wine. A serving *girl*, nearly blind and crippled by swollen joints, spilled more wine into his tub than into his cup. The Khan didn't seem to notice, or if he did, care.

"How does *Muktaka* have it? When see you mountains walk, and mountains are walking, and see you them because they are walking, then does a Tribesman understand that mountains truly walk 'cause they are *always* walking."

"But *I say*: When mountain walks people get rocked!"

He drained his deep cup and laughed. "A bit'o wine and I'm as good a master of proverbs as any Yadish Duke. Better, by Almighty."

Not a few in the upper tower room were surprised that the befuddled Khan was able to quote from the *Runehayana*. Of course, not a few believed that the *Muktaka*, the last Book, was mostly the gibberish of idiot priests driven insane by the Almighty's silence. Perhaps the Khan in his final stages of *kittim* madness actually understood it. An Akkadean proverb had it that only the mad were able to grasp the last words of the Lord on High. No one knew if the proverb came from the Khan or the Grand Duke. If it didn't come from the Khan, it should have had.

The Akkadean nobles waited for more golden words. And the Khan did not disappoint them. He called for more wine.

Grand Vizier Abdullah cleared his throat. The Khan ignored him. The Grand Vizier waited patiently. He ventured a cough. When this had evaporated into the silent air he finally risked a word. Many words, to be accurate.

"Such wisdom, oh Khan. Such an eloquent summation of a book, nay, ten books, distilled in single sentence. We mere thirsty men, oh Khan, and you a deep tankard of spirit. Let us drink wisdom from your mouth, oh Khan."

Belching and grunting, the oh-Khan rose from the tub and called for his robe. Another *girl*, silver haired, corpulent, and brown as old bark, hurried to cover her Khan and master of proverbs. He waddled to his divan and wearily sank into the pillows, sighing heavily as if he had walked for miles.

Abdullah approached cautiously. "Now, if Khan grants, to subject of Zub'lin Tribe—"

Fixing the Grand Vizier with a singular watery stare, (his right eye having been closed from an old wound and his good left eye barely able to focus), the Khan raised his left eyebrow. He looked completely imbecilic, as if he should be cast into a cage and left to howl, as the saying went. Another Akkadean proverb proclaimed, however, that in the howls of the mad one might find the seeds of wisdom. But only after a diligent search. No one believed that either had originated with the Khan, though he claimed credit for *every* proverb ever uttered in Akkad, and for those that had yet to be uttered.

"Whaa-t 'bout em? Can't trust 'em, know you. Slimy bastards—"

"Yes, oh-Khan. But—"

A disturbance erupted at the far end of the hall. The double doors flew open and Orlok Agni burst into the room. He wore his field gear: thick blue-dyed cloth jacket and trousers, with patches of tough leather shielding the arms and legs. He also wore a vest of rusted chain mail. He bore a tribal scimitar belted at his waist. It was a dull ceremonial blade, hardly a weapon. Weapons were forbidden in the high towers.

These days (those days long past), most Akkadeans nobles had learned to despise Agni. Not a few mocked him, always careful to do so behind his back. The main reason was that he'd been beaten by a woman—a girl, merely—on the training fields. No one mentioned it. Everyone knew it. After all this time it still burned deep.

The youngest of the Orloks, Agni came from the last generation of Akkadeans before the Almighty's Curse fell upon the Tribe. Devorah, the Khan's daughter and only child, came from the same generation. She no longer lived in Emerald.

A sneer turned Abdullah's lips. "Perhaps Orlok, young as he, forgets rules that govern Towers."

Ignoring him, Agni gave the Khan a perfunctory bow and said: "It's spring, Great Khan. Lotus Moon is on the rise. How odd that Lesser Wind still sweeps down from the north."

"And what need of a weather forecast?" asked Abdullah.

"Vizier spends too much time sleeping off indulgences, he does. When has Lesser Wind arisen this late into spring? Yesterday Greater Wind came at dawn. The Two Winds still come, even in the spring. Know you that?"

"What of it, oh-Khan? Everyone knows old calendar's rotten. Foolish priests. Think they know everything there is to know about heavens, and without looking up. Can't look up with nose in a scroll. Why should this concern our glorious Khan?"

"There were *kittim*!" Agni boomed. A crack of thunder seemed to shake the tower walls. "Saw 'em with my own eyes. They took a woman near the Min-vena Gate. Dissolved her in seconds. Didn't leave a bone. Just a pool of black water."

"Must we endure such nonsense? Agni's temper clouds judgment. It makes foolish, like Talib over there."

Asleep beneath a ragged blanket at the far end of the tower, Talib poked his head out and cried: "Lame-foot! In all Akkad is he of pale-face known. Even Almighty knows. But ain't no fool—" He threw off his blanket, jumped up, and ran to Agni. Turning a somersault, he landed in heap at Agni's feet. He stuck out his tongue and rolled his eyes.

"Don't go out in *kittim* shower, says I. No, no, no..."

"Call out horde, Great Khan," Agni demanded. He aimed a vicious kick at Talib, but he missed, lost his balance, and almost fell on his face. The Jester scampered away, laughing, drooling, rolling his head from side to side. "Oooo, very dangerous, play with fire it is. Kilt his own brother, we heard—fire, fire, fire..."

Agni gripped his scimitar. Talib cowered. "Any man dressed like a spring violet ought to be castrated!" Agni growled.

"Oooo...no man gots balls to cut, dank the Lord!"

Abdullah interrupted, "March against *kittim*?" He hobbled to the Khan and whispered into his ear, as if divulging a state secret: "Warned 'bout Agni's sanity, didn't I? Ever since Devorah married Vishnu."

Agni heard.

"Devorah is not here," he said quickly. "When have Winds come this late in season? When have *kittim* fell except in cold weather?"

"Heard such things from priests," said one of the nobles standing next to Abdullah. He was the one they called old Guthman. He hated Abdullah and Agni both, equally and without prejudice for one or the other.

Guthman believed that he should have been Grand Vizier. He'd spent a lifetime maneuvering for the position. It was rumored that he'd poisoned the previous Vizier, Selim Birdlegs. He'd attempted the identical career advancement strategy on Abdullah during a feast in the East Tower. But that very evening Abdullah suddenly announced that he'd decided to undertake a cleansing fast of indeterminate length. The Khan praised him and called him Grand Vizier of Health, Akkadean Discipline, Master of the Kitchen and Bed-chamber. Guthman would never have believed that Abdullah, he of large belly and crocodile teeth, could go without Banalis wine for a single evening. Abdullah, however, surprised him. Unfortunately, later at night a serving *girl* dropped dead in the kitchen, for no apparent reason.

Abdullah's fast ended on the second day.

"Of course priests lie," Guthman added. "Lie every time they take an oath." He glared at the Grand Vizier.

"That's not uncommon," Abdullah observed airily. He ignored Guthman. "Do it so well, they do. Convince themselves. Some in this tower, oh-Khan, might find it profitable to learn lessons from priests."

A few old men and serving *girls* laughed heartily. The underhanded reference was to Agni, of course, who was known to consort with wandering *sramanas*. Not a few laughs concluded with a fit of coughing.

"Some already have," Guthman said through gritted teeth.

Agni's thick body trembled as if he were about to explode. He hissed like one of those old Nepptali boilers venting steam: "There's more. What if entire Zub'lin Tribe's done disappeared? And the same for Ra'bim—which includes thy daughter, *oh Khan.*"

The Khan called for his uniform and rose to his feet. "What're you say? What's this 'bout *kittim* and Zubs? And…Devorah…?" He struggled to get into his military tunic which had become a size too small, and not for any reason having to do with the tunic.

"Call out horde," Agni bellowed, "the years much weigh, yet Akkad cannot ignore such a threat. *Yadish are on the move.* Grand Duke Rudra marches north at the head of an army. He's destroyed Zubs. He marches on Ra'bim. Akkad's next. Akkad cannot let the Grand Duke have its daughter. Why ever did Akkad give her to old Vishnu? She is last fertile woman in all Greenbottom."

Even the half-deaf found it difficult missing the note of pain in his voice, and for those whose eyesight still worked reasonably well, the look of agony on his broad face.

"My Khan, what does Yadish Grand Duke have to do with *kittim?*" Abdullah asked innocently. "Agni seems confused. First he's worried 'bout winds and *kittim.* Next he's talking 'bout lost Tribes and Yadish invasions. How does Orlok know what goes on outside Akkad?"

"A priest told the Nepptali and the Nepptali told us. King Reuben's Road cuts through Zub'lin and Ra'bim lands. Priest wanderers…uh, wander up and down."

"Priests lie," Guthman observed once more. He waited for laughter but when none was forthcoming he added, "Everyone outside Akkad lies."

"Yes, yes... Everyone lies. But if everyone lies, how can an Akkadean believe anyone? Everyone lies—must be a lie."

Guthman looked puzzled. "My Khan," he said, "Agni's confused. Been drinking again."

The Khan seemed to be staring at Agni with his good eye. "Devorah has conceived, yes?"

"NO! How do... know?" For the first time Agni sounded uncertain, and, something he never sounded, embarrassed.

"Tis doubtful," Abdullah observed, enjoying Agni's discomfort. "Vishnu would've announced it far and wide. Would make that one King. Might even be declared Almighty. Would be first birth in all the Tribes of Men, in...ah, a long time."

"Devorah would NEVER submit to him," Agni said.

"How might an Akkadean know such a thing?" Guthman asked. "Ra'bim concoct all sorts of potions and medicines to heat the flesh—like those *somas* they peddle—"

"Because she respectfully declined our glorious Orlok's energetic efforts," said Abdullah. He grinned at Agni. "She probably heard stories of his wild youth, especially his wrestling matches in Borassus."

This brought another round of rasping laughter, even from the Khan. To everyone's surprise, Agni held his temper, but his broad face puffed up like a fish out of water and his small eyes bulged.

"Listen! Grand Duke is up to something," he said, the strain in his voice. "Somehow Yads have learned to control *kittim*. Who can say how? Nepptali say that they killed all Zub men and stole all women, like legends tell of Yakashas. Even now, my Khan, your only daughter is a concubine of lust-crazed Grand Duke Rudra. Even now he reaches for her—"

Exalted Father

"What's this?" The Khan shouted, suddenly enraged. "*Kittim* have taken Devorah? I sold her to Vishnu."

"No, no, not *kittim*. Yads, Yadish Tribe. They're a mortal threat."

Agni paused and drew a breath. Silence settled on the room like smoky night creeping in through the windows. He waited for what he hoped would be the maximum effect. Then, judging that the moment was ripe, he declared:

"*Rudra claims he met Almighty Lord of Lords in steppe. And... Almighty named him... Exalted Father.* All women of Tribes of Men are his. So says Almighty Lord of Lords. *I say...only Akkadeans can stop him. As we did in the past. Call up the horde.*"

Abdullah shook his head in disbelief. "Agni... Agni really should have been priest. What imagination—"

Orlok Jebe, the greatest living warrior in Akkad (and the oldest, making him over one hundred), approached the Khan, who'd risen from his tub. Many thought of a fat whitefish recently taken from the lake. Jebe glanced at Agni and looked Abdullah up and down.

"Great Khan, if Agni says the truth, even half-truth, we must fight. We cannot allow Grand Duke's kidnapping women of Greenbottom. He *did father a son,* once. If he finds other fertile wombs he will reclaim King-title and tax us to death. Our survival is at risk. Remember, no Akkadean child has been born in over forty years."

"Khan sold daughter to Ra'bim!" Agni exploded, unable to contain himself. "Wonder if she really was *Khan's* daughter—"

It was said among the Tribes of Men that Devorah had been born in the Khan's old age. Her mother had been his Third Wife, Hagar. Devorah resembled her quite closely except for her light skin which was honey-colored rather than the brown bark of Akkad. Some Akkadeans openly questioned the legitimacy of her birth. Those few the Khan had executed by the most imaginative, fiendishly clever means. He had especially enjoyed these executions, taking an active role in them.

Abdullah sighed, "That's what this is all about—"

"The Great Khan was well paid." The Khan's appearance seemed to magically transform. A wide smile of broken yellow teeth twisted his mouth. He looked sly and cunning, and carnivorous.

"And can always make another. Some mud from the river, a mold, some white *soma*, maybe one or two *kittim*, ground up of course, a little bit of wind, of breath..." He clutched at his hidden genitals, smiling wickedly. His shriveled penis was barely visible beneath his huge belly, and as far as anyone could see, he was missing his testicles...as every man.

Talib the Fool laughed: "Well paid, well paid—" He quickly backed away, his eyes on Agni. "Well paid, well pained, bloodsucker Khan..." He laughed and drooled and grabbed his own penis as if trying to masturbate. Naturally he did not succeed. This was, after all, Akkad and the Tribes of Men at the close of the Third Kalpa.

No one spoke. The Fool reminded them of the Lord's curse.

The room passed into shadow. Female servants of the Khan rushed to light quartz lamps. Half of the lamps fizzled and died in the first minute. Two servants threw a thick blue robe over his body. Outside, Lesser Wind created white caps on the surface of Lake Emerald. The Wind commenced its half-hour blast of freezing northern air.

The Khan's good eye seemed to gleam with its own light. "Yes, yes, well paid...quite profitable...but have plenty of *soma* for another."

"Great Khan, please—" Agni was in real pain. He didn't like the crafty look on Talib's narrow face even as the Fool still fumbled in his purple trousers.

Abdullah looked uncertain. His snickering grin vanished.

The Khan turned his back as if dismissing them all. "Ah, mountains walk. When an Akkadean see the mountains walking, that one *will know*. Are these not One Lord's words? Have Yakashas come upon us? Or Yadish *kittim*? Ha, ha, ha, ha…"

"I've seen 'em. Oh yes. They mount Stairs of Akkad. They come down. They go up. Up and down they go, from Greenbottom to Kingdoms of Heavens and back to Greenbottom. Thousands of 'em. Not Yakashas, not *kittim*, not Yads. Flood of Lords."

Agni backed away shaking his head.

Jebe stepped forward. "As Orlok, we declare gathering of horde in name of Khan. Akkadeans must march against Grand Duke, Exalted Father, Tyrant. Khan wills it." He glared at the Khan, trying to catch the Khan's good eye. The Khan seemed to feel his glare, though he did not see it.

"Yes, yes, Great Khan wills it… Climbing to Kingdoms of Heavens, up and down, always up and down, marching, marching—"

He turned and made a frightful face at Talib, baring broken yellow teeth, twisting his mouth, sticking out a black tongue. The Fool howled and ran out of the room. People heard him yelp as he slipped and tumbled down the winding stairs. Rasping laughter once again filled the room, and as before, many laughs ended in a fit of coughing.

Agni did not laugh. Instead, he shouted: "Thus speaks Great Khan of Akkad. Akkad *marches* on Grand Duke Rudra."

"Yes, yes, march, march… up and down," the Khan agreed. "First, more drink."

THE BOOKS OF MARDUK

BOOK OF SILENCE
<u>VERSE 1.2.2</u>

That very night, following a meager communal supper of salted whitefish and black bread, Agni, Jebe, Abdullah, and three Lords, Sallie, Omar and Guthman, held a meeting in the Beehive, the monumental edifice of Emerald City: government building, library, art gallery, weapons depot. Like the pale blue of a new spring sky, its gargantuan dome dominated the cityscape.

(Let us pause and speak of earlier times, *those times past*.)

All roads led to the Beehive, Akkadean poets said. It was the circular hub of the great wheel which was Emerald. Wide roads (in these days, broken clumps of brick and shattered rock) formed spokes of the wheel. Poets sang of it as one of the two moons fallen from the sky. Some poets claimed that a sacred tree once grew in its center. Merely touching the tree brought unbounded fertility to men and women. A woman who hugged the tree became impregnated instantly. How this actually happened, the mechanics of it, the singers did not sing. "Like priests, all poets are liars..." said the Khan—proverbially.

Once a congress hall of a thousand Orloks, the Beehive now stood empty, abandoned for uncounted years. As the population declined, the great dome became, almost by default, a museum, a museum with few patrons.

Inside, rich tapestries covered its walls. These works of antique art depicted glorious triumphs of mighty Akkad. The most famous series of tapestries, created by the artist Pliny (his name was all that anyone knew about him), told the history of the Great War against the Yads.

Exalted Father

The present Khan (his given name was *Kutchem*, but few if any Akkadeans remembered it—except Jebe) had been born about fifty years after the Great War. The first panel portrayed his father, Manuel Khan, called the *Bastard Khan*, leading mounted Akkadean warriors south. The next seven panels illustrated his seven great victories. The eighth tapestry, the famous eighth panel of Victory and Everlasting glory of Manuel, renamed Conqueror, depicted the battle of Ai. At Ai, Manuel smashed the Yadish lines and with them the myth of Yadish invincibility.

The scene, now dirtied and worn, depicted a thick, black cloud rising from the field, which seemed to spread like a blanket of ash, blotting out the daystar. Poets wrote that so horrible was the slaughter on that day that the daystar hid its face. Only once before in all history had this happened, and that was three Kalpas ago when the Lord came down to the Holy Mountain of Elsseleron. Poets claimed that the horse species went into extinction on this single day. And while poets exaggerate, as has been said many times, in this they told the truth (which, truth be told, seems absurd).

Akkadean lore has it that the last Yadish King, one named Joseph of unknown number (in Akkad) threw away his crown on that day. It is further claimed that after Ai, he renounced war and swore a vow of peace. The present Khan believed that he went raving mad on that day when the skies became black and the rivers became blood, and the noble horse perished forever. From then on he was known as the Laughing Duke. He laughed at the Unified Kingdom and at his former title of King. He laughed at politics in general, at honor, glory—truth itself. He laughed, and he lived past a hundred, to a hundred and twenty, the Yads said. He died laughing, although a few poets said he cried. But poets are confused.

Other tapestries depicted more ancient times when the Tribe took part in the Lord's Holy Wars. Here one could gaze upon the grisly destruction of farvels, those strange cat-like creatures whose fur seemed to change color as they walked. One might ponder the victory over the Rakashas, desert demons supposedly related to Yakashas. Akkadean cavalry slaughtered both. If the viewer had the stomach for it—in the past every Akkadean did—another tapestry pictured a battle line of infantry armed with working L-guns burning to cinders strange beasts, no more than quivering lumps of fur, which nonetheless looked unpleasantly human. These colorful panels were particularly vivid. Somehow they resisted the omnipresent dirt.

EXALTED FATHER

BOOK OF SILENCE
VERSE 1.2.3

This night, five old men, and one just past forty, sat at a broad blue table and plotted a new war against the Yadish Tribe. Where once there had been electric lights set in the ceiling of the dome, blazing like starlight, in these days sputtered quartz lamps that gave off foul smells and uncertain, flickering illumination. How far had the Tribe—all the Tribes—fallen.

(Needs be, gasping their plot requires more context, alas.)

Oh yes, poets said, the Yadish Tribe had created a Unified Kingdom, a worthy tribute to the power and glory of Men, like the Kingdoms of the Heavens. But it became a Yadish tyranny. The other Tribes were forced to make a yearly *donation* to the cost of maintaining a massive Yadish bureaucracy and an outrageously expensive court at Haran.

The first Yadish King, Joseph, called Dreamer, claimed that the priesthood possessed records of past Kingdoms of the Tribes of Men. Begotten of the Lord on the Mountain, they said. The evidence for such Kingdoms, however, was buried in the early books of the *Runehayana*. Higher priestly exegesis was required in order to extract it from layers upon layers of nonsense. Priests were always able to make sense from nonsense. Akkadean Khans laughed and called such histories "lower priestly nonsense." There was nothing funny, however, when such histories were used as justification for "higher donations."

During the period of the Unified Kingdom, towards the end of the Second Kalpa, most priests—and always the archbishop of Nalanda—came from the Yadish Tribe. The priests themselves had little to say about such an unusual coincidence, except to observe that "the laws of randomness are random—you know."

The Lord spoke of Kingdoms numerous times in the early books—after priests recalculated the Runes—with one exception, and this exception seemed an odd admission coming from Yadish priests. Those other Kingdoms which had flourished ages ago, even before the First Kalpa, *did not exist on the continent Jambridvipa*. They had been founded in the Lord's Heavens, from which He descended and came to the Holy Mountain Elsseleron.

Now, if this entire notion seemed, well, a bit nonsensical—Kingdoms in the Heavens—it fell off the edge of the world when priests revealed—actually the heretic priest Suthralane divulged the secret—that *the Kingdoms in the Heavens had fallen one by one, like stars going out.*

Ironically, this crazy idea, for which there was not one grain of evidence or passage in the *Runehayana*, sparked the rebellion of the Tribes against the Yadish King, Joseph of Unknown Number, later styled Laughing Duke.

Khan Manuel the Bastard took the lead. *"As in the Heavens so on the continent of Jambridvipa,"* was his rallying cry. The Yadish Unified Kingdom collapsed like a house of straw. The terrible battle of Ai sealed its fate. Soon afterwards the Lord ceased speaking to the priesthood in Nalanda.

Yadish sympathizers within the priesthood claimed that the Lord turned His Holy Face from humanity, "as the daystar itself, so too the Lord." The barbarous bloodlust of men disgusted Him. He regretted having created men. Thus did the Almighty send floods of *kittim* to wash away all human corruption. Priests dated the barrenness of women to this time.

Among the Akkadeans, the legend grew that *Suthralane the Liberator* (as they named him) had been of Akkadean blood. Suthralane discovered the great secret of the priesthood: that the Runes which appeared beneath the *Lordpool* in Upper Nalanda *were not* the words of the Almighty at all. Rather, a hidden mechanism controlled by the archbishop caused Runes to appear as though by magic. The entire *Runehayana* was no more than a priestly forgery. Suthralane jokingly referred to it as the *Priestpool*, the *P-pool*.

The Lord on High never spoke to anyone, announced the heretic priest. The Lord's words were not the words of the Almighty. They were *P-words*. Suthralane thought all this quite amusing.

The Khans of Akkad called them *Y-words* from the *Yadish Source*. The whole *Runehayana* was a *Yadish Source*. They were not amused.

Khan Manuel the Bastard, renamed Conqueror, took an unprecedented step. For the first (and last) time in Akkadean history he actually *believed* a priest. For, Khan Manuel said, Suthralane told the truth when he said that Kingdoms fall. *Kingdoms do indeed fall.*

The priesthood declared Suthralane a heretic. The Yadish archbishop at the time, Athanasius II, had him imprisoned and tortured. They put him on the rack of screws and straps, wheels and gears, pinchers and spikes. They tortured him most cruelly but did not kill him. In fact, they released him to live out his days in agony. From that time on he bore terrible deformities. He concealed these wounds with a thick black robe which he wore no matter what the season. People who saw him, and they were scarce, said he limped.

Realizing that his mercy had been a bad miscalculation (despite his suffering, Suthralane wandered Greenbottom teaching his blasphemy—he is said to be the father of the wandering *sramanas*), Athanasius II ordered him seized and burned at the stake in Lower Nalanda. It was winter, and before they lit the bonfire a freakish storm of *kittim* slammed into the monastery. Many priests died agonizing deaths—including the arch-villain Athanasius II.

Suthralane's fate is left to the imagination of poets.

Some poets say that a large green and blue *kittim* resembling a double-winged butterfly came down to Suthralane and wrapped itself around his broken body. It bore him down from the stake and up out of Nalanda into the dark skies.

So he disappeared from the eyes of men. Yet he did not die.

He wanders the world still, say Akkadean poets, invisible to men. And he will come again, when the time is fulfilled, to liberate humanity once more from the oppression of wicked men—such as Yadish Grand Dukes who steal women.

EXALTED FATHER

BOOK OF SILENCE
VERSE 1.2.4

(In those times...)

Agni took a special interest in the legend of Suthralane. About five years ago, a *sramana* Agni's own age and dressed in black rags, wandered into Emerald. He told an odd variation of the legend, one Agni had never heard.

This strange *sramana* seemed far too robust and healthy for an ascetic. He acted quite foolishly, if not downright insane. He marched directly to the Khan's Tower and demanded wine. A woman took pity on him and gave him a brimming cup from the Khan's own cellar. He acted offended and told her he didn't drink. Didn't she recognize an ascetic? He refused food at first, but later gorged himself at the Khan's own table. He even called out for mutton, although there was only fish, and he drank wine by the gallons. How strange that no one noticed him. Agni alone seemed aware of his presence (and perhaps the woman who offered him wine, for he may have bedded her).

Only later did Agni learn that Devorah had seen him too. What he did not learn, but suspected, was that she'd fallen in love. It was too crazy a notion to take seriously. An Akkadean warrior princess falling in love with a wandering priest.

Agni concluded that he was a priestly spy—and therefore a Yadish stooge. Yet, he possessed long black hair and the brown, nut-colored skin of an Akkadean. He might have been from Agni's own generation. Still, while there was no denying his physical appearance, the *sramana* could not have been Akkadean simply because there had been no other children born in Akkad.

For some reason he was never able to articulate, Agni took a liking to him, although the wandering priest seemed cold and aloof even when he was most charming. Agni certainly would have never admitted his own feelings to anyone. He refused to admit them to himself. There was something. Perhaps the (relatively) young ascetic reminded the Akkadean warrior of himself, which would have been more than strange.

The *sramana* said that he liked to wander Greenbottom telling tales of Nalanda and the *Runehayana*. He had no name, he said. Like the Winds, he could be Greater and Lesser depending on the time of day. Agni had no idea what the fool meant by this. Agni did not believe, as many people did, that one heard wisdom in the ravings of the mad. *One heard only ravings in the ravings of the mad*, he said, a proverb the Grand Duke would have loved.

The crazy ascetic told the following tale:

"Now Suthra, for such was he named in the beginning, was a priest of Nalanda. He should have been archbishop, for great was his scholarship. But he was Akkadean, for he was dark-skinned and he loved his wine." The *sramana* drained his goblet as though to demonstrate.

"A wine-drinking ascetic," Agni observed.

"No, he was a priest."

Agni shook his head.

"*You.*"

"Me?"

He put the goblet on the table and looked very confused. "What do you mean, noble Orlok?"

Agni waved a hand. "Irony seems not a priestly trait," he remarked. "And I'm not Orlok, yet. Continue. Be quick about it. Patience is not a virtue of mine."

EXALTED FATHER

"Well no, of course not. Important men have no time for patience—as I've had the opportunity to observe many times and in many places—"

"*The story!*"

"Well yes, of course."

He took the cup and set it down again. Twice he did this.

"Priest Suthra read in the *Runehayana* about the Kingdoms *in* the Heavens, you know. And he wondered if there was a *there in* the Heavens *where* no Kingdoms existed—'

"What?"

"Is there a Heavenly place without Kingdoms? Is there a place of...no-kingdoms, no-things, an empty place...?"

"Must be," Agni said. "In the Heavens Kingdoms fell like stars, it is written. If they fall in Heavens then Yadish Kingdom falls here on Jambridvipa." He repeated the old Akkadean formula.

"Yes. So it is written. Just *where* in the Heavens did all these Kingdoms rise and fall? And where was no-thing?"

"Look you at night sky."

"Yes, tis a big place. All those stars. The Books say they're infinite. Not exactly infinite because the real infinite cannot be complete. The Books mean, uh, unfinished...*to have no end*...but this no-end is a limit and thus complete. So, the Heavens are infinite, wouldn't you say? So, *where* could there be a *there* that's any different from any other *there*? How could there be a *nothing*? I mean, not just an empty place, no-thing, but *nothing*. I mean, the word makes no sense. What if the Kingdoms were not *in* the Heavens *someplace*? Instead they were *of* the Heavens everyplace? *They were the Heavens*. The Heavens were made up of Kingdoms as, say, your face consists of mouth, chin, cheeks, nose and eyes. Did the Heavens change when they fell? And...is there only *one Heaven* of which the *Heavens* are parts? So, if the parts change does the whole also change? What would the whole Heaven change into? Not-Heaven? So, is Not-Heaven this senseless *nothing*?"

The Books Of Marduk

Obviously the *sramana* was mad, if only in a mild, harmless way. He spoke nonsense of course. Yet Agni had to admit that he was amused. The *sramana's* cheerful nonsense reminded him of the court jester, sneaky Talib, except Talib's nonsense was hardly cheerful.

"Because, well, if Heaven is simply a receptacle, like empty space, then how can anyone think of Heaven without something *in* it. If it is unthinkable as empty, well, then, the *nothing is unthinkable too*. But if Heaven is more, say it *is made of* the Kingdoms, then if the Kingdoms fall the Heavens fall—I mean, well, there must be some effect? I mean, well— if the Heavens fall, they cannot be *Heaven*. How can infinity be diminished? Even if one subtracts infinity from the infinite does not infinity remain?"

"A real puzzle it is," Agni commented dryly.

"Yes. And Suthra couldn't solve it. So he decided to ask the Lord."

"Runes did not appear on the surface of *Priestpool*?"

"No. Yes, not *His* Runes. He went to ask the Lord on His Holy Mountain."

Agni's heavy jaw dropped. "He...he dared Elsseleron?"

"Yes. And the Lord of the Mountain maimed him for his efforts. From that time on he limped from the effects of a displaced hip. So he's named Suthra the Lame...Suthralane."

Agni hardly breathed. "He...met the Almighty?"

"Guess so. The Lord became very, very angry, so angry that He cast him down from the Holy Mountain which is how he injured his hip. Haven't you been listening?"

"What exactly did he ask?"

"He asked the Lord if there was such a thing as *nothing*?"

Still hardly breathing, Agni whispered: "What did Lord say?"

"Don't know—" The *sramana* grinned. "Said *nothing*. I mean, no-word, no-thing... I mean, the Lord Himself would have trouble resolving the Suthra paradox, don't you think?"

"What foolishness is this?"

EXALTED FATHER

"I like wandering about Greenbottom telling the story. It has a certain, uh, special quality. You know, a priest face to face with the Lord. Think of all the questions a priest might ask. The give and take. No more taking things as they were written. You know, Books are really dead. That's why I like *telling* the story. The *Runehayana* is dead. Conversation is alive. And think of this: When the Lord makes some foolish declaration—like His Kingdoms *of* the Heavens—the priest is able to cross-examine Him. Put Him to the test. Argue with Him. Show Him how stupid He sounds. Tell Him to shut up about *nothing*, for example. No wonder the Lord got mad.

"Priests like talking…with anyone who will listen."

"But you don't know—" The spell broke and Agni sighed.

The ascetic sighed too. At that moment he looked like Agni's twin.

"Go," Agni said heavily. "Tomorrow morning, after Greater Wind. May *you* go seek the Lord on His Mountain."

(Did Agni's sarcastic, off-hand remark plant the crazy idea in that befuddled mind?)[3]

The mad *sramana* left in the morning *before* the coming of Greater Wind. About a year later, Agni heard from the Ra'bim that a *sramana* had suffered fatal *kittim* poisoning on the road to their capital city of Tholos. They surmised that he might have been Akkadean.

So the Legend grew as legends are prone to do. Suthralane had met the Lord of the Mountain. Finally came a spring when the Winds refused to die, the kittim failed to depart for colder climes, and Grand Duke Rudra had met the Lord in the steppe. *And lived.* After

---

[3] This obvious interpolation is found in the oldest manuscripts. The others, all designated with(…), come from later redactions.

sleeping for nearly a Kalpa, the Lord had suddenly become visible, and even accessible.

Agni believed none of it. Had he known, the old archbishop of Nalanda shared his view.

EXALTED FATHER

BOOK OF SILENCE
VERSE 1.2.5

Agni planned to outflank the Yadish by attacking them from the east. In order to accomplish this maneuver, the Akkadeans would have to cross the Pearldew, turn south, and march a good nine weeks—considering the average age of the army was around eighty—through the Yakashas Steppe.

Agni assumed that there wouldn't be *kittim* in the summer. He did not believe—he could not believe—that the Grand Duke had discovered a way to harness their deadly powers. The late season plague of *kittim* was coincidence, he told himself, and the others.

"So Akkadeans are agreed enemy is Duke Rudra?" Abdullah asked.

"Akkadeans believe something destroyed the Zubs. A *priest said* so. Must be Yads. Is a logical matter of plausible belief."

"Never known Akkadeans to believe in priestly tales," said Jebe. "How is it logical?"

"This priest is a coward," Agni said.

"Ah, so Agni *persuaded* this priest to tell truth?"

"Akkadean frown is enough. *That priest* squealed like a Yadish pig—"

"Know that one," said Salim the Wretched. Salim had earned this title by mutilating and killing his wife for her barrenness. This was long ago and his guilt had never been proven. He testified in court that he'd seen a Yadish warrior—he could tell from the soiled golden coat—fleeing the scene. The disgusting Yad had raped and dismembered his wife. Her body was never discovered. The court believed him. It sounded just like something a Yad would do. It was logically plausible.

"Jacob Ox, that one's named. Call 'em snake instead of ox. Evil looking. Poisonous. Always hanging around Emerald, ogling women. That priest's no *sramana*, for sure."

"Aye," said Omar One-armed. Omar had lost his arm in the Yadish War, he claimed. Just as he was about to strike the son of the Yadish King, a cowardly Yad had taken off his sword arm from behind. No one believed this tale of bravado. The Great Yadish War had occurred a hundred years ago. The common opinion was that his arm simply withered and fell off, following the path blazed by another member, one that he missed even more than his arm. Many Akkadeans believed he'd been *kittim* poisoned.

"People say this Jacob visits all Tribes along King's Road. Duke Rudra once had that priest whipped for fondling a Yadish slut."

"So, Agni, that one's a useful priest after all," Abdullah observed.

Agni brushed back his long black hair. He was the only Akkadean whose hair had not yet turned white. Unlike the others, he was clean-shaven. He made it a point to emphasize his relative youth. Unfortunately, his face was heavy and his eyes always appeared half-closed—which caused him to look older than his forty years.

"Priests can be useful, not only for pawing old Yadish women. Need to know how to read priests. First principle is nothing a priest believes is true. If a priest believes something, then that something must be false thing. If a priest *does not believe* something, then that something must be true thing. Priests believe that Lord Almighty wrote *Runehayana*. Therefore, Lord did not write *Runehayana*. Jacob Ox says Rudra met Lord Almighty in steppe and Lord ordered that old man Duke to found new Yadish Kingdom. Jacob the Ox does not believe Rudra. Therefore, Rudra is planning new Yadish Kingdom. So it is proved."

The old men laughed like a gathering of cackling chickens.

Abdullah said: "So, does Agni agree that Rudra *met the Lord?*"

"No."

"Doesn't Agni violate his own principle? Jacob does not believe it?"

Agni scowled. "There are exceptions."

"Then…what? What priest does not believe must be true, except the part Agni likes not?"

"Akkadeans must plan campaigns on more solid information," Jebe interrupted. "Agree, all Akkadeans, Rudra is threat. So, given Akkadean resources, this Orlok says Akkadeans march straight down King's Road. Gather allies along the way. No one likes Rudra."

The others agreed, except Agni. "Rudra anticipates a direct assault. Rudra might think Akkadeans are Yakashas if they attack from the steppe."

"What if there really *are* Yakashas?" asked Omar One-armed.

"Examine east tapestry."

"Aren't those Rakashas, desert devils?"

"Same thing. Just another priestly lie in *Runehayana*. Books confuse the two. When priest writes Yakashas, priest really means *Rakashas*. Akkadeans destroyed 'em as any Akkadean can see. Yakashas is geographical term for the steppe. Priests confused the word with some desert species of carrion feeder, a desert scavenger."

"How does Agni know such scholarly details?"

"A *sramana* told me. Maybe the only priest who doesn't lie."

"And here is Agni again. All priests lie, except when *Agni* decides otherwise."

"He says priests really did read words of Lord Almighty, so he lies enough," Agni shot back, his voice rising. "*Priests read words because priests create words.*"

THE BOOKS OF MARDUK

BOOK OF SILENCE
VERSE 1.2.6

Sunrise. Greater Wind blew with all the icy force of winter although it was spring. Dewdrop Moon rose in the north like a huge glowing wheel. The Akkadean *horde* gathered in Gibhorim Square, a wide rectangular parade ground that formed the southern entrance to Beehive. In the days of power, when children still played on the tree-lined avenues of Emerald, thousands of warriors, horses, and battle chariots filled the square.

On this day a few hundred old men and women stood rubbing their eyes and complaining about the chill. The rest of Emerald's population heard the summons, rolled over and went back to sleep. Not a soul from the hinterlands marched into Emerald, if there were souls (or bodies) fit to march in the hinterlands.

The elderly needed their rest, many complained. Others moaned that the damp cold froze their joints and wasted muscles. Early morning was no time for the gathering of the horde. What if there were still *kittim* this late in the season? It was so cold.

They were armed with rusty scimitars (mostly family heirlooms), a few L-guns, bows, pikes, assorted kitchen knives and garden implements.

Why had the Khan awakened them at this preposterous hour? And with Greater Wind still sweeping down from the north?

At long last the Khan arrived. In ancient times he would have ridden in a chariot, or possibly on a war horse. Today he sat in a rusted sedan chair carried by creaking skeletons in Akkadean battle gear. These days battle gear consisted of heavy cloth fatigues fixed with leather guards on the arms and legs. A few wore chainmail, but chainmail made from bronze instead of light silvery kerdofan. No one worried that chainmail might prove deadly in the summer heat

Exalted Father

beneath a relentless southern daystar. No matter what the weather, the elderly were always cold.

Just as they entered Gibhorim Square, the strength of the bearers gave out and they set both Khan and gilded chair down with a crash. The jolt served a purpose. The Khan woke up.

Assisted by Orlok Jebe, Supreme General of the Horde, he mounted a platform at the north end of the Square and addressed the throng.

The Khan wore kerdofan chainmail armor underneath a blue cloak trimmed with gold leaf, colorful lapels, and the gold Akkadean symbol of Lotus Moon on his pocket. A silver kerdofan crown decorated with crossed scimitars sat askew on his bald head. Like the other warriors, a wide blue stripe was painted down his forehead to his sparsely bearded chin. Blue war paint encircled his good eye. He wore a patch over the other. A younger man might have looked formidable and dangerous. The pear-shaped Khan resembled an aged clown who had forgotten how to be a clown yet was nonetheless uproariously funny when he put on a mask of deadly gravitas.

"Akkadeans of the Blue Horde—" he cried out in a thin, reedy voice, not at all what one would expect from a man of his girth.

Greater Wind blew the words back into his face.

"What'd he say? Speak louder!" The horde was in a foul mood. As previously noted, this was no weather for older gentlemen and a few older ladies.

"Yakashas have come—"

"Yadish," Jebe hissed into his ear. "Grand Duke Rudra."

"Yakashas have abducted this Khan's dear daughter Devorah—and are planning to eat her. But fear not. Your Khan makes another out of mud—"

Jebe clambered up and shouted at the crowd, "Duke Rudra destroyed Zubs. That one threatens all the Tribes. Is mad, that one. Claims Grand Duke speaks to Lord of the Mountain, that one. Akkad *fights*!"

Greater Wind howled through the square, growing stronger. Many people turned away, shaking their heads, laughing and cursing at the same time. At this precise moment the daystar rose over the waters of the lake and the square was illuminated in dazzling light. The brilliance was painful to ancient eyes. Many cursed the new light.

Dawn was brief. A black cloud suddenly appeared in the north and swept over the lake like a tightly-packed flock of blackbirds. Instantly, the cloud blotted out the morning star and night abruptly returned.

"*Kittim!*" someone cried.

"Yeah. Those too," said the Khan.

A crazy melee of panic-fueled confusion erupted in the square. People screamed and shouted, mindlessly bolting for cover. Gibhorim was vast and age-stiffened legs no longer ran with the swiftness of past glory. Many people hardly recalled what it felt like to run, much less bolt. Some collided with their neighbors and rebounded like rubber balls, flying this way and that. Some fell and were trampled. Others dropped to their knees and cried out hysterical prayers to the Almighty. Still others shouted profanities at the Khan, Jebe, Agni, the priesthood, Rudra, anyone. A few added the Lord for good measure. Having fallen asleep on their feet, not a few suddenly awoke. "Shut up and let an Akkadean sleep!" they cried. "Are minds lost?"

Agni drew his scimitar and slapped the most hysterical with the flat of his blade. His anger burned like the blue fire of an L-gun. He was about to turn the sharp side of the blade on the crowd when a strange thing happened.

The *kittim* seemed to halt in mid-air and then, executing a well-timed maneuver, began to dive in a blizzard of wild forms and colors. It was as if a cloud of dead leaves had suddenly become self-propelled. In moments Gibhorim Square resembled a battlefield. The horde looked as if it had been decimated by L-guns.

Exalted Father

Few *kittim* actually alighted on a person. Most swirled down randomly and dissolved into the dirt and broken tiles. Some seemed to burn up in the daylight like morning dew.

The Khan continued speaking—something about mountains walking.

Vizier Abdullah popped up suddenly as if out of thin air. He screamed at the Khan to "find cover, fool!" and clawed his way through to the platform. Just as he reached the Khan, a blue and green *kittim* changed direction and sailed towards him. It resembled a child's box kite: gossamer wing-like panels of various shades of blue and green, random geometric designs, all bound together by yellow tendrils, without head or tail.

Attracted by his call, the thing shot in his direction like an arrow. But that was impossible. How could plant-leaves, alive or dead, be purposeful?

He turned and threw out his arms.

Too late. The *kittim* appeared to come apart as if someone untied several knots causing the tendrils to fall away. It wrapped flexible sheets of silk about the Vizier's torso, smothering him in a gentle embrace. Then, like salt in a cup of water, both *kittim* and Grand Vizier melted away leaving a moist stain on the wooden panel of the platform. A stream of dark fluid watered the ground.

The Vizier's melting (priests called the process "somatic reduction") seemed quite natural, even painless. The Wind continued to blow. The daystar mounted the sky. The universe did not notice.

The Khan noticed. Abdullah vanished in a suit of *kittim* silk before his eyes, close enough that he felt droplets of moisture on his skin. He halted in mid-sentence and fixed his good eye on the expanding puddle at the platform's base. "What'd in hell…" he muttered.

A yellow *kittim* of intersecting hexagonal planes suddenly seemed to change course from its lazy wind-fueled spiral. It flew directly for the Khan. Half the size of its box-kite cousin, it managed to soak into his neck and most of his chest, penetrating his chainmail like thrusting a scimitar into the waters of Lake Emerald. In the time it took for him to expel a breath, the thing soaked through metal and cloth into his skin.

The Khan gave a strangled yell. He clawed at his neck trying to tear away the chainmail. Flailing his arms like a bird struck by an arrow, he toppled backward off the platform.

Agni had not moved a muscle. A look of incomprehension spread across his broad face. He watched the Khan fall.

"Khan's poisoned!" he shouted at last. His own words surprised him. "To Khan—"

Before he could take a step, a moth-like *kittim* abruptly changed course and came for him.

EXALTED FATHER

THE BOOK OF SILENCE

CHAPTER THREE - Tholos

VERSE 1.3.1

The procession wound through the narrow streets of Tholos. The Days of Spring had begun. It was morning. Greater Wind had come and gone. *Kittim* had neither come nor gone.

The bride, who had been confined to the Women's Compartment throughout the winter, was arrayed in white and lavender silks, as befitting the wife-to-be of the Triumvir of the Ra'bim Tribe. A crown of red and pink flowers encircled her black tightly braided hair. In spite of her light brown skin, she looked like a spring flower in full bloom.

Ten squat, lumpish men bore her golden sedan chair. They were the ministers of government. Ladies-in-service followed, dressed in simple white cotton gowns and soft white slippers of dog-skin. Everything was done in accordance with the most ancient traditions of the Ra'bim Tribe.

The procession followed the Grand Canal which flowed west through the city after it branched off from the Pearldew River. Two parallel canals bisected Tholos. The Grand Canal was the main artery that led to the heart of the city. This heart was actually an artificial lake named Urlock. The smaller, Gihon Canal, split off from the

Grand Canal about half way to Lake Urlock. It made a large sweeping circle and returned to the river outside the city walls.

Lake Urlock, usually filled with river barges, gondolas and small fishing craft, was roughly circular. Its northern arc touched a large open square named for the Fourth Book of Starmirror (*Sariraka*), the *cleansing*. A brick pyramid constructed in three distinct tiers dominated the square. This was the true heart of Tholos, called the *Mountain,* home to the Triumvirs as well as the offices of government.

Standard Tholos architecture consisted of squat, single-storied buildings, crammed together in square warrens divided by the narrow thoroughfares. It was rumored that the inhabitants lived not in the buildings themselves but chambers beneath where, like troglodytes, they labored in chemical factory-caves. Plants grew on the tops of buildings. The Ra'bim manufactured medicines, dyes, spices and tinctures, and above all, deadly poisons. They were artists, it was said.

The procession made its way slowly to the *Sariraka* and its Mountain upon which Triumvir Vishnu awaited his new bride. The spring daystar shone brightly on the polished stones of the square setting them ablaze. Other Tribes claimed that the Ra'bim had purposefully constructed the *Sariraka* to mimic Lordpool in Upper Nalanda, which also seemed to catch fire when the Runes of the Lord appeared beneath its crystal surface.

Vishnu was pleased. He was almost happy (if such a thing were possible). He bragged to all who would listen (which was, of course, the entire Tribe) that there would be children once again playing in the streets of Tholos—for the first time in over a hundred years.

His new bride was none too pleased, and far from happy. The somas her *dear father* had initially administered to her in Akkad had worn off. She was positively livid, although she could not show her extreme displeasure. She'd been imprisoned for the entire winter, confined to a miserably tiny and drafty room on the north side of the pyramid. Her ill-named "ladies-in-service" had attempted to administer foul tasting medicines—to make her fertile and more beautiful, they said. She responded by breaking the neck of the Over-mistress with a well-practiced blow. The repulsive old woman, cadaverous, hairless, oily, and squat like all Ra'bim, had been particularly foul-mouthed and mean. Like all Ra'bim, she smelled of rotten fish. They tossed her body into the canal.

After this episode, they bound the bride to her bed. The gentle ladies-in-service forced her to drink a particularly noxious fluid that burned her throat and gagged her. She did her best to spit it up. They almost drowned her, which would have made for a rather gloomy wedding day, daystar or no.

Her strong body became like soft rubber. She lost control over her bodily functions. The new Over-mistress and her ladies-in-service were forced to scrub out her cell every day. They forced more medicine down her throat, "to ease her anxiety," they said.

Because of the drugs, her rage on this happy day of her marriage was more akin to cloudy discontent, an unfocused gloomy feeling, anger siphoned through a dense fog. Things might have been worse had she known that they'd bribed her father to *medicate* her drink even before she arrived in Tholos.

When the ministers of government perceived her pouting frown and droopy half-closed eyes, they berated the gentle ladies-in-service. The ministers scolded in the tongue of the Ra'bim, which in the ears of the other Tribes sounding like a series of sharp squeaks, clacking sounds, and guttural barks, more animal than human. The language itself seemed to vibrate with viciousness and spite. The sounds would have caused her to shudder, had she been able. Things being as they were, she simply looked miserably unconcerned.

The Ra'bim claimed that they spoke the original language of the *Runehayana* before it had been corrupted by the priesthood. One of the Khan's marriage negotiators had pointed out that the Lord's words originally appeared as Runes in the Lordpool and therefore no one knew how they were pronounced. This off-hand observation nearly ruined the marriage contract between the Khan and Vishnu (neither of whom were present).

Outraged, voices seething with anger, the Ra'bim ministers replied that *they, and only they, heard the Runes speak*. Well that is quite remarkable, the Akkadeans observed, given the fact that all the Tribes read the Books in vernacular Sandi. The Ra'bim refused to yield an inch. They *heard the Runes through the translations*, they barked. Does not language transcend the forms it takes?

"Make her as a spring bride ought to be!" the ministers snapped at the ladies-in-service. "And be quick about it."

One of the ladies rushed to the sedan chair and brought forth a small brown-glass bottle. "Drink, drink, my dear," she squealed. You'll feel oh so much joy—"

Unable to resist, the poor Akkadean girl (actually she was nearly forty) drained the bottle.

In a few seconds she was smiling sweetly. Her dark eyes softened and glowed. She was like a doe in the springtime gazing upon her newborn fawns. Like a mosscat with her cubs, a farvel with her pride. Unfortunately, the treatment was only temporary.

Deep in her mind, where the Ra'bim drugs could not penetrate, she cursed the hideously pale women. She cursed this day. She cursed Vishnu with especially vicious thoughts. She cursed her father the Khan as she always did. She recognized how close she was to wanting to kill them both, but naturally she could not cross *that* boundary.

While still a child, she'd taught herself to stop thinking of the Khan as a father. No matter how well she did in the martial arts, besting his best warriors, no matter how brilliantly she succeeded in her studies, no matter how powerful her will to rule the Tribe, she could never please him. He responded with harsh words, cutting remarks and insults. More often, he simply laughed. She would always remain a weak little girl, he said. And he sold her when the first opportunity arose. She came to hate all men, save for the strange *sramana*.

Beyond all reason she craved a priest, a wandering ascetic. Only when she thought about him did she experience the burning desire, the delicious fire that had nearly gone out among the Tribes of Men. Otherwise, she hated men.

She cursed her father, and all men, and never tired of it.

At last the wedding procession entered the vast courtyard named *Cleansing*. It could have easily accommodated several thousand people. Today, a little less than three hundred stood waiting for the wedding of the great Vishnu. Like underground grubs, white and bloated (the other Tribes called them a Tribe of maggots), they blinked in the sunlight and huddled together in a compact cluster. They wore thick white coats and still complained about the chill air, even in the brilliant spring sunshine.

A hastily constructed wooden ramp mounted to the first tier of the pyramid. It appeared none too stable. Wooden bridges had not the solidity of stone. A wide platform supported three shrunken figures seated on polished cedar thrones. These *were* the Triumvirs of the Ra'bim Tribe. Two were dead and mummified. Desiccated in vats of special salts, then wrapped tightly in linen bandages soaked with resin, the two deceased triumvirs sat upright, surveying the scene with empty eye sockets.

The third Triumvir also watched the procession intently. He looked dead and mummified, but he was very much alive.

He was Vishnu, the oldest living human being in all Greenbottom. Naturally this claim could not be verified. Contact had been lost with many Tribes for over a century. So there were none to dispute the assertion.

THE BOOKS OF MARDUK

BOOK OF SILENCE
VERSE 1.3.2

Vishnu had spent the winter undergoing all sorts of pharmacological experiments. The greatest herb-masters and physicians worked ceaselessly in subterranean laboratories. There had been many failures. At one point, Vishnu flew into a rage and executed several of his chief physicians.

Their deaths had been particularly gruesome. The combination of drugs and precise surgical instruments invented by the finest minds in Ra'bim kept the victims alive while at the same time heightening their agony.

Vishnu was an enthusiastic participant. "On with it," he would shout gleefully as blood splashed his face and screams filled the catacombs of the pyramid.

Among the physicians Vishnu spared (apparently on a whim), two were quick to note that at such times, during those "moments of the patient's maximum treatment," they said, Vishnu's ancient flesh responded favorably. His testicles reappeared. In one case he nearly reached the intended goal. He nearly achieved an erection. Such observations actually led to a great breakthrough.

The herb-masters had been giving him a solution of maryweed mixed with pepper. His continued drinking of this potion would eventually, they hoped, raise his blood pressure. Of course they couldn't afford to raise his blood pressure too high as the treatment might result in organ failure or a stroke. Then Vishnu himself came to the rescue.

During those bloody executions, the good doctors thought that they perceived in Vishnu a kind of temporary madness. They diagnosed Low Grade Insanity, in Ra'bim medical terminology. It seemed as if some other being, a slumbering personality deep inside the Triumvir, suddenly awoke. The evil thing staged a revolution and overrode his normal personality. The blood flowed, the flesh ripped, the screams reached that impossible volume, and the *being-within-Vishnu* came to surface. Only death appeared to satiate the thing. Perhaps it simply lacked endurance, the physicians observed. At the patient's death the being within went back to sleep.

But Vishnu had achieved a momentary erection. There was hope.

Their goal became to awaken the sleeping *being-within-Vishnu*—only partially, however, because they didn't want him killing his new bride.

Deep in the cellar of a certain herbalist, locked away in a finely made Nepptali chest of iron and silver, passed down through the family generations of this particular herb-master, there was a talisman of such power and malevolence that the Lord of the Mountain Himself had forbidden its use. Written in silver on the surface of the chest was a passage from the Book of *Aitareya (Forbidden)*, which was said to be the Lord's death-curse on anyone who opened the chest: "on that day will you die" (or something to this effect since the priests could not agree on its proper translation into the Sandi).[4]

The chest contained bark from the cursed Whittling Tree.

Out of desperation, and out of fear, this particular herb-master dared the Lord's curse and forced the chest open. Actually the sealed chest surprised him. Its unlocking proved to be a less formidable task than he expected. He simply lifted the lid.

The herb-master extracted a finger-length piece of shining bark that seemed more like the skin of a black snake than the bark of a tree (ancient lore had it that the trees grew in swampy areas, usually about slim-covered ponds).

---

[4] In their primitive form, the Four Major Runes were transcribed: **XΛIV**, as found in recently discovered papyrus fragments.

"Though I'm cursed of the Lord and will surely die this day, I gladly surrender my life for my Triumvir Vishnu," he croaked, sounding like a bloated albino frog. Albino frogs were poisonous and still inhabited the river valley. Ra'bim herb-masters had adopted the frog as their secret symbol during the First Kalpa.

"How very brave of you," one of the physicians commented. "What if the Lord's curse extends to Vishnu?"

"Would the Lord punish the innocent for the sins of one man?"

"I suppose not. The Almighty cannot be a serial killer. I was thinking about the bark, not the Lord, fool. Is not the bark of the Whittling poison? As bad as *kittim*?"

"Perhaps. Have you any better solution?"

No one did. They ground up a tiny bit of bark and mixed it with the secret drink named Yellow Soma. They then tried it on a lady-in-service—at age sixty-eight the youngest lady-in-service. They waited an entire day. There was no visible effect.

One of the senior chemists convinced the herb-master (who was still quite healthy despite the curse) to add a slice of the sacred mushroom which was grown in the dank cellars of the chemist's guild.

They forced this mixture down the throat of the new Over-mistress of the ladies-in-service. It took five physicians to hold her down. She immediately went into convulsions and was dead in minutes. She bled from every opening in her body.

A second before she gasped her last breath, this unfortunate Over-mistress began shrieking about frightful monsters tearing at her flesh. Huge, hairy, man-like slavering beasts with massive horns and gigantic phalluses ravished her, she screamed. Her hips jerked convulsively, her body seemed to quake as a series of spasms shot through it, her eyes bulged and her screams broke glass. Then she died.

EXALTED FATHER

The physicians were quite encouraged. They congratulated the senior physician, but gazed suspiciously at the herb-master who refused to expire.

They tried two more experiments with different combinations of ingredients. Both subjects died. With the third attempt they were successful. Except, her behavior was so bizarre and lewd—she actually grabbed the testicles of one of the physicians and twisted them until the man fainted (being in his eighties he died later from the shock)—that they had to administer a sedative. Unfortunately, the sedative killed her.

So the winter passed. Two weeks before the wedding they finally achieved what they called a success. The woman survived, both the treatment and the required sedative. The herb-master remained alive, in fact he seemed younger and more energetic. The physicians suspected him of sneaking samples of the whittling-mushroom-yellow-soma medicine. So, they poisoned his wine and said that his untimely death was the result of the Lord's curse, though the good Lord had been a bit tardy in carrying out the execution.

A week before the wedding they gave the concoction to Vishnu, telling him it was a solution of vitamins, sugar, minerals and other nutriments. At once he achieved an erection. It was strong enough to actually enable him to penetrate a lady-in-service. That she died of shock did not concern the physicians. The Akkadean bride was far younger and stronger than any living Rab woman.

Vishnu began acting strangely. Such odd behavior was to be expected, the physicians told themselves, when the oldest man in all Greenbottom was about to wed the youngest woman—and, perhaps, the last fertile woman in all Greenbottom.

BOOK OF SILENCE
VERSE 1.3.3

The boatman spat into the sluggish canal waters. He adjusted his broad-brimmed hat, fearful of what the spring daystar might do to his skin.

"Strangers 'er forbidden in Tholos," he snarled at the imposing figure standing on the rotted pier. "Specially priests."

"*Sramana*," said the traveler. "No priest. *Sramana*. No *sramana* either. Both. Neither."

Standing astride a gondola, hands on his hips, the boatman struggled to look fierce and imposing. Half the height of the traveler, he looked more like a stuffed white frog trying to frighten a lion.

"*Sramana?*" he said shrilly, "what's the fuck that?"

"Wanderer," the man on the pier answered.

The pier was about a hundred meters up the canal from the Pearldew. Here the canal surface was less turbulent than the swollen waters of the springtime river. Here, too, the canal water stank of refuse and oil, chemicals, garbage and the Lord knew what else, if the Lord really cared to know. He would have had to hold His divine nose the smell was so bad.

"*Sramana*, wanderer, ascetic forest dweller, as the most ancient Books of the *Runehayana* have it."

"Ach, books," laughed the boatman. "Only us here knows the ancient tongue correctly. Priests lie. Say youse ain't no *sree...ana* either?"

"*Sramana*," the stranger corrected him.

"Ain't no fuckin' difference. Juss 'cause youse wears them black rags and walks about with downcast eyes and hood so no one can see youse wretched face—"

The traveler carefully pulled back his hood.

Exalted Father

The boatman nearly lost his balance and capsized the narrow gondola.

"Well ain't this special! An Akkadean priest."

The traveler did indeed possess dark skin and long black hair, as well as bright green eyes, a rare feature even in Akkad. Beardless and youthful, his face was friendly and pleasing to behold, a smiling mouth, high forehead, straight nose and expressive eyebrows. He was beautiful in his simplicity—and he was the youngest person the boatman had ever seen, younger even than that brown Akkadean slut who was about to marry the great Triumvir.

He inhaled deeply to regain his composure.

"Don't need any more Akkadeans in Tholos these days," he said peevishly. "High and mighty, and better'n us normal people. Begone!"

"Ferry me into the city," the *sramana* said. "I'll pay you well."

"Oh yeah? How well?" The boatman looked suspicious.

"Whatever is the going rate. And a bit extra."

"Well, ain't no going rate. Don't get many customers anymore. Other a few Yisskur merchants come to visit the herb gardens inside the city. And I tell you what—" he glanced about furtively as if he were about to divulge a state secret "—I think some of them garden's for growing stuff that ain't for medical purposes."

He dropped his voice so he actually did sound like a river frog croaking, besides look like one. "I thinks them is poison plants. The Yisskur Tribe's a bunch of slimy bastards. But they've money, so they kin corrupt even our most decent herb-masters. Some of their stuff messes with your mind. Great Vishnu says that the Yisskur gives it to Duke Rudra of the Yads which is why the old Duke sees stuff. And know what? The most corrupted of the bunch of herb-masters—and it's the fault of the Yisskur, mind you—make nets to catch *kittim*. Who knows what they does with them? I seen my fair share of drug-lords on this very dock—gruesome lookin' bastards."

He stopped and gazed at the *sramana* with a look of puzzlement on his face as though he'd forgotten something.

"And they paid me well indeed," he finished lamely.

"How much?"

"What'd youse got?"

The *sramana* loosened the black belt that held his priestly robe in place and brought forth a small cloth pouch from an inner pocket. The weathered garment parted revealing a blue-black stain that ran from the base of his neck (which his long hair had concealed) down to cover his entire left shoulder.

The boatman gasped. "Well, ain't that just something. And talk about *kittim*. How'd youse ever survive that? I heard tell of a few that did, but I ain't never believed it."

The *sramana* grinned and covered himself. "Must have been a different kind of *kittim*," he said offhandedly. "I do suffer side-effects, though."

He emptied the purse, spilling a half dozen gold coins into the boatman's open palm. They were quite old, Yadish coins from the time of the Unified Kingdom. They bore the likenesses of ancient Yadish Kings.

Beneath the shade of his wide hat, the boatman's wicked little eyes bugged out, causing him to look more froglike than any frog the *sramana* had ever seen in all his wanderings up and down the river.

"Ain't that special."

"Will these do?"

"Thought youse was some kind of ass-cetic."

"I found them. People can discover lots of things when they learn to look. I've found much more during my travels, but I've no use for the stuff. Just weighs me down—"

The boatman laughed. "Well, if youse ain't the strangest priest I've ever seen. An Akkadean that don't want no wealth? Ain't that special. Here, if youse don't want 'em hand 'em over. I'm happy to relieve youse of the burden, I am."

"You'll take me into the city then?"

"Sure, sure—" The boatman leaned against his oars and pushed the gondola up against the pier. "Here, here, hand 'em over."

The *sramana* dropped the coins into his open hand.

"What's your name, good boatman?"

"Calls me Drang, my boy. It's the noise the oars make in the eyelets…drang, drang, drang… And youse, my good Akkadean priest?"

"We leave names behind. Names are not real. They never change. They repeat the same thing again and again, forever if that were possible. This world is about coming and going, appearing and disappearing—from one moment to the next."

"Is that so? Well, maybe your *kittim* poisoning is the slow acting kind, drives a man insane before it kills 'em. Heard about them sort'o poisons from an old herb-master. Didn't believe it then. They is always bragging about their skills and powers. Could be he was telling the truth—"

"May I?" The *sramana* stepped off the dock and into the gondola. The vessel almost sank. He pushed past Drang and seated himself beneath a canvas awning at the center of the craft. Miraculously the gondola stayed afloat.

"Ain't much of an ass-cetic, as I said before." Drang peered at him from under his hat. He pocketed the coins, grasped the oars and turned the vessel about. Slowly, he began pulling the weighted craft through the dark waters of the canal toward the city walls.

"Come for the wedding, huh? Visitors ain't welcome in Tholos except for Akkadeans selling their women." He chuckled at his own jest.

The *sramana* remained silent.

"I seen her from afar. When she came down King's Road. Didn't think much of her. Too skinny, far too young if you ask me. Oh and that dark skin—" He stopped himself. "I mean…I likes my women seasoned and filled out—and white. Vishnu paid a fortune too. And he could have any woman in the Tribe. It's 'cause she's fertile, they say. But how would anyone know that?"

"How could you know?" The *sramana's* voice was quite low, barely audible.

"What? Well, tell youse what, I don't like mixing Tribes either. Tribes have been apart for a long time. No telling what might come out of it. Youse ask me, I think them Akkadeans is barely human—and I tell you what, those Yads ain't nothing but a bunch of monkeys dressed in gold suits and robes—"

He stopped himself again, suddenly realizing—too late—that the priest might be offended, even though Drang was simply telling the truth. Yet, when he considered it, he figured that the priest had already paid for his services—so what did he care?

"Oh, they're human," the *sramana* said softly. "I've been to Emerald and Haran both. Other *sramanas* have also. They're as human as you."

"Well, ain't that special."

They neared the arched opening in the wall where the Grand Canal entered the city. A single guard stood on top of the wall dressed in a white military tunic with a black officer's sash and silver fluting. He wore a broad brimmed hat like Drang, but unlike the boatman he carried an L-gun.

Drang leaned on his oars and brought the gondola to a standstill.

"He's gonna want a name and wanderer or priest ain't enough.

The *sramana* sighed. "Give him Marduk. Marduk, priest of Nalanda."

EXALTED FATHER

BOOK OF SILENCE
VERSE 1.3.4

The guard waved them in. Drang docked at the first wharf. A host of river barges were tied up here, many had not been unloaded. In fact, by the looks of things, the rotted hulls, frayed cables, and thick coat of sickly algae, they had been tied to this wharf for many years.

"Walk from here, my boy. Unless youse got more of them coins weighing you down."

The *sramana* shrugged and stepped onto the uncertain footing of the wharf. In a second, four white-coated guards surrounded him. They bore pikes and sabers but no L-guns.

"What's your business in Tholos?" one of the guards demanded. He wore a red armband and was the tallest of the group. His tone might have sounded gruff, even dangerous, had it not been for the unintended squeak leaking out like air from a ruptured balloon.

"Nothing. No business. Just wandering the River Road and stopped here. Heard there was a wedding. It is the nature of wanderers to wander."

"He's lying!" Drang abruptly shouted. He's an Akkadean spy, sent here to snoop out the wedding. Got a thing for the Khan's daughter. Toll me so. See? He don't look like no ass-cetic to me. And he's young."

"What are you saying, pilot?" asked the guard.

Drang pushed the gondola back from the wharf. They had difficulty hearing him. He began to shout.

"Are youse deaf youssell, sergeant? Ass-cetics don't look so healthy. And he says he ain't no priest neither. He's Akkadean, don't youse know. Ever hear tell of Akkadeans giving away healthy kids to the priesthood?"

The sergeant fixed squinting eyes on Marduk, peering up at him as if filtering perception through a newly formed sieve of suspicion.

"He had money too," Drang went on, all the time pulling further away. "And he's got the biggest bug wound I've ever seen. Look at his left neck and shoulder. Should be dead—"

The sergeant reached for the ascetic's shoulder. The *sramana* backed away quickly, and collided with another guard standing behind him. The collision sent the surprised man headfirst into the canal.

The guard screeched, then began choking. His coat began smoke even as water soaked into it. It seemed as if he were burning, although he floated on the surface.

He thrashed and screamed and choked. The tightly woven cotton fabric appeared to unravel at the seams. In a moment the coat disintegrated. Then a most horrible thing happened: his skin began to peel, actually dissolving from his body as though he were being boiled.

His screams became whimpering, then gurgling. He turned completely black and sank from view.

"Seize that murdering priest!" the sergeant cried.

The two other guards hesitated. The sergeant screamed at them to bind the priest's arms and if he resisted to run him through— or push him into the canal—or cut off his arms, legs, his head, anything the sergeant could think of. When they still did not move, he cursed them for their cowardice and swore that he'd see them drawn and quartered (although all of them knew that this was an empty threat since there were no horses in Ra'bim, nor in all Greenbottom, nor had there been for over a hundred years).

The sergeant raged on, though he made sure to keep himself at a safe distance—at least what he guessed was a safe distance.

"No need for such drastic measures," said the *sramana* calmly. "Spring comes of itself." He offered his hands to be bound. "I'll come peacefully. You must know I had no wish to harm your companion. His fall was an accident. A monk came wandering, and he fell."

"Bind the assassin," croaked the sergeant.

Reluctantly, yellow eyes wide with fear, they slipped flexible metal cables about his wrists. The metal looked thin and worn. It was old Nepptali make, and it seemed that the big *sramana* might have easily twisted and broke them.

Drang, who had stopped his craft to observe the doings on the wharf, yelled back in a high-pitched voice: "That priest-boy is the girl's former lover. Admitted to me himself, he did. I weaseled it outta him. She jilted him, don't youse know. For our glorious Vishnu. Toll him she wanted a real man. So he's here to kill Vishnu. Can youse believe it?"

He swept his hat off and bowed, nearly upending the boat. "Lucky I remembered just now. Youse'll tell the centurion how I saved our beloved Vishnu. Name's Drang. Drang the Boatman. I'm sure the Triumvir will wish to reward me with a great reward."

THE BOOKS OF MARDUK

BOOK OF SILENCE
VERSE 1.3.5

They marched the young *sramana* through deserted streets. A block before the street they followed terminated at The Cleansing, the sergeant turned right and dragged the thus-named Marduk into a squat cube-like house made of white brick and stucco. Inside, the house smelled of formaldehyde, ginger-root, resin, and other pungent spices unknown to him. The experience was quite unpleasant.

A vicious shove in the back sent him stumbling down cut stone steps into a wide cellar. The surface of the steps was slippery. They were made for shorter legs and smaller feet. But the *sramana* kept his balance—quite an athletic feat—and reached the ground floor unharmed.

An enormous cavern opened before him, stuffed with tables, sinks, tubs, and rows upon rows of shelves bearing a confusion of bottles, jars, boxes, beakers and test-tubes of every shape and size. Nepptali quartz lamps bathed the cavern in yellow light.

A large man arose unsteadily from a feather mattress. He was frightfully obese but tall (for a Rab), coming almost to the *sramana*'s chin. He pulled on a white guards-coat trimmed with gold and covered with ribbons.

"Who the hell is this?" he complained, fixing the sergeant with a baneful glare—although it was in truth difficult to determine just where he fixed his yellow eyes as they were sunken and enfolded by rolls of puffy white skin. The glare *felt* baneful.

"Over-colonel Dmitri, I bring you an Akkadean assassin."

The Over-colonel grasped a saber and looked thus-named Marduk up and down.

"Are you fuckin' crazy, Sergeant Hari? This here's a priest."

"He killed a guard."

Exalted Father

"What?"

"Done killed old Yang-I. Pushed 'em into the canal. He's here to kill the Triumvir and steal the Akkadean slut."

"Vishnu's wife?"

"Aye, Over-colonel. The mad Khan lied to us. She's no virgin. Been married for a long time. To this one."

"To a priest? Shit! They're a bunch of castrates."

"He's an Akkadean assassin in the disguise of a priest."

"You there." The Over-colonel fixed his gaze upon the assassin-in-disguise. "Did you kill poor Yang-I?"

The *sramana* shook his head. "It was an accident, my Over-colonel. The man—Yang-I? —slipped on slime-covered wood and fell into the water. I don't really know what killed him. His coming, his going, like Lesser and Greater Winds."

Sergeant Hari yelled: "Lies, lies…nonsense! Done pushed him in. He knew all along that the canal's deadly. Been spying on Ra'bim for years."

"Take him over there." Dmitri pointed to a large wooden frame that stood vertically between two tables.

Hari and the two other guards shoved the *sramana* up against the frame. They tore off his priestly robes and left him naked but for his loincloth.

"Well look at that!" the Over-colonel exclaimed. "Ain't never seen a bug stain that big on someone who's still breathing."

"Dmitri shuffled over to a bookcase. He examined row after row of dark glass bottles. At last, after careful consideration he selected one and walked back to the frame upon which the guards had bound the *sramana* with leather thongs.

"Drink this, Akkadean. Drink or I'll cut you so you'll never want another woman again."

Sergeant Hari and the two guards snickered.

"My hands are tied," said the *sramana*-assassin innocently.

"Yeah, well, here, I'll help." The Over-colonel reached up and put the bottle to the ascetic's lips. He gazed in astonishment. The Akkadean assassin drank the entire contents without hesitation.

"I was thirsty. What was that? Tasted a little sour."

Over-colonel Dmitri took a backward step

The others stopped snickering.

They waited—for a quarter hour. In the meantime, the *sramana* closed his eyes and appeared to take a nap. When he opened them again, they were still bright green and clearly sane—for a priest.

"What the fuck!" The Over-colonel went to another shelf and retrieved a large beaker of purple fluid. "Drink this."

"I don't drink—wine."

"Ain't no fuckin' wine. Drink it or I slice a few important pieces from your dirty hide."

Thus-named Marduk obediently drained the beaker. They waited. This time he didn't take a nap. He stared at them in curiosity as if awaiting an explanation.

"I believe we're missing the wedding," he said finally.

"Shit..." Hari breathed. "Shouldn't he be all bloody and bleeding from every pore? Babbling everything he knows and then some?"

The Over-colonel spun suddenly and smashed the hilt of his saber into the sergeant's face. The Rab's features seemed to come apart as if exploding in slow motion. Blood shot from his nose, mouth and ears. His eyes bulged as if they were about to pop. He collapsed with a wet, gurgling cry.

"Get that incompetent maggot out of here and throw him into the canal!"

Over-colonel Dmitri turned back to the assassin. "The wedding's over and Vishnu's otherwise occupied. There's a banquet later. I'm invited which means you're invited too. You done killed *two* Ra'bim guards, Yang-I and Hari. Ain't nobody ever seen no one drink Purple Soma and remain sane. You done drank enough to put down an

EXALTED FATHER

entire Tribe. Vishnu's gonna see you before I slit your throat. Come to think of it, you'll be my wedding gift."

The Books Of Marduk

BOOK OF SILENCE
VERSE 1.3.6

The banquet hall was located in a vaulted cavern deep beneath the pyramid. The Ra'bim, it was said, only felt safe and at ease when they were underground. Quartz lamps hung from thick wooden beams and heavy tapestries covered the vaulted walls. A long table dominated the hall, and behind it double doors opened to a spacious, heated kitchen. The dinning area felt damp and musty and smelled of rotted things.

She was dimly aware of sitting at the head of the table, seated alongside a disgusting, bloated maggot of a man. The day had been a blur of images, sounds, and unfocused feelings. They kept feeding her things that looked like pieces of candy. They forced her to drink from brown-glass bottles. She was helpless to resist their medications.

It was fortunate for them (and the ancient maggot-man seated next to her) that they kept her drugged. Had she been free she would have killed them all, and she would have needed nothing except her bare hands. She would have felt no remorse.

The somas could not erase her memories. She wondered if the somas changed them. Somehow, although blinded by the soma fog, she understood that memories were the anchor of her sanity. She dared not doubt them.

From the moment she was able to walk, she wore the blue leather vest, the blue coat and stripped trousers of an Akkadean officer. Jebe, the greatest soldier since the days of Khan Manuel, taught her the art of the scimitar, the bow, the L-gun and dagger, the staff and net, and all the lethal martial art techniques that had been developed for two Kalpas by the greatest warriors in Greenbottom.

She'd shaved her black hair and exercised daily. When not in military uniform, she dressed in the black style of the assassins' guild.

Her father the Khan laughed.

She'd grown up without girlfriends. There were really no girls her age to be her friends. She despised Akkadean womanly fashions. She refused to learn the feminine occupations of the Tribe from her mother Hagar and her aunts. In everything she'd tried with every ounce of determination to please her father. By the time she'd reached her teens she realized that her father *would never* be pleased. Unconsciously perhaps, she began to feel sad (her word at the time) towards him. It seemed to her that he never wanted to be her father in the first place. In time sadness became resentment, then disgust, at last hate.

While still a small child, until the age of twelve or thirteen, she'd sensed a strange, invisible presence that seemed to hover around her and follow her wherever she went. At dusk, dawn, in a dream, in the shadows of a grove of white birch near the lake, she felt the presence of a being, a man she believed, she began to call her *protector.* Her mother told her that it was the spirit of the Lord, but she doubted that.

Her protector had the dark skin and long black hair of an Akkadean. Usually, he dressed in the blue military tunic of Akkad. Sometimes he was young, sometimes old, bearded, hobbling along as though lame. He seemed to drag his left leg, although sometimes it was his right. She was certain she'd known him *before*—but *before* what?

Once when she was swimming in Emerald Lake, she ventured too far out and got caught in the lake's powerful undertow. She would have drowned had not her *protector* intervened. Suddenly she felt strong hands grab her arms and pull her to the surface, and then into shore. Gasping for air, gagging on lake water, she turned her head hoping to gaze upon her rescuer. She saw nothing.

She never saw his face, but she was certain she'd know him if she did see him. Then, about twelve or thirteen, he disappeared. Deserted once by a man, the dark part of her soul grew and expanded like lake sludge. She recognized the black stain, knew what it meant—and welcomed it.

Agni was the closest to her in years. Although Agni might have wished differently, she treated him as a competitor in everthing. And—she bested him: in sports, in training, in endurance and strength. She ran faster, fenced better, fought harder. She even learned to read and write with ease, where Agni struggled. Had there still been horses, she would have made the better equestrian.

There was a moment in her middle teens when she felt a stirring, when her world suddenly transformed into something very different, quite strange and frightening, yet wonderful as well. Suddenly she wanted Agni, not as a competitor, but as something more. It almost drove her mad and she feared that she was losing herself. It was like drowning in the lake. It caused her to sweat on a cold day, shudder on a hot one. She dreamed of Agni and her together, felt him, tasted him, loathed and loved him at the same time. Then, one fine day, she woke up and felt—nothing. The frightening craving had vanished, and with it the beautiful exciting wonder.

(Later, the sramana revived it, but then it became something quite different, something far more intense...poets sing.)

Soon after her longing for him had dissolved, during combat practice in which she'd bloodied his nose, Agni tried to seduce her.

They were resting on a grassy slope overlooking Lake Emerald. The warm summer sun, the gentle lake breeze, and the exhilaration of the contest, conspired with him, causing her to doze. She was dreaming, not about him.

Abruptly she came to full awaking. Agni cuddled close. He muzzled and kissed her neck. His hand had crept inside her black silk shirt and was gently caressing her small firm breast. A pinch of her nipple had brought her to awareness.

Her first reaction was incredulous laughter.

In a husky voice, he whispered in her ear: "Who is there for you in all Akkad? Only *me*, Devorah. I am for you."

She rolled over and faced him. She was still laughing.

His fingers explored. He said: "Yes, you feel it, don't you? I have for many years. And beyond that… In a past I cannot remember, we were together."

She stopped laughing, but she still grinned, pitying his complete incomprehension of how close to death he was at this moment.

"Remove your hand, Agni my foolish boy," she advised calmly. "In a moment it'll be useless to you. And worse will follow as certain as Greater Wind in the morning."

Sudden anger, like liquid fire, surged through his veins. She saw it. Then he perceived the danger and he withdrew his hand quickly. He wanted to strike her. But, oh, how well he knew her capabilities. Fear stopped him. Humiliation followed.

"If not me, who?" he asked bitterly.

She grinned but did not answer. Her craving for Agni had vanished, and there was nothing to replace it. Her desire for men disappeared. She knew that this was true of many women of her Tribe, and she suspected it was so in many other Tribes. There were some, she knew, who'd gone completely in the opposite direction. In not a few of these few, lust drove them to madness. For this was the Third Kalpa, the age of male impotence and barren wives.

"Don't you feel them? Memories that have no form or substance. We have them. Of other times, strange, far-away places?" Agni asked.

She had no answer. Not that she hadn't felt the need…oh, but the opposite was true. How powerful and insistent her need had been. And, she knew the unformed memories of which Agni spoke.

Agni had been someplace in the dim past. A different Agni, in another...another kind of being.

"Who?" he asked again.

"Who? Not *you*."

Slowly, with agonizing difficulty, fueled by a deadly will born of memory, she turned her face to the ancient mummy and whispered: "Not *you*—"

It was true. Not Vishnu.

Her memory of the wedding ceremony was far weaker. Bits and slices of experience remained like a dull aftertaste. Horrendous singing and endless speeches—in a language that sounded like the death-cries of lizards. A long ascent to the throne room of the Triumvirs—lying naked on a bed that smelled like rotten wormwood, burned barleycorn, and tamariska root. Vishnu, ghastly white, a decaying corpse, mounting her. His screams of failure. Her own satisfaction at his failure.

"What'd you say, Akkadean?" Vishnu asked. He sounded irritated and surprised. She'd actually spoken the words. How could that be?

"Thought you said she couldn't talk," Vishnu complained to the man seated at his left hand.

"Yes, sire. She shows resistance to Yellow Soma."

"Thought I said I didn't want 'er talking?"

"Indeed, sire."

"Especially when I'm hard at work. And I tell you, Roman my boy, I was both hard and at work most of the afternoon."

This brought forth laughter from the table and another round of toasts.

"Does she remember?"

"Not much. Yellow Soma especially affects memory. Thus are we able to write in a new personality...we think."

"We *think*!"

Roman the Court Physician studied Vishnu closely. He could tell that the old man had failed. His skin was cold and a shade of white below white, the color of empty. This meant their prized Whittling potion had failed. He perceived signs of side-effects. Unlike the intended object of the treatment, the beast-within was rising up. Why had the potion failed after all those successful tests?

It had to be the Akkadean slut—

Vishnu glanced at Devorah and frowned. That is to say, he frowned within a frown. His face appeared frozen in a petrified frown. The hanging jowls, bloated nose, always wet, always dripping, the droopy eyes, faded yellow and watery, great hanging ears, lumpy dome of a head—all together constituted one great frown. Everything in existence bored him, everything caused him pain, everything was a struggle against inertia—all was sour and bitter and not worth the effort.

He turned back to Roman. "Now what's this entertainment you promised?"

The Court Physician rose from his chair and gave a signal to the guards at the double doors at the far end of the hall. Immediately, the the doors swung open and Over-colonel Dmitri entered. A dark man followed, naked but for a loincloth, bound and surrounded by guards with drawn sabers. The man was Akkadean, and young, younger even than the bride. Spreading down from his neck to his shoulder, and touching his breast, was a large blue-black patch of discolored skin. *Kittim* poisoning.

Roman turned to Vishnu. "Sire, an Akkadean spy and assassin. We thought you'd like to witness its execution."

"*An Akkadean assassin!*" Vishnu screeched. His anger mounted and Roman feared he'd suffer a stroke. "Bastard! That old bastard

Khan. Next time they ask for medicines, give 'em a barrel of Purple Soma and kill the whole fucking Tribe."

"We'll begin with this one." The Court Physician turned to Over-colonel Dmitri and said: "Administer the death-drink."

Dimly she felt his presence. She really couldn't physically see him, but she felt him. He was gazing at her. She knew it. His eyes, green, young like the spring, his body, strong and supple like a sapling, his hair long and black. Him?

"Then who?" She heard the words, in a place of hearing beyond hearing.

They untied his hands and gave him the cup. Drink, the Over-colonel ordered. Public executions among the Ra'bim were always suicides.

He smiled and drained the cup without resistance. All the time watching her, drinking far more deeply of her, smiling all the while. Then the smile faded, for he remembered the old vows. Now he focused on the reason he'd come. The farvel had spoken to him in a dream. The farvel had given him words, and he spoke them exactly as the farvel had instructed, to *her*, to Devorah of Akkad.

"And he said aloud: *"Oh Devorah of Akkad, what binds you?"*

The Ra'bim around the hall stared at him in disbelief. He should not have been breathing. How could he be talking? No one actually paid attention to *what* he'd said. It was nonsense. Except Devorah of Akkad—

His voice, it richness and strength—she *heard what he said*. Her mind came alive with his words, like the daystar breaking through a dark cover of clouds. She became filled with rage. Tears came to her eyes and her heart began to race.

He spoke again as the farvel had instructed: *"Devorah of Akkad. What binds you? Arise and go from this place."*

"You are the dark soil itself, the trees and fields, the river and even the red desert. You belong to this world. What binds you?"

His new voice, so deep and loud, was over-powering. The Ra'bim guards backed away, holding their ears.

Abruptly he ignited. He blazed, his skin, his hair, his entire body. He became a pillar of fire.

Dmitri cried out and shielded his eyes. All the Ra'bim shielded their eyes. It was impossible that he should live.

"What binds you?"

The *sramana* turned and walked back through the doors. Not a single bloated Rab moved to stop him. The shock was too great. The soma should have killed him. The soma should have burned him from the inside. Soma was unpredictable, the herb-masters often said.

Minutes passed. No living being should have able to resist such a soma. No Rab could endure the brilliance of his burning.

Vishnu lurched to his feet. His yellow eyes turned red.

"Kill him!" he screamed.

THE BOOKS OF MARDUK

THE BOOK OF SILENCE

CHAPTER FOUR - Nalanda

VERSE 1.4.1

The oldest architecture constructed by human hands was the monastery called Nalanda.

All roads lead to Nalanda, priests said. In actual fact, one road led to Nalanda.

(But everyone knows how easily *one* becomes *all* in theological discussions.)

King Reuben's Road ran parallel to the Pearldew wadi and terminated at Nalanda.

(Forgotten *in these days* is the full name of the road: King Reuben's Road of Victorious Harmony and Final Peace Beloved of All the Tribes).[5]

The priesthood liked to say that the road began with Nalanda. The Tribes protested. Like rivers, roads do not flow south to north. King Reuben's Road began in the Blackdiamond Forest where the

---

[5] Both scribal interpolations come from later manuscripts and are not found in the oldest.

Exalted Father

Blue and White Pearldew merged as they meandered down from the northern Blackdiamond Mountains. No human being in three Kalpas had visited these lands, which means that no human being had ever seen these places.

Outside of the Yadish, the Tribes preferred to call the road *King's Road*. *Reuben* reminded them of the Unified Kingdom. This name they wished to forget.

Overlooking a shallow gorge, Nalanda sat on the southwestern tip of Red Lake. The lake was shaped like an inverted teardrop. The Pearldew flowed into it from the north and exited from the southern tip where it then split into a web of capillaries that fed into the Windward Sea. Across the Windward Sea was Starmirror, the Southern Continent, the Holy One's continent, home to His Holy Mountain Elsseleron. Priests of the First Kalpa claimed that Elsseleron meant *Needleglass*. [*In those days*] no one trusted priestly translations—or said another way, by the end of Third Kalpa people had learned to doubt anything a priest said. One might say that the Akkadean disease had spread among the Tribes as thoroughly as the barrenness of women.

In truth there were two Nalandas, upper and the lower, much as a tree-line divides a mountain. Upper Nalanda was bare and windswept, a perfect square of stone walls enclosing a single tower. Weather-beaten and very ancient, the stone walls resembled denuded bone. In some places they had caved in, creating random heaps of shattered debris, as if some giant had taken a sledgehammer to them.

After an exhausting climb (for priests) of steep rock stairs that tacked in one direction and then another like a ship making sail against the wind, the traveler discovered that the tower was really a series of square boxes, one resting on the other, each a tiny bit smaller than the box upon which it sat. The tower resembled a massive wedding cake, [*in those days*] a confection seldom, if ever, seen among the Tribes of Men.

The Books Of Marduk

A winding stairs tracked the inside wall of the tower. It led to the topmost room. The upper nest was the cell of the archbishop, chief prelate of the monastery, master of the priesthood, keeper of the *Runehayana*.

For two Kalpas, among nearly all the Tribes, Upper Nalanda was the most honored and holy site in all Greenbottom. According to the priesthood, the archbishop's tower reproduced Elsseleron, the Holy Mountain. *According to the priesthood.* Since no one had ever seen Elsseleron, this assertion had to be taken on faith. [In these times] faith is like the memory of a deathly fever.

Deep in the rocky foundation of Upper Nalanda was buried the greatest gift of the Almighty to men. Cut into the roots of the false-mountain (false meaning artificial) was a vast hall which housed a subterranean crystalline lake dubbed Lordpool. The Tribes named it Priestpool.

Rising to the surface of the pool (Lord or Priest), like stars appearing on the surface of a pond, the Four Major Runes of the Lord would suddenly and unpredictably manifest in line after line, row after row, without word breaks, paragraphs, or punctuation. In times past, the Holy One made known His divine will to human beings. Priests duly recorded the words of the Lord in the *Runehayana*. Until the Third Kalpa.

Lower Nalanda resembled a military fort with rows of barracks constructed from northern cedar and oak, supposedly harvested from the Blackdiamond Forest and floated down the river. It was whispered that some of the building materials included wood from the cursed whittling trees. Many Tribes believed that this claim was almost certainly priestly foolishness. Many suspected that it was some pitiful attempt to impress the Tribes and win back their respect.

Whittling trees had been cut and burned during the First Kalpa. No one knew what their wood looked like. The Rabs said that they preserved samples of whittling bark in their laboratories, which were really dungeons of wickedness and perversion (according to the priesthood). Rabs were hardly human anymore (according to the Tribes). They'd devolved into a nest of bleached maggots. They lied with finesse, although cynically and not with the sincerity of the priesthood. Which species of lie is the most evil became a celebrated priestly debating point.

Priests and novice monks inhabited the barracks of Lower Nalanda. A massive Cathedral in the shape of a truncated cone—another copy of Elsseleron, said the priests (unknowingly confirming their own ignorance since it looked nothing like the archbishop's tower)—sat in the middle of the barracks square. The Cathedral, dubbed Convocation, once served as the gathering place for the Twelve Tribes of Men. In the Third Kalpa of Silence it had become decayed and empty.

The Lord of the Mountain no longer spoke to His children, and so His children no longer spoke to each other—said the priests, speaking among themselves.

THE BOOKS OF MARDUK

BOOK OF SILENCE
VERSE 1.4.2

On this particular spring morning, archbishop Theophilus sat alone in his tower cell and gazed north. He sipped his first brandy of the day. Dewdrop moon faded as the daystar overwhelmed its borrowed light. Torn clouds from last night's storm floated south across a brightening sky. The last gasp of Greater Wind rattled the shutters of the tower's windows.

The archbishop glanced down and noted that a few stray *bugeaves* had fallen into the courtyard. These were exceedingly large, perhaps the largest he'd seen in all his hundred and twenty years. Colorful too. Mostly light green, blue, light purple, a thousand shades of yellow and an especially brilliant shade of red—like blood, he mused—they swirled in vortices and shot down like sparks. Dissolving into whatever they touched, they left a deep penetrating stain, generally some shade of blue-black, even in soil and stone.

He sighed and sipped his brandy. Never had they come this late in the season and so far south. Never had they seemed so... He permitted himself a chuckle. *Purposeful?*

As if *anything* in nature had a purpose. Scribal inventions, priestly desires, hopeful biases—such words as *purpose* and *meaning* sprang from wistful dreams. He knew this well enough from long experience. Propelled by imagination, words such as purpose (also meaning, justice, fate, soul) found homes in nature itself. Like the moons, they owed their existence to borrowed light.

As if mere longing proved the existence of a thing. As if desires nature could never fulfill pointed to the existence of a better world in which *all* desires were fulfilled. Theophilus felt the warmth rising from his stomach. Such *proofs* were symptoms of mental illness. He couldn't recall exactly when he'd reached this conclusion. Subsequent experience only served to make it stronger.

A flimsy chain of cause and effect, another superstition—

Watching *bugeaves* drift about the monastery drove the archbishop's brandy-born thoughts to memories of Marduk. The *sramana* may have possibly been the only human being to survive a *bugeave* poisoning, although Theophilus had heard rumors that some Akkadeans, the old senile Khan for one, were also immune.

Marduk was relatively young and strong. Although the archbishop could not be absolutely certain, he suspected that Marduk came from the last human generation born in Greenbottom. That would make Marduk's age somewhere in his forties. There was no way of being sure. The Tribes had splintered terribly since the Great Yadish War. He was certain that some had disappeared. And others—? Who knew what they'd become?

Theophilus closed his eyes and pictured the long-haired *sramana*, beardless and smooth skinned, with the deep tattoo of bug-poisoning covering the left side of his neck and shoulder. For an ascetic, Marduk appeared *too* healthy. He never stumbled, never shuffled like other *sramanas*. His steps were steady and dignified as if he were always walking downhill. Theophilus believed that he'd once caught him floating. Of course the archbishop had to be mistaken.

Yet, there was something *cold* in Marduk. He appeared aloof from the concerns of other men, even priests. He spoke in riddles, if he spoke at all. He laughed on the most inappropriate occasions, as though he were slightly (perhaps more than slightly) mad. Theophilus thought of him as a man who lived *somewhere else*. Despite all this, he was the greatest scholar of the age.

His last visit to Nalanda had been some five years ago. Or was it last year? The archbishop found it ever more difficult to keep track of the time's flow. It didn't seem to matter anymore. Yesterday might have fifty years ago. He was beginning to suspect that time too was a mental illness.

The young ascetic arrived in the evening guided by the soft light of Lotus Moon. There had been a deluge of *bugeaves*. They seemed to accompany him. Without explanation, he disappeared into the catacombs of Upper Nalanda's library.

The library stood separate from the main tower but was connected to it by a long causeway. When he had not surfaced for a week, the archbishop—who hated the library as much as he despised Lordpool—went looking for him.

He found Marduk in the oldest section, which was in fact a basement beneath the squat single-floored rectangle that housed the main collection. Chill and damp, it resembled a crypt. If only it were a wine cellar, how much the better.

Square shafts, like tombs, were dug into the ground. Instead of a sarcophagus however, each shaft contained a ceramic jar. Fifteen such shafts and jars, divided into groups of three, made the floor look like a huge checker-board. Long work benches with oil lamps sat along the walls. Quartz lamps were unknown in Nalanda. It was unknown how long they'd been unknown, although the archbishop guessed it had been a very long time—although it could have been yesterday.

Each jar contained a scroll of animal skin taken from extinct antelopes. Runes covered the parchment scrolls and were inscribed with gold and red ink. Shelves along the walls contained codices, books that represented the work of two and a half Kalpas of priests as they calculated and transliterated the Runes of the Holy One. The main library in Lower Nalanda contained translations, histories, theological tomes, and various commentaries: thousands upon thousands of volumes of priestly writings (Theophilus could only guess the number, and he easily avoided the temptation of looking through the codices) dated back to the beginning of Greenbottom.

EXALTED FATHER

Theophilus knew one thing for certain. *Not a single Rune came from the Almighty, The Holy One, the All Powerful, the One Lord, or any being remotely resembling such an absurd concept.* He'd heard rumors that the Nepptali hoarded their own thousands of volumes, far older versions of the Books. From where, he'd wondered, had these come?

After a lifetime of dedicated scholarship, and after much internal resistance, the archbishop had succumbed to this fateful conclusion. Non-belief had arisen in him like an irresistible compulsion, not unlike infatuation. It was identical to love for a mysterious and captivating woman. Naturally the archbishop saw the irony in such a comparison and wondered at the foolishness of anyone who might dare make it. What did priests know about women? Except in their dreams. He laughed at the thought.

As a young man he had fervently believed. Oh how he had believed. Belief was a fever that banished all other desires—even the desire for a woman. He laughed again. How is it that women keep popping up in priestly narratives?

Through sheer determination and almost super-human dedication he made himself into the greatest scholar of the Kalpa, until Marduk. A kind of madness drove him. He was Lord-intoxicated said many priests and *sramanas*. He very nearly destroyed himself, his health and his sanity, in order to know the *real* and *true* Almighty in the *real* and *true* divine language. He craved the All-Powerful Lord of Lords more than he'd ever desired anything.

Perhaps in the end his own obsessive desire betrayed him. One day he fell asleep on the crystalline surface of Lordpool. Wearing his old patched black cassock, he looked like a dead leaf floating on an absolutely calm lake.

A dream came to him. He only remembered distorted images. He saw strange creatures, golden furred cat-like things that seemed eerily human. They were watering and tending strange trees…but not really trees…more like pulsating shafts of light…like vertical staircases filled with strange beings going up and down. The trees encircled dark green, almost black, stagnant ponds, not unlike Lordpool upon which he slept. He felt the Winds, saw the Moons, tasted the air. And when he awoke, staring into the black depths of the dead pool, he knew with unquestionable certainty that his life-long quest had come to a conclusion. Lordpool was a polluted pond. Lord-language was nonsense, the hopeful croaking of frogs. Mountains were just mountains, in no need of Lords.

Non-belief was like gravity holding his body to the pool's dark surface.

Later, he came to the conclusion that the beings from his dream were the source of his compulsion to *not-believe*. And—to his surprise, which he quickly dismissed it as coincidence—he discovered accounts of such beings buried in dusty histories of long ago. Dubbed *farvels*, the histories said that they were not of the Lord. All creatures *not of the Lord* the Lord ordered hunted down and destroyed. The Lord never said *why* farvels were not of the Lord. He apparently left it up to the priests. Priests are never lax when it comes to finding good reasons for the Lord's worse crimes. Theophilus had forgotten the reason (or reasons) for the slaughter of the farvels.

Odd that he should dream of a long dead race of beings, cursed by the Lord, while sleeping on the crystal surface of the Lord's own pool. He stuck with odd and went no further.

The archbishop made a vow that before he died he would take a sledge hammer and smash Lordpool. It would be like breaking ice. He vowed to uncover the Rune-producing mechanism invented by the first priests (those scoundrels). He would show the Tribes the machine that randomly ground out meaningless symbols, symbols that set men howling like wolves in the wild and wailing like children in the night. He would demonstrate how the long dead held the living in thrall. He would become the liberator of men. He would wash their minds with the truth.

EXALTED FATHER

How foolish a notion was this? He grimaced and drank some brandy. The truth was different. The histories shouted the truth. The truth was that the truth would drive men and women howling into the streets. His job was to expand and strengthen a stupid transparent *lie*.

In his later years he came to realize that truth would make no difference. The *idea* of the Lord drove men mad. No human being possessed the strength to resist it. While people might come to know that there was No-One-On-High, the knowledge would create a new No-One-On-High, only stronger—a High-No-One-On-High

The non-existence of the Only-One took some time to internalize—and not without the aid of a little brandy. The One and Only was a sneaky bastard, slipping in the backdoor of emotion. Unbelief was like a *bugeave* stain; it went no deeper than the skin. It took time to soak into the guts.

He took another sip of brandy.

Seated at one of the work benches, Marduk bent over a scroll containing the Book of *Bhavana*, Great Tribal War, the Fourth Book, gathered together in a huge jar labeled the *Books of Jambridvipa*, which the priests took to mean *Human History*.

Marduk was writing on what appeared to be another ancient scroll.

Despite the fact that the emaciated archbishop was as transparent as any ghost and could be invisible to human eyes when he so desired, Marduk instantly sensed his approach.

"What an awful shadow floats above these Runes," the *sramana* whispered over his shoulder. His voice broke at each syllable as if he sobbed the words. "Relentless as death—

"Suthra the Lame,

Cursed by priests and men,

And the One All-powerful.

Why climb the mountain?

Only to find rock and snow,
Only to find your answer,
A bruised hip."
Marduk looked up. "Or is it a broken leg?"

Theophilus coughed and pulled at the few remaining strands of his once-generous archbishop's beard. How often had he heard Marduk complain that not a single priest in all history had correctly calculated and translated the Runes? In the presence of the archbishop he wondered aloud if the whole *Runehayana* was nothing more than an exercise in creative (and destructive) mistranslation? Which is why he became a wandering ascetic, Theophilus guessed—although to tell the truth he really didn't know.

"The old legend of Suthralane again. And how came you to this translation, my good *sramana*?"

Marduk gazed upon the whispering ghost who seemed quite at home in this tomb.

"Recalculation," he said. "Another law haunts these combinations. Who has grasped it? There is a rule. It is not mere guessing of the fractions, which dishonest priests call intuition. Perhaps the fraction-combinations of the Runes immediately preceding the next string of Runes actually limit the possible selections of the next numbers? And these would govern the Sandi selections. The Runes may contain their own rules of combination *that have nothing to do with the letters of Sandi.*"

"So in three Kalpas of the greatest minds in human history only *you* know the correct calculations?"

Marduk ignored the question and continued. "These few lines here in *Bhavana*—"

"Yes?"

A sneer turned Marduk's thin lips. With his sharp nose he resembles a bird, the archbishop thought. He is like a hawk that soars high above the world and sees everything. But he never lands.

"Not the words of the Lord,

Not the words of priests.
From the outside, the cold, airless emptiness.
The Kingdoms *of* the Heavens,
Rise and fall, come and go,
Spoke the silent mountain,
To Suthra the Lame."

Over the years, the archbishop had come to realize that Marduk cultivated an ability to invent cryptic verses that sounded as though they came from the Books themselves. He was doing it now. Many priests were in awe of this ability. They babbled about how lyrical, profound, elegant, even inspired, Marduk could be. It was almost as if the Lord spoke through him rather than the dead *P-pool* beneath the archbishop's tower. There were other priests, of course, who hated Marduk and suspected him of deceit—and overweening pride.

The archbishop knew better. Marduk invented verses, true. But somehow he convinced himself that they were real translations of the Runes into Sandi as the symbols had originally appeared beneath the surface of Lordpool. So much like the old priests, like Theophilus himself in those happy days of belief.

The verses undoubtedly came from Marduk's fertile imagination—which may be the only fertility left to human beings.

Taking a sip of Banalis brandy, he sighed. "Marduk, my boy, you were my best student. Pretty good for an Akkadean. Oh, don't look so surprised. Green eyes, dark skin, hawk nose—Akkadean for sure. Why they sacrificed one as healthy as you to the priesthood still puzzles me. Now look what you've become. A crazy *sramana*, wandering about, imagining all sorts of hidden knowledge, plots and conspiracies, mysteries and prophecies—inserting your fantasies into the scrolls. Yes, yes, don't blanch. Your scribbling sounds incomprehensible enough to be authentic. You may fool yourself but you don't fool me. *They are your words.*"

The old man shook his head. "Like every other priest in history—"

Marduk put his stylus down, turned and smoothed his black scholar's robe. He rolled up the scroll and slipped it back into its urn. Then he rose, grabbed his knotted walking staff and started for the stairs. But halfway there he paused and turned back to look at Theophilus. His green eyes flashed.

"You're wrong, my father. I don't know the things I write. The numbers seem to exist somewhere in another world. They come to me like smoke from a fire. They are waiting to be discovered. I swear to you the method exists *inside* the scrolls...brought from the outside..." He drew a breath. "Somehow..." he finished lamely.

He sighed. "Suthralane found *something* on the Holy Mountain. And it was not the Lord."

Theophilus raised his bushy eyebrows in mock surprise. "Do tell? I've never heard *that version.*"

Marduk stared at him as if reading the Runes in the old man's glassy eyes. The archbishop's mockery did not seem to divert him—if he even noticed that the archbishop was mocking him.

"Suthralane found... *Not-the-Lord.*"

Theophilus felt the brandy heating and scattering his thoughts.

"And Suthralane asked his question," Marduk continued, "Do the Heavens fall with their Kingdoms?"

He glanced away and mumbled to himself, but loud enough for the archbishop to hear: "And the Holy Mountain was stone silent. And Suthralane never learned the answer. And it is not recorded here. If an answer exists, *I will find it—*"

Theophilus laughed. "Well, my boy, this is a new one for sure. But tell me, doesn't one cancel the other? Not-the-Lord and the Lord equals zero. So, ole Suthra the Lame found nothing at all. The Nothing seldom answers questions, I suppose—and, what ears hear it if it did?"

Although he kept staring at the old man, the black haired ascetic appeared not to have heard. He repeated the question "If Kingdoms *of* the Heavens rise and fall, do the Heavens change?"

"Is that your question, or did Suthra ask it of the Lord on the Mountain?"

Marduk turned and took three sheets of papyrus from his inner pocket. He walked back to the table and spread them out for the old man to see.

"Look here, archbishop. The Runes combine differently. The old translations into Sandi were wrong. I've used decimals in place of fractions. And look, this one never ends. Many never end. The decimals keep spinning out new places. Endlessly. No repeats, as least as far as I can calculate. It might take years, centuries, Kalpas of calculation to see if they repeat or conclude. The possible fractions must be limited. How can they be infinite?"

"So? How do you translate infinite decimals into finite Sandi letters? You should know that. One takes it to the third place and calls a halt to the calculating."

Marduk ignored him. He said in a soft voice: "They are *impossible numbers*. Impossible numbers mean that the Lord did not answer Suthralane. The Lord could not answer him because—*He forgot*. No one, not even the Almighty, can remember a number that does not end. Who can recall infinity? It destroyed His mind and He forgot. He forgot the language of the Kingdoms of the Heavens. He forgot their histories. He craved the limit. So he came here, to this world, and created us so there'd be a limit. But he can't change the law of numbers. Therefore He ended up speaking nonsense. And then He went silent... And became Not-the-Lord. He became the *Nothing*."

"So, this terrible *Nothing* smote poor Suthra?" The archbishop was enjoying himself. "*Nothing* sure has a temper."

"Yes. But why?"

"For climbing Not-the-Lord's Holy Mountain?"

"No. Had that been the case the Lord would have never heard him out. He would still be the Lord, not-Not-the-Lord. It is because of the numbers. What if one drops the Sandi number translations?

What if one simply takes the Runes? Is there some pattern in the Four alone? The Nepptali thought so and they worked it out, the rumors say."

Theophilus chuckled. "Oh yes, I've heard all about the Nepptali."

Marduk scribbled two strings of Runes on the third page.

"The Nepptali claimed the Runes come in pairs. They match up, **X** to **'I**, and Λ to **V**. Each string of Runes can be divided into groups of three, and these pair up with the next string by the law of matches. According to the Nepptali *they cannot be assigned fractions nor can they be transliterated into Sandi. They translate into something else.* Look here:

XXX VVI 'IVΛ TTI ΛΛX
TTI ΛΛX XΛV XXX VVI

The pattern seems meaningless. If The Lord's Runes do not transliterate into Sandi letters, then what?"

"Indeed, a great mystery," the archbishop said in a brandy-soaked voice. "What secrets you've discovered. What puzzles you've unraveled. And only you, my boy. And maybe the Nepptali. But nobody, not even priests, understands the Nepptali. Do no further seeking, my son. Rather, create new verses and bring back life's happiness, as in the days when the Lord spoke to Men, directly, through us. How glorious. How the Tribes will admire and love you—and us. You, Marduk, teacher of the world, savior—"

Marduk smiled and the smile creased his face, revealing deep lines where the skin seemed smooth and young. Smiling altered his looks completely. Now he seemed old and weather-beaten, leathery, sinewy, like an authentic ascetic, a true *sramana*. The transformation went deeper, as if an entirely different person had stepped into those road-worn priestly slippers.

EXALTED FATHER

"Oh my good archbishop, do you really think so little of me? It's all in jest, you know. Just now. An inner law of Runes. How ridiculous. I like to tell stories of Suthralane, you know. Some say I make 'em up. And maybe I do. I like to come here for new material." He crinkled the pages and stuffed them carelessly into a hidden pocket of his black *sramana* robe.

Laughing he turned and scrambled up the stairs, leaving a thoroughly confused archbishop in his wake.

That very evening, the pale light of Lotus Moon his lantern, Marduk left Nalanda. Lesser Wind brought a furious storm of *bugeaves* that blanketed the Monastery. Not a single one landed on the black-haired *sramana*.

Before he left he paid a final visit to the archbishop who by evening was as thoroughly drunk. Drinking brandy himself—a very odd behavior for an ascetic—Marduk told stories of King Joseph the Dreamer, and of the pride of the Yadish. They shared a hearty laugh. Marduk appeared young again, almost as if his physical appearance changed with his mood. He seemed very happy.

"Look, archbishop, I've worked out our little puzzle." He tossed the crumpled three sheets of papyrus on the archbishop's desk. "It's another possibility. The Runes combine with themselves. There is a pattern. It is not the Nepptali Law of Runes."

The archbishop studied the pages, gave it some thought—and more brandy—shook his head and peered owlishly at Marduk. The *sramana* met the archbishop's gaze and his green eyes seemed clouded, though not from brandy.

"There's still a missing piece," he whispered into the old man's ear.

He would say no more.

Later, he went out into the storm of *kittim*, the name by which the Tribes know the poison *bugeaves*—taking the pages with him.

(This was the night of his second *kittim* poisoning, the poets sing.)

Exalted Father

BOOK OF SILENCE
VERSE 1.4.3

From high in his tower cell Theophilus gazed north. King's Road was now fully bathed in spring light of the daystar. The road sparkled clean and bright, and empty as it always was.

Snippets of light broke into his gloomy cell, illuminating corners and crevices. Stacks of dusty papyrus books, partially read, filled wooden bookcases. Plates of hard moldy bread and black cheese lay scattered about the place. Old candles sat moldering on his desk, while his archbishop robes hung in an open closet, which was home to moths and poisonous spiders, and a strange species of river-worm known to leech onto the skin and bleed a person dry.

The archbishop rubbed his eyes. His memory was far more vivid than his perception, for as he peered down he saw a strange, unbelievable thing that he remembered could not exist.

Human figures traveled the road. He could not say how many. The brilliant daystar made it impossible to tell what color they wore and therefore what Tribe they came from. In the glare they looked like an army clad in golden armor. For a moment he thought they might be a pack of farvels whose multi-colored stripped fur rippled gold in direct light (according to at least one translation of the Books).

He rubbed his eyes a second time and looked again. Now he perceived individual jets of flame in human form. They were like white hot sparks blown south by Greater Wind, on the way to incinerate Nalanda.

White light. White... They wore white. White flowing robes, billowy dresses, skirts and shawls that caught and reflected the daystar. White... *Ra'bim*. White was the color of the Ra'bim. It was the color of the Rabs themselves, a people who spent their lives beneath the ground. He'd heard they raised all sort of noxious herbs above and beneath the ground, and they raised serpents too, from which they extracted all sorts of poisons. For such evil the Lord had cursed them and made them into shrunken, miserable creatures, white as death (according to priestly commentaries).

Slowly the figures on the road came into focus. He saw their diminutive stature and deathly white skin. One wore a wide-belted white gown and soft white leather boots. Another wrapped *herself* in a white fur cape. The fur looked new as if it had been recently harvested from a gaum, those oddly-shaped, lumpy white creatures that once lived on the banks of the Pearldew. But gaum had been extinct for at least a Kalpa and the Books were very vague defining the phrase *oddly-shaped*.

A band of women from the Ra'bim Tribe came down King Reuben's Road to Nalanda. Old barren Ra'bim women, hairless, stunted, misshapen. Except for one, the one leading them. The light favored her. She seemed to soak it up, leaving the world about her in shadow. She was young, her skin as dark as the fertile soil brought downstream with the spring floods. Her hair was starless night, close-cropped and tightly curled. She was dressed in a long cape of white fur beneath which she wore some sort of white body-suit that might have been Ra'bim armor, for all the archbishop knew about such things.

Spellbound, he stared at her. She could have been an illusion. An Akkadean woman dressed in a Ra'bim garb on the road to Nalanda, a fusion of three impossible things before he'd eaten breakfast.

A sudden banging at the door broke the spell.

Theophilus shuffled painfully across the small cell and yanked on the heavy oak door. It barely moved.

"Archbishop," a frustrated voice cried from the other side, "let me in. Please. I need to talk to you."

The archbishop took a backward step. "Come on in."

Grunting and wheezing, a massive body forced the door open and lumbered into the cell. An immensely corpulent priest filled the tiny room. His scholar's black hat covered a large hairless dome. Droopy eyelids, dark eyes that appeared unfocused and dull, blank expression—at first glance the priest brought to mind a mindless cow content to graze and chew.

Theophilus knew better.

This scholarly ox thought of himself as the cleverist priest who ever lived. This definition was beyond debate for he'd settled the issue in his own mind years ago. He couldn't even imagine it being an issue.

"Ah, my dear priest Jacob. What new teachings do you bring to your foolish archbishop this fine spring morning?"

Theophilus loved to bait him. Jacob never sensed the bait. He was like an eyeless scrub fish, the only remaining species of fish that still inhabited the river.

Jacob's voice sounded condescending and peevish at the same time. "Archbishop, I must inform you of a particularly strange activity on King's Road. And, in reference to this very inappropriate event, I must humbly request you bestow upon your loyal priesthood proper direction and leadership as is delineated by the Lord-on-High in the *Runehayana*. If you wish, I will quote the exact book and verses. These are—"

"Thank you, priest Jacob, that will not be necessary. Everyone is aware of your vast erudition."

Jacob grinned (or grimaced, the two were indistinguishable) and puffed out his chest. At least Theophilus thought he puffed out his chest, for it was difficult telling exactly where his belly ended and his chest began. He just as well might have swallowed something—say, an archbishop.

"Then I'll get to the point. An occurrence has—occurred—of which there is no historical precedent. This morning, in the Third Kalpa of wickedness—a fact I think highly significant—the occurrence of an outrageous violation of the monastic rules is about to—occur—"

"Yes, yes a gaggle of Ra'bim women led by an Akkadean tigress has come upon us," the archbishop said. "I can still see you know. Beware, my dear celibate priest, they may well be out for rape and pillage."

Jacob cried. "Oh Lord, what a danger! Nalanda sacked? What will we do? How will *you* behave in such circumstances? A man's very being, not to mention his esteemed office, is defined by his action. For just as the word *being* takes its form from the verb *to be*, so too must the acting person take its meaning from—"

"I'm on my way out to see what they want," Theophilus interrupted him.

"Women? What can they want? They cannot *want* anything—to do with the spirit. They must not be allowed to violate the precincts of holiness!" Jacob's voice climbed to the lower sphere of shrill complaint, threatening to rise to the upper sphere of hysteria. "Our monastery is a sanctuary from the profane world, and women, driven by earthly things, base and frivolous and mundane and lustful—"

Theophilus snorted. "Ah, Jacob my boy, see how hot and agitated you've become, almost as though you were truly alive. Perhaps we'll assign them to your barracks."

"Archbishop, really. How outrageous. This is no time for immature jesting. And from a man of your age. Your responsibility requires that you act—responsibly. Responsible responsibility requires a responsible response. *You* must turn them away—responsibly."

"Jacob, you are surely joking. I think I'll name you Jacob Jester."

"I could not be more serious. They're a plague the Lord has sent to plague us."

"There are no plagues, except one." The archbishop suddenly sounded very solemn.

Exalted Father

Jacob wasn't listening. "And The Lord-on-High has cursed them for their corruption—with barrenness, with diseases and madness, and—much more."

Theophilus laughed. He donned his old faded-red archbishop robes. Then, moving nimbly for petrified wood, the archbishop squeezed past the Lord's own portable mountain and hurried out the door. Jacob was proof that mountains walked.

"The Lord and His curses," he said beneath his breath, "His holiness, His purity. We and our offenses against Him. Lucky for Him that He doesn't exist."

"Archbishop, wait! I didn't catch all that. Purity and holiness, yes, just as I said. But what else?"

BOOK OF SILENCE
VERSE 1.4.4

The archbishop hurried down the rock-hewn stairs to lower Nalanda. His robes flapped like the wings of some prehistoric bird. Painful knees and wasted muscles forced him to take one stair at a time, gingerly leading off with the same foot.

Jacob rumbled down the stairs like an avalanche.

Frightened priests ushered the women into Convocation Cathedral. Lower Nalanda erupted into a frenzy of agitated priests. Like a disturbed wasp's nest, priests buzzed about the Cathedral in a chaos of aimless activity. No one could recall women in the monastery profaning its holy grounds. And such women. Led by a fierce Akkadean, they boldly entered the Banalis Gate and loudly demanded an audience with the archbishop.

The army of women numbered—*three.*

Poor flustered Father Leo, second in age only to Theophilus, and looking the worse—a striking combination in one person of old age, disease and death—had taken it upon his authority to deposit them in the Cathedral. After all, he reasoned, long ago the Tribes gathered there in happier times, before the Unified Kingdom and the Silence of the Lord.

Father Leo met the archbishop at its arched entrance. "My dear archbishop, please forgive me. I...I didn't know what to do with them. That Akkadean woman... is...terrifying."

"Foolish old man..." Jacob had never moved so quickly and for such an extended duration of time, at least that he could recall. "Depravity—profanity and filth—infinite filth. What have you done allowing them into the Cathedral? They should've been turned away. Their depravity—depraves."

"They seek refuge," Father Leo said defensively. "Surely the *Church* is a place of refuge if it is anything."

Theophilus gave him a quizzical look. "*Church*? What an odd, archaic word, Leo my son. Whatever have you been reading?"

"The *Church* is not archaic!" Jacob interrupted. His impatience with the archbishop was becoming unbearable. He was sweating and out of breath.

"Marduk invented the word. He lied and said it was old. He's always making up nonsense words."

Leo proved tougher than he appeared. "It was always there. Marduk discovered it. It is another word for the Kingdoms of the Heavens. It fell with the Kingdoms, he claimed. Maybe it fell here? And became Nalanda."

Pulling his beard, Theophilus gazed at Father Leo. Unconsciously he dug for his flask. Its weight told him that it was empty. "Leo, *what* have you been reading? The First Book, *Isa*? Not so?"

Leo bowed his head. "Marduk's translation. It is the most accurate."

"Well, it is nonsense!" Jacob thundered. He drew himself up proudly. "The Kingdom of the Heavens is more than books and Runes, monasteries and *Marduk*. It lives in its people, but only if they merit it. We don't use the word *Church*. I know it is false because Marduk is prideful and full of arrogance. I am correct because I am pure and humble—"

Theophilus groaned. "Enough. The One Lord probably went crazy listening to such shit."

"Foul mouth!" Jacob howled. "You, archbishop, are not worthy of your title—"

"Oh, so it's to be archbishop Jacob then?"

"Who else? Him?" Jacob pointed at Father Leo who seemed to praying.

"It is my birthright after all. I was born to royalty, you know."

"And royalty abandoned you to us—"

"Not abandoned. When the day finally comes, the King and archbishop will both sprout from the same source and rule Greenbottom, as two eyes and one brain. In a Unified Kingdom. And then will the Lord-on-High resume speaking to humanity." He suddenly clamped his mouth shut. His dark eyes squinted in worry as if the Lord, or someone, had overheard him.

The archbishop laughed. "Who says priest Jacob doesn't have a sense of humor. Again I say that we ought to call you Jesting Jacob."

Jacob fixed his eyes on the Cathedral and stubbornly refused to respond.

The archbishop gathered his robes and proceeded through the Cathedral's archway. "Do you wish to come, my loyal priest?" He asked Jacob.

"I would hear these women," Jacob muttered.

"Thought so. Father Leo, see what you can do to get these bothered priests and monks back to their occupations. There'll probably be a few dreams about women in not a few naps this afternoon."

"In a monastery all dreams are about women," said Father Leo.

EXALTED FATHER

BOOK OF SILENCE
VERSE 1.4.5

His voice— reverberating inside her body, like the beating of her own heart. She heard it even now. It seemed stronger as they entered the Cathedral and beheld the Lordpool.

How long ago had it been since she heard *his voice*? Days? Weeks? A year? A hundred? She knew *his voice*, knew it as a child, knew it before she'd been born. Vishnu and his somas no longer ruled her. She was free—of the rule of men. Of every rule.

She knew that this was not *the* Lordpool. She knew that it was a replica, a working copy true enough, but a copy nonetheless. Like its father, it too had gone dead.

His voice was a copy—from a place in her memory that was hers and not-hers at the same time. But the copy was very much alive. Speaking to her. His eyes, his hair, his nose, the line of his jaw, how the artery in his neck pulsed with life...his skin, the *kittim* blemish. On him it was—beautiful. She'd seen him here, in this world. She knew him there. She knew she loved him.

She couldn't recall the precise words he spoke in the dim vault of her wedding feast (Vishnu's wedding feast!). She so much wanted to recall them. They were a fever pulsating through her veins. His words drew the poison. Her protector had returned. What had taken him so long?

His voice—*His words*— the antidote for Ra'bim medical treatment.

The somas had made her passive, defenseless— a puppet, a dog beaten into abject submission. "*Civilized*," the old Ra'bim women said. "The medicines'll civilize you. You'll be fit for proper society,

Not an Akkadean banshee—" What had the *sramana, her protector,* said? What had he said to her before she was born?

Through Zub'lin, Yadishland, through deserted villages, and towns, desolate farmlands, to Nalanda where all roads lead.

The *sramana* liberated her. There was power in his voice. Magic in his words. Wretched Vishnu was helpless. The Ra'bim, helpless. Their somas became water. Freed of them, free from men—

Despite everything, doubt clouded her mind. How can mere words, sounds traveling through the stale air of a Ra'bim tomb, physically change flesh? Or did the somas—the medicines—simply wear off? She was young, her body trained and honed, her mind disciplined. Her body had waged a long struggle with the somas, like fighting a chronic disease. Was it Vishnu's ridiculous attempted rape? How can mere words change flesh?

What did *he* say?

Ra'bim oppressors were powerless without their somas. Clear-eyed, she gazed upon Vishnu. The brilliant white and gold uniform could not hide the hideous nature of his true appearance: squat, bloated, cadaverous, his head a skull thinly wrapped in rotting flesh. Dead eyes, drooling mouth slack and wicked, he cried in a thin, reedy voice:

"Kill him!"

"Kill him," she answered in her voice of the black soil.

All eyes turned towards her—including those of Over-colonel Dmitri who had unsheathed his saber and was preparing to execute Vishnu's orders. *Her voice* stayed his hand.

In that moment of hesitation, which was an eternity for her, she struck. As quick and nimble as a mosscat, she sprang. The poisons oozed through the pores of her skin like sweat. Her dress became a second skin. Soaked in soma, its fabric transformed into a shiny body-suit as hard as stone, yet flexible and brilliantly white.

She was pure movement, flowing as does the Pearldew in Spring. She moved within time but not as its slave. She was free of men, free from reality itself (but isn't this mental illness?). Around her, like an expanding vortex, time's flow slowed to a crawl, and empty space bent like rubber.

She sped past Vishnu. To him it seemed as though Lesser Wind had suddenly entered the vault of the pyramid. The Wind reached out and gave him a powerful kick to the head. He fell face first into his favorite noodle dish. To her it seemed that he fell as fast as the grass grew. Had she killed him? Why didn't she make sure? The question would haunt her. But she was in a hurry, and one well-placed blow to the head should have been enough.

Lesser Wind smashed into the Over-colonel, knocking the saber from his hand and sending him spinning like a top. The Wind, an invisible force lifted him off his feet and threw him onto the table where he crashed amid cups and plates and bowls. The guards raised their L-guns.

She leaped upon the table. With cat-like springs, delicate and powerful, she crossed its entire length without disturbing a single glass.

No Rab in a million Kalpas would have entertained the thought that the Akkadean woman was immune to Yellow and Purple Soma. No one would believe in a million Kalpas that she'd suddenly vanished, although many had seen her abruptly spring forward as the crazy *sramana's* voice drifted across the table. The herb-masters must have put some strange soma into the wine, the sort that produced hallucinations. Despite all evidence to the contrary, every witness at the wedding feast, including Vishnu himself, swore that someone— an Akkadean spy to be sure— had spiked the wine with Red Soma.

The Akkadean bitch escaped. The perfidious Khan had struck into the heart of Tholos. He'd even attempted to assassinate Vishnu.

But the Lord had intervened. How else could he have survived a mortal blow to the head? How had the Khan learned the art of the Red Soma?

An Akkadean assassin in *sramana* disguise had stolen Vishnu's bride under their drugged noses. Almost instantly, blame fell upon the shoulders of the Over-colonel. And although he loudly proclaimed his regret, Ra'bim law forced Vishnu to execute Dmitri. For negligence—the Over-colonel should have killed the *sramana* at first sight.

She leaped off the table and headed for the tunnel. The *sramana* had disappeared. Her protector, vanished again. Was he laughing at her? Because she was unworthy?

The doors were open. He'd fled this way. The pyramid seemed deserted. Lesser Wind was blowing at full strength—more than full strength.

She walked the narrow streets of Tholos, retracing the wedding procession from earlier in the day. It was like unrolling time, cancelling her previous existence. A few Rabs were out in the streets. They felt her passing. She was Lesser Wind, wind of the evening that comes from the north and sweeps the valley known as Greenbottom for a half hour. They hurried indoors.

She found *him* on the east wharf of the Grand Canal. A single gondola was moored to the wharf. A boatman stood at its bow, staring at the *sramana*. He appeared terrified.

"Well now, who'd have foreseen it?" The boatman tried to sound unfazed but his voice was quaking. "Don't be upset, now. I was only having a little fun. Only joking—Why look, and here she is!"

The *sramana* turned.

The boatman shrank back, nearly overturning the gondola. The woman frightened him. He shook so badly that he couldn't grasp his oars and paddle away.

She knew him before her birth, before her many births. In other times, other worlds, when they were together. She knew every inch of him, the cut of his jaw, the curve of his neck, the curl of his hair, every single strand—she knew his voice, his smell, the brilliant green of his eyes. This meeting here at this moment had happened many times before, will be happening in countless future nows and places. Yet each was different. Each was uniquely *now*, brand new, without precedent.

The question haunted her: Was this not an illness? Worse than any soma?

She'd departed the world of reality.

She came to him, not really knowing what it was she would say. Did she not hate *all men*?

He took a step back.

She paused. She had no memory of backward steps.

One more step and he would plunge into the canal.

"Drang!" he cried in a voice dense with authority. "Bring the boat here."

Yellow eyes wide with fear, Drang grasped his oars and managed to push the boat to the wharf. The black-haired *sramana* stepped in.

"To the river," he ordered.

She stared at him dumbfounded. Surely he knew what she knew. Those other times. Those other whens and wheres.

Distressed, she called to him: "Why?"

He glanced at her and quickly lowered his eyes.

"*You are for me*," she said.

"I am...*sramana*," he said softly, speaking to Drang. "I only did as the farvel requested. It is finished and so I go—"

She heard. She would always hear, even if he spoke from a distant star.

He waved an arm over the canal. "See the world? Our house is falling down, as you can plainly see."

"Am *I* not of this world?"

He ignored the question. He gazed through her as if she wasn't there. He gazed through her as if searching for something she did not possess.

"I seek an answer to a riddle," he said.

"What riddle?"

"To the river!" he said sharply to Drang. He gave her one last look. "I go where none may follow—"

And with that he was gone.

She grew suddenly angry with him for being so stupid and willfully ignorant. He must know. How could his voice have touched that deep core where she was stronger than any soma?

It was in his eyes. In the moment he gazed at her. Until then, she'd never thought such a thing possible. How could she have forgotten it?

Why couldn't he see? That they'd been together, in other worlds, in different bodies. Bright, sun-filled days, warm, passion-filled nights, holy nights of love, like strong wine and perfumed breezes. Spring and summer, gentle autumn with its gradual, dignified slipping of the light, winter like a whispered conclusion, a final sigh of contentment—together.

Was she going mad? She brushed the question aside.

Why were things so different *here*? Was it in the nature of the priesthood *here*? In the crazy Books of the *Runehayana*? Watching him fade away like a soul being ferried out of the world, *out of her world*, she wept, and the darkness within her soul wept.

Then she made her vow. She would go to Nalanda and learn the Runes. She'd find the key to the lock that would open his mind. She'd follow him to that place where none may follow.

And so Devorah took King's Road out of the lands of the Ra'bim and headed to Nalanda where all roads lead.

She walked all night until the grey of morning fog brought her to the river.

The Road mounted a gentle rise giving her a clear view of the Pearldew. A breeze brushed her face and hair, reminding her that hour long Greater Wind was coming to greet the dawn. Her senses became sharp.

Rab women squatted on the river bank washing their clothes. They wore ragged cotton shifts like the clothes they washed and beat on the rocks.

Their task was nearly finished. Two sisters, Tera and Kera, looked up.

"Is this not the Akkadcan Queen?" Tera asked in surprise. "See her washing dress. What has become of it? It is like white armor. Like a second skin. See how it blazes! She is like silver fresh from a Napptah forge."

"Indeed sister," answered Kera. "But what is she doing here?"

"Come to help us finish our work," Tera cackled.

Her sister laughed along. Then both simultaneously shrugged. They were turning back to their work when Devorah called to them.

"Follow me... what have you?"

The other women raised their heads and stared at her. They squinted and rubbed their eyes unable to bear the blinding light for more than a few seconds.

"Why is she to order us?" one asked in a peevish tone. "We do not listen to fish." It was a light joke, we do not listen to outsiders, aliens, all outsiders was where and therefore fish.

"She is not Queen," said another.

"She's Akkadean," a third said.

"Has old Nahum planted his seed in her do you think?"

All laughed except Tera and Kera.

"I will make all of you free of men," Devorah said.

"And I say who are you to make us anything?" asked Mistress Peevish. "Get you back to Thebes and service your husband! I've heard it said that he paid quite a price for his Akkadian slut."

Again they laughed—except Tera and Kera.

Devorah said, "I am free. Follow me."

Without a backward glance, Tera and Kera dropped their wet clothes and climbed the river bank.

The other Ra'bim women snickered. "See how she calls the idiot sisters," they said to one another. "See how they obey fish, 'cause they are fish." Then they turned back to their labors for Greater Wind was upon them and they had to get back to the city.

"I wonder if old Vishnu knows his whore is a fish?" observed Mistress Peevish.

The women never made it back to the city. As Greater Wind mounted to full force, a vast cloud of *kitten* appeared in the east. The *kitten* sailed across the river and fell upon the women. All were consumed, none were spared.

Another cloud swept over the walls of Thebes and covered the city like a winter snowfall. It was said among the Ra'bu who survived said there were few that these *kitten* were quite strange and terrible. They could soak through flesh, wood and stone. Thebes suffered a devastating massacre, it was said.

And following the devastation wrought by the *kitten*, an army of Yahudim appeared in the east and overran all of Ra'bah. The Yahudim killed every Ra'bu in sight, including with enough the women.

(Israeli past historians have never been able to verify these events.)

Obviously commentary written centuries between that wife situation was obviously a marginal note. It

EXALTED FATHER

BOOK OF SILENCE
VERSE 1.4.6

Once every year, for two Kalpas, the Great Lords of the Tribes of Men took their places in the seats of the First Circle. They came as always to see and hear the Words of the Lord. Today, in the Third Kalpa of Silence, three women came, and not to see or hear the Words of the Lord.

They sat above the crystalline surface of Lordpool. The impenetrable pool formed an ellipse which was divided into squares like huge glass tiles. Because of the geometry of squares within ellipses, the tiles along the curved edges were bounded by arcs. Ancient priests taught that Lordpool reflected the eternal laws of the Kingdoms of the Heavens from which the Almighty came. This was nonsense of course. Any eternal law of Heaven had to make a perfect circle. Even the dullest Yadish serf knew that.

Dark green, almost black, the flawless surface gave a feeling of depth, as if a person stood upon a frozen lake and could see only a few feet past the surface. As green faded into black, one experienced the disorienting feeling of gazing into an abyss without the support of a solid foundation.

The Lordpool of the Convocation Cathedral was an identical replica of the true Lordpool beneath the archbishop's tower in Upper Nalanda. They were so alike that priests engaged in debates over which was *real* and which was the artifact. Such discussions usually spawned entirely new arguments over the authenticity and identity of the Lord's words. Were they alike in Upper and Lower Nalanda? The

---

should also be obvious that there is another source here, interpolated by some unknown scribe into the account of the events in Nalanda. It interrupts the narrative flow, which picks up again in 1.4.6., though there are modern scholars who challenge this:

Runes had once appeared in both pools simultaneously according to ancient priests. Why should the archbishop's tower take precedence? The ancient priests agreed that the archbishop's Lordpool was the original. But why? The Runes were the same. How could the testimony of the hoary past be an argument?

Priests loved to argue. Too bad all their arguments became moot when the Lord stopped speaking to men.

"When the Lord became a mute," archbishop Theophilus once joked with Jacob (who found nothing funny when it came to the Lord), His servants did also. They still go on as if they are really speaking. They are the dead who've forgotten to die. You know that antique word—What was it?"

"*Dead*," muttered Jacob. "Either you're dead or not-dead."

The archbishop laughed. "Jacob, you've become dangerous. A logical priest."

In the Cathedral, the archbishop's throne sat imposingly on the south end of the ellipse. Black and polished to the point that its surface resembled the perfection of a diamond, the massive throne was carved from an unknown, vanished species of tree. Its wood never seemed to age. A series of inlaid silver Runes covered the arms of the throne. When the archbishop touched them in the proper mathematical sequence, Runes would appear just beneath the surface of the pool like stars floating up from the black depths of the heavens. In both Lordpools the mechanism had failed early in the Third Kalpa.

As if challenging the Lord to speak, a dark-skinned Akkadean woman stood in the middle of the pool. She was comparatively young, from Marduk's generation perhaps. The archbishop saw that she wore a strange white body suit that seemed to mark her as a Rab. However, her black eyes, shinning black hair and dark skin (what was still visible) cried Akkadean, even though she was the lightest Akkadean he'd ever seen.

"Fishing for the Lord, my girl?"

"My dear archbishop," her voice resounded like a living gong, "we are not on a fishing trip. We have come here in this hour which is also the hour of our need."

"Beware," Jacob whispered into the archbishop's ear, "such beauty is deadly. Who among us can endure such beauty? Hers is of the kind that drives men mad. Such beauty must be unnatural, therefore wicked. Do not look at her directly—"

"Beautiful indeed," Theophilus murmured. "Like a young lioness. Maybe a farvel, hey? She's in need, Jacob my boy. For what, I wonder?"

Jacob screwed up his bloated face, which required great effort. His normally red cheeks became pale, and he looked about to explode. His eyes were open as wide as was physically possible.

"Beware, one word and your reason is lost. You and fate, she means to take your soul, old man."

The archbishop raised his voice so the woman could hear. "Had I a soul to forfeit I would happily surrender it. As things are, I have found little need for a soul—"

Her oval eyes widened. They were so dark it was difficult discerning an internal structure.

"Surely you, archbishop, understand the soul. I know it. I have experienced it. It is like a mirror. It takes my breath away. You'll see countless others reflected in it, from other places, other times. The living and the dead. I see them. They speak to me. He came and spoke to me, and washed my soul. I'm free of men."

"Preposterous!" Jacob blurted. "Mysticism and nonsense passed in the mind of a simpleton."

"Oh, I should probably not expect a priest to understand. Weak, blind you as does the sunlight a mole. I'm Lotus Moon an owl. I'm Dewdrop Moon a worm." She raised her hand over the Pond and made a sweeping motion as if to dust debris from its surface. "What a poet I am."

"What seek you here?" asked Theophilus. He was thirsty and hated to admit that Jacob was right about nonsense. She spoke and her enchantment evaporated. He became disagreeably sober.

The woman went on as if she'd not heard his question. "You believe that the Lord is silent. Oh, but He is not. Oh no, no. He is always talking. *You are deaf. He is everywhere. He is inside too, with-us.* Only when we come to know ourselves will we know *Him.* I am *with-Him, He-With-Us.* These women are my followers. I am their *protector.* They have heard as I have heard. They know as I know. Feel as I feel—"

"This feeling... Is it a warm feeling?" the archbishop asked dryly.

She did not hesitate for a second. Her wide eyes narrowed, however, just as Marduk's did when he caught the archbishop mocking him.

"It warms my heart."

Jacob groaned.

"Allow me to rephrase my question. Why does a...warrior woman like you seek refuge in Nalanda?"

"Archbishop," she said solemnly, "you should not mock what you do not understand."

"Apologies, my dear girl. I forgot the *feeling—*"

"Oh, am I so humble? Feeling is exactly what you do not understand." She turned her head. "Is this not so, my disciples?"

Tera and Kera responded in perfect harmony: "It is as you say, *Devorah, our protector.*"

"Oh yes," she said off-handedly, "I am also that—"

"A woman of many titles," the chorus at her back sang.

"Devorah?" Jacob exclaimed. "Devorah of Akkad? Daughter of the Khan? Wife of Triumvir Vishnu?"

The archbishop cocked his head. "Well, aren't you full of surprises my dear priest Jacob. Maybe you will become archbishop after all. How know you such things, I wonder—"

The archbishop's faint grin became a wide smile. His hollow face decomposed into a denuded skull laughing diabolically at the living: *think not, foolish ones, that you will avoid my condition...* She did not notice the transformation.

"So...you don't know? Yet you seek this *sramana*? Is that why you've come here? Perhaps to experience, uh, more vibrations?"

"We have climbed the road to this place. We seek the Mountain of the Lord."

"The Mountain of the Lord?" For the first time the archbishop sounded as though he'd been caught off guard.

"My *sramana* journeys there. We know not the way. So we seek the knowledge here. It is our need of which I speak. Of the one who came before."

"She's talking about Suthralane," Jacob gasped. "He's been dead for centuries, if he ever lived at all—"

"Was this *sramana* whose voice sends shivers through your body named Suthra?"

"He's has many names. Beyond the many I know the one—"

"This is absurd," Jacob snorted as he struggled to maintain his superior composure. "A sly woman you are...and false. What is your real purpose?"

"Perhaps she fears that Vishnu will come. Demand payment, if he's up for it—"

Theophilus chuckled to himself.

Jacob winced and looked away.

She drew herself up. Her distracted, dreamy demeanor vanished instantly. Now she was an Akkadean warrior woman, laughing haughtily. "I do not *fear* anyone, least of all Vishnu. He's ball-less and soft. He could not penetrate water. Nor do I fear Grand Duke Rudra who, if the rumors are true, is *up for it*."

"What is this about the Grand Duke?" Jacob's voice shook as if he were suddenly having a seizure.

"You have not heard of the Grand Duke's prowess?"

Jacob glared at her.

By now Theophilus strongly suspected that he was dealing with a madwoman. "Why come here then? We poor ignorant priests and monks cannot protect you from Vishnu, or the Grand Duke, or any tribal chief."

"I come here to prepare. That is my need. *I will follow him to the Mountain of the Lord. I must study the Runehayana and find the path.*"

Jacob cried out: "*A priestess? This foolish woman wishes to become a priestess! What heresy is this?*"

"A—what?"

"You wish to become a priestess?" The archbishop was laughing.

She gazed past him, to the dark pool. "I remember many things. I follow He-With-Us and these women follow me."

"Back to Suthralane," Jacob snorted. He'd calmed down, apparently coming to the archbishop's conclusion: She was mad.

Theophilus sighed. "Is your *He-With-Us* called Suthralane?"

Her eyes glazed over. "He asked a question. He would ask this question of the Lord on the Mountain."

Her eyes cleared and she peered at Theophilus. "Though he wore the black habit of a priest he was young and strong, long-haired and beardless, an Akkadean to be sure. His voice was *truth*."

Jacob was as silent as the Almighty.

Theophilus gave a start. His droopy eyes opened wide, which took considerable effort. "This *sramana* who taught you the…*truth* was Akkadean?"

She smiled. Her teeth were brilliantly white. Her loveliness became almost unbearable and both priests were forced to look away.

Jacob glanced at the archbishop. "*Marduk!*" he said. He sounded as though he'd spoken a blasphemy.

BOOK OF SILENCE

VERSE 1.4.7

Later that evening, after [illegible] the archbishop [illegible] Jacob to his cell. The angry priest [illegible] and demanded to know why the archbishop had given [illegible] to that woman and her so called [illegible].

"Jacob, my boy, we need [illegible] I suggested that they begin their [illegible] the [illegible] the [illegible] called [illegible] another [illegible]."

Jacob looked [illegible].

"You've [illegible]"

"I [illegible] him."

"May I inquire why?"

"He [illegible]."

"You've heard him?"

"It's not important, archbishop. He [illegible] everything and everyone [illegible] He [illegible] and in the same breath [illegible] you know [illegible]."

The archbishop [illegible] of his [illegible].

[illegible]

must go out on the road and find Marduk, and bring him back here. Look for him in the ruins of Machpelah at the end of summer. I need to know what nonsense he's been teaching the weak-minded."

(All these events occurred in the first year of the first decade of the ninth century of the Third Kalpa as reckoned by the priests of Nalanda and recorded here.)

Neil H. Fenna

THE BOOK OF
WINDS

PASSAGES FROM THE RUNEHAYANA

EXALTED FATHER

3. Priests caught the fish, attempted the calculations (Runes come in four), and transcribed the results. [*Runehayana*] in the Sandi (the Lord's song to the Tribes of Men). They did holy work.
4. Two Kalpa passed as measured by the (greater) Star Wheel. (Alas, at the beginning of the Third Kalpa) Lordpool went (dark, silent) [.........]. The One Lord ceased His holy speech."
5. Some priests (oh, blasphemy!) remarked that the Lord had become senile [...] a stroke, emigrated, gone home, to (the Kingdoms of the Heavens).
6. Cursed is the Third Kalpa, called the Kalpa of Silence, the Kalpa of the Winds that bring (messengers) of death.
7. Divine Silence, oh faithful ones (that trust), is deafening.

" Note in the hand Theophilus (the guest!): *This verse and the two that follow are also interpolations according to the priest Marduk since the dates are confused. It could be, however, that the Lord's Silence came earlier than is generally accepted.*

THE BOOKS OF MARDUK

THE BOOK OF WINDS

CHAPTER ONE - Yadishland

VERSE 2.1.1

The nearest Zakelm village worth raiding was Cinneroth. The village lay nestled in the Ramah Stairs, a ladder-like series of hills and gullies that gradually climbed out of the Yadish valley west of the river. According to *sramana* travelers, who in this case, a rare case to be sure, agreed with Yadish poets (some call them chroniclers, others historians), the distance from the Yadish capital at Hatan to Cinneroth was about three days march. Five during the heat of summer.

Grand Duke Rodu calculated that for men of an advanced age, not a few pushing the century mark, the *sramana* estimation was woefully optimistic. Priestly ascetics were known to be weak of mind as well as weak of limb. Habitual starvation does little to improve observation and reasoning powers. Yadish poets had no such excuses except weak mindedness, or no mindedness at all, in the Grand Duke's tough minded opinion—and a proverb. The Yadish army would probably require weeks. They might even have to winter in Cinneroth, if they got that far.

The army that gathered in the Plaza of King Bashoka this brilliant summer morning disappointed the Grand Duke—now he

143

The Zub'lin people, their northern neighbors, were harmless farmers and sheepherders. With the backing of the Akkadean Khan, whose fine hand manipulated events from afar, Triumvir Vishnu at the head of a massive Ra'bim army had marched south and taken their lands. At this moment the Ra'bim were massing on the northern border of Yudishland. And see: "Today the Zubs, tomorrow us."

Not one of the upper aristocracy asked for evidence for such a claim, and Rudra offered none although he was prepared, had someone asked, to cite an unknown *sramana* (but then every *sramana* is unknown) who'd wandered into Haran some time ago—he could not recall exactly when—and had given him the news.

The Grand Duke's most persuasive argument was the threat that *he* would take *their* lands and distribute them among *their* peasants should they refuse his summons. His *expert political maneuvers*, as he explained later to Miriam, amounted to reminding the nobles that he was still Grand Duke and could do with their wealth and titles what he pleased, and should they not vote war, redistribution pleased him immensely.

Because old noble gentlemen and gentlewomen found it beneath their dignity to argue, they acquiesced without protest. Too much debate might key them up and ruin their sleep. The Privy Council voted unanimously for war.

The rest of the Tribe proved more intransigent. Peasants were busy in the fields tending their crops, orchards required constant watering and care, fishing nets always needed mending, and artisans were always behind on their orders. And—as the Grand Duke surely remembered—peasants hardly knew the first thing about soldiering.

Much to his displeasure, the Grand Duke was forced to wage what the priests would have called an *information* campaign. Once he'd formulated the information, he happily discovered that he believed every word of what he said, and he said quite a lot. Therefore he no longer lowered himself to mere information, which he knew could be challenged. No, he promoted information to truth.

her. *And we knows why. So he thinks it's time to plug a fat Zub'lin tart even though they're all stuffed with diseases—*"

"Still your damned tongue, old hag!" The messenger, a viscount, was unaccustomed to such abuse from a peasant. Of course, he'd not talked to a peasant for many years.

She laughed mockingly and went back to hacking at tough and blighted millet, which was midsummer's meager harvest. After a few swipes she stopped and pointed her scythe at the wasted plants.

"Look here, fool. Ground is barren. Soil mocks us, refuses to yield life like our bodies. We'll soon be gone. But we hears of others, of *farvels, queeri, gaum, Yakashas* in the grasslands beyond Red Lake. There're whispers in the night of stranger beings not mentioned in your precious books...."

She dropped her voice as if these beings might be listening. "—and whirling trees, and the Winds, and *kittim* in the heat of summer whose lightest kiss is death."

Her words changed, became a chant: "*They come in the Third Kalpa, while we fade into the shadows. And diminish. We're ancient ghosts, spiteful and mean, insubstantial and powerless. We live in the netherworld of an old age that never seems to end....*"

"Those are not your words, old witch. What peasant speaks thusly? This sounds like priestly language. Who comes here and twists your feeble mind?"

"Ah, truth's name is feeble nowadays in Haran?"

"The Lord is truth and He has revealed Himself to the Grand Duke."

"Ah ha, what of old books?"

"Priests never translated them correctly. How could they? Their sin is grave and they are an outrage to the Almighty. He has chosen a new vessel, our glorious Grand Duke Rudra."

The viscount hoped he repeated the words exactly as the Grand Duke had pronounced them.

"How convenient for Rudra."

THE BOOKS OF MARDUK

The viscount became frustrated. "Mind your tongue, hag. You verge on treason. The Grand Duke may turn his army on this miserable village before he destroys the Ra'hm."

She laughed again. "Be gone with your idle threats. We've heard *He With Us*..."

She seemed to catch herself. Turning her back on him and bending at the waist as if inviting him to address her ample hindquarters, she returned to her whacking at the unforgiving plants.

From insignificant hamlets to larger villages that once called themselves cities, the Grand Duke's messengers met with similar, if not identical arguments. Refusal was universal, and wherever they went they heard of *He With Us*.

The decay is deeper than we guessed, they reported back to the Grand Duke. The stupid peasants fantasize about some *protector of peasants* who wanders from village to village teaching nonsense. One would hardly label it nonsense. One must begin with sense before one negates it (which was a proverb of the Duke). Added to this bit of wisdom, no one knew the precise nature of the nonsense *He With Us* taught. They only knew *He With Us* taught it.

The Grand Duke nodded knowingly. He understood quite well the iron grip of delusions on Tribal minds, "especially on minds drowning in baseness and despairing silence..." he remarked knowingly.

Sixty men mustered in King Bashoka Plaza. Almost all of them came from the aristocratic families of Haran. Thirteen sad-eyed, joint-creaking, lung-gurgling, disease-wasted peasants answered the summoning of the Yudah feudal host. Six bore antique pikes and rusted swords. The rest brought pitch-forks, rakes, scythes, shovels, and other farm implements. No one brought a crossbow or a longbow, and no one bore an I-gun. Three carried provisions for a few days march, mostly fallow deer jerky, hard rolls, and skins of

soldiers tumbled down like dead trees in a strong wind. They snored contently in the dust.

Miriam and three other noblewomen stood in the shade of the colossal arch which served as a formal entrance to the Plaza. King Bashoka's Arch was dedicated to the great King's victory over the Rakashas, a species of desert creature called in the colloquial tongue *black desert imps*. Yadish historians claimed that King Bashoka had annihilated the entire species as the Lord had ordered in the Book of *Narayana*.

At least four other Tribes claimed credit for this holy slaughter. They were envious liars according to well informed Yadish historians who had closely examined the evidence, which came solely from the war memoirs of King Bashoka—and therefore could not be counted as fairy tales.

Miriam and the other women laughed loudly. Ignoring them, Rudra concluded his speech:

"Let us march to great deeds. I have met the Almighty beyond the Pearldew. I have heard His words. *The Lord wills it!*"

"The Lord wills it," the host responded in forlorn voices.

"Follow me."

They hefted their weapons and with some grumbling, but mostly sighs, they filed behind the Grand Duke and marched like a funeral procession out of the Plaza. They headed in the general direction of King Reuben's Road. The peasants dragged their pikes in the dirt, like lifeless tails.

The women continued to laugh. Miriam called after them: "And how shall old men give pleasure to women so young and fruitful?"

The other women took up the mocking cry.

"*So young and fruitful—*"

Miriam snorted: "When you go to them, you powerful men of Yadish, don't forget your mighty swords..."

After two miles of fields sparsely populated by mustard bushes—groves of fig and lemon trees once grew here in abundance—the terrain became broken and hilly, rising in elevation as the land climbed out of the Yadish bowl. A series of blunt ridges and shallow gorges formed the so-called Ramah Stairs. King's Road followed a particularly wide ridge that twisted and turned but led in a general northern direction.

Rudra believed that a good day's march would bring them to the little Yadish town of Misar which sat on a level plain north of the Ramah Stairs. The city lay on the border of the Zob'lin Tribal lands. It would serve as the jump off point for the conquest of Cinneath.

His messengers had neglected to visit Misar, or *small town*, the meaning of the word. The place was poor and sparsely populated, a dismal backwater of dirty streets and dull peasants. His father, the Laughing Duke, had not even bothered to collect feudal rents, and Rudra had followed his lead. Today he would make up for the neglect.

After frequent rest stops, two desertions, and what seemed to be an unending litany of complaints—Rudra halted the march to have one particularly obnoxious peasant whipped for insubordination—they sighted the dozen or so square buildings of blistered brick and rotted wood. Taking a narrow overgrown path that intersected Reuben's Road, they headed towards the town, marching through fields of broken rock, wild mustard, thorny weeds, and patches of yellow grass growing like tufts of hair on a bald man's head.

The daystar slipped behind the western hills casting the fields into shadow so that it seemed the ground were covered by a blanket of broken bones and smashed headstones. To Rudra, it was like walking into a vast graveyard after robbers had pillaged and desecrated the tombs, leaving the bones to bleach in the sun.

Issuing from Misar, ten living cadavers appeared on the road ahead. They wore patched peasant blouses and smocks, broad brimmed hats and yellow leather boots. Two were men, the rest women. All were silver haired, yellow skinned and pot bellied. They shambled on stick legs. Every one walked in a stooped fashion, dragging down the path as though they bore massive weights. A few seemed to be missing limbs, and one, a woman—or so Rudra guessed—displayed an empty eye socket. She didn't bother to wear a patch. They reminded him of a funeral procession.

Rudra halted the army, drew himself up as tall as possible—his back hurt terribly and his gut felt as if someone had stabbed him with a sharp blade—and addressed the good citizens of Misar in the formal manner of their sovereign Grand Duke:

"Where the hell is your mayor? And why the hell aren't these damned fields planted?" He wanted to bellow the words, but they became a peevish groan.

A shrunken fossil of a woman stepped forward. "I am called Myss," she said sounding like a broken flute. She gasped for air and spit her words.

"My husband was mayor but he's gone back to the mud, many seasons now.... Where all will follow," she added as though she'd forgotten the closing verse of a prayer. "We've gardens north of town. Nothing grows here, as you obviously see."

"I do see," snapped Rudra. "There's no excuse for Misar not paying its damned feudal dues."

The branch of dried wood named Myss gave a screech that startled the army. Actually, she startled the nobles. The peasants simply stared at her with dull eyes. They were too tired to be startled. They could have taught her a few things about feudal dues had they the strength.

"Be gone from this place," she squawked like a wounded sparrow falling from the sky. "Devils haunt this land by night. They kill the men and make their flesh into bread, and blood into wine. They leave the bones that turn to stone. They slaughter the men. The women they take...."

"Men they eat. Women they take...men they eat, women they take..."

"But nothin' comes of it," Myss added.

The Grand Duke opened his gold-threaded summer coat decorated with silver buttons and silver epaulets bearing Runes spelling the words: "the Yadish King." At least this was how the priests translated them. The Laughing Duke once joked that the Runes meant "Yadish prick."

Rudra drew his ceremonial short sword and waved it in Myss's face.

"Enough, crazy old witch. Escort my men to shelter before Lesser Wind is upon us. Make sure they get a hot meal. Now! Or you'll learn what it truly means to be split by an icy prod that burns. We march on the Zuba tomorrow..."

At his shoulder Count Vladimir whispered "Lesser Wind does not come in the summer."

"I say it does," Rudra growled in a dangerous voice. The good count thought it best not to argue the point. Why lose one's life over a weather forecast?

Myss dropped to her knees. "Oooo..." she wailed. "Zuba are gone...taken."

On cue, the chorus took up the cry: "Men they eat, women they take..."

"SILENCE!"

Rudra's voice was a howling wind.

"I forbid you to utter such nonsense. There are no damned Yakashas. There is only double damned Vishnu. He took the Zuba."

Rudra was enraged. He saw that his aristocratic soldiers, and now the blank-eyed peasants, were fearfully looking this way and that as if at any moment the frightful Yakashas would arise from the shadowed plain and devour them all. Viscount Vladimir and The Marquise Rurik produced L-guns. The weapons had not been used in over a century, perhaps since the Great Tribal War. No one knew for

Once in the room, dusty and full of mold, she unbuttoned her smock and twisted her face into what at first glance appeared to be a horrid grimace, but what she meant to be a look aflame with passionate desire.

To Rudra she was a skeleton shedding its remaining flesh. What the Lord on High might want with such a woman—she was fairly typical of all the daughters of men—puzzled him greatly. But very quickly he gave up thinking about the Lord.

"Take me, oh Great Duke," she purred. "We have not witnessed a birth in Misar for eighty years. Take me, oh please. Please! I have not known a man—that I can remember. Are you not called Rudra the Strong? Father of hundreds, of thousands, like the grains of sand in Palam? Has not the Lord spoken to you? Oh don't look surprised. Your story is known up and down Greenbottom. I've heard it said that the Lord restored your manhood. Oh, take me! Pierce me! Oh please, I will die…"

Repelled by her body, he found to his immense surprise that her words excited him. She came closer. He reached for her left breast and cupped it in his hand. With his other hand, he lifted her smock and slid his hand up her thigh…

"Restored, reborn, remade, refitted… Oh yes!" She moved close, pressing her naked body to his.

A wave of revulsion swept over him. Her skin was cold and clammy, spongy like mud from the river bottom. Beneath the vile perfume she smelled even worse, as if nothing could banish the smell of decay. She spread her legs and began to grunt like an old wart hog.

Then she went berserk.

Tearing at his crotch with frenzied claws, she grabbed hold of his penis. She pushed him back to the dirt-covered bed and tried to mount him. She grunted and wheezed, drooling, and grinding her hips into his. She even tried to bite him.

"Give me a child or I shall die!"

In less than a minute she pulled away choking for air. She was laughing.

"Look, look..." she cried, laughing hysterically, "how small and shrivelled. Like a worm baked to death in the sun. No balls either. Father of thousands, father of thousands..."

She laughed and laughed, and it was difficult distinguishing her laughter from her screeching.

"Oh Lord, please..." She fell to her knees and tried to stuff him into her mouth. She gagged, gurgled and cried out: "Oh Lord, I'll die!"

"What magic spell of impotence is this? Get the hell out of here, crazy old witch." He pushed her away.

She fell on the dirty floor, still moving her hips, still crying... "I'll die..."

He staggered up from the bed. He howled as though she'd wounded him. "What've you done to me..."

She gazed up at him continuing to laugh. Then she cursed him: "Look how you've made me waste the last of my Ra'him perfume!"

She got up, put on her smock and went out the door. Behind her, like an afterthought, she left a croaking chant hanging in the air: "Men they eat, women they take..."

THE BOOKS OF MARDUK

BOOK OF WINDS
VERSE 2.1.5

Morning had come on the dismal wings of low, heavy clouds. The Kamah Stairs were buried under layers of chilled mist as if clouds sprouted from the cold ground like vaporous weeds. A strong wind swept down from the north.

"Greater Wind comes in the summer," observed Count Trevor One-toothed. In actual fact he had two teeth, but one was broken in half. He whistled his words.

King Reuben's Road climbed hills and descended gently into the deepest gorges. Now it presented them with an incline that quickly taxed their strength. Greater Wind conspired with the steep climb.

"It is not Greater Wind," snapped Rudra. "There are no summer Winds."

"But my Duke," said Marquis Rurik in a quivering voice, "that bright spot on the northwest horizon must be Dewdrop Moon—"

"It is nothing but a break in the fog. And Greater Wind does not blow." His tone forbade further discussion. The moons changed with the seasons, of course. Dewdrop Moon should have been a barely visible sliver. The old calendars were notoriously inaccurate (thanks to drunken priests, Rudra said). It was better to gage the season by the weather. But the weather had become notoriously chaotic in the Third Kalpa.

An hour passed and the Wind died just as hour-long Greater Wind always did in the winter. No one mentioned it. Nature dared not contradict the Grand Duke of the Yadish Tribe.

Marching into the cold wind on an exposed road that continually gained elevation, and then dropped precariously, exhausted the army. They had not come prepared for winter. Threadbare peasant blouses and thin aristocratic coats, no matter how thickly embroidered with

assembled in a Nepptali factory. He set the stock firmly in his shoulder and pointed the silver barrel at the nearest tree.

Vladimir pulled the trigger. A sharp snap, then a yellow fizzle of sparks...and a puff of black oily smoke. The mist swallowed the smoke. He shook it and tried again. Nothing.

"Almighty help us! Look, they have fangs like knives. And claws. Tails..."

"Fools! Idiots! They're fig trees!"

Rudra spun on them and shook his sword. Near him, Count Vladimir tossed the J. gun away, threw up his hands, and bolted down the road. Rudra aimed a wild swing at his neck. The strike was meant to decapitate him. But the Count was surprisingly quick for an old man of wasted muscles and shagging belly.

The Grand Duke swung with all of his strength. His sword assumed a life of its own as though some other hand wielded it. It spun him off his feet. Swinging in a circle, the sword struck back, nearly taking off his dazed head...had he not fallen on his face.

The Yadish army disintegrated. Many tripped and fell down the slope. Sharp rocks cut and stabbed their frail skin. Old bones snapped and empty heads cracked like nuts. The land itself seemed to rise up with spear and sword, slashing and hacking at the Yadish soldiers.

Rudra flew into mindless frenzy. Picking himself up, he slashed and cut and chopped, attacking anyone or anything in sight. His blade finally found flesh...his own.

He'd planted his feet and aimed a mighty blow at the base of a fig. His hands and wrists were painfully stiff. He hit the tree with the flat of his sword. The blade rebounded and cut deep into his left thigh.

He cried out and collapsed like a falling cedar.

"The Duke is down," Vladimir shouted hoarsely. He'd heard Rudra cry out. He was running with his back turned and did not actually see Rudra fall.

THE BOOKS OF MARDUK

"Oh my Lord! Devils stabbed him!"

And then, too frightened to look back—and too frightened to know where he was going—he turned and ran in the direction of Moab.

"Men they eat—" He cried once. Then he was out of breath.

A battalion of *kittim* fell (landed). In a well-organized phalanx it advanced upon the fleeing Yadah. In a few minutes the battle was over and the once-glorious Yadah army was nothing more than puddles and streams of syrup-like liquid that soaked into the hard ground of King Reuben's Road.

They spared Grand Duke Rudra, probably taking him for mortally wounded and not worth the effort. How the Grand Duke would conquer the Tribes, resurrect the United Kingdom, and bring all the women to the Lord as the Lord had ordered—only the Lord knew.

THE BOOK OF WINDS

the Middle Sea began to boil. Or, he believed that's what he saw. That's what he'd been taught to see.

Priestly astronomers said that the daystar circled a roughly spherical planet. As it swung out over the Middle Sea it heated the water, they said. Agni thought this a bit silly: Lake Emerald's temperature changed with the seasons, it was true, but never with the rising or setting of the daystar. Today, shivering in the summer, he remembered (and not for the last time) that if priests believed something then it had to be false.

The mad black-haired *sramana* once told him that the ancient priests were incapable of calculating the positions and movements of the two moons—even with the help of the Lord (meaning the *Runghayang*). Naturally they claimed that their (divinely inspired) celestial mechanics were precise and absolutely trustworthy (as befitting the divine author). But secretly they suspected that the moons (and all other heavenly bodies) would in time diverge from their appointed paths. And diverge drastically.

If they didn't trust their own calculations, why should Agni?

Lesser Wind began with a whisper. In a few minutes it blew full force, bringing crisp air from the dark Blackdiamond Forest in the far north.

The Winds stubbornly refused to obey the seasons. Apparently they failed to note that summer had come to Greenbottom. Agni wondered if his own summer chill might be due to *kittim* poison racing through his veins. Soon he'd be dead. Like the Khan.

considering various defensive measures—when, *apparently* he collapsed.

They buried him where they'd found him. *Defensor Emeraldi.*

Livia forbade an autopsy. Her reasons were beyond dispute. An autopsy would mean bringing Ra'bim physicians into Akkad. No one wanted those disgusting maggots snooping about Emerald. Serya had been suffering a severe case of hemorrhoids, she said.

A stray *sramana* heard of this and brought the news to Yudishland. It was on this occasion, some say, that the Laughing Duke uttered one of his most famous quips: "Hemorrhoids must be very dangerous in Akkad."

Livia died two years later, almost to the day (given that Agni remembered the day his father died). It was whispered that she'd died given birth a third time. But this has never been confirmed. The Khan forbade an autopsy—naturally—and for the same reason: no Ra'bim physicians were allowed in Emerald. No one mentioned hemorrhoids.

And so the Khan brought Agni into his household and raised him as the son he never had.

Naturally Devorah hated the interloper and did everything in her power to make his life miserable.

Ironically, Agni proved her best ally in this enterprise. The boy took after his mother. But what was fiery ambition in the mother became a violent temper in the son. The boy could be menacing. There was menace in his unpredictability. A cold fury might erupt at any moment into murderous rage. Once he nearly beheaded his gentle old tutor Nikolas who'd make the mistake of correcting his Sandi grammar. There was no telling how hot the fire burned on any given day. Generally, he controlled it. Still, it simmered behind his dark eyes, lingered in his perpetual frown (he was never happy), and often announced its presence in his habit of sneering at almost everyone.

Devorah quickly learned to manipulate him as easily as the Nepptali raised the temperature of their boilers. She never teased him outright, yet she found it easy to insinuate degrading insults that drove him to near madness. Worse, she bested him in all things. She ran faster, wielded the blade with greater skill, outsmarted him in games; she was not quite as strong but her quickness was deadly. It was said that Talib the Jester learned his tricks from her.

Agni's fatal flaw saddened the Khan. He longed to see the other Orloks pledge allegiance to the boy as Successor, but he knew that this would never happen. The title would probably pass to someone like Jehu. Deep inside he knew that his successor should be Devorah, but this he could not admit to himself, nor would the Tribe accept it. Never in history as far as anyone knew had there been a *Khan-anah*.

It was out of desperation, then, that he sold Devorah to Vishnu. The Ra'him tribesmen were experts in the chemical and biological arts. Perhaps a grandson would come of the union. Khans do not inherit their title through the female line according to ancient Akkadean law—which the Khan chose to ignore when it suited him.

Despite it all, Agni loved him as a father. Fittingly, Agni was with him when he died.

The Khan's last moments haunted him. Disturbing images of his horrid death refused to recede into the stagnant backwaters of memory no matter how hard Agni tried to push them away.

The Khan lingered for a day in terrible pain. Agni remained by his side in the Beehive where the Khan had insisted they take him to die. He wished to die surrounded by the past glories of the Akkad, he said.

"I see the other Khans," he said between gasping breaths. The wet rattle deep in his chest made it difficult for him to speak. "I see them, Agni...really I do. Back to the founding of Greenbottom..." He coughed and spit up bloody phlegm.

they are young and vulnerable, a brutal father abuses them, or they're burdened with a weakling...a thousand other things cause them to weep, to feel heartbreak, and instantly the world is to blame. The world is the cause. They imagine a better world in which sadness does not exist. The ills of the world are banished by a power beyond human abilities. Is not this other world a judgment and a condemnation? Hatred? Our life is evil, they say, and they gnash their teeth and curse life itself. The world is profane, they howl, and they gnash their teeth. The world is without purpose, meaning, hateful place. Everything is worthy of destruction."

"Agni, you sound like a priest." The Khan was listening.

"I've observed them, that's all," Agni shot back. "I've listened and thought about what I heard. Despite themselves, they are great teachers. They reveal much without intending to."

"Ah, Agni, how much you resemble your brother. Even your language. You no longer speak in the manner of Akkadean."

"I have no brother."

Despite his pain and difficulty breathing, the Khan forced a smile. "You know him, we think. He took after your father. He deeply disappointed your mother. He was a man of the towers, so to speak, a city man. Your father took his side."

Agni frowned. He'd heard rumors of his dead sibling. His mother had said that the baby died within days of birth. And she'd never told him its sex.

"What became of my brother?" He still sounded unconvinced.

The Khan slipped back into his demented rambling. He began to mutter: "I will live again...and again, again, again..." He paused as if considering his own words. "Life lives..."

Then he squawked: "*They come for me. Do you see the kittim? They fill the dome.*"

Agni jerked back startled. In the poor light of the sputtering quartz-lamp much of the cavernous Beehive's interior remained in agitated darkness. For all he knew, *kittim* had found a way to soak through masonry and stone and fill the vast spaces above their heads. He held his breath, feeling the dull smoldering ache of his own wound. The *kittim* had merely brushed his arm during what was now known as the Battle of Emerald. It left a stain no larger than a fingertip. Yet, Agni knew that he was doomed.

"They come for me—"

The Khan moaned: "Trees flow and waters take root, mountains walk and clouds sing. As they once did, before us. It is night and the lights blaze brightly. Did you know that light shines brightest in the dark?"

The Khan had become delusional. The final stages of *kittim* poisoning—he'd seen it a few times before when the victim had not immediately dissolved but lingered on in unbearable agony. Except—the Khan did not seem to be in the slightest pain. He appeared happy, almost blissful. Agni knew that insanity had many levels. The entire priesthood was mildly insane, the *sramanas* more so. For years after his first poisoning the Khan teetered on the edge of madness. Now he dropped like a rock into the abyss.

"Promise me, Agni—"

Agni waited but the Khan did not complete the sentence. His good eye closed.

"Promise what, my Khan?"

No response. The Khan was barely breathing.

"My Khan?"

"You'll free *her*—"

"Who?"

"*Her.*"

"Your daughter?"

"*Not mine...but I love her still.*"

The Khan took a breath. He exhaled. Agni waited for another. It did not come.

At once the air was filled with *steam*. Agni jumped back, overturning his chair. He tripped on the chair and fell. In a panic he scrambled to his feet.

The Khan had disappeared. The bed was soaking wet.

EXALTED FATHER

BOOK OF WINDS
VERSE 2.2.3

"Lesser Wind!" Agni cried, shaking himself from his reverie. "Find shelter. Quickly. One of those shacks—with a roof. *Kittim* come—"

"You're not Khan," Omar One-armed shouted.

"Then remain here and inform the *kittim* when they arrive."

Omar looked to Jebe. The Orlok was Field Marshall of the Horde and technically the highest ranking officer after the Khan and the Grand Vizier. Jebe was also the oldest among them now that both the Khan and Vizier were gone, and Jebe had shown signs of instability since the Khan's death. He had begun to act like the Khan, muttering to himself, looking confused, behaving erratically. Agni wondered if he'd been poisoned.

Jebe gave a high-pitched, belly-shaking laugh. "I wanna see 'em, I do. They're all so different, so colorful—" His tone sounded childish, his voice high and piping, all of which seemed totally at odds with his scraggly white beard and leather-skinned face.

Omar and the rest of the Akkadean horde (under a hundred warriors—there'd been some desertions since they'd left Emerald) hesitated for a heart-beat and then darted for cover. It no longer mattered whether Agni thought he was Khan, or even if he believed himself the Lord on High.

Gusts of Lesser Wind swept through the empty streets of Bethsham howling like a pack of Blackdiamond white wolves (although no one had ever heard such a sound since white wolves had been hunted to extinction during the First Kalpa). Darkness descended suddenly as if the fire of the daystar was extinguished as it dropped into the Middle Sea. The abrupt darkness was neither dusk nor night. Clouds of *kittim* attacked from the north, an army mounted on the Wind. Only Lotus Moon peeking above the eastern hills of the Akkadean Ladder made it possible to see.

Surely not by design, Omar and Agni found themselves beneath the same stone arch. They hugged the polished wall. A symbol was carved into the stone: a hammer and an engineer's ruler forming a cross. Beneath the symbol were Runes, and then Sandi lettering that spelled out the word: "Nepptali."

"The Winds come before summer surrenders its heat. *Kittim* too." Omar glanced at Agni, as though he expected an explanation.

Agni closed his eyes. His face contorted in pain. He seemed to be having difficulty breathing.

"How is it, Lord Agni, that you survived *kittim* poisoning?"

Agni opened his eyes and stared at the oncoming *kittim*. They rolled up the horizon like black storm clouds. His eyes were glazed. The fire that once burned in those black coal-like orbs had died down into dying embers. From black, their color changed into a watery green, like the sluggish waters of the Pearldew when they reflected the foliage of trees on its banks.

"Don't know." He slumped down against the arch.

A sudden inspiration seized Omar. His inspiration was born of a calculation. "The Lord must have chosen you," Omar declared. "He marks you for a great task. You are…reborn."

Agni scowled. The inner fire had not totally died. "Chance makes most choices—"

"Oh no. Search for Almighty's clues." (Omar thought himself as talented as any priest when it came to making up fantastic yarns about the Lord) "Why do Winds come in summer? Why don't *kittim* melt in summer's heat? How, you've survived *kittim* poisoning? These are clues, pieces of puzzle that you must assemble. The meaning of your life hides within them. It is duty you owe the Lord. And I can help—"

Agni gave him a suspicious look. "I owe Him nothing…"

EXALTED FATHER

He fixed his attention on the swirling *kittim*. They were larger than ever, more colorful than ever, if that were possible. Their geometric designs were infinitely more complex and chaotic. They came in impossible forms, as if multiple dimensions were joined together. Then silken panels emerged and vanished into invisible planes seemingly beyond normal space. They popped out of the air and instantly disappeared. Appearing, disappearing, reappearing, reborn... a dance. The poison racing through his veins surely affected his perception. Shaking his head did not banish the eerie vision.

"Priest madness," he muttered.

"What's that?" Omar asked. "Be quiet! Maybe *kittim* hear." Omar pressed his entire body against the stone.

Agni was no longer paying attention. Nor did he seem to care about the *kittim*. His mind suddenly slipped into the past. *Do I really have a brother?*

Omar glanced at him. Perhaps Agni was not the Lord's chosen. If not Agni, if not Jebe—then why not Omar the One-armed?

"Clues—point to *me*!" Omar declared.

Agni came awake. "What the hell are you jabbering about—"

A monstrously large *kittim* slammed into the arch. The thick stone shook as if it had taken a hammer blow. Agni closed his eyes and waited. One more poisoning and he'd be dead, like his father the Khan. Omar's eyes were wide with terror. He glanced at Agni and saw a strange smile. But Agni never smiled.

A *kittim* suddenly popped up behind Omar. His last thought was that it must have come around the wall. Common sense said that the *kittim* were mindless sheets of filmy silk. They acted more like dead leaves than living things. Possessing neither head nor tail, they floated about randomly. They knew neither coming nor going.

This one acted as though it possessed a purposeful mind driven by a malevolent will.

Omar gave a shriek and tried to bat the thing away. The *kittim* embraced him. For a moment it looked as if he had acquired a patchwork cloak of hundreds of pieces of hundreds of colors. Then, both man and *kittim* simply melted into porous stone.

Agni remained untouched. He glanced around the wall.

Jebe stood in the middle of the road, arms raised as though to embrace the Wind. *Kittim* swirled about him like a swarm of giant butterflies. He was actually trying to grab the things. The *kittim* swooped in and out of his clutching fingers, evading his grasp. They were playing with him. He laughed like a small child with a shiny new toy.

There was a sudden flurry of color and motion, and Jebe was gone, leaving only child's laughter in the Wind.

And then the sky brightened. And the *kittim* army arose in unison and sailed south. They'd defeated the horde.

EXALTED FATHER

BOOK OF WINDS
VERSE 2.2.4

Heads hanging, a smattering of Akkadeans continued south, out of Nepptali and into the lands of the Ra'bim Tribe. A few wailed and cursed their fate. One or two muttered something about retreat. Allied with kittim, Grand Duke Rudra was invincible. The majority simply shrugged, resigned to the absurdity of their quest, more numb than afraid, too old to care.

The Battle of Bethsham (as it was later named) decimated the horde. The force was reduced by half. In the day that followed the epic battle, the half was halved. Agni could not be sure if the cause was desertions or abductions. Perhaps Yakashas really existed. Perhaps the Grand Duke himself followed them commanding the Winds, ordering the dead leaves. Rudra, Lord of the *kittim*.

They passed Tholos, the great Capital of the Ra'bim. They came to Canal Bridge where the Grand Canal intersected the Pearldew. If the Ra'bim were going to mount a defense it would be here.

During the time of the Great Tribal War that destroyed the Unified Kingdom, the Ra'bim had heroically halted a massive Yadish army at this bridge. For seven days they kept the Yadish at bay, preventing them from crossing. It was the first time since the creation of the Unified Kingdom that a Yadish force had been checked. And though the Yads finally broke through and slaughtered the Ra'bim defenders to the last man, the myth of Yadish invincibility was destroyed for good.

The glorious Rabs had fought like devils out of Edom—in the words of Ra'bim historians. Akkadeans knew better.

Rab alchemists had poisoned the waters of the canal, including much of the Pearldew. Yads died in the thousands when they drank the deadly waters. A foul stench arose from the canal and river both, and many Yadish soldiers fell ill by simply breathing the air. A few Tribes—the Yadish, of course—claimed that the curse of infertility began on that day. The once life-giving Pearldew spread the evil disease up and down Greenbottom.

Agni might well have believed it. (In these times) the canal was choked with a black slimy substance that resembled an oily tar. It stank worse than a thousand corpses. Beyond its high walls, Tholos reeked of similar decay. A yellow haze hung over the city. There were no signs of life. Not even a single bird flew above the necropolis. Not a single insect buzzed about the dead canal.

The Akkadeans rushed across Canal Bridge and never looked back. Many suffered vomiting and fever for days afterwards. Some died, further reducing the ranks.

(Thus concluded the Battle of Tholos, the third great battle of the Akkadean campaign against Grand Duke Rudra, false prophet, liar, blasphemer...and so on.)

They followed an ancient wadi that cut through the Ladder of Akkad and ran parallel to King Reuben's Road. Overhanging rock formations and an occasional cave offered protection from the *kittim*. Agni feared that not even solid stone could stop them. The *kittim*, it seemed, were able to penetrate anything.

A dozen warriors bore L-guns they'd salvaged from Nepptali workshops. No Akkadean understood their manufacture, and certainly none knew the art of repair. It was said that the Nepptali themselves had lost the knowledge centuries ago. L-guns looked dangerous, however, and just the sight of them might be enough to frighten the Yadish to death.

Greater Wind blew at dawn, and black clouds of *kittim* rolled in from the north. But none fell. They passed over the heads of the horde and headed south. To feast on Yadish, Agni hoped. They'd certainly fed well upon Akkadean.

The Ra'bim seemed to have suffered the same fate as Tholos. Towns and villages were deserted. Not a trace of human life remained (if one could call them human). It seemed that no one lived here for a very long time. How could that be, Agni wondered? Yet, like the Nepptali, a blanket of gray ash covered the ruined buildings. The conflagration had to have been the work of Yadish L-guns, Agni guessed. Yet for reasons he could not name he doubted what seemed to be a quite sensible explanation.

Agni remembered the Ra'bim. He vividly recalled how repellent the Tribal members appeared. Picturing them in his mind, he populated the streets with crowds. An unhealthy pasty white, lacking a single hair on their entire body, the Ra'bim were stunted creatures who seemed to have been pressed and cut from moldy dough. Squat, given to oily fat, they exuded an odor of spoiled meat. They spoke in nasal voices and glared at a person through yellow eyes. And they never seemed to age. Triumvir Vishnu was the oldest living human being in Greenbottom.

In the past, Vishnu aroused the deepest disgust in Agni, setting him into a murderous rage. At such times he was capable of slaughtering them all without the slightest regret, easily convincing himself that they were not human beings at all but a plague of nauseous insects. Surprisingly, on this day he found it difficult to gloat over their demise. He even felt a bit sad.

Talib the Court Jester was happy to be rid of them.

"Duke Rudra be praised," he cried. "Cleansed Greenbottom of maggots, he did. I piss in his honor."

He actually attempted to urinate into the canal. But his stream was weak and he was too far away. He nearly hit Agni's boot. The others tensed, expecting Agni to fly into a rage and strike off the fool's foolish head. But Agni appeared distracted and simply stared at him.

"How do we know Duke Rudra did this thing?" Agni asked.

Talib looked puzzled. "*You* said! The one named Ox toll you."

"If a priest believes…" Mechanically Agni repeated the mantra. He sounded bored.

"He knows lots about the Grand Duke, Ox does."

Agni gave the jester a pained look. His head throbbed and the whole left side of his body burned.

"Maybe Ox is really Yadish," said Talib frowning. The frown made him look uncharacteristically clever. Perhaps he realized his mistake for he quickly reverted to his idiot's grin.

"Who really knows about priests? Tribal cast-offs, abandoned for some reason. The few that survive become priests…"

Agni sighed.

"What Tribe now-a-days would abandon a child?"

Talib squeezed his eyes shut concentrating. Sweat beaded on his forehead and he drooled. "Oh my Khan, you ask a most difficult question."

Agni grinned. There was no malice, no sarcasm in his look. Talib grew fearful. His audition as the new Khan's court jester was not going well at all.

"Traditions that once made sense become ridiculous in another age. Sometimes they become deadly. In a barren age no child is expendable. How is it that there's even a priesthood?"

Talib snickered, "Oh that Ox! He's a Rab for sure. A bloated snake he is, all pasty white and filled with venom. Remember that *sramana*—forgot his name—who's a pretty solid fellow? Beardless, black hair, brown skin, green eyes— Is he Akkadean? Could be your twin, Agni. Why'd the old Khan donate him? For brandy? Nalanda's well stocked with Banalis brandy. So he traded 'em. Like when he sold Devorah to the Rabs."

Talib instantly regretted his final comment. He was trying to be witty. Trying too hard. It pained him to even think about his dear Devorah. Agni would surely strike him down. Court fool, *dead man—*

EXALTED FATHER

Then a great miracle occurred. Agni did not draw his sword. Rather, he held his breath.

"Ah yes, quite a mystery here—" Talib quickly added. "We'll have to ask that *sramana* when we see him again."

Agni stared at the clownish face. The bastard really was a jester. "After we've taken Nalanda," he said.

Talib frowned.

"A joke," said Agni. "Call me *Jesting Khan*."

BOOK OF WINDS
VERSE 2.2.5

Towards evening of the next day they crossed the famous Wall of Ra'bim into the Tribal lands of the Zub'lin. No more than sections of broken stone overgrown with weeds, the Wall had been a casualty of the Great Tribal War. The Akkadean horde had destroyed the Wall. Tribal historians were wildly at odds, and nearly every Tribe—except the Ra'bim—claimed responsibility for the destruction. The Ra'bim said that the Wall's destruction was due to an earthquake.

They had yet to encounter a single living soul. There may have been plenty of dead ones, yet there were no bodies.

Provisions were low and canteens no longer hung heavy from belts. Since the Canal, they feared to drink from the river.

It was late summer. No people meant no harvest. Unless the horde took what grew wild—but they were not peasants after all. They were Akkadean soldiers. And what army halted a campaign to engage in field labor? And—hard manual labor might kill old men, a fact Talib himself pointed out—and he wasn't jesting.

The next day they turned east from the ancient Wall and followed the road to Ai, the capital of the Zub'lin Tribe.

As luck would have it—or the Lord's providence, considering how the Lord had worked His purposes on Omar One-armed, among so many others—they met a traveler on the Ai road.

A *sramana* wearing a loincloth and dirty black scholar's robe was apparently traveling in their direction. They caught up to him just as he had seated himself on a flat rock at the side of the road. He was wretchedly thin and sickly-looking, his bones stuck out all over his body. His skin was like bark and his eyes shone dull green like two algae-covered ponds. His head seemed too large for his body. He smelled of wood fire and pungent spices.

Exalted Father

The *sramana* jumped to his feet. With an exaggerated flourish he bowed to them as if he had been expecting the horde for lunch.

"Hail, mighty Akkadeans," he sang through broken teeth.

"Hail, *sramana*," Agni responded. He smiled. "Who is it who does the hailing on such a fine summer's day with a great harvest in full swing?"

Talib looked offended. Agni was obviously clowning—again. But Agni *never* joked.

The scarecrow leaped down from his rock and danced a bow-legged step. "A simple *sramana* passed by this day, his life a coming and a going—"

"Does this simple one have a name?"

"Oh, he does," laughed the *sramana* happily. He danced another step, lost his balance and nearly toppled over. "Yes he does—" He winked at Agni as if inviting him to join a conspiracy.

The other warriors snorted, except Talib whose expression went from offended to envious. His bulging eyes became narrow slits. He recognized serious competition when he saw it.

Agni waited patiently. He thought he knew this one. The horde also waited. They waited for him to fly into a rage and cut down the *sramana* with his scimitar.

"The name?"

"What name?"

"Do you mock us," snarled an elderly Akkadean warrior.

"Mock you?" The madman sounded genuinely surprised. "Oh no—"

Agni sighed. "Well, my good *sramana*, it really doesn't matter. Perhaps you've forgotten your name. You do seem familiar to me.

"We are Akkadeans, if you care to recall our Tribe. We seek the daughter of the Khan. She was wife to Vishnu, Triumvir of the Ra'bim, but they've disappeared. Have you seen them in the course of your travels?"

The Akkadean horde stared at him dumfounded. Was this truly Agni or had some changeling taken his place? By now the *sramana* should not have had a head to be answering questions. Nor the time. He should be quite preoccupied searching for it.

And since when were they searching for Devorah? She'd probably died in Tholos. Weren't they on their way to slaughter Yads?

"Vishnu!" the *sramana* exclaimed, "I know him. Very formidable man, as powerful as the Grand Duke of the Yadish. The Duke looks like the Almighty, or so they say. Maybe the Almighty's older brother. Venerable and wise— Vishnu is pure white, like snow on the mountains, the foam on the ocean—"

"Do you know Devorah of Akkad?"

The *sramana* staggered back a step and looked as if he were about to faint.

"Do I know her? No, I don't *know* her, but I've seen her. Dark lady of the night. Durga she is named in the *Runehayana*...so young, so beautiful. Starless nightshade hair, like the mystery of the Lord's mountain. Eyes like a farvel, black and mysterious, yet shining too. She smiles like a farvel. Her skin is like satin, finer than the wings of a bugeave, luminous and dark at the same time, moist like fertile soil awaiting spring seed—

"Ah, all descriptions are false, foolish man. Words are webs of dew that cannot hold the slightest weight. The very presence of such beauty drives a man mad. And what man having seen such loveliness can endure another second without it?"

"All priests are mad," Talib observed, shaking his head. "Especially *sramanas*. It's vows. After a while, sheep become nymphs and *kittim* dancing girls. From the looks of him I'd say he'd tried fondling a *kittim*, maybe even tried plugging one, although priestly pluggers squirt about as well as L-guns—"

Agni stared at the lovesick wraith. "All Greenbottom's mad," he said.

"No more than Almighty Himself." Talib regained some of his confidence. "Really, why live on desolate mountain when you've the pick of the choicest spots? Why not a beach? Warm breezes keep the *kittim* away, you know—"

"Silence, fool—" Agni said without anger. "You, *sramana*, have not answered my question. Who are you? Again, I say, I seem to know you."

"Who am *I*? Who is this I asking? Who is this I who asks who is this I that asks who I am? I cannot find this one. When I seek myself I run from myself and retreat behind another. I find someone else, but it is this I that finds an object I. I want I that finds. I cannot be the object which I seek and still remain I the seeker! I, I, I... Ooo...it hurts I's head!"

"Do you have a name?"

"I do not need a name."

Again, Agni waited. Again his companions wondered why he suffered the *sramana* to live.

Tears rolled down hollow cheeks. He shook his matted locks of hair disrupting the peaceful lives of a few thousand lice. The robe slipped from his shoulders revealing the tell-tale blue-black tattoos of *kittim* infection. They appeared old and deep.

"My name is..." Perspiration gathered on his brow, "...Suthralane."

Agni took a backward step. His hand went to the hilt of his scimitar. For a second he resembled the Agni of old. The fire of anger ignited in his eyes. Then he saw the *kittim* discolored skin. As if drenched in a sudden cloud-burst, but from the inside, his inner flame went out.

"*You...are not he...*"

The *sramana*'s demeanor changed in that infinitesimal moment between thoughts. He laughed like a child and danced another step. "Could be. Could not be. Which is it, oh Lord of the Inner Fire?"

And just as quickly Agni found himself laughing along. His abrupt and shocking mood swing caused Talib to winch. Once more the fool experienced the pain of envy. There existed other fools in the world prepared to challenge him for the honor.

"I recall this Suthralane. A legend. Is he not titled Liberator? He was well-muscled and dark, they say—Akkadean to be sure. That was long ago. Some call him a myth. You are twice confused, my dear ascetic. And why call me Lord of the Inner Fire?"

A crafty look twisted the *sramana*'s features into a mask. It reminded Agni of the hideous death-masks worn by the half-human Tribe of Li'may who lived on the banks of the White Pearldew on the edge of the haunted Blackdiamond Forest.

"Do you not burn from the inner fire brought down to you from on high?"

"What?"

"Ah—" The *sramana* covered his discolored skin with the threadbare robe.

Agni stared at him.

"This is not Suthralane," Talib declared sounding uncharacteristically grim. He glanced at Agni and then back to the *sramana*. "It's useless banding words with an imbecile. You there, fool, we are on the road to Ai seeking the Great Khan's daughter Devorah. As you can see. Have you come from there?"

"Ah—" the *sramana* repeated, chuckling at some personal joke. "Yes, Ai. No one's there. The men are dead and the women have fled. To Nalanda they go. Seek you her among the priests." He laughed as though he'd just told a joke.

The court jester was long past laughing.

EXALTED FATHER

BOOK OF WINDS
VERSE 2.2.6

Dusk came and Lesser Wind brought its usual clouds of *kittim*. Now, however, they appeared to arise in the darkening east and ride the upper currents, like rows upon rows of colorful cavalry. Then they executed a wheel-like turn in perfect formation and sped south. None fell on the Akkadeans. None deviated from the formation. They appeared more purposeful than ever, a flock of giant birds driven by a single will. Passing high above, they soon disappeared into the haze of the steppe.

The next day the horde entered Ai. The town was deserted, although it showed no sign of sack or burning. The population had seemingly decided to pack up and leave. Storehouses and silos were filled with all sorts of grains, bean, corn, olives, lemons, apples and figs, even while the fields around the city looked as though they'd gone untended for the whole summer.

A stray cow crossed their path. It regarded them with a combination of surprise and forlorn reserve, and then continued down the road as though it had urgent business elsewhere.

That evening the Akkadeans discovered a vast winery stocked with hundreds of unopened casks. They spent the night feasting and drinking in a large building. Massive fluted pillars supported the imposing structure. With its vaulted barrel ceiling and wide portico, it appeared to be the Ai town hall.

That evening, the *sramana* who called himself Suthralane disappeared. Agni wandered through Ai in a half-hearted search. Failing that, he found himself outside of town climbing its eastern hills.

He came upon a grove of elm and birch. The trees appeared vibrant, filled with dark green leaves with serrated edges that reminded him of *kittim*. He found a lone elm growing on a green-carpeted rise at the edge of the grove overlooking a small valley. Seating himself beneath its canopy, he faced east and watched real *kittim* cavorting in the fading light.

The strange sensation of spatial elasticity was intoxicating. Space seemed to bend and fold as *kittim* spiraled in and out of the normal three dimensions. The phenomenon resembled heat waves shimmering in the light. Here space was moving and undulating. Space itself was doing the shimmering.

Agni smiled. Then he laughed. He laughed at himself for laughing. His *kittim* wound was warm but not unpleasantly so. At least bug poisoning made you happy before it killed you. Unlike Ra'bim medicine, for example. He knew this from experience. Once, aged twelve, he came down with a severe fever. His mother gave him a Ra'bim potion. It tasted bitter and made him feel worse. In a few days the fever left him. It seemed to have departed on its own. The medicine ruined his digestion for months.

Another old memory popped into his head. It was more vivid than the previous one. He was a disembodied spectator, outside time and space—

He was fourteen. A powerful Akkadean warrior— a younger version of Jebe—was leading him into the circular building of cut stone and immense columns called the Shrine. Built upon the northeastern shore of Lake Emerald, its full title was the Holy Shrine of Borassus. Borassus according to the priests meant "tree of life." But no trees grew anywhere near the place.

He shivered in the chill dampness of the place. He saw himself step through the entrance into smoky shadows where a fearsome warrior woman stood waiting for him. She was a giantess, ancient yet powerfully muscled, as thick and solid as ancient oak. She stood completely naked, like a living statue. Steam rose from her. "You and I," she announced. "We visit the great mystery of Beginnings—"

She brought him to the center of the Shrine. There was a shallow pool of green. Instructing him to shed his clothes, she led him into surprisingly warm water. And then reciting a litany he could not remember she took him into herself. At the height of that divine moment when the liquid fire erupts—the same liquid fire, she said, that burns in the stars of heaven and in the fields of the earth (this was part of the liturgy)— Agni's own inner heat failed.

And now he knew that the *sramana* was mistaken. He possessed no real inner fire, only the false flame of anger. He heard her mocking laugh, even now. He felt the heat of her, smelled the rich odor of her like a verdant forest—even now.

The memory pushed aside his quiet joy. He no longer laughed. Foolish boy! Was he born a natural ascetic? What of Devorah? He bowed his head.

The sky turned blue-black as the *kittim* departed for the southeast. They passed over the steppe and flew on to the Edom desert. In the north, a full Lotus Moon rose and bathed the grove in pale light, turning the elm leaves silver.

Someone was there beside him.

As if he'd suddenly emerged from a seam in empty space, the strange *sramana* was quietly seated next to Agni in an odd, cross-legged way, staring off in the direction of the Pearldew.

"You are not Suthralane," Agni said, studying him closely. The memory of the Shrine still lingered in his mind. "Suthralane probably never existed, or if he did, nothing like we think."

The *sramana* shrugged. The dirty robe hung loosely from his bony shoulders and Agni saw dark patches of *kittim* infection. Close up, they appeared even deeper, far worse than Agni's or the Khan's.

"I have strange dreams," the *sramana* said. "In each I am someone else— you have not dreamed so?"

A still small voice in the recesses of Agni's mind angrily protested such priestly nonsense. Agni marveled at how faint the old voice had become. Born of repeated habit, it had been like stone. Here now was a rushing river, flowing, overwhelming stone, wearing it away. He marveled that he did not draw his scimitar and water the tree roots with *sramana* blood.

"Perhaps we dream here," the Akkadean remarked off-handedly.

"Perhaps we dream this grove," the ascetic said. "Did you know that here on this spot there was once a great forest of elm and birch and oak and poplar—and another kind of tree. That *other* tree—one could see inside the body of that other tree. One could see the pulse of life flowing like a living flame, up and down, from earth to heaven and heaven to earth. Fire sap—" He laughed. "And the leaves, thick and fleshy, some were the size of a man. There was a pool too. Of dark green. And every so often a plant-like thing came to the surface, many of them, oddly shaped, of different sizes."

"Whittlings," Agni breathed. "You dream—of whittlings?"

"Hated of the Lord, destroyed by man..." The *sramana* recited the familiar verse from *Sariraka, The Book of the Cleansing*.

Agni had heard the whittling verses, but he couldn't recall when or where, or from whom.

"The land needed to be cleared for agriculture," he said without conviction. "The Lord never gave reasons for His commands. Why should the Almighty need to give reasons?"

The *sramana* seemed to concentrate on the growing darkness. "And there were farvels who tended the forest—" His voice became a childish piping, in stark contrast to his aged and emaciated body.

"Forests walk on, as clouds float and cover the sun.
Everything is produced; everything is extinguished,
When creation and extinction are extinguished,

Things are as they really are."

"From the *Runehayana*? Agni asked. "What Book?"

"It's a recalculation of the original Runes. A new translation into the Sandi. The archbishop rejected it of course. It comes from *Murdaka*, the *Third Book of Elsseleron*."

Agni furrowed his brow, "Who has not heard that Suthralane was the greatest scholar of his age, and the greatest blasphemer. Some blame him for the Lord's Curse. Are you a second Suthralane?"

"Look there," the *sramana* said. He pointed down into the valley.

THE BOOKS OF MARDUK

BOOK OF WINDS
VERSE 2.2.7

A cold mist was rising, milky white in the pale light of Lotus Moon. At first, Agni thought that the ascetic was pointing at a colony of wild flowers. Then a breeze came and parted the mist. And he saw the creature.

It sat back on its haunches like a huge mosscat: a long, sleek body, extended, lipless muzzle, wide, triangular ears on the sides of a round head resembling furry birch leaves. There was something funny about the mouth. The lower jaw was more pronounced than that of a mosscat and its overall line gave the creature a kind of perpetual grin—or a snarl. Agni could not be sure.

With almost supernatural grace, the creature stood up and faced him. Bands of fur covered the body and seemed to change colors with movement. In the soft moonlight and pale mist Agni had difficulty identifying the different shades as they passed one into another, but the overall impression was gold. A large golden mosscat wearing a bemused smile, silently watching him.

Agni peered directly into the face. The shock was like a physical blow. The eyes were totally incongruous with the body—*human eyes*, large and round and shining with intelligence. The moonlight gave them a light green tint. The creature stared back as if teasing him, challenging him. *What am I?*

Scar tissue from an old wound half-closed the creature's right eye.

Agni sprang to his feet. The creature vanished. One second it was there, grinning, and the next it was gone. Like the passing of a shadow, a sudden gust of wind, a brief motion at the very periphery of sight, he never saw the thing disappear. *When you see mountains walk...*

"*Sramana*, did you see that?"

"Ah, so you see them—"

"Them?"

"Old habits do not poison easily—"

Agni shook his head and took a long breath. "I saw a creature... something...strange and familiar at the same time..."

"A farvel. Beloved of the world, hated by the Lord. They speak to me, you know."

"They were exterminated. Our histories say in the First Kalpa. We Akkadeans claim the glorious distinction. We hunted them ruthlessly. We pursued them into Edom and from there to the Windward Straits where they drowned in the Reed Sea."

"Well then, we must be imagining things."

"You saw it too?"

"Perhaps illusions are contagious." The *sramana* threw back his head and laughed as if he were having a seizure. The *kittim* stain that covered his neck and shoulder glowed in the moonlight. Agni felt his own infected skin tingling.

"Look again, my Akkadean brother." The *sramana* pointed.

Lotus Moon was approaching its zenith, speeding southwest in order to make way for the coming of Dewdrop Moon in the morning. The valley passed into darkness as black as the depths of the Middle Sea. They saw King Reuben's Road shining brightly on the far ridge. It looked like a band of light rising out of the waters.

The Road was not empty.

Thousands upon thousands of farvels filled the road. They were headed south, a farvel army marching south, as if on pilgrimage to the monastery named Nalanda.

Agni stared in a trance. Hours may have passed, but he had lost all sense of time's flow. Hours might have been seconds. Suddenly he remembered.

My brother...

Marduk!

He spun around as though to seize the *sramana*.

The Books Of Marduk

Marduk had disappeared.

Exalted Father

THE BOOK OF WINDS

CHAPTER THREE - Upper Nalanda

VERSE 2.3.1

The Runes defeated her. Not even old Vishnu had been able to humiliate her like this. Not even her father. Since everyone acknowledged Marduk a brilliant Rune scholar, this was reason to hate him even more.

The old archbishop had granted her access to the main library of Upper Nalanda. He had even provided a room in his own vast tower. Kera and Tera found quarters in Lower Nalanda. The three women will henceforth be scholar-priests, priestesses, the archbishop announced.

The old Khan had taught Devorah the fine art of reading and writing in Sandi. The two Ra'bim ladies had gone without lettering, as the Rabs say. They were from the plebian class, as the Ra'bim named their peasants. For plebs lettering was a waste of time.

In Lower Nalanda, the priesthood gave Kera and Tera the chance to acquire the gift of literacy. Unfortunately, the gift quickly became burdensome and boring. The Rab females soon discovered that they lacked other gifts, such as concentration and determination. And they soon discovered that the priests themselves were more interesting. A few of the younger priests (those still in their sixties) were able to achieve erections, if only for a short time. Tera and Kera felt a tiny bit guilty for being the cause of these brief erections—but their feelings were brief.

Father Leo chastised the two ladies for luring pure ones into sin, as Father Leo labelled these momentary lapses into virility. He was quick to reassure them, however: celibacy, he patiently explained, was profoundly religious symbolism and not meant to be taken too literally. The erring priests were, of course, victims, if willing ones.

Devorah knew her Sandi. The language of the Lord was another matter. The countless rules seemed ridiculously chaotic. Theophilus did his best to tutor her. Yet, she simply couldn't understand how mathematics found its way into literature. The steps appeared arbitrary and unnecessarily complicated. She was quite prepared to accept Akkadean opinion that the priests made the whole thing up.

The archbishop sighed and called it a mystery of the Lord on High. He added with a laugh: "When a priest speaks of mystery it usually means he hasn't a clue." Agni might have said that, she mused. "The Lord is unknowable," Theophilus added, "which is what we know about Him…" He winked.

As her interest in the *Runehayana* (and the Kingdoms of the Heavens) sagged, her fascination with Marduk surged, along with her hatred. She felt his presence in the library. Hour after hour she sat, lightly brushing her fingers over pages he'd written. They made little sense to her. Strings of numbers were intermittently broken by words. She found the Kingdoms of the Heavens sandwiched between long numerical calculations. She found the Lord, Suthralane, some Tribal names (but not Akkad), and a word she'd never seen before, *Earth*. When she queried the archbishop, Theophilus threw up his hands and laughed. Not even the Lord Himself can make sense of Marduk's writings, he advised her.

Exalted Father

She felt his presence most strongly in those cast-off sheets. She strained to recall his green eyes, his not-quite-a-smile smile, his dark skin, his long black hair and beardless face. And especially his voice.

She heard him as though he were still speaking. She felt the depth and richness of his voice. It seemed to her that he spoke from another place, a wholly other place. In her mind, like an audible dream, he spoke of times long past, of people long dead, of her (and himself)—but the words escaped her understanding and she knew not their content, only the yearnings they aroused within her. In that wholly other place and that wholly other time (in many others) they'd been together. She knew it deep in her body, in her body's cells. But what places? What times?

She had a revelation. *He'd been mocking her.* Her liberation was mockery—all priests were liars. All men betrayed her...her father, her protector, Agni, now Marduk. For all this and more, she discovered that she hated him. He'd die by her hand, and with him all men.

BOOK OF WINDS
VERSE 2.3.2

Devorah fascinated the archbishop. He discovered all sorts of reasons to visit the library, even after she'd given up the Rune tutoring sessions.

She possessed a mysterious appeal, an uncanny attraction that sprang from her physical beauty but was not wholly dependent upon it. She was the youngest woman he's ever known. Her dark eyes, flawless skin, lithe and strong body might have driven a younger man to the brink of desparation. Except—there were no such men remaining in Greenbottom in the Third Kalpa. He wasn't counting *sramanas*, of course, for they had their vows.

There was something else about her. Theophilus for all his knowledge and years of experience found himself at a loss to name it.

Autumn came riding the cold winds like an army from the north. *Kittim*—bugeaves—rained down upon Nalanda daily. Not a few priests were caught in the open courtyards and were reduced to shallow pools of water soaking into the ground between cobblestones. Many such unfortunates were caught coming from the quarters of Tera and Kera, located at the far south end of Lower Nalanda near the Edom Gate. Sadly, priest Thomas was one of the first.

EXALTED FATHER

BOOK OF WINDS
VERSE 2.3.3

One gray, chill morning after Greater Wind, the archbishop found himself in the lower levels of the Tower. He wandered into the library. Devorah was there, studying a priestly history (in Sandi) of the Unified Kingdom.

She glanced up as he entered. He marveled at how mesmerizing her look could be. Her white body-suit seemed molded to her like a second skin. It caused her to appear naked. She'd taken to wearing priestly robes over it. She was surely aware of her attraction, yet she didn't seem to care. *That* (which had become Tera's and Kera's new occupation) did not seem to interest her in the least. Of course he was an ancient celibate priest, but he doubted she would have acted different with a younger man, say someone like Marduk.

He permitted himself a sip of brandy. As of late, the drink no longer seemed to do anything for him. He experienced neither warmth nor light-headedness. He wondered if the Banalis had forgotten the art of distillation.

"Our Orlok Agni says that when a priest writes something, the opposite must be true. And this is a truth more dependable than the laws of nature. What say you, oh archbishop of liars?"

Theophilus found it amusing that she'd adopted the black robes of the scholars. Strange how shapeless wool actually added to her dark beauty, making her a thousand times more desirable than the Ra'bim body-suit. How captivating her mystery—concealment inflames the imagination. Revelation is boring—apparently puzzles and mysteries were more enticing. He wished he had the time and youth to ponder this paradox.

"Your Agni would make a fine priest," he said, chuckling.

Her eyebrows raised and wrinkles appeared in the skin of her forehead. She blessed him with a slight smile. Suddenly he felt drunk. How dare he doubt the art of the Banalis Tribe.

"Does Marduk lie?" she asked.

"Marduk is a *sramana*, my dear girl. No longer a priest-scholar."

"He was a priest, not so? *Sramanas* are really wandering priests. Agni says they're spies, which makes him a liar and a deceiver."

Theophilus laughed and shook his head. "Oh what odd tales travel up and down King's Road these days. Let's say Marduk's a *sramana* who's given up the priesthood out of frustration—"

Her black eyes became wide and her breathing heavy. "Frustration with—"

"Don't misunderstand. Marduk was the greatest scholar of this Kalpa. Perhaps of all Kalpas. The Runes melt in his mouth, so to speak. That's why they torture him. Their uncertainty tortures him. So he became a *sramana*."

"This history... Is it *his* work?" She raised the bulky folios.

Theophilus glimpsed the craggy script that covered the papyrus leaves.

"His indeed," he said.

He marveled at her reaction. Her transparency fascinated him. She didn't even try to hide it. Disgust.

She stared at the ragged page. "I feel it... It lives... in me... But I don't understand..."

"What is it you're reading, my girl?"

"The Legend of Suthralane."

"Ah—" The archbishop danced a step. He swept the skullcap from his head and bowed to her.

"Don't read another word. It's mush. You have your answer anyhow. Why Marduk quit the priesthood."

"Why?"

"Why? Why oh why? Why oh why are there so many Suthralane legends? Why oh why do they not agree? Not a single one with the other. It drove him crazy."

"Why not stick to the oldest. Should not the original be the truth?"

"Why, why, why…? Even the originals may be lies."

She was growing weary with such nonsense. "That's not an answer, old man," she said harshly.

Her anger amused him. It made her more beautiful.

"Ah my girl, the oldest need not be the most accurate, even if the ancient priests were exceptions to your Agni's natural law—I mean your greater-than-natural-law law. Even if they were eye-witnesses. The time is too short. Events need time to simmer in people's minds. It takes generations before they become history. Not even then. How many second thoughts? Reconsiderations? Sudden revelations? All inside a person's head. How much worse is it when it's all coded in the Runes?"

"Marduk became a *sramana* because of that?"

Theophilus dropped his eyes. "And for other reasons," he said softly.

"What other reasons? Don't lie to me, priest!" Suddenly she was the fierce Akkadean warrior ready to pounce.

He knew that she was capable of anything. He'd heard that a certain priest, one named Paul, had approached her a few days ago with something less (or more) than simple monastery business on mind. The *kittim* took him that day, but rumor had it that he was dead long before his final demise into a puddle of black fluid.

"What other reasons?" Her voice was full of calm menace.

"Because he was ill—*kittim* poisoning."

"*Liar!*" She leaped out of her chair.

Interesting, the archbishop briefly thought, that I should die at the hands of such beauty—

"He cured *me* of the Purple Soma," she said.

"I've heard the story."

"He cannot cure himself?"

"He seeks another cure."

"So he went to Tholos, city of physicians? Let me tell you, archbishop, he found there nothing but corruption and filth."

Theophilus nodded. "I know. The *kittim* madness has him now. He sees farvels. They speak to him, tell him things. He wanders aimlessly. His crazy illusions may be the cause of his own destruction."

"How so?"

"He seeks to repeat the crime of Suthralane. You're following him, not so? He goes to Starmirror. To confront the Lord on His Holy Mountain, which is forbidden to men—and women, I'd guess." The archbishop grinned. "He's completely mad, you know. He takes a crooked path to the mountain...through the Nepptali lands, I'd guess...maybe Ai, Yadishland...who knows? Where he goes you cannot follow."

"I do follow." She stood straight like a soldier at attention. "*He-With-Us*," she added.

He did not ask her why. He already knew. He saw it in her eyes. How she fascinated him. Perhaps it had been like this with Suthralane. Those *other* stories, the ones that told how women followed him because he'd captivated them with his cheerful absurdities and profound-sounding drivel. Nonsense in the name of higher things is alluring. Those *other* stories about the gift of Suthralane.

The archbishop nodded. "Go with the Lord, my dear."

Exalted Father

BOOK OF WINDS
VERSE 2.3.4

This particular scouting party had come up out of the fly-infested marshlands of the delta. Captain Menes ordered the main army west. He was worried about his northern flank. The entire campaign depended upon the scouting party covering the exposed flank of the main army.

"Fail me," he barked, "and it will go worse for you than the Tailless."

The subaltern whose name was Teapat groveled in the dust at his feet. "We'll not fail you, great Captain," he squeaked. "Their flesh will we tear and rend. Their females will we take—"

"*NO!*" Captain Menes barred his teeth. "Their females are for the White Lord. Touch them and you die!"

Teapat whined deep in his throat.

"No—"

"No? No?"

Menes was powerfully built as Redfolk went, which meant that he was a little taller than an Edom lemon tree sapling in the spring. He grabbed Teapat by the scuff of his neck and lifted him off the ground like a dead branch.

"No. You will not follow the White Lord's commandments."

Teapat howled and wiggled like a worm on a hook.

"No, no... I meant—"

"Still no, maggot?"

Menes grabbed him with both claws and sank his fangs into Teapat's neck. The subaltern shrieked in surprise and pain. Then Menes twisted his head viciously and bit again, this time tearing out the jugular. Blood pumped from the wound splashing the Captain's face.

Teapat tried to fight back by raking his talons across the Captain's chest. But the life drained from him and his efforts were feeble. In moments he was dead.

"Who will obey me?" Menes snarled.

Another of the Redfolk stepped forward. He was roughly Teapat's size, maybe a bit larger. His narrow eyes gleamed with wicked intelligence.

"I, Serrati, will most certainly obey the great Captain."

"Then do as I have commanded and you shall become a subaltern."

"I am yours, great Captain. What you wish is my one desire. What you say my only thought."

Menes glared at him.

"Do it then, and shut-up about it."

"I do it. I do it. The males we will kill. The females we will capture. For the Lord."

He smiled showing his yellow fangs. He dropped his voice to a throaty growl.

"And the choicest female shall be yours, Captain Menes."

Menes grunted. "Then see to it."

BOOK OF WINDS
VERSE 2.3.5

They caught her scent before they saw her. They knew her. As surely as the longer wind brought blowflies in the morning they knew. Her scent was of the season. Every season. Such was the way of the tailless. Seasonal time did not matter to them.

Her odor was of the black soil, moist, rich, warm and fecund. Not a few experienced a swelling between their crooked legs.

Serrati snarled a warning: "She is for the White Lord." He drew a rusty blade given to him by Menes. "Touch her and die."

The others showed their teeth and snarled back. The odds were in their favor: nine to one. Serrati was devious. He wielded a knife of the Lord. He was somewhat bigger than the average Red Yakashas. Naturally, the wrath of the Lord terrified them.

She appeared to be headed towards the delta. That was strange. No Tailless female ever came this far south.

A bitter odor drifted over the dying autumn grasses among which they hid. It was not of her, but it clung to her like a cloud of blowflies. Perhaps it arose from the black shroud she wore. They'd never heard of Tailless females wearing the beggar's shroud.

Serrati growled instructions. They crept forward on all fours, meaning to encircle her.

She stopped suddenly.

The Redfolk froze. Her features were hidden by the shroud's hood. Her smell was overpowering. It drove them to the edge of madness.

She reached inside the shapeless shroud and drew a weapon. Serrati had never seen the like. The blade was exceptionally long. Shining. Wickedly curved. It made the Lord's knife look like a sprite's toy—he guessed it looked like a toy, there'd not been a sprite born to his people in his lifetime.

He whistled the order. He was too late. Her weapon was free and she crouched in a fighting stance. Too fast for Redfolk eyes, she'd thrown off the cumbersome shroud.

Poor Yakashas. A number simply went mad. She was nothing like the heavy-breasted, wide-hipped females of Gad. She wore a strange white material that covered her body completely. Or perhaps it was her skin, like that of the White Lords. She was perfect of line and form, a dream come to life. And how the Redfolk could dream—of other places, other times, different bodies, when they were creatures of dignity and stature.

Her terrible beauty destroyed their minds as her sword did their bodies.

In a blur of motion, she cut down the nearest soldier, slicing him from groin to neck, splitting him in half.

She leaped over him before he hit the ground. With fluid grace, she drove between the next two astonished Redfolk. Spinning around like a top, she took their heads off with a full sweep of her razor sharp blade.

She danced among them, a smile on her lovely face, slashing back and forth, without wasting a single move, not a flourish in vain. At once she was beautiful and deadly.

Four more Redfolk died. Two screeched and fled.

Serrati stood frozen, his knife forgotten—it slipped from his claw. He stood utterly dumbfounded.

She towered over him. Her blade was wet with the black blood of his kind. He could not move.

"So, there're Yakashas after all," she remarked casually.

He stared at her wide-eyed. His stringy moss-like hair hung past his narrow shoulders. Naked but for a worn black vest, he looked as though he'd been assembled from branches and twigs. His large triangular ears stood erect, his ferret face twisted in fear. Next to her he resembled a small wooden puppet painted red, the sort of toy the Zubs made for children a Kalpa ago.

"Do you understand my speech, Yakashas? I would answer the question before I kill you."

He collapsed as if someone had severed his puppet strings. Face down, he wailed: "Oh pleassseee, Great Queen, spare this humble servant of the Lord."

"Who is the Lord?"

"He is Lord of Lords—" His voice sounded like the sizzle of a wood fire doused by water.

"Speak up. I'm losing patience."

"Oh, oh, thou art loved—touching my heart, washing it in wine—"

"What foolishness is this? Tell me of your Lord before I wash the ground in your blood!"

"He is—Lord of Lords—He rules the Mirror—"

He lifted his eyes. They were black, eerily human—human eyes set in an animal face dominated by a long muzzle and ears as big as the small head. He barred his fangs. Despite the vest reaching his knees, she saw that he had an erection.

"Come," she said, her voice serene and full of danger, "try my skill. Test me, foolish imp. For I am Devorah of Akkad, Mistress of Time, Washer of Souls— Destroyer of Desert Imps. Come, test me."

He howled: "Oh no, great Queen! You wrong your servant. Do not judge me according to the others…foolish…Desert Imps, as you say. Serrati, servant of the Lord am I. Yes, yes, yes… No, no, no…"

He paused and dropped his eyes. His ears flopped over as though all life had drained from them. Even his tiny phallus seemed to shrink.

"I am…a guide. Yes, yes, yes…"

"Go on," she said.

"He, the Lord, knew of thy coming, oh Queen. The Divine One sees far and deep, He does. Hears far and wide, He does. Knows far and deep too, He does. He welcomes His Queen."

At times Serrati found himself surprised by his own cleverness.

His jabbering drivel made no sense to her. But it didn't matter. The chance encounter was not chance at all. Forgotten until now, it was there in her mind. Not the details, not this place, this creature, this time, yet she remembered. Met a thousand times, on a thousand roads—

"You, my guide, will take me to Him," she said.

"Yes, yes, oh yes, beautiful Queen. Will this humble servant's reward be great?"

"Of course. As it has been in the past."

She turned and strode to the place where she'd dropped her black robe. She wrapped it about her body. It was like putting out a fire.

He sighed. Redfolk skin was rough as bark. But the chill of the northern autumn was still hard on such creatures from the south. How unlike the queeti with their thick pelts of fur and massive bodies, poor Redfolk. Why had the Lord been so miserly when He'd designed them?

"Follow your servant," he said, joy and hope in his reedy voice.

"What of your companions, Master Yakashas, who were not as wise as you?"

"Food for blowflies," he said.

"Let the dead bury the dead."

(All these events occurred in the first year of the first decade of the ninth century of the Third Kalpa as reckoned by the priests of Nalanda and recorded here.)

THE BOOK OF PLAGUES

THE BOOKS OF MARDUK

PASSAGES FROM THE
RUNEHAYANA

Aitareya Book IV, Section I. *The Books of Elsseleron* (The Lord's Holy Mountain)

The following is a re-calculation, transliteration, and translation into the *Sandi* by the *sramana* Marduk, former priest of Nalanda.[9]

Verses From the Second Chapter:

1. When the Lord (walked on) Jambridvipa, He found the land choked with thorny shrubs surrounding stagnant ponds [...] also named whittling groves. He found nameless beings He did not *make* (fashion, as on a potter's wheel).

2. The Lord caused (urinated) a rain of sulfur, bitumen, and

---

[9] In the hand of the queeti poet-historian Theophilus: Roughly speaking, there are two methods of translation. The first is to focus on the target language; in this case Sandi is given priority, and the Runes of the Lord are rendered in subservience to their meaning in Sandi. In the case of the Runes, this requires the strange priestly mathematical scheme of arbitrarily assigning fractions to a given Rune in a given passage as it appeared in Lordpool, and using these fractions to transliterate the given Rune into a Sandi letter. This method betrays the source language (and hence the Lord). The second method gives priority to the source or root language, which in the case of the Runes is not a language at all but a random list of four symbols. This method's drawback is that there is no method, since there doesn't seem to be a discernable order to any given appearance of the Runes. Only the Nepptali (and Marduk) believed otherwise.

EXALTED FATHER

mercury. He cleansed the Land.

3. And the Lord caused the waters to well up beneath the soil [...] and He caused them to flow into two channels. And they merged into one, which is the Pearldew (also read *four rivers*).
4. On the banks of the Pearldew did the Lord [...] a garden. And the Lord said: *"Behold, the garden Greenbottom is a gift of the Pearldew."*
5. Behold, everything that comes to be has a cause. Every cause is also an effect in time and must have a cause. But the Lord is uncaused. Therefore, everything does not have a cause. But this is impossible. [....] the Lord did not come to be. Is the Lord out(side) time? But life presupposes change in time. Out(side) time is no life. Life, then, is impossible. (Is the Lord impossible?)
6. "Behold," said the Lord, "*I am impossible. Yet, I am.*" And the Lord laughed (at his own Joke?). Who heard the divine laughter?
7. The Lord placed (threw down, plopped down) man and woman in the garden Greenbottom. What was the model (original)? What was the (shadow)? [From the Impossible?]

Verses From Book V, Section III:

8. The Lord wished to be known. (Wish implies lack. The Lord cannot wish.) He formed (planted) the man.
9. Is not the Lord's hand (foot) found in the language of plants? In the two Winds? In flower fairies and desert imps? Why did the Lord create? Why did the Lord destroy?[10]
10. To be known (or to be clean, say the ancient sages.) Does not

---

[10] In the hand of Theophilus: In Verse 8 Marduk seems to abandon his translation principle. The Runes (given the highest probability of their chosen fractions) say: *inject genetic codes*, whatever this means. Marduk translates "to create."

the Lord know Himself? Is there a need in the Lord? But He cannot need, for such is a lack.

11. The Lord knew *her* in the Heavens. And so He planted a garden for *her*. Was […]?

THE BOOK OF PLAGUES

CHAPTER ONE - Machpelah

VERSE 3.1.1

Jacob found the high citadel abandoned, as it had been for many decades. The place smelled of death.

From this elevation he caught a wavering glimpse of the shining surface of Red Lake in the west. The setting daystar appeared to sink into the dark waters turning them red. Strange that Red Lake should be named from the perspective of someone in the east. The *Runehayana* implied that the first humans who entered Greenbottom came up from the south. They'd fled Starmirror because they'd angered the Lord. The Books never specified the nature of their sin, exactly what they did to anger the Lord. It must have been terrible.

Coming from the south, they would have experienced the daystar rising over the lake, its waters sparkling white as tree shadows surrendered to its effulgence.

The name *Red Lake* suggested that the first settlers came out of the Yakashas Steppe. Since the *Runehayana* said otherwise, the logic of the eastern approach had to be mistaken. Alternative explanations had to be discarded when they contradicted the *Runehayana*, which was a priestly rule-of-thumb.

Satisfied by this bit of weighty analysis, Jacob scrambled up the citadel's massive ramp. He sought shelter from the Winds.

Machpelah, *cave-in-the-hill*. Jacob had visited here before. Unlike other Yadish towns which were constructed from red brick and wood, Machpelah's walls and towers, and not a few of its homes, were built from cut stone and a kind of hard stucco found nowhere else in Greenbottom. Rising high above the rest of the town, its citadel resembled a mountain of headstones and ornate burial crypts. Broken walls and ruined towers still provided ample protection from Lesser Wind.

Jacob had heard from senior priests that Marduk loved high places like Machpelah. Outside of Nalanda, the citadel boasted the highest elevation south of the Ramah Stairs. From this height, Jacob could watch the east road. He'd heard the old priests refer to the road as *Sramana* Path, or sometimes Ascetics Way. The climb was difficult on world-deniers, they added sarcastically. Fortunately for Jacob, such claims were exaggerated.

Officially the road was named the Way of King Ephron. According to Yadish poets, King Ephron had destroyed an especially bestial steppe race called the queeti. He built the citadel to guard the Yadish from future attacks coming out of the desert. Some unknown disaster had befallen it, which the poet-historians did not record.

None of this history appeared in the *Runehayana*. Therefore, none of it mattered to Jacob. *What was not in the Runehayana was not worth knowing,* he often said. He prided himself for having invented this saying. How witty he was. He'd surely become famous for this saying (and many others) someday—he said. Jacob, priest of proverbs.

A ragged band of Akkadeans had spotted Marduk near the Zub capital of Ai. They'd come to Nalanda seeking asylum. Everyone seemed to be seeking shelter in Nalanda (these days.)

Somewhere east of Ai, the Akkadeans said, Marduk had crossed the Pearldew into Gad. The Akkadeans had been poisoned by

EXALTED FATHER

bugeaves, the leader too, a young warrior from the same generation as Jacob himself. The court jester, apparently, was the one exception.

Jacob thought this so-called jester more irritating than funny. He tried to be funny, but lacking the imagination, he struck Jacob as pathetically dull and vain, and his jokes were more rudeness and bad-temper than clever. He resembled an old bird with his beak-like nose and wide-set eyes. His ill-fitting jacket looked as if it had been assembled from rags cast off by the Tribes, each piece of a different tribal color. Skinny, old, looking as though he'd been slowly roasted over a fire, the jester acted childish, which slid into infantilism, mere attention seeking.

Jacob doubted Akkadean testimony. The man they described was surely not Marduk. Physically, Marduk would never be taken for an ascetic. The Akkadean leader, one named Agni—absurd name, Jacob thought it—spoke of an older man, starved, diseased, near death. This was not Marduk. Akkadeans were such liars. When an Akkadean spoke you could be sure the opposite was true. Someday, Jacob would be famous for this proverb too.

The Winds were rising, the nights were colder and the bugeaves more plentiful than ever. Marduk often *went into retreat*, as he called it, in Machpelah. Jacob's chances were good. He sharpened his blade and waited.

THE BOOKS OF MARDUK

BOOK OF PLAGUES
VERSE 3.1.2

Jacob sat beneath the lentils of a broad portico that led into a massive square mansion of turrets and vaulted ceilings. Its wide frieze was decorated with statues of former Yadish kings. A few had toppled over losing their arms and noses. Some had lost their heads.

He watched Dewdrop Moon set in the northwest. The mansion sat just inside the crumbled wall. Nothing obstructed his view of the road. (How can nothing *obstruct* something?)

This morning, Greater Wind brought a huge cloud of bugeaves. Jacob watched them spread over the sky like a phalanx of clouds rolling in from the north. He considered writing down "like a phalanx of clouds," given how brilliant the imagery, as he judged it. Yet, he did possess a scholar's memory and therefore knew that, in his own words—his memory would remember.

Suddenly a formation of bugeaves veered west and sailed over the lake like a brightly colored flock of marsh fowl (yet another brilliant image.)

Jacob knew for certain—because it was written in the Books—that bugeaves were nothing more than leaf-like spores in shapes of children's kites. Bugeave origins probably had something to do with an unknown plant or tree in the Blackdiamond Forest, but this was priestly speculation, and Jacob didn't take it seriously. Bugeaves had most likely consumed the Min-vena and the Li'way Tribes, the northern-most Tribes in the Second Kalpa (more speculation). In recent times bugeave behavior had become quite odd…*purposeful*, Priest Thomas called it. But Jacob hated priest Thomas so this could not be true.

Jacob knew the true cause. He bowed his head and sighed. The Lord had deserted the world, abandoning it to wicked powers. And the Lord had good reason. Marduk was only the latest of those blasphemous scholars who had tampered with the infallible translations of the early priests, the pure ones, those who translated with the Lord's breath still in their ears, in their mouth, in their mind, in every cell of their body. Jacob fervently believed that the Lord's Word was changeless and absolute. It was *truth* forever and for all time. Marduk and his ilk, going back to the arch-devil Suthralane, had changed that truth. Their pride was overweening, and because of their pride the Lord on High cursed the world—for pride, Jacob believed—and because Jacob believed, and his belief was strong, it was true.

Two monotonous days passed. Jacob watched the road until his blurry eyes grew so heavy they refused to remain open. One afternoon he succumbed and indulged in a long nap. Afterwards, feeling refreshed, and more bored than ever (one requires energy to be bored, he said) he explored the ruined fortress town.

As luck would have it, he discovered an old wine cellar in the basement of a nearby stone house along with a fully stocked storehouse. He was able to relieve the monotony sipping wine and consuming vast quantities of dried sweet-meat, salted salmon, anchovies, and even such delicacies as aged goat cheese and a kind of lake trout. Not luck—since nothing happened by chance, the Lord must have guided him.

Wine and good food provided the occasion for deep theological thinking. Jacob was always ready to indulge in this pleasant pastime. It was his only vice, he said.

He dragged a large marble table into a bright and airy atrium on the south side of the mansion. The atrium was partially covered by a vaulted canopy. A small pool sat in the center of roughly circular floor with a fireplace on the north wall.

Comfortable and content, he indulged in deeper theological thinking.

Jacob rejected the idea of luck or chance. Such words were mere labels that denoted human ignorance, he said (he hated to admit that he was not original with this bit of wisdom). All things, every random cloud, wisp of air, drop of rain, roll of a wave on the surface of the lake—life and death—were governed by the unalterable will of the Lord. Time itself flowed according to His permission. That the laws of nature continued to operate without pause even after the Lord deserted the world did not concern Jacob. Somehow the Lord ruled everything even in his Divine Absence.

One bright morning, invigorated by the sharp bracing air, the brilliant autumn sky, the soothing silence of the citadel (not to forget well-aged wine and copious amounts of food), he inadvertently discovered a contradiction in this (unoriginal) bit of wisdom.

Had not the Lord ceased speaking to men? Had He not abandoned the world? But if the Lord truly abandoned the world then why didn't His natural laws cease working and the world collapse back into chaos? *How did the world continue to exist without the Divine Presence?*

Now here was something he had not previously considered. Maybe high places in the autumn were valuable retreats after all.

Furrows appeared in the normally stress-free skin of Jacob's forehead. Beads of sweat dripped into his eyes. The paradox took him hours to solve. After several (he lost count) glasses of wine, the tension finally broke and Jacob saw the answer.

Yes, the Lord had abandoned the world, but not for all time. The Lord had chosen according to His will and His justice to abandon the world to evil powers. Evil ruled the world by His permission. Chaos remained by His Divine permission. The old archbishop once quipped that the Lord's silence was due to the fact that He became so angry with Suthralane that He'd suffered an apoplectic seizure rendering Him speechless. Jacob thought this ridiculous. Now he saw that it contained a tiny grain of the truth.

The answer—Jacob drained his glass—*his* answer was brilliant in its simplicity: *silence proved the Lord's divine rule!* The Lord's silence and neglect were aspects of His rule. *He ruled by means of neglect. The world continued because He'd neglected it.* For those like Jacob—and how few there were, maybe only one—who saw with clear eyes, The High One's silence was a revelation. It was a pronouncement of justice upon sinful priests like Suthralane and the unbelieving archbishop.

As sometimes happened in the past during those moments of calm relaxation, Jacob sensed the presence of the Lord all around him, in the Winds, in the bugeaves, even in wickedness. Even in death. All those opposed to the Lord's Will were in fact *the Lord's Will*. He saw the answer as clearly as he saw the daystar drop into the lake. His own brilliance amazed him.

That evening he began scribbling theological notes. Such discoveries deserved better preservation than fragile remembered aphorisms. He moved a sleeping divan close to the fireplace and made the large atrium into his own archbishop's cell. His marble table became an altar, his act of writing a sacrament.

There was something about the high places that cleared the mind and made complex ideas marvelously simple. He had to give some credit to Marduk. Unfortunately, the *sramana's* mind had become too simple and stumbled off a precipice.

Although Jacob's scratching deteriorated as the night wore on, he was quite confident that someday, when men were once again holy, his writings would be studied assiduously by all true believers.

Jacob came to realize that his thoughts were the Lord's revelation, the voice of the All-powerful.

He could not say that he heard the holy words. Rather he felt them. He wrestled with them and they seized his very being until they soaked in and pervaded every cell of his body. The words came not from his brain, although they achieved form there. They were a roaring blaze consuming him. Compared to the priesthood's clumsy translations of the *Runehayana*, they were as the daystar in a room full of candles—the glory of Elsseleron compared to the squalor of Greenbottom.

Jacob became the mouth of the Lord Who'd finally broken His divine silence. Jacob was His voice, Jacob *Golden-tongued*.

Alas, Jacob found himself in a quandary. The *Runehayana* was still the One Lord's revelation. It was true and its truth was eternal. Logically then, his own revelation could not contradict the contents of the Books and still be *true*.

After a rather large and satisfying dinner (of especially well seasoned lake trout, washed down by gallons of Banalis wine from a special cask), an inspiration seized him.

The Lord's truth was absolute and eternal—yes—but it had been revealed only *partially* in the Runes. Now, here, at this moment in history, during the Third Kalpa, and with *him*, The One Alone had shown a way to *deeper theological thinking*. Yes, yes, not contradiction. Rather elucidation. *Deeper theological thinking* uncovered new and surprising depths in the Runes, and beyond the Runes. The Lord's truth was like an infinite well from which the believer could draw the ever-fresh water of renewal.

The depth of satisfaction, its intensity, made Jacob queasy. For the first time in many, many years he thought that he actually felt desire for a woman. A vision of Devorah passed before his eyes. He gasped. For the second time in his life his penis awoke (the first time had been when he was an adolescent and an older priest had rubbed up against him in the dormitory).

No! He quickly drained his wine glass and struggled to replace Devorah with the vision of himself as the new archbishop. Grudgingly she retreated into the shadows of the mansion. His penis, however, remained awake.

He resolved that after he'd finished this business with Marduk, he would compose a massive summation of his thought in multiple

Exalted Father

volumes. For the present he would bask in the sweet ecstasy of his breakthrough.

(Queeti poet-historians ask: What was Jacob's tremendous theological breakthrough?[11])

The Four Major Runes looked very much alike. Jacob had always found this quite perplexing. They were constructed from vertical, horizontal, and diagonal strokes. When they appeared on the surface of the Lordpool, they arose from a deep green darkness. They appeared in strings without break that expended all the way to the edges of the pool. At the edges, they simply faded away and recommenced on the opposite side. There was no discernable order to the Runes or to the Rune strings. Sometimes a Rune seemed to break into pieces as if limited by the size of the pool.

No one knew the origin of the strange method used to transliterate the Runes into Sandi. In the beginning of the First Kalpa, as the story went, ancient priests developed a habit of assigning fractions to each Rune. The fractions, later transcribed in decimal form, were from 0 to 1, but never greater than 1.

In any revealed passage, which was the single appearance of a jumble of Runes at a specific time, priests assigned each Rune a fraction given the frequency of its appearance *in that particular passage*. The higher the frequency the greater the fraction. But since the Runes often broke off at the edges, and it was often difficult deciding on the identity of the specific Rune, this fraction was usually assigned arbitrarily, at the whim of the priest (the ancient priests referred to this operation as *collapsing the Rune*).

Priests transliterated the highest fractions in any given passage (which changed from revelation to revelation) into Sandi vowels (of

---

[11] Obviously an interpolation, this section was most likely a marginal note that later scribes inserted erroneously into the text.

which there were 5 short vowels, 3 medium, 6 long, and 3 half). They assigned the very highest fractions to the vowels that were used most frequently *in Sandi*. The next highest fractions were assigned frequently used consonants (there are 23 total consonants in Sandi.) Fractions from 0 to .5 were generally the least used consonants, with 0 as a break in the words, giving any Rune a *no-value* in any specific passage. The specific value of the fraction varied according to the decision of the priest doing the transliteration and translation.

Usually the first run resulted in nonsense. Priests would then fiddle with the fractions until they came out right and the Sandi passage became comprehensible. Successive generations of priests built upon earlier work. But since it was possible to engage in endless recalculations—there appeared to be no end to denumerable fractions—endless versions of the Books were also possible.

The terrible flaw, as Jacob perceived it, lurked in the fractions assigned to a given Rune. Despite all the pious hymns sung to divine guidance, the whole process appeared arbitrary and artificial. It began with the predilection of the individual priest—not the Lord's words, but how the priest transliterated and translated the Lord's words. Not what the Lord meant, but what priests decided the Lord meant.

When all was said and done, the priest-scholars relied upon nothing more than their own minds. Jacob knew the sins of men, the corruption and confusion of men's minds, and the impiety of the priesthood.

[Of course, Jacob's understanding of the collapsing method was weak. In his eyes, this was a good thing.[12]]

---

[12] Many scholars agree that the scribe, possibly a queeti poet-historian inserted an editorial comment that does not appear in the original manuscripts, upon which this version is founded.

Exalted Father

By the Third Kalpa the transliteration of Runes into Sandi letters, as well as the translations of the Books, had become authoritative through convention and tradition. Over time, and through continual use, tradition more or less cemented translation.

Jacob understood the inequity of men and the frailty of human reason.

There were always renegades like Marduk who claimed that they had discovered some previously unknown law within the Runes themselves before they were transliterated. Jacob had heard that the Nepptali claimed something similar.

Jacob understood Marduk's arrogance and especially his impiety. The Nepptali were cursed of the Lord.

Jacob saw the *truth*.

From the desolate mount of Machpelah Jacob saw the truth clearly. *As if human choice had a say in the composition of the Word of the Lord. As if the human being spoke for the Lord.*

Jacob knew that there had to be a hidden variable.

The hidden variable was Jacob himself.

Deeper theological thinking filled in the gaps. The hopeless confusion of the Runes pointed directly to the pristine clarity of Jacob's own theology. He was the New Revelation.

His reasoning went like this.

He had always been a poor student of the Runes. And why? Because the *Runehayana* was a mere glimmer of the Lord cast into the darkness of primitive men. It belonged to the childhood of the race. It was written for children. *He* was not a child.

The light of *Jacob's truth* swallowed the *Runehayana's* dim glow just as the daystar blotted out the frail light of the night stars. By allowing his mind to remain uncorrupted—which explained his dismal attempts to become a scholar—the Lord had prepared him for greater truth. In fact, priests mired in the old revelations were actually in rebellion against the Lord.

THE BOOKS OF MARDUK

The so-called brilliance of scholars was rebellion against the Lord— another aphorism (*proverb—the word is uncertain*) for which he'd be famous, he was sure.

Intelligence brewed pride. Men's words, not the Lord's. Men's minds, not All-powerful omniscience. Intelligence was never humble. They laughed at *him*. They mocked *him*. Because he *knew*.

Jacob knew that Marduk visited the Tribes, spreading his unholy plague. Are not false teachers worse than thieves and murderers? Did they not deserve death?

Jacob unsheathed his beautifully crafted Yadish knife. Its polished blade shone gloriously in the firelight—another piece of evidence, a gift given to him by the Grand Duke himself— he who had spoken face to face with the Lord. Was it a gift for services rendered? Or, was it a prophecy? A gift that would reveal its purpose when the time was ripe.

The Lord spoke to the Grand Duke. And this day the Lord had chosen Jacob to be His voice. Wickedness destroyed, the truth made known, and once again the women of Greenbottom would bear fruit. He, Jacob, was the fulcrum.

He felt hot.

Toward evening of the next day, a little before the start of Lesser Wind, Jacob spied a lone figure climbing the Machpelah Road.

BOOK OF PLAGUES
VERSE 3.1.3

Marduk had become quite portly since Jacob saw him last. His old priestly travel cloak was stretched tight over his belly. Head down and wheezing like an old hog, he trudged up the road.

The Lord has delivered into my hands—Jacob offered up a silent prayer of thanks, briefly bowing his head to the south, in the direction of Holy Elsseleron.

Lesser Wind started to blow. Already the Winds brought the cold winter air of the north. For the first time in Jacob's memory, however, the Winds also bore scents of the great northern forests, the heavy, pungent odors of fresh pine, oak, and maple. The world, it seemed, was changing.

Jacob cared nothing for the world. Marduk, on the other hand, loved nature. It was one of his many weaknesses. He loved the world but not the author of the world. He'd corrupted the Books. He'd composed his own poetry and claimed it was from the Lord. For such sins—and others too heinous to even contemplate—*he had to die.*

Jacob took the Yadish knife and hid it in his black robes. He rose, scrambled down the portico stairs, and ran down the road to give the blasphemer a proper greeting.

Lesser Wind swept the Machpelah acropolis. The verdant odors of the far north were like perfume administered to a corpse. In the west, just at the farthest reach of human vision, Red Lake burned like a wild fire on the steppe. The fall sky went from violet to purple to dark blue. Not a single cloud marred its perfection. Not a single bugeave danced in the upper currents.

As he lumbered down the path, Jacob called out to the ascetic: "So, Marduk, by the looks of things the world of the flesh quite agrees with you. The begging season must have been highly productive, especially among the Akkadeans."

Marduk raised his head. His green eyes were enfolded by puffy red cheeks. It was a miracle he could see at all. His mouth hung open. He gasped for air and his heavy jowls quivered with effort. He leaned heavily on his walking stick.

"Jacob, brother," he cried, struggling to breathe as he fought the irresistible pull of gravity on his dense flesh. "So, you've given up your studies? Become a *sramana*? A wanderer's life is quite uncertain, you know."

"It appears to agree with you, my brother. And, oh my brother, I've learned why you come to Machpelah each winter, and it's certainly not for the women. No, no, my brilliant friend. What a collection of well-stocked wine cellars. The place is wealthy—in its wealth. Why did the Akkadeans abandon it? Why would anyone abandon such riches and leave this high place in—abandonment?"

"Too much weight, brother?"

"Ah, jesting Marduk. How is there freedom from plenty in a world of want?

"Don't know." Marduk studied him as they proceeded to the mansion.

Jacob laughed. "Marduk, you are quite a character. Here you're not free to starve. That's true. Come, we'll discuss your ravings indoors. A little wine, some food in your gut—maybe a gallon of wine—and perhaps you'll start making sense. But seriously now, I've always admired you, you know, and respected your mind—what a free mind it is."

Marduk acted as though he hadn't heard. He stopped and gazed north. "They're coming," he said softly, "lovely *kittim* to paint the world. They must have an offering, *you* understand. "He glanced back at Jacob and winked. "*You understand—*"

Exalted Father

Jacob smiled. "They shall, my beloved brother and fellow *sramana*. For now do not trouble yourself with sacrifice. The Lord will provide."

BOOK OF PLAGUES
VERSE 3.1.4

Jacob burned finely crafted cedar and oak furniture in the great fireplace. He set a hug feast on the marble table: salted fish, cheese, olives, figs and other dried fruits—and deep pitchers of wine. Marduk nibbled a few olives and cheese but touched neither fish nor wine.

Jacob used his fancy Yadish knife to cut the fish into strips. He set it down close at hand. "The Lord has provided," he said.

Marduk looked at him, nodded, but made no reply.

"So, Marduk, who has wandered the length and breadth of Greenbottom like you? What interesting things you must have discovered in your travels?"

Marduk looked away and stared into the fire.

Jacob tried to wait patiently. Patience not being one of his strengths, the idea suddenly came to him that he ought to slit Marduk's throat before the false ascetic could utter one more blasphemous word. Jacob ignored the idea, he was curious. That stupid Akkadean slut Devorah had given voice to strange ideas, ideas that seemed to Jacob like empty shadows of fleeing thoughts. Anti-ideas, Jacob thought them. No woman possessed the slightest ability to think theologically. Better burn the *Runehayana* than teach it to a woman. They must have come from Marduk, no doubt, and no doubt in exchange for something hardly abstract.

"What hear you of the Ra'bim? Of the Akkadeans?"

A shadow passed over Marduk's face. His eyes became glassy as if he'd consumed a barrel of wine.

"It is said that the Akkadeans are an especially handsome people," Jacob continued. "The Ra'bim are a race of cadaverous grubs, it is also said. I've heard that Akkadean females are still fertile, perhaps the only flowers yet blooming among the Tribes of Men, as it is said."

Marduk shifted his considerable bulk. "They are beautiful," he agreed. "They're perfect of limb, strong, graceful. Their eyes are the blue of bright heaven, the dark of heaven's vault, the green of fresh fields. Their voices are the music of the spheres, their lips red figs through which flash pearly teeth, their breasts like pomegranates. I sing of them with great praise."

Jacob grasped hold of the blade. Marduk failed to notice.

"Especially of *her*—"

"Devorah?"

Marduk turned his head, exposing his neck, begging for the stroke, it seemed. Jacob's body tensed—a serpent rising out of the high grass of the steppe. His fingers squeezed the ornate Yadish handle—

Marduk's eyes changed. They flashed brilliant green.

"Devorah...more beautiful than the dawn, more mysterious than the dusk when shadows merge and sharp lines are smoothed and all fountains sing as one—when mist rises from the fields and fog descends from the mountain. I sing of her with great praise."

"And after all this singing, what nonsense did you teach her?" Jacob croaked—a river frog from the Ra'bim canals.

"Can't recall exactly..." Marduk sounded embarrassed. "*That one* may have spoken of Suthralane. Or of the heavens, the Kingdoms of the Heavens, from which the Lord came. *This one* doesn't remember, brother, what *that one* said—"

"Tis sinful to speak of Suthralane the arch-heretic. He dared Elsseleron, sacred to the Lord, forbidden to men," Jacob lectured. "Be he cursed and forgotten."

Marduk sounded happy, like a child giddily describing a new toy. "Yes, yes...priests, I agree, are sinful louts. Forbid us something and we want it with a greater passion than ever. It's our special calling, it's why we're priests—and *sramanas*. Cursed be Suthralane for divulging our secrets."

The solid feel of the knife in his hand may have prevented Jacob from slipping into a fit of apoplexy. "We are a sinful lot—" was all he could manage.

Marduk drew his knees up to his chest and stared into the fire. He'd thrown off his cloak.

Blurry eyed, his head throbbing, Jacob suddenly noticed that the *sramana* no longer appeared fat and well-fed, but emaciated and starving. His ribs could be easily counted and the vertebra of his backbone seemed about to pop out of his dark skin. The bugeave tattoo covering his shoulder and neck glowed as if smoldering.

"*That one* was in Tholos, the capital of the Ra'bim," Marduk said as though recounting a dream. "She'd just been married to old Vishnu. Vishnu isn't up for it. Now there's a *sramana* who'll never break his vows—" Marduk chuckled for a moment and then his voice became barely audible, "*that one* saw her and felt the fire of the world burning inside, perhaps for the first time. *That one's* vows were like *kittim* in the Winds, *that one's* mind shattered like glass beneath a sledge hammer. *Do you understand? Do you feel it?*"

The knife slid from Jacob's fingers. Breathing became painful and his heart beat dangerously fast, pounding like a hammer, like his aching head, about to explode.

Marduk sighed. "But *that one* had his vows— Since then, *that one* has become fanatic about vows—"

Marduk turned his head. Tears moistened hollow cheeks, flowing from sunken eyes, yet glowing bright green.

"*That one* slunk out of Tholos, a shadow sulking through the darkened streets, a leaf floating on the Grand Canal, a dark cloud racing to catch the daystar. *She* tried to follow. *That one* spurned her, *that one* is *one-who-has-fled*. And Greater Wind brought *kittim* by the thousands. *That one* welcomed them as one welcomes death. And they covered *this one*, brother, head to toe. Yet *this one* did not die. Why?"

"You imagined it all, a grand delusion—"

"We'll make a test," Marduk cried. "Tomorrow at dawn. *This one* will stand outside in Greater Wind. Naked— Naked and helpless this one came into the world. Tomorrow, naked and helpless *this one* will leave it."

Jacob got up and groped his way to the old divan he'd dragged into the atrium. He sheathed the Yadish knife. The Lord had spoken. Marduk was the sacrifice. The Lord did indeed provide.

The Books Of Marduk

BOOK OF PLAGUES
VERSE 3.1.5

In the middle of the night Marduk suddenly began speaking:

"Many years ago before I took to wandering, I recalculated a number of passages from the *Book of Bhavana*. These were the passages that contained the legends of Suthralane."

"The arch-blasphemer himself." Jacob yawned and stretched out on the divan. He'd been asleep rolled up like a scroll, as he liked to say. "Why must you be so annoying?"

Marduk ignored him. "Priest Suthra was the only human being to see the Lord face to face. He dared to climb Elsseleron. And God maimed him for his daring. The Lord cut his left hamstring. It never healed properly. He limped to the end of his days. Suthra the Lame, so he is named."

"What of it?" Jacob scowled. The imbecile's prattle irritated him beyond endurance. Perhaps now was the time for the sacrifice after all. "Everyone knows this. Who needs a new translation—"

Marduk went on, happily oblivious to Jacob's desperate need for rest. How little empathy he possessed, not at all like Jacob himself—Jacob thought.

"Suthralane saw the Lord face to face. He would pose his paradox of the Kingdoms of the Heavens to the Lord, but the Lord preempted him. And the Lord put him to the test:

> 'What think you of my world, man of my making?
> See how the seasons turn according to the Sky Wheel?
> See how the Two Winds blow?
> The bird flies and the fish swims?
> Feel, you, the daystar's warmth,
> And the cool mystery of the Two Moons?

Is it not good?'

Now Suthralane was as clever as he was audacious. 'What you have said is true, Mighty One. Let no one blame the Lord. He is powerful and He is humble, the most humble creature in the universe.'

'Well said,' said the Lord.

'Indeed so, Divine One. But what of, say, the farvel? Golden furred beast, silent, wise, always watching? Why have you set your face against the farvel? Why have you commanded your people to destroy every last one?'

'It is a wicked creature. It does not worship the Lord of Lords,' the One Alone complained. *'Nor do I recall its making.'*

'Well then, it deserves to suffer,' Suthralane agreed.

'It does. As do many who reject the Lord of Lords,' said the One Alone.

Suthralane put on his most doubtful expression. 'Ah, if *I do not suffer then I am righteous*? If others suffer then they are wretched?'

'Well said, frail man,' the Lord agreed.

'If I should feel compassion for those that suffer, those that are slaughtered in the Lord of Lord's name, those that hunger and are diseased, then am I too a wicked one?'

'Well said, man of limited understanding,' The Nameless One agreed.

'And if I am righteous beyond dispute and yet I suddenly become ill? Or my dear child suddenly dies? Or, if someone strikes me? Wounds me so that the wound never heals? Or, if I, righteous though I am, should destroy another—indeed, an entire species from the oldest farvel to the smallest farvel cub—as you command? And if I murder the innocent along with the guilty?

'What then? Is it all a test? To test me that I will still praise the Lord of Lords? To see if I will abandon belief? Is it instruction?'

'It is,' the Lord agreed. 'And more. For such is the mystery of the Lord.'

Suthralane gave the Lord a hard look, yet the One-on-High did not seem to notice.

Suthralane said: 'When I eat, others starve. Is this not so? I offer praise to the Lord for my food—do I not also praise the Lord for allowing others to starve? When I am healthy—praise be the Lord! Am I not at the same time praising the Lord for another's disease? Praise be, he is sick and not I! A child dies, but not mine. Praise be the Lord my child lives! So, whenever I praise the Lord for my good fortune do I not also praise the Lord for the suffering of others? And if suffering is the divine gift for sin, does not all praise of the Lord also condemn?'

'Well said,' said the One.

And then Suthralane spoke in the voice of millions: 'Why, oh Lord? Surely not so many. The innocent, the young, those whose eyes have not yet opened. The trees, the grasses, the flower people—do they not all groan and cry, and yet You do not hear? What am I to learn from such horror, such widespread, senseless suffering? What am I to learn that I cannot learn in some less gruesome way?'

And then Suthralane spoke for himself: 'To offer praise for such things, even to one so powerful as the Lord of Lords, is to worship a lunatic, a moral monster blinded, self-obsessed, infantile— Is this not true my humble Lord?'

Then did the Lord rise in fury, severed his hamstring and cast him down from the Holy Mountain.

As he fell, the Lord called after him: 'Where were you, puny man, when I sheared the peak from this mountain as easily as cutting cake? Who was there to witness the fire of my coming down from heaven? Foolish man! The eyeballs in your head would have popped like kernels of corn thrown into a simple wood fire. How dare you question the purposes of the Lord your Lord!'"

EXALTED FATHER

Marduk paused and stared into the dying fire, as if daring the Lord to cook his own green eyes.

"Was Suthralane right? Was the Lord of the *Runehayana* insane from the beginning?"

Jacob dozed, on the edge of sleep. He'd only caught snippets of the tale.

"Tell me, Jacob, is the Holy One crazy?" Marduk's voice took on a tone of urgency.

"Heretics are like children whose minds have yet to mature," Jacob replied groggily. He repeated the familiar liturgy. "Evil powers rule the world. They are opposed to the Lord. They and they alone are the source of every ill. Yet, without them we would have no free choice in the matter—free choice to obey or disobey, to love or not love. The choice between good and good is not a choice. Thus the Lord allows evil. Evil makes choice meaningful. Otherwise we would be like the bugeaves, blown about by the Winds without wills of their own. We could not know holiness, blessedness, and our death would be our end, complete and final... Now please shut up. I'm exhausted."

Jacob turned his back and fell into a deep, satisfying sleep. If he dreamed a dream, he did not recall the slightest detail.

Marduk watched the fire burn down and felt the chill creep into the deserted mansion. He huddled in his old priestly traveling robes. These days, it seemed, the garment had magically grown in size.

He feared sleep. His dreams were quite often nightmares, nightmares of Yakashas armed with fangs and claws, and razor-bladed knives that cut human flesh like warm butter. Then, although rarely, he would dream of bright spring in the trees, soaring forests of pine, oak, elm, maple, holly, and whittling—of beautiful farvels tending vast gardens and dark green ponds beneath a brilliant daystar, cooled by gentle breezes that carried the scents of a thousand spices. And of a woman, light-brown and sinewy, dancing on the soft green carpet.

The Books Of Marduk

BOOK OF PLAGUES
VERSE 3.1.6

Hidden in the tall grasses of the steppe, they watched the flickering light on Stonehill. They smelled the wood fire. They debated whether Stonehill had been resettled.

It had been a century in Redfolk years. The oldest among them, the elders, recalled the sack.

In earlier times the Tailless wielded the thunderbolt. Great swaths of burning decimated the Redfolk ranks. The trees, the bushes, the wildflowers, even the grasses suffered the burning. How little the Tailless cared for life. And then, at Stonehill, the thunderbolts fizzled and went out.

Redfolk died in droves. Redfolk courage did not falter. The White Lord of the Straits, he of mighty Zell, ordered it. They served him selflessly.

The thunderbolts failed and Stonehill fell. The males and male children they killed. How they relished the screams, the cries, the whimpering and pleading. The little ones especially, those who could not comprehend it, how utterly guileless were the innocent. The females they took.

As always, coupling failed. The Tailless were too big and heavy. The Redfolk too small—if only their members were the size of their tails. The females fought like the vicious farvels. *Redimps* (the name by which they are known to the White Lord) are fragile, ephemeral beings. They broke like dried twigs. They were crushed like new grass. Captured Tailless porcine females died in a few months. It was said that Redfolk food was poison to them.

They sniffed the wood fire and chattered excitedly. Now it was different. The Tailless monsters no longer wielded the thunderbolt of heaven. Their ranks were thinning. Their males were impotent. The Great Lord cursed them. Their bodies were dry. Their sacks undescended and fruitless.

Scouts returned to the main body of the army. It would be light soon. The foul northern Long Wind would come bearing the poison blowflies. The touch of a blowfly meant instant death.

"Retreat to caves—" barked Captain Menes. Next to the late Captain Mose, he was the largest Redfolk from the steppe. Besides, Menes was the only officer who'd spoken to the White Lord face to face. He was the nearest thing to King of the Redfolk. His orders went unchallenged.

There were female queeti in the caves. They'd been taken in the south. They were far worse than the Tailless. Larger, more primitive, they fought like wild animals. They killed the Redfolk. Many avoided capture by committing suicide.

The White Lord desired Tailless females, not queeti. Who among the Redfolk, even Menes, could fathom His wishes? The White Lord's kind was indeed fearsome. With their heads they brushed the heavens. They broke stone and crushed grass.

There were lights again on Stonehill. The Tailless had returned. *Their males were impotent but their females were fertile.*

They waited in the damp caves. They wailed, chattered, barked and growled, and they killed the last of the queeti females. The Lord of the Mountain, greater than the White Lord of Zell, beyond *great*, remote, isolated, unapproachable— Why should He create such a creature as a queeti?

Why grant them, male and female, such fertility? Queeti numbers were beginning to fill the Starmirror. Soon they'd spill into Jambridvipa.

If only Redfolk members were the size of Redfolk tails.

THE BOOKS OF MARDUK

THE BOOK OF PLAGUES

CHAPTER TWO - Edom

VERSE 3.2.1

Never in the past had they dared march this far north. White Father of Zell forbade it. Never in the past had there suc a Hetman as Green-eyes. Only this summer had Blue Mother chosen the powerful young bull. As Hetman of the Reed Sea Clan, his first act was to declare war on the hairless red monkeys of Edom, those odious desert wisps.

The Reed Sea Clan was vassal to White Father Rekhmire, Overseer of the Straits, Lord of Zell. No more than six dreary villages of thatched huts, mud bungalows, and dark caves belonged to Rekhmire's fief. The Reed Sea Clan struggled each year to meet their feudal dues. White Father Overseer for his part refused to protect them from desert wisp raids. It was almost as if White Father Rekhmire permitted the raids as a form of punishment. As if the red monkeys actually *served* White Father.

This past summer's raid had been especially destructive. The old Hetman Bristle-back had died trying to fend off a wisp horde. Many females had been taken, many pups slaughtered. Among the captured females was Pink-coral, Green-eyes' mate.

Green-eyes was the youngest Hetman ever. There were two major reasons for this.

Exalted Father

Pink-coral's first cub had been born with six fingers on each paw. The Clan believed his birth-mark auspicious, a sign of Heaven's favor. Secondly, Green-eyes had killed three red monkeys during the raid. One monkey's neck he snapped like a dried twig. The other he struck squarely in its hollow chest with a well-aimed blow of his root-hammer. This one had been a wisp chief. It bore a bronze sword and wore some sort of shiny vest. Green-eyes relieved him of his weapon, observing that the chief, as far as Green-eyes could tell, would not have further need of it.

The Blue thought Green-eyes quite clever. His language skills were well developed for a queeti. He was from a new generation, a generation that seemed to master the mysteries of articulated words, like a Grey, no longer dependent upon gestures, snarls, grunts, and growls.

Green-eyes proved that there was more to him than mere wit. The blade may have passed as a sword among the wisps, but it looked like a toy in the paws of a full-grown bull such as Green-eyes. He proceeded to break off the wooden handle so that only the bronze remained. Then he took a fishing harpoon, which was no more than a blackwood pole, split its end, and inserted the blade. He bound it up with strips from a tough reed plant that grew in the delta. He melted the Supreme White Father's copper coin (destroying the engraved visage of the Supreme White Father in the process) and poured the molten metal over the binding.

"You a sacrilege have committed," growled old Moss, the most pious of the Clan, believed by some the likely successor to Bristle-bark. He barred his fangs.

Green-eyes did not back down. "I see not a sacred in copper discs," he snarled.

"They are signs"—Moss waved his arms to indicate the word *signs*— "of Father's protection."

Green-eyes shook his gleaming harpoon. "Slavery signs! We are slaves to fear. Now lost is my beautiful Pink-coral. Think on it, you. Think you what'll I do to the filthy monkeys with this—"

He made a sweeping motion with the harpoon. The blade whistled and cut through the smoke of the village fire. Many bulls, and not a few females, even some cubs imagined the heads of red monkeys flying from their shoulders.

Moss should have awarded him a hard cuff as one might a disrespectful cub. But the sight of the bladed harpoon in Green-eyes' paws caused him to think better of it.

So the Blue elected Green-eyes Hetman. That night he dreamed. A strange being all in white came to him while he slept on the ground. The being was female, tailless like a queeti but lacking fur. She was very tall. She reached down and grabbed his head with both hands. He experienced a dreadful pressure and it seemed that his head would burst like a ripe fruit. He saw a mountain, its flanks glistening in the sun. Creatures descended from the mountain's sawed-off summit. A multitude, thousands upon thousands. He felt an immense loathing. They were like a horde of carrion-eating maggots, like river muck sliding down the sheer slopes, like an infestation of biting gnats that sometimes invaded a queeti's pelt, leaving large patches of exposed skin.

He tried to twist out of her grasp. Barring his fangs, he sought to rip out her throat. She spoke words, words he'd never heard and only vaguely, if at all, understood. Then she disappeared and he heard himself howling—whether in his dream or waking life he could not tell.

The next day he called out the bulls from all the villages. They would invade the desert in force. They'd put an end to the red monkeys' raids forever. Exalted Father, King of the Mountain, had spoken to him in his dream, he said. He, Green-eyes, was Exalted Father's judge and scourge in this world.

EXALTED FATHER

He failed to mention the strange female. Nor did he say anything about the disgusting plague that oozed down from the mountain. He knew, however, that he'd dreamed the mountain of the Exalted Father. Which was enough.

Fall came to the world by the time they were ready to march. The Overseer of the Straits knew nothing of their intentions. He'd abandoned his fortress-city of Zell on the Windward Straits for the winter season and journeyed south to Tharas Major. There he would spend the winter with other White Fathers, in the presence of the Supreme White Father. There he would be far from the cold rain and winds, and giant butterflies.

They crossed the Windward Straits during the dry season, at the beginning of fall. The Winds of Morning and Evening came down upon them. Butterflies fell in colorful showers. Some alighted on the Reed Sea People's thick fur. The Reed Sea People smiled and gently brushed them off. They could not understand why White Fathers were so terrified of such beautiful, fragile creatures. They understood very little about the White Fathers, even Lord Rekhmire.

A hundred adult bulls armed with root-hammers of various sizes, led by Green-eyes of the Shining Spear, crossed the Windward Straits and advanced into Edom Desert. They trusted Green-eyes' leadership. Only Moss had reservations. They trusted because no one dared question a Hetman, especially one Exalted Father, Father of the Mountain, had called.

Exalted Father made a path through the Sea of Reeds for his people.[13]

Green-eyes trusted his nose. Desert wisps left a most foul scent. Their odor rode the Great Winds. A pup could follow it.

The second day into Edom, they came upon a large outcropping of black obsidian that looked as if it had fallen from the heavens

---

[13] Modern scholars understand this phrase as some sort of ritual saying, and probably scribal interpolation.

rather than having risen from the ground. Here, once-sharp peaks had been weathered down to blunt stubs by Kalpas of sandy winds. Black surfaces were polished like mirrors, for numberless Kalpas.

A small carpet of faded green and brown desert grass surrounded the miniature mountain. Nearby, a few stunted palms and junipers grew around an alga covered pool.

They were overjoyed. Unerringly the Hetman had found the red wisp stronghold.

Hetman Green-eyes set them in battle formation. Thirty bulls he sent north, around the stronghold, in order to block escape attempts. The remaining force circled west. Green-eyes planned to flush the wisps out of their lair and drive them east into the Reed Sea. The Reed Sea people would slaughter them on the beaches like an avenging tide. Hopefully Short Wind would bring a shower of butterflies.

At the first whisper of Short Wind, over fifty bulls launched themselves upon the black mountain, screaming and roaring, barking and growling, a maddened swarm of desert devils. They invaded every crack and crevice, every opening, forcing their huge bodies through narrow spaces meant for wisps. Not a few left tufts of brown fur on black rock.

They found the caves deserted except for several dead wisps whose frail red bodies had turned bluish-black. Limbs were snapped and broken, heads smashed like grapes.

The Reed Sea People howled and screeched as if in terrible pain. Not because of dead wisps. They discovered many of the Clan's kidnapped females. Wisps had killed them all. Pink-coral was not among them.

They fell into mindless frenzy and tore the wisp bodies to pieces. They smashed the remains with heavy root-hammers. They beat and beat until the wisps became pulp, and they continued until the pulp became mist, and finally separated into the primary elements of matter.

After Green-eyes restored order, they salvaged wisp swords and set to work. Many bulls bore fishing harpoons into battle. Shortly, many bore shining spears.

That night they lighted a victory fire, and while they mourned the females they also celebrated their victory over the red demons of the Edom Desert. Such a thing was unprecedented. Such a thing seemed impossible. Incomprehensible. As if natural law was overturned. As if clods of mud, grains of beach sand, had suddenly shot up and become stars of heaven.

Green-eyes dimly wondered who or what had killed the wisps.

Old Grey, the crazy shaman, opened his sacred bag. He drew forth the long-stemmed pipe and filled it with Red Onion herb taken from the fire trees in the south. He lit it with a faggot from the victory fire, inhaled deeply, and passed it to the Hetman. The Hetman filled his lungs and passed the pipe around to the others.

Soon they entered into that place when the outward senses shut down and thoughts ceased their usual flow, like a river that stops and abruptly reverses course. As mouths are drawn to fire, their minds swirled down and were consumed in that eternal fire that heats the world, and beyond the world, the fire that burns in the athanor, the dark sweat of Exalted Father, residue of creation. They came to that place and time when the world was new and their species was young and did not know the ways of the White Fathers, before the coming of the White Fathers — at the coming of the Exalted Father to His Mountain. They dropped into the very core of the planet, into the heart of existence itself. The planet whispered to them in a tongue only Shaman Grey could understand.

As their heads lolled and their eyes stared beyond sight, into eternity, Shaman Grey spoke to them in the queeti tongue, translating incomprehensible words.

"Count not time in this place," he purred like a mosscat. "We journey. We are free. Here will we hear once again the Legend of the Lame Wanderer."

Exalted Father

BOOK OF PLAGUES
VERSE 3.2.2

Darkness descended as the victory fire began to die. They were not conscious or unconscious, awake or asleep. They dreamed a dream more vivid than the obsidian mountain, more real than the oasis, more stimulating than the crisp air of fall. The night itself leaned close to catch Grey's soft words.

The words, the voice in which he spoke, like nothing they'd heard. Did they understand?

Grey said: "The rod of the White Fathers falls hard upon the backs of our people. The same is true for all other queeti, those who inhabit the lands of the Topartz, the Redrain, Tharas Major and Tharas Minor, even the southern jungle. Exalted Father sits upon His Holy Mountain in the east. He does not stir. Who is there to speak for the queeti?"

"None—" they mewed like newborn cubs.

"None," Grey acknowledged. "Yet have we not crossed over to another shore? Are we not free of the old world where the White Fathers rule and Exalted Father is like silent stone? But, ah, this place is young, my brothers. Its memories are young. These memories awaken others, and more, until like digging a well, we come to water, pure and clean and primordial. Behold, my brothers, these waters are your deepest mind. For the young are rooted in the old."

The pipe made its round once again. Above their shaggy heads the star-wheel continued its remorseless rotation. Time did not matter. It did not touch them. They'd come to a place beyond all turnings, a place they'd always carried within them but never knew, a once-sealed chamber where resided ancient memories, memories shared by all.

Grey unlocked the chamber.

Grey said: "There are beings in this new land across the straits, those who once dwelled with Exalted Father in the highest heavens. They are not wisps, nor of the White Fathers' kind. They are children of Exalted Father. They dwell where the lands become green and blue. A great river flows in that place, and there Exalted Father planted a garden. But He turned His face from them and cursed them. He cursed the land and every creature great and small. Who will explain it—?"

He whined like a cub.

"The wanderer was of that kind. He came among us when we were young. We were newly emerged from the southern jungles. Our heads still swayed back and forth, and we walked sometimes on two legs and sometimes on four. We came to the valleys and groves, to the hills and mountains, and finally to the sea. We became vassals of the White Fathers who inhabit Tharas Major and Tharas Minor. Thus did we surrender our freedom—"

A collective sigh arose from the gathering.

"*He* came to us, but none remember *His* coming—the coming of *He-With-Us*. None remember his gift. Were we not young? Too young, perhaps, to grasp the power of his words? Or have we forgotten? Listen, it is *His* language, the language of *He-With-Us*. Poor queeti, we do not speak *his* language, only here, in this place, which is no-place, which is nowhere, alas, poor queeti.

"His words come to us now, here in this no-place. Are they not as the waters of life? Do not other words enslave us? Words of the White Fathers? Words are different, but words are still words. They work magic upon the mind. They work magic upon the body. For when we discovered words we shed the beast and stood upright, and gazed upon the heavens. Words liberate and words enslave. Is it not strange, my brothers? Is it not a mystery? It is not a question of good and evil, for all things depend one upon the other. Without night there can be no day. Without sleep no awakening. Without words that bind, no freedom. So how is it we are bound?

Exalted Father

"Behold, my brothers, this is the great mystery, the darkness in the deepest part of the sea.

"When we were young, the wanderer, *He-With-Us*, came to us and revealed the mystery of words. *For he had seen Exalted Father face to face.*

"He was a child of Exalted Father, the most blessed of all creatures. Exalted Father was very generous, but He forbade His children one thing. No child may climb the Holy Mountain of Exalted Father. On that day the child will die. Neither White Fathers nor red wisps, neither angel nor devil, neither old nor young. On that day they will die.

"My brothers, the wanderer dared break Exalted Father's law. We know not why. And he discovered Exalted Father's secret, which is the mystery of words. *Which even Exalted Father knew not.* In our youth did the wanderer come among us. He taught us.

Brothers, what did *He* teach?"

THE BOOKS OF MARDUK

BOOK OF PLAGUES
VERSE 3.2.3

"The wanderer was an ugly creature. It wore black skins, like the coat of a short-hair desert dingo. It was larger than a wisp but just as thin, and it lacked a tail. Old and wrinkled, its skin was nut brown. A tangled black main of hair covered its large head and reached down to its shoulders. It was something between a wisp and a White Lord.

The wanderer bore a hardwood staff and limped favoring its left leg.

It came to a certain village in the fief of the Overseer of Sheep. It came from the northeast. Serfs working in the fields thought it a ghoul. They sought to kill the creature since ghouls steal babies. Something stopped them. Perhaps it was the creature's limp, perhaps something else.

The wanderer laughed and seated itself on a large rock. Then a miracle happened. Purple flowers sprouted at its base and a gush of water erupted and flowed outward. It soaked the parched ground. A queeti may still see a grove of purple-barked trees bearing lavender flowers on this spot.

The wanderer's voice was deep and resonant, a gong on Tharas Major. The very vibrations of its voice seemed to penetrate their bodies. Some would later claim that they felt the turning of the star-wheel in that voice.

The wanderer said: "Sages teach that life is suffering and so it stands condemned. The world, they say, does not satisfy our deepest needs. Something is always missing. In one's youth the missing piece is very small, yeah, nearly invisible, and always in the future. So was invented the form of speech that points to the future. In later years the missing grows to become as big as the Holy Mountain.

Exalted Father

"Some shrug and labor on. They seek the missing piece in the world: in things, in anxious activities, or even gazing into the mirror of a calm pond. Hither and thither they turn, frantically searching, compulsively grasping, in a mad rush to find that *something*.

"The sages say there is a better world, the Kingdoms of the Heavens from which Exalted Father came."

The poor serfs shook their shaggy heads for they understood nothing about this nowhere, which is no-place.

Therefore the wanderer spoke in a language taken from the life of the serfs.

"Poor serfs, poor clods of mud. The soil yields thorns and weeds, and all your labor is fruitless. Your flocks are thin, few are the lambs.

"Your Exalted Father is the great physician. From the Heavens He came. Out of pity, sympathy and love comes He to Needleglass. Heaven would He bring to your world, you poor clods of mud. Was not Heaven the missing piece? You, oh mud, must worship Him, serve the White Fathers who come with Him, and serve not the old world. Therefore the sages despise the world, mock it, and seek its destruction.

"Such was the teaching of old. But I say unto you—

"Behold, children, a wanderer came and tested Exalted Father on His Mountain. Behold, children of innocence, Exalted Father lies, the sages lie. They lie without guilt for they have convinced themselves that their falsehoods are true.

"This wanderer dared the mountain and put the question of suffering to Exalted Father. In His lies did He tell the truth. It is like this.

"A bull serf, young and strong, comes to a tiny village and calls for the shaman. 'I cannot see,' he says, yet he looks at the shaman with closed eyes. 'Do the blind see the color red?' asks the shaman. 'No,' replies the bull. 'Open your eyes. Look now as the daystar sets on the western horizon. What color?' 'Red,' says the blind bull opening his eyes. The bull pauses and then shakes his shaggy head. 'I was wrong,' said he, 'blind do see red.'

"So it is with the Exalted Father. 'You feel suffering,' said He to the wanderer. The wanderer replied: 'What does my feeling prove?' Exalted Father said: 'That the world stands condemned.' The wanderer laughed. 'Feeling proves nothing. Rather, *You are condemned.*'

"Exalted Father exploded in fury and smote the wanderer, and wrenched his left thigh bone from his hip socket. Behold, children, Exalted Father knows how to maim those who dispute Him.

"Why, then, your suffering, my children? Once you lived naked in the jungles, happy and unknowing. A woman came to you. She wore a white shining garment but her skin was dark, her hair black, her eyes darker yet. Black and mysterious, like the vault of Heaven. Do you remember? She shaped you from the jungle mud. Life did she breathe into your nostrils. Words did she breathe into your mouth. You arose and spoke, not the grunts and growls of beasts, but the words of Exalted Father. You were transformed. Are you not *queeti?*

"But she left you, when you were the most vulnerable.

"There are fisher folk, the Reed Sea People. They use nets to capture fish. Many fish escape, of course. The tightest woven nets cannot capture all. What queeti is foolish enough to think nets *are* fish? It is true that without nets you cannot catch fish, and without fish, nets are empty. It is also true that one does not eat nets. Such is the secret of words and the reason for your suffering. Think on it, my children. Why did she not tell you?

"Behold, the wanderer climbed Exalted Father's mountain. He learned Exalted Father's secret. *Exalted Father is the greatest of all empty nets.* He is so large that He is unable to trap a single fish. Every fish swims right through.

"I charge you therefore to swim through. Empty nets cause not the suffering of fish. Leaky nets do not condemn the water.

EXALTED FATHER

"Know then that you are free. You are not vassals. Nor are you lesser beings. Do not suffer needlessly. Your world lacks nothing. It is just as it should be. You are liberated when you see this truth. When you experience this truth. When you embrace this truth—"

THE BOOKS OF MARDUK

BOOK OF PLAGUES
VERSE 3.2.4

Grey stopped speaking. The others had fallen asleep. None had been able to follow his account of the wanderer. He doubted any had even listened, or if listened, would remember. Only he, Grey, and all the Greys past, and all to come, knew the legend. Grey was the oldest. His journeys went the deepest. His language the best. The generation of Green-eyes would change that, he knew.

He sank like a stone into the swirling eddies of time. Grey witnessed the fiery descent of Exalted Father as He came down to rest upon the mountain named Needleglass. He watched the truly marvelous rebirth of thousands, of tens of thousands, like the stars of the Heavens.

It took some time before he noticed that the lame wanderer was sitting next to him, staring into the embers of the campfire, near the red wisp fortress of black rock.

The lame wanderer glanced at Grey with sad eyes, brilliant green.

Grey frowned. "What is the secret of Exalted Father?"

The wanderer smiled a weak smile. "Do not force me to tell you what is best left a mystery."

Grey shook his silver mane. "Is this not my vision? You must show me if I demand it."

"Ah child, it is best not to know."

"You are my vision. You will show me."

"Look, then, into the fire and know the secret of Exalted Father, Lord of the Mountain."

Grey looked and recoiled at the horror.

EXALTED FATHER

BOOK OF PLAGUES
VERSE 3.2.5

In the morning they discovered that the Shaman Grey had died. His eyes were still open, staring into the cold ashes of the campfire. His wizened face appeared frozen in a mask of sheer terror. Greater Wind gently brushed his silver fur. Colorful butterflies danced above him but none alighted.

Green-eyes snatched a butterfly from the air. The fragile thing instantly dissolved in his paw. He licked his wet fur and sighed. How strange his dreams. How little he remembered. Vague forms, odd images, strange nonsense words—how he wished Grey were still alive to interpret it all. He whined loudly and long, his whine ending in a howl.

They buried Grey in the caves with the rest of the females. They howled for him, but not overmuch. There would be a new Shaman, another Grey.

"We go north," the Hetman declared. "There are females yet rescued to be. And justice visited upon the wicked wisps."

"What of Overseer Rekhmire?" Moss inquired.

The Hetman turned and shook Shining Spear. "This for the White Fathers," he growled, "if they dare—"

"Dare what?"

"Dare stand between a queeti and his mate."

"Queeti? Sounds stupid. Stupid word."

Hetman Green-eyes rose to his full height. "*He* gave us this title. Is dignified name. Thou shall not take the name in vain! Or I shall smite thee, slice thee to pieces. Thy flesh will be food for worms and maggots. The carrion birds shall pick thy bones."

Moss shrank back. Green-eyes spoke Grey's language. Yet he lacked the Shaman's dignity.

The rest of the war party gathered to wail for Grey. The Hetman turned on them as though he were about to massacre them all.

"Grieve not for Grey!" he roared. "He lives still. He is the land. Its bones are his bones. Its soil his flesh. His bones the bones of the Reed Sea People. And their Hetman. We claim this land. For we are *queeti*."

The others looked dumbfounded.

Moss recovered his courage and said: "Forget not that Moss shared Grey's dream. Such was not the wanderer's teaching. Teaching no one understand, the wanderer's. He was mad."

The Hetman's broad face became a terrible mask of anger, more frightful than any beast of the jungle. He lowered the metal spear tip and pointed it at Moss's chest.

This time Moss did not flinch. "Grey showed us a silly creature who limped. Foolish creature. A fool. It spoke of fishing, but of the sea nothing it knew."

"*Thou art the fool!*" Foam gathered at the edges of the Hetman's mouth. "We are *queeti*. We are the highest of all that walks, flies, and crawls. I am Hetman. I am highest of the high."

Moss moved with surprising quickness given his advanced age. He delivered a powerful blow to the side of the Green-eyes' head. Green-eyes eyes went blank and he crashed into the sand.

Moss threw himself upon the Hetman beating him with his fists. He grabbed for Shining Spear, as it had slipped out of the Hetman's numb fingers.

Blood flowed from his nose. Moss's onslaught had completely taken him by surprise. Green-eyes was still one of the largest bulls of the Reed Sea people and far younger than Moss.

Moss raised his clenched fist to deliver the killing blow. Green-eyes' arm shot up and seized the older bull by the wrist. Calling upon his considerable strength, he slowly bent the wrist back.

With a loud crack it snapped. Moss gave a high-pitched howl and tried to roll away.

Green-eyes bit off a finger. Moss shrieked and tried to hit him with his free paw. Green-eyes chewed off another finger.

Moss clubbed him on the top of his head. The Hetman yelped and released his hold. Both scrambled to their feet. Moss was not quick enough. Green-eyes snatched up Shining Spear.

Whimpering, Moss backed away.

Green-eyes leaped upon him. With all the might of his powerful shoulders and arms, he plunged the spear into Moss's chest and ran him through. Then he wrenched the blade free with a mighty pull. Blood and gore splattered his face, chest, and arms.

The Reed Sea People gave a collective wail. Never had a Hetman killed one of the Clan.

"I am Hetman!" screamed Green-eyes. "I am queeti. I am highest. I claim this land. We march now to destroy wisps and anything else that contests my rule."

"What of Moss?" muttered Ram who was a sturdy bull about the same age as Green-eyes.

"Let the desert consume his flesh. Let the sands drink his blood."

Thus did a thing occur that has never happened in the life of the Clans. And this thing-that-has-never-happened was soon followed by another never-happened. For on this very day, one of the newly-christened queeti, one named Log, discovered a real flesh and blood creature that was neither White Father nor red monkey, just as Grey had described.

The creature had been cast into a pit.

THE BOOKS OF MARDUK

BOOK OF PLAGUES
VERSE 3.2.6

They came to the fringe of the grassy steppe.

"The season of cold begins," observed young Ram, one of those who'd shared Grey's pipe. Yet the grasses are still tall, conceal our passage they. We go on four legs as in the days of our youth."

"No!" barked the Hetman. "We are queeti. We go on two legs, as do the White Lords."

"But wisps will discover us."

"Let them."

"What?"

"Let them see and despair. Let them know fear. The queeti come now. The future belongs to us."

"Perhaps it is better they know fear after we have surprised and slaughtered them," observed Ram.

"I am Hetman. There is no more discussion."

"Are you as great as the White Fathers?"

"The queeti are great. I am Hetman. I am great."

"But—"

"*No more discussion!*" The Hetman shook Shining Spear. "Would thou share the fate of Moss?"

Ram did not answer.

And so Green-eyes, the Hetman of the Reed Sea People, entered the steppe upright, striding on two legs. On the fringe of the steppe stunted by the desert, the yellow and brown grasses came to his waist.

Log lagged behind, as did a number of the others. When the Hetman was not looking, they dropped down and scampered on all fours.

Exalted Father

In the afternoon the Hetman spied another rocky outcropping, far larger than the obsidian fortress and its opposite in color and texture—a grayish jumble of ragged stone with sharp spires and jagged edges.

"Behold," bellowed the Hetman, "the stronghold of the steppe wisps."

Paying no mind to military tactics—such a thing being beneath the dignity of a queeti—the Hetman ordered an assault upon the mountain of shattered rock.

The queeti army sprinted towards the stronghold in a disorganized, bowlegged run. Screaming, growling, barking, screeching, swinging root-hammers and shaking spears (though some were not sure how spears were actually wielded in battle), they resembled a stampeding herd of cattle.

Except Log who hung back and rested on his haunches, hidden in the grass.

Living near the sea, the Reed Sea People should have understood how tricky the perception of distance could be. In a landscape like the steppe, and in the late afternoon, the mountain of gray rock appeared closer than it actually was. They ran and ran, struggling to stay on two legs, and yet it seemed to them that the rock kept one step ahead as if for every step they took the rock took another—

In a short time they were gasping for air.

The Hetman continued on, screaming at the top of his lungs about queeti dignity and majesty and so on. But his words soon splintered into inarticulate grunts and moans. The rest of the army simply halted, paws on knees, barrel chests heaving as if to explode.

At that moment the wisps struck. Crouching in the grasses, their red leathery skin blending with the soil, they sprang up on all sides of the queeti as though they came from the ground itself, from beneath the ground.

The slaughter was terrible. Green-eyes stabbed a wisp, but his spear lodged in its rib cage. Before he could wrench it free, an avalanche of red bodies fell upon him. Fangs and claws tore him to pieces.

The rest of the Reed Sea army was annihilated in the same manner. Only one escaped.

Log turned and fled blindly, remaining on all fours.

He didn't see the pit, which was no more than a narrow shaft dug in the hard ground and covered by brown grass and sticks. He crashed through the covering and fell in. The accident saved his life. Above, the wisp whirlwind blew past.

The fall dazed Log. On his knees in mud and water, it took him several minutes to realize what had happened. Suddenly he noticed that something else occupied the pit.

The strange creature was nearly hairless, except for a silver-black beard and long braided hair falling from what appeared to be an over-sized head. The creature was larger than a wisp and unlike a White Father it lacked a tail. It hugged a mud wall and silently regarded him. Then he saw that it wore a coat, not unlike those long coats of the White Fathers. This coat, however, shimmered with many colors. Like a farvel.

It took a step towards the center of the pit and glanced up. Log saw that it limped.

EXALTED FATHER

THE BOOK OF PLAGUES

CHAPTER THREE – Green House

VERSE 3.3.1

"Come Rudra, tell me," Miriam said. Her habitual mocking tone was oddly lacking. She'd gathered her hair into a pony-tail. The gown she wore this morning was ill-fitting, nonetheless it was clean and of fine golden silk, far nicer than her usual soiled brown smock. Beyond unusual, she'd bathed.

He was sitting in the library garden, in the shade of sickly looking elms and red burree trees, the latter named for their bulbous fruit, dark red in color and about the size of a person's head. A few had fallen and split open. Inside was a purple meat-like substance, slimy and oozing, which if eaten brought on stomach cramps, dizziness, and sometimes even paralysis. Yet the smell they emitted was like perfume.

He sat on a cushioned bench, his bandaged left leg resting on a low stool. He'd braided his hair in the style of the old Yadish Kings. An unbound book of papyrus pages lay open on his lap. The wind lifted a page and floated it towards the library, as if intending to return the book page by page.

Rudra had been snoozing. He dreamed a vivid dream but was unable to recall any of it, not even an image.

"Do you really believe that the Lord of Lords called *you*?" Miriam asked.

He looked at her. Had it been in another life when he loved her? In that other life, as if in another world, there had lived two people quite different from the two in this garden. For a time they loved each other, and when they loved one another their world made sense. Those two people slowly died, although they remained unaware of the event. Their love died with them, and their world became dull.

Somewhere from a nearly forgotten archive of memory he called up a forgotten shadow. Vaguely, possessing only the slightest resemblance to the living person, the shadow settled in Miriam. It gazed out at him through the windows of her eyes. Once in another life he'd loved that person. For the briefest of moments that one stood before him, and then, as when a cloud passes over the daystar, the shadow vanished.

Rudra sighed and pulled at his beard. He wanted to scratch his left leg, but he feared he'd re-open the wound. He found himself unable to extract a proverb from the memory.

"I've tried to make myself believe. I really want to believe. Today, it no longer seems very important—"

"Oh Rudra, so dramatic." She laughed yet there was no malice in it.

He sat for a time in silence. "It was foolish, Miriam. There is nothing to conquer. The Tribes of men have passed away. I never was Exalted Father, nor will I be King—"

"So dramatic."

He laughed and his laugh was not bitter.

She joined him for spell. Then she became serious. "Perhaps it was not a delusion. Something is happening in the world. Women sense the subtle signals, especially when they have to do with birth."

"After all these years you still hate me because of *him*. What can I say? You've heard all the reasons and excuses countless times before."

"Indeed I have. I do not hate you, my Grand Duke. Today your effect on me is far too weak. Hate requires much more."

"He still lives, our son."

"I know."

"He is not aware of his origins, of course."

"Say no more, Rudra. You make me wish I was wrong about effects. I have not the will to hate."

"Love, then?"

"Be serious!"

"Forgive me. There was something just now, a gesture, a word, a tone, that reminded me of someone for whom I cared a great deal a long time ago."

A tear glistened on her blotchy cheek. "Damn you, Rudra—"

"Sorry."

"Damn you."

"You were saying? Your feeling? A sense known only to women?"

She forced a grin. He noticed that her teeth appeared a little brighter, no longer dull black but light brown. It must have taken her hours to clean them.

"Not only women. You have it. But in you it assumes a different form and wears a different garb. You see power and authority, order, meaning, purpose, goals. You see the Lord. For me it is less distinct, more like...the Winds, the *kittim*, sounds in the high grasses, movement in the trees. The world is pregnant. Something has conceived. Something will be born."

He looked down at his book. "This is Yadish poet-history," he said. "It tells of the *Runehayana*, how the priests lied about the words of the Lord. It tells of Suthralane—"

She emitted a cackle. "I frighten you, don't I? Women are a threat to you Rudra. Perhaps you are thinking of becoming a priest."

"Perhaps," he agreed. "If not King, why not archbishop? Or something greater."

"Like Exalted Father?"

He grinned behind his beard. "I saw the Lord and suffered this wound. Suthra gazed upon the Lord and was maimed for his efforts. His left leg, this poem says—"

"He wounded himself so he could claim that he encountered the Lord. Like you. And like you he never became a father, exalted or not."

"Ah, that may not be true. I discovered this book in Green House. Who has searched the library since the fall of the Unified Kingdom?"

"Who? No one," she said. "Not even during the Unified Kingdom."

"This poet-history quotes lost books. No, not lost, censored. Books rejected by the priesthood and never included in the *Runehayana*. Perhaps they contained the true words of the Lord."

"So, despite your bravado, you still desperately grasp the will to believe."

"Yes!" He said the word with such force that his wounded leg began to throb. "I *will believe* what this book says about Suthralane."

He read from the page:

EXALTED FATHER

BOOK OF PLAGUES
VERSE 3.3.2

"Thou shalt not climb the holy mountain Elsseleron, nor shalt thou set foot upon a single rock of the holy mountain, lest ye die. For none dare gaze upon the face of the Lord and live. On that day they shall surely die."

"Who heard that?" she asked. "Sure you're not making it up as you go?"

Rudra glanced up. "Comes from *Aitareya*," he said, "*Forbidden*." He chose his words carefully. "I have it on good authority that the passage is authentic. It is the work of the greatest scholar of the Third Kalpa. Our Yadish poet here paraphrases the source. How he came by it I do not know."

"Ah—" Her tone was slightly mocking, perhaps for the first time. "Well now, from our own library too. Brought here by a spy, huh? At last we poor Yads have something to be proud of. We steal from priests without their knowing."

He did not fly into a rage, nor did he chastise her as he usually did. The wound in his left leg was throbbing again. He quoted from the book:

"*Personal names do not persist in memory, oral or inscribed. But titles do, especially when they describe—sometimes prescribe—a belief about the person named. From mere substitutes, such titles morph into names and ultimately things in themselves. Blame is often placed on the lying pens of scribes. Alas, it is really forgetfulness, laziness, self-deception, long before names are innocently recorded. Words are lies after all.*

"*None know his original name. All have heard of Suthra the Lame, Suthralane.*"

She laughed. "It's always Suthralane. Suthralane, Suthralane. Talk long enough with a priest and you'll hear Suthralane. Even among the Akkadeans, so I've heard. Suthralane. So, my loving Grand Duke, Father of Thousands, you truly have joined the priesthood. Or are you Akkadean?"

Rudra continued to read:

"He was sramana from the start, not a priest of Nalanda. Like the cry of the blue owl that once echoed through the cedar forests of the north, the word 'sramana' reverberated through the Kalpas. In the first stage the Tribes heard the 'shraman,' later, fainter, they heard 'shurna,' then 'surtha,' and finally in a still faint whisper, 'suthra.'"

"Suthra really was a *sramana*," she said, becoming interested in the legend despite her purpose. For she'd not visited the garden to listen to ancient readings. Lurking behind one of the golden elms was a hunched figure dressed in white. The shadowy presence awaited her signal. It bore an Akkadean curved blade of the finest Nepptali steel.

"Not all *sramanas* are priests," she mused. "He may have come from any Tribe. Perhaps even Yadish—"

Rudra continued:

"Suthra broke the greatest of all the Supreme Lord's commandments. He climbed Elsseleron seeking the face of the Lord. None may see the Lord and live. Yet Suthra gazed upon the Divine Form and survived. Oh believers, was the Lord not powerful enough to stop him? How could this be? How is it that the Supreme Power permits such wickedness among men?

"Descending the Holy Mountain, he slipped on the glassy surface and dislocated his left hip, wrenching the thigh bone from its socket. Was he perhaps blinded by the Holy Light?

"Behold, tradition is stronger than reason. Like water, it wears away sharp arguments, sharper observations, razor sharp thinking. It is an amorphous fog of the early morning. It rises from the cold damp ground and erases distinctions. How may one reason without distinctions?

"That Suthralane existed is all ye need to know.

EXALTED FATHER

"Did he know the great law of the Supreme Being? Had he forgotten? Was he arrogant, conceited, prideful?

"Some Legends tell of a cryptic saying attributed to the arch-lawbreaker. On the right bank of the Reed Sea a rock once stood, twelve feet high, five feet wide. It has long since vanished, worn away by spray and wind. Legend says Suthra carved a verse on its glass-like surface:

The Supreme Being is Eternal.

He came down from the Kingdoms of the Heavens.

But if He is Eternal,

How could He come down?

"In order to answer this question, Suthra scaled Elsseleron."

He stopped reading and pondered crumbling Green House. A greenish-brown moss that smelled of rot and corruption covered the once bright stone. Wooden carvings of animals, mountains, trees and flowers once graced the triangular pediment, but all of it had vanished long ago, and there were no living artists to affect a rebirth. Thick vines encircled the fluted columns like monstrous serpents. How often over the years had Rudra ordered the building repaired?

Heavy clouds came together and sealed the pale sky. In the north they heard a low rumbling.

Miriam drew a silver cord from an inner pocket. The cord was made from that fine flexible metal called *kerdofan*. The secrets of its making belonged to the Nepptali. She'd been saving it for a special occasion.

THE BOOKS OF MARDUK

BOOK OF PLAGUES
VERSE 3.3.3

Rudra sighed. "The first account breaks off here. Another hand seems to take up the pen. Not the hand of a priest, or a poet. Not even Yad."

"A literate peasant then?" Miriam sounded surprised.

"Perhaps. Listen to this:

A Kalpa ago—a day of the Lord which by human reckoning is a thousand years—a strange being appeared in the fields of the Lord's Tribe. On the west bank of the Pearldew.

The hard-eyed peasants regarded it with suspicion. It had come from the direction of Edom. But it was no Yakashas.

The creature was a man, naked save for a worn loincloth made from homespun. He tottered on spindly legs, yet his chest, shoulders and arms were powerfully muscled as though he'd performed peasant labor all his life. Old, broken-toothed, nut-brown, piercing eyes, the smell of old leather, he had a foul disposition, or so peasants imagined. Deformed too, his ears were like mosscat's, or like the wicked farvel, and they swiveled independent of one another.

The good peasants named the old man Long-ears. He accepted the title happily. Scratching and belching, he inquired after dinner. 'When do we eat', his first words.

The suspicious peasants were wary. They'd work to do. The spring fields were golden, wheat freshly sprouted, and some corn—and a few rows of cabbage—in constant need of watering, especially here on the edge of dry Yakashas Steppe. Water had to be brought up from the Pearldew and made to flow through narrow canals. Water-wheels, forever turning, driven by human energy. Wooden aqueducts, in constant need of mending.

Farming here was difficult. There was little time for conversation.

'What have you in exchange?' they inquired.

'Oh!' he laughed and skipped a step. 'A story. A tale. A joke.'

If some still thought Long-ears a Yakashas, this belief quickly dissipated.

It was early morning, the daystar at his back, Lesser Wind in his face, kittim falling around him like colorful snowflakes. The work-weary peasants glimpsed madness in his eyes.

'Kill it, I says.' One of the older women, a matron of fifty or so, brought her knife out, prepared to follow her own advice. Her companion, a decade-older wizened farmer, grasped his sharp-bladed hoe, prepared to do her biding.

'No!' cried the foreman, waving his stave at her. 'Let us hear his stories and especially his jokes. If the stories are good we feed it. If the jokes are bad we kill it.'

'Is Yakashas, I say!' She hissed like a serpent in the grass.

'Silence, wench!' The foreman was not accustomed to having his orders challenged. The women outnumbered the men and they bore weapons of various kinds: knives, pitchforks, staves, scythes. He feared them more than the strange creature Long-ears.

'I said we kills it if its jokes are bad.'

This seemed to mollify the woman for the time being.

The foreman, whose name is recorded as Papias, addressed the creature. 'Speak, Long-ears. For breakfast or for death.'

Long-ears grinned foolishly. He appeared to be enjoying the spectacle. 'Long-ears. I like that. Better than being called Old-cripple.'

Only then did they notice that he limped on a lame left leg."

Rudra paused. "See there. Lame—and the left leg." He felt his own leg wound. It itched now instead of burning.

She glared at him. How had she ever loved such a ridiculous man? She couldn't remember. It seemed to her that she'd hated him for a life-time, until at last she found no more energy for hatred. Perhaps the love had been there before their son. It didn't matter now.

"I grow weary," she groaned.

"I'll not weary you further."

"Oh why not? Has there ever been a time when you haven't?"

He gave her a wry smile. It was quite unexpected.

"You know, Rudra, I liked you better before you met the Lord of Lords. At least then your anger was predictable. I like good mad rage in a man. Why, a person might have believed you half-alive. If only the upper half—" She snickered and winked.

"The account breaks off anyway," he said serenely. "I mean, there're still fragments, but they make little sense—"

"So, is there some conclusion, Grand Duke Limp?"

"He told them a story that made them laugh—"

He stopped again and stared off, past the library, to the Pearldew, to the steppe.

"And—" She was quickly losing patience.

He pulled at his beard. He studied the book. He did not respond. She fingered the silver death-cord but kept it hidden from him.

Rudra read: *"Behold I will tell you a great mystery. Though you are women of the Tribe advanced in years, you shall yet bear children.*

And all the women, together in a chorus, laughed out loud. 'Are we not past the time of pleasure? Are we not withered? Our men too?'

Papias shouted at them to be quiet. To Long-ears he said: 'Explain yourself.'

"A tale and a joke,' Long-ears replied.

Frowning, Papias stared at him. He saw the toothless grin, the ears twitch, dark eyes twinkling. And he exploded with laughter."

Celestial rumbling came closer. Rudra looked up. He closed the book.

"Thus they adopted him into the Tribe," he said, "and many women came to him willingly, in search of the great mystery. And many did not. For as it is written, he was very ugly and dirty, covered by layers of grime and sweat. He was lame, thin as a river reed, and smelt vilely. The ones that refused he took by force, for they had a special attraction for him."

"Priest and rapist combined. A worthy model to emulate, Grand Duke Lame. Why, you're half-way there."

He stared at her. For perhaps the first time in their countless years together she thought that she perceived a look of surprise—and for lack of a better word—*doubt* cloud his face.

"The willing ones bore children," he said, rifling through the pages, "and they were healthy. The unwilling shut their eyes, and after they bore children they became barren. And their female children were barren, their male children impotent—"

His voice fell to barely a whisper. "The author here says that he went to all the Tribes, and the same events transpired. And after many ages barrenness infected all the Tribes, for few were those with eyes wide open."

"Because women refused rape?" she spat. "Because they refused to smile and gaze lovingly at their rapist? What sort of perverted mind would imagine such a thing?"

"Suthralane was merely the instrument of the Lord's curse upon the Tribes." He touched the bandaged wound and winched. The leg was healing cleanly but it was still sore. "Have I been called to undo the damage caused by Suthralane, to open the wombs of women?"

With a guttural cry, she leaped upon him. She looped the silver cord around his neck and hissed into his ear: "Try fucking when you can't breathe!"

BOOK OF PLAGUES
VERSE 3.3.4

The cord shut off his cry for help. She twisted the flexible kerdofan and gave a mighty yank. He tumbled backwards off the bench, his arms flailing and his feet kicking out.

Miriam's strength was almost superhuman and her agility was not far behind. She increased the tension of the cord while at the same time avoiding Rudra's frantic hands. He thrashed about and clawed at the cord around his neck. All in vain.

"How little people appreciate breathing," she said, taking her own deep breath. "There ought to be a holy book dedicated to it. Is it not more precious than silver and gold, titles and offices? The good air, breathed by Dukes and peasants alike. Ah, but to be without it."

He kicked furiously, but his bad leg burned and his strength began to ebb away like water from a leaky jar.

A flash of lightning split the sky followed by a deep boom of thunder.

"Do you hear your Almighty Lord, my dear husband. He's laughing at you, oh Exalted Father!"

Rain began to fall, first in small drops. They steadily increased in size and intensity.

Her own lungs burned. She grew hot and sweaty as though she were in the throes of passion. "Your Lord weeps for you. Why does he not rescue you? Perhaps He's less potent than you imagined… less potent than you. Best ignore Him. Pray to the Lord of Breath. Alas, there is no Lord of Breath. How unfortunate."

He could barely hear her. Nor did he feel the rain soaking his clothes. The cord cut into his neck, bringing a trickle of blood. He felt himself plummeting into a deep abyss.

"Maybe the priests will compose a hymn to breathing. You must remind your son, when he meet him in the nether world—"

"*Miriam, no!*"

A strange heavy-set man burst from the grove behind them. Half the size of a Yad, he was dressed in a white peasant blouse and white baggy trousers. His skin was coarse, almost bark-like, and his white hair long and shaggy, like the mane of some extinct cat.

He seized her shoulders with rough hands. "Do not kill him!"

She shook him off and stared into his face. His features appeared bloated, puffy, like spoiled dough, yet oddly beast-like. He appeared to be growing dark sprouts of facial hair.

"Justice demands it," she cried.

"Even if his sins are infinite, and so, too, the demands of justice, mercy trumps them."

"The Lord demands justice—as the priests have it."

"Then mercy is an argument against the Lord's existence."

"But not against *my* justice."

"Then kill him," he said evenly. "Remember though, to kill a man according to the claims of justice means that those claims are infallible. The person making those claims must also be infallible. Are you infallible, Miriam?"

She hesitated. She liked this one better when the madness took him. Her grip loosened ever so slightly. A tiny wisp of air found its way into Rudra's lungs.

"If you would be Queen begin your reign with mercy. Let justice follow later. After they believe."

She released the cord and Rudra dropped to the ground unconscious, but still alive.

"Damn you, *Vishnu*," she muttered.

Vishnu [but, queeti poets ask, how could this be he?][14] scowled. He grasped Rudra, who was nearly twice his size, and heaved him onto the bench.

"Bind his hands and feet. And better gag him too unless he suddenly wakes and calls out for help in the powerful voice of his."

The rain began to let up. There was no more thunder.

"And cover him. Completely. That old cloak—the one worn by the Kings of the Unified Kingdom, the one of many colors—does he still have it?"

She snickered. "He keeps it by his bed, but he never wears it."

She bound his hands with the flexible cord and stuffed pages from the silly old book into his mouth. Vishnu swung the limp body over his shoulder, again demonstrating surprising physical strength, and proceeded up the path to Green House. Miriam went in the opposite direction to the palace.

When she reappeared at Green House she bore the King's coat of many colors. It had faded over the years, yet one could still see that it was a mass of patches representing the colors of all the Tribes of Men.

Lesser Wind commenced to wash over the southern lands.

She found Vishnu in the vast foyer of the library. He'd found a chair and was reading from Rudra's book. Rudra lay at his feet still unconscious.

Vishnu looked up and grinned. His yellow teeth seemed oddly fang-like. She wished the inner beast would take him.

"Tomorrow morning, after Greater Wind, we'll take him into the steppe and dump him in a pit. I noticed an old trap on my way here. A grave just waiting to be occupied. It shouldn't take too long. We'll

---

[14] An obvious queeti editorial comment, which is why it is bracketed. Some scholars believe that much of this chapter is of queeti invention, further redacted over the millennia. What hovering ghost heard the conversation? they ask.

tell the Tribe he got lost on one of his little excursions. If the Yakashas didn't get him, the *kittim* did, we'll say. And it'll be true."

"Why all the trouble? Why not kill him right here?"

"What if there really is an Almighty Lord who demands justice?"

"You can't be serious!"

"Ah, Miriam. If you really would be Queen you'll need to be far more subtle. Don't spill blood needlessly, at least by your own hand. If you must, let someone else do it for you. Whatever falsehoods you perpetuate in the name of power you must believe them yourself. Thus others will believe. Thus whatever you say will be the truth."

She scowled. "He may be dead already. He's almost as old as you. Shock finished the job."

He sighed. "If that's so then I'll give a very convincing funeral oration."

"Vishnu, it's been a long time… You've changed. You were the most cynical and brutal of men—granted, this new demon-within attracts me—but I like you better without this useless priest-talk. What's happened to you?"

His grin abruptly vanished, replaced by a frown. It might have been the Akkadean tigress…the blow to his head that nearly killed him, and all but drowned him in his favorite noodles. He'd capture her yet, even if it took every last Yad. More probably the somas scrambled his brains. They'd transformed more than his body. He had to admit that the Akkadean woman-man no longer seemed so appealing.

He remembered the day Miriam came to Tholos, the young Grand Duchess seeking Ra'bim potions of fertility. The herbmasters soon realized that they had the Grand Duchess of the Yadish in their power. They gave her potions, but not of the fertility kind. They brought her to Vishnu whose many wives had died, one at a time, as quickly as he mounted them.

He remembered how she looked then: the thick powerful body, ruddy complexion, long black hair, brown, half-lidded eyes—how she literally reeked of the black soil, wet and furrowed, prepared for the planting. How wild and violent her passion, how he plunged into velvety thatch of her fire and was consumed—after all these years he could still feel the moment, and especially now as the whittling soma spread through his body, soaking into every cell.

She'd stayed for the summer. Had the Grand Duke even noticed her long absence? Finally she returned to the Yadish. The next year they heard from a wandering *sramana* that the Grand Duke had an heir. So they charged him double the going price of the fertility potion, for the heir was male—which he gladly paid.

"Ah, you are so transparent, old man. Perhaps you've fallen into your own trap. Perhaps you do have one belief. Ah, Vishnu, you've become boring. *She's* beyond your grasp. Gone into the steppe, *she has*."

"And now you become irritating, Miriam. Do *you* cultivate a belief too? That your womb may still bear fruit?"

"It did once, as you well know. Why not come and see?"

She led him up a winding staircase to the balcony where couches moldered between tall bookshelves beneath a crystalline dome. *Kittim* circled outside the dome.

She loosed her hair and shed her clothes, and lay naked on a couch, a lumpy thing, dry and wrinkled. He placed a hand on her breast and with the other pried her legs open. The desire mounted in him as it had not done in a hundred years. The terrible thing inside awoke. It surprised her. She had come to believe that the Lord's curse did not inhabit the bodies of women, men were without balls. However, neither Miriam nor, apparently, the Lord on High had made the effort to study Ra'bim chemistry. Somas took time to work in cells.

If there truly was an Almighty Lord on the mountain called Elsseleron, He might have benefited from studying the art of the Ra'bim physicians.

EXALTED FATHER

BOOK OF PLAGUES
VERSE 3.3.5

King Joseph stadium stood empty and unused for longer than anybody could recall. Old men and women generally do not have much interest in competitive athletics. The Laughing Duke once tried to hold two weeks of games. This was after he'd read a musty old history of the Yadish Tribe's most notable sports feats. A sizable number of aristocrats attended (the choice was: games or a flogging). But after two died in a four lap race, the games were called off. The Laughing Duke laughed. He did not participate, although he did brag about his wrestling prowess and how he trained diligently (as reported by the Grand Duchess). However, there'd been no challengers.

Today, over five hundred filled the stadium. The entire population of Haran turned out. The local peasants, of course, should have been working in the fields. Yet many decided to attend and let the fields work themselves. For all it mattered, the rotten crops might be better off without human labor. Not a single Yad from the outlying villages appeared. They'd grown accustomed to ignoring summons from Haran.

The crowd came to see the Triumvir Vishnu, the oldest living human being in Greenbottom.

Many asked the question: How could this person be Vishnu?

A stocky, brutal looking man wearing a Yadish golden ducal uniform mounted the winner's platform in the center of the stadium.

The late autumn afternoon hastened to evening, aided by an impenetrable cloud cover. If this Vishnu character didn't get on with it Lesser Wind would start to blow, and the *kittim* would come.

He spoke with little effort. His voice seemed overly strong and deep for a man his age, and it carried around the stadium.

"I am Vishnu, Triumvir of the Ra'bim. I am Triumvir no longer, because the Ra'bim Tribe is no more. The Zub'lin Tribe is no more—the Nepptali, the Gads and Akkadeans and all the others. All have succumbed to a Great Plague.

"Behold, my dear friends, this Great Plague has come to the Yadish."

A few aristocrats gasped. Peasants began to wail. There were also some skeptical snickers, and a few outright laughs. An ancient peasant woman called out: "Your Great Plague came here long before you, ole man!"

"What might that be?" Vishnu responded. He appeared very serene and not at all put out by her rude interruption.

"Are you a fool? Do you jest? See you any young ones here?"

"I do not," Vishnu acknowledged.

"Has not jealous Lord stolen the seed of men?"

"Am I a priest? I know nothing about the doings of divine beings. I speak of neither the impotence of men nor the barrenness of women." He crossed his arms over his chest. "I only speak of what I know:

"Alas, two days ago in the steppe, a swarm of *kittim* took your beloved Grand Duke Rudra. He dissolved like dew on the grass."

Stunned silence settled on the stadium. Yads looked at one another in disbelief. Even the peasant crone looked surprised. Standing behind Vishnu, a step lower on the platform (reserved for second place), Miriam forced herself to shed a tear.

"*Behold, the Great Plague of which I speak is kittim!* It has raged through the northern Tribes throughout the summer. Now it creeps south. Have you not seen them on the horizon? They are the dark clouds of every storm. Have you not seen their size? They are like living sails, like the sails that once brightened yonder Red Lake."

The breeze suddenly felt colder. The sky appeared darker. In a short time Lesser Wind would come and with it the terrible plague of *kittim*.

"What are we to do?" The crowd howled as one.

Vishnu smiled. "It was written long ago that Triumvir Vishnu is the preserver. It is written that in times of need, he comes to all the Tribes. He is their savior. He is greater than any King."

"Where's *that* written?" cried out the old woman. She'd apparently recovered from her initial surprise. "It's easy to quote from books nobody else has read, or able to read."

"Shut up, old hag!" snarled people standing close to her.

"Are you such idiots? This is not Vishnu. The real Vishnu's a hairless ball of white fat. He's off chasing his Akkadean wench who passed through these parts last summer." She raised her face to the man on the platform. "What've you done with the Grand Duke? I bet I know what you're doing with the Grand Duchess—"

A peasant standing next to her—he might have been her husband—turned and hit her in the face with a hoe. Behind her, another slammed her on the back with a shovel. She screamed and collapsed in a heap. Bellowing like maddened beasts, the crowd fell upon her. They kicked, punched, gorged and stamped. Blood flew like juice from a melon.

"Peace, my dear friends," Vishnu called out. "It is written that men should honor and respect one another, and one should love his fellow Tribesman." He was smiling.

Lesser Wind began, but no *kittim* fell. The cold and damp evening brought a deep shiver to thin skin and old bones. The Wind seemed to drain the anger from the crowd. Many gazed upon the old woman's mangled corpse in horror. "What strange madness seized us," some exclaimed, "that we should do such a thing?"

A half-hour passed and the Wind fell. The crowd remained frozen in their places, although the night had come and sane people feared the darkness. Many whimpered in terror, but none moved. At a secret signal from Miriam, two peasants produced a large quartz lamp and hosted it on a pole above Vishnu's head. Standing a circle of yellow light, he appeared larger and frightfully imposing.

Old nearsighted Marquis Baldwin stepped up to the platform. His family claimed descent from the younger brother of King Joseph I. Green-house library contained a separate archival section dedicated to genealogy. But the thousands of volumes crammed with tables were notoriously inconsistent and fragmentary. And the last Keeper of the Archives had died nearly two centuries ago. No one knew how to read Imperial Yadish, which had been the written language of the archives. And—besides—weak-minded, drunken poets had done all the scribbling.

The Marquis was a gloomy, morose man, who never smiled, never joked, and never produced an heir. His gravelly voice always cared a tone of complaint.

"If indeed the Grand Duke is consumed—" He gave Vishnu a suspicious look. "—then the title rightly passes to our family."

Cries of protest erupted from other aristocrats in the crowd. Counts, Viscounts, and even a few Earls shouted: "No, no... It is ours! Our family! My grandfather, granduncle..."

And so on and so forth, citing names of long dead relatives, as well as characters from myth and legend, even bastards and sons of famous concubines, many taken directly from popular romances, and not a few from trashy novels. Some even claimed descent from Suthralane, which made no sense but of which they appeared quite proud.

Miriam pushed forward and elbowed Vishnu aside. She stood a head taller and the breeze caused her white-streaked hair to shimmer in the yellow light as though she wore a golden crown. Lightning seemed to flash directly above her and her voice was like thunder.

"THE LATE GRAND-DUKE HAD A SON. WE THOUGHT HIM DEAD. BUT I HAVE REASON TO BELIEVE THAT HE STILL LIVES."

Vishnu's eyes narrowed ever so slightly. He seemed to shrink in her presence.

"You know this for sure?" the Marquis Baldwin asked, suspicion visibly oozing from him like steam from his bald head. He was having trouble locating her due to his bad eyesight and the glare.

Miriam ignored him.

"BY LAW I AM REGENT. I APPOINT TRIUMVIR VISHNU AS CO-REGENT. WE COMMAND THAT THE ENTIRE TRIBE MOVE SOUTH, BEFORE THE COMING OF WINTER. BECAUSE OF THIS PLAGUE WE WILL SEEK REFUGE ON STARMIRROR."

Vishnu spoke up: "And along the way, we will pay a visit to the monastery named Nalanda. The priesthood is responsible for this Plague. It was their foolishness that brought the wrath of the Lord down upon our heads. The Lord demands that we cleanse the land of their blasphemous stench."

Marquis Baldwin was about to protest, but Viscount Donatien drew his short sword and placed its sharp point in the middle of Baldwin's back.

"My family has better claim than any bastard Marquis," he shouted. "Lost children carry no claim. Show us this son!"

"And mine, and mine..." More swords were drawn. "Show us this son—"

The Viscount added: "Should he even appear before us, how could we know this son is Rudra's?"

Miriam gave Vishnu a worried look.

"Have you not heard?" she replied in a different voice. "*Have you not heard the promise of the Lord?*"

The crowd fell silent.

"Our beloved Grand Duke walked with the Lord. The Almighty, the One, demanded that he, Blessed Rudra, bring the Tribes of Men into a Holy Land that the Lord would show him. Alas, the Plague of which Vishnu speaks took our sweet Duke before he could complete the Lord's work. And so, before he died, he passed the calling to Vishnu—unless Rudra's long lost son should reappear—"

"This is a different story," said Donatien.

She looked directly at him and smiled. "Oh, it is the same, only more detailed."

"Where is this Holy Land," he asked peevishly.

"Is it not written that Starmirror is a Holy Land? Rich, fertile, lush and sweet? A Holy Land without *kittim*, without Yakashas, without all those creatures cursed of the Lord—"

Vishnu interrupted her. "Follow me and the Lord will reward your families with more than empty titles. *Yadish nobility will become wealthy beyond their wildest dreams.* And even you peasants—you too may become nobles in that Land."

Donatien sheathed his sword as did the others. The Marquis Baldwin stepped aside and turned to the Viscount. He smiled, perhaps for the first time in his miserably long life. Donatien smiled back.

"This *is* a new story," he observed, "one I like much better than the first."

"It has the ring of truth," Donatien acknowledged.

Miriam shouted: "THE LORD WILLS IT!"

A slight pause, and then "THE LORD WILLS IT!" filled the stadium.

Miriam laughed.

EXALTED FATHER

THE BOOK OF PLAGUES

CHAPTER FOUR – Stonehill

VERSE 3.4.1

A messenger arrived in the small hours of the morning. He was young, his red skin had yet to acquire that leathery wrinkled hide of the desert. He'd been born without a tail. This odd mutation had appeared in the generation before his. It seemed to be increasing in frequency. Some said the Redfolk imps of Starmirror were all born without tails.

Smoke hung in the cool night air. Smoke arose from Stonehill. Had the tailless giants returned? Did they still wield the thunderbolt?

The caves were alight with torches. The messenger winced at the sight of the queeti corpses. One body was that of an especially large female wearing a pink coral necklace.

Captain Menes was old, thick about the middle, yet still a formidable warrior, at least by reputation, which had not been put to the test in recent years. He carried a dagger of bronze, given to him personally by Lord Rekhmire, Overseer of the Straits. The Lord had bestowed upon him this singular honor in recognition of his ability to quell recent queeti rebellions.

The messenger whose name was Tark bowed stiffly.

"What's this?" Menes grumbled. He'd been asleep on a soft bed of straw. Joints creaking, he forced his old body to stand as straight as possible in order to receive the worship as was his due.

"Oh great Captain," Tark addressed his feet, "a thing has happened that has never happened in all the turnings of the star-wheel—"

He hesitated and cringed slightly, fearing a hard cuff to the ears as the great Captain was prone to do to those who dared to disturb his rest.

"Get on with it," Menes yawned.

"Lotus Moon cycle past, a pack of queeti came up from the coast and invaded Red Desert. My master, the great Captain Amon, determined that they'd come to rescue females *you* took summer past."

Menes drank a full cup of fermented berry juice brought by one of his aides.

"Amon, you say? Proud, arrogant, very stupid. What'd he do? Flee from a pack of queeti? Yes, of course, tail between his legs. Left a trail of pee, I'd guess, for queeti to follow—"

"Scared the piss outta him," the aide commented. The officers who'd gathered around them roared with laughter.

Tark cringed. He dared not contradict Captain Menes. He feared a beating or worse. The lowly know instinctively how often their telling of the truth brings on anger, fear and resentment—and violent retribution. He'd heard it said somewhere, perhaps, or perhaps not.

"Forgive me, Great Captain, but my Master Amon engaged them in battle—and emerged the victor. As you know, he is the most humble of Redfolk. So humble, that I'm afraid his virtues go unrecognized by the great and powerful, such as yourself."

Menes frowned. Suddenly he realized that he quite disliked this upstart sniveling idiot.

"Captain Amon set a trap. Oh, how difficult is such maneuver in the desert, as you obviously know. My wise Captain used Black Rock as bait. He'd hunted those traitors—you know—the ones that stole the Lord's females—and killed them at Black Rock. The foolish queeti seized the place and thought themselves the victors. As Amon suspected, they went north from there. Great joy, he took them. Ah, the slaughter was terrible. The daystar itself hid its face. Even Northern Wind failed that evening. Not a single blowfly dared alight. The red soil drank deep of queeti blood—"

"Why wake me with frivolous tales?" Menes complained. His irritation was slowly giving way to distress. He began to feel old and helpless. He had to do something. Tark did not cringe and grovel as he should. His story was an obvious pack of lies and nonsense. Worse, he appeared to draw pride and strength from it.

"My Master thought you should know that he discovered a very strange creature. North of Black Rock our scouts came upon an old pit, once a trap, on the edge of the steppe, in the land of the tailless. Oh, great Captain, it was not empty as one might expect—"

"Get to the point," Menes snarled. This Tark was in love with the sound of his own voice, and he'd learned to speak quite fluently. Like Amon, if Menes remembered clearly.

"Two creatures inhabited the pit. One was a queeti bull. The other was a male tailless, tall and rather plump, with a thick beard but no hair on its head—poor thing. A chief, no doubt—"

"What genius decided that?" Menes wondered if he were having a nightmare.

"It wore a second skin, almost identical to that of the White Lords. But its skin was not white. It was of many colors, like legends say of the fur of the haricat."

Menes shot a nervous glance at his aids. They were listening intently.

"Did Amon kill it as he should?"

"Oh no, great Captain. My Master is humble as he is clever. At this very moment he takes them both across the straits to the castle Zell of Lord Rekhmire. He would not presume to take such momentous action on his own. His only wish is that the Overseer acknowledges his qualities."

"And reward him," Menes added sourly.

"Oh no. He only does his duty." Tark paused. "What Redfolk Captain has ever discovered such a thing? Not even the great Mose. A tailless one who wears the skin of a haricat?"

"What indeed—"

"Clever Amon—how brilliant is my Master—took the second skin of many colors away from the tailless chief in order to present it as a gift to our Lord Rekhmire."

Menes' aids cast quizzical looks upon his once-august person now grown old. He knew what they were thinking.

"Why does stupid Amon inform *me* of his splendid success?" he snapped.

Tark dared raise his face. He stared boldly into Menes' once-brown eyes, now become milky white.

"Captain Menes has heard of the lights on Stonehill? Amon believes that this chief was a scout. The tailless have returned to Stonehill. Do they still wield the lightning bolt? Let not the great Captain Menes, to whom all praise is given, attempt anything rash—"

"As, say, attack Stonehill and steal the glory from Amon?"

"My humble Master would never think such a thing. The lives of all Redfolk concern him, especially *yours*. I've heard him often singing your praises. His is true affection. I've heard him call you *brother*."

"*Indeed!* Well, winter is no time for campaigning in the steppe. The blowflies would be on us like rotten meat. Tomorrow we depart for Edom and the Straits. Blowflies burn up in the desert. I for one will mix their ashes with my berry juice and drink to their long life."

An aide broke in, one as old as Menes yet half his size and weight: "Great Captain, was it not your intention to sack Stonehill?"

Menes turned upon the skeletal creature and struck him a frightful blow with his fist. The unexpected blow took the aide on his temple and smashed his skull. His arms went loose, his bladder emptied, and he dropped like a stone.

"See how I am surrounded by traitors and scoundrels?" Menes howled. "My long-suffering patience has its limits."

Tark bowed his head— to hide his grin.

"Is this not so, my friends?"

The other Redfolk acknowledged the Captain's truth.

BOOK OF PLAGUES
VERSE 3.4.2

They set out the next day heading south. Menes questioned Tark as to the location of the pit and the road Captain Amon would probably favor. Tark, of course, begged ignorance.

Menes forced the pace. Brave Captain Amon requires our aid, he explained to his tired troops. If his captive is indeed a great chief of the tailless, there will undoubtedly be some sort of rescue attempt.

"Strange times," remarked Tark. "In all the generations of Redfolk, since the time we came into the steppe, none have ever encountered a force of tailless this far south."

"Strange times indeed," acknowledged Menes. He doubled the pace. Shortly, no one had the breath to talk.

That evening they set camp in the shadow of a small hillock. Menes set guards, but the day's exertion quickly overwhelmed them and soon they were asleep.

The next morning they discovered Tark's body. His throat had been slashed. There was no sign of a struggle. Apparently he'd been murdered in his sleep.

"A lone queeti out for revenge," Menes observed. He didn't appear surprised.

"We saw nothing," the two guards protested.

Barring his fangs, Menes eyed them. They cringed beneath his glare, fearing for the worse. At last he shrugged.

"Queeti are devious beasts. We'll need to post more guards."

"What do we do with Tark?" asked an aide.

"Leave 'em for the blowflies."

"The winds bring no flying maggots this far south," an aide remarked.

"It is well, then." The Captain sounded disappointed.

"Looks like a blade did the work, a dull blade," said one of the guards. His red tail snapped like a whip. "Queeti carry blades? How can that be?"

Menes fingered the hilt of his dagger. It had lost its former luster. Although Lord Rekhmire had given him the weapon, the White Lord had apparently forgotten to include instructions on its upkeep.

"Strange times indeed," he observed.

The Books Of Marduk

BOOK OF PLAGUES
VERSE 3.4.3

Jacob's patience evaporated like bugeaves on a hot summer's morning. He considered carrying out the sacrifice himself. He hated polluting the beautiful ceremonial Yadish knife.

The days dragged on and Marduk consumed vast amounts of food and drink, more drink than food. He cursed his ascetic life—his former ascetic life—and how he'd suffered. Jacob's own long suffering patience, about which he constantly bragged, and over which he'd nearly come to blows with not a small number of priests who dared question his claims, also suffered.

Marduk cursed, and then told more stories about Suthralane. Jacob had never heard a single one. They became more unbelievable the more wine—mostly wine, but also a thick brown whisky—Marduk consumed.

The days grew colder, the winds biting, especially on their exposed summit. *Kittim*, bugeaves in the constipated language of the priesthood, filled the pale yellow autumn sky. One evening Jacob noticed a dark bugeave cloud moving south *against* Lesser Wind, like leaves in a rushing river pushing upstream. Such a thing contradicted common sense and the testimony of ages, not to mention the sacred texts. Therefore Jacob dismissed it. Too much wine, perhaps. Something had to be causing him to see distortions, or was distorting his vision, or confusing his mind, or—something.

One night, after a miserable day of iron skies and steady, freezing rain, Jacob decided that the time had come to use his knife for something other than slicing bread.

Marduk's custom was to stand on the wide portico every morning and observe bugeaves whirling and cavorting in Greater Wind. This particular morning a seamless curtain of clouds hid

EXALTED FATHER

Dewdrop Moon. Below, the barren land bore patches of white frost. Jacob determined that the sacrificial moment had arrived.

He rubbed the sleep from his eyes and donned his black traveling cloak. It had grown tight about the middle. He grasped the Yadish knife. Marduk, true to habit, had gone out onto the portico. His back was to Jacob. He was studying some pages of old parchment he'd tried to hide from Jacob (Jacob was far too clever to be taken in by the clumsy ruse). You can always count on habits, Jacob thought.

He lumbered to the arched doorway. His hands were shaking. His heart beat faster, his breathing was ragged, his stomach bloated and painful. The Lord wills it, he kept repeating.

Greater Wind blew fiercely. He drew the cowl over his head and focused on his slipper-clad feet as he negotiated the slick marble. He'd discovered a pair of red slippers in an upper bedroom that fit his swollen feet perfectly. Wearing them somehow caused him to feel taller and even more dignified. Patches of ice shone like mirrors. His head was down. He prepared to strike.

Marduk had vanished.

The rain drew a curtain over Jacob's eyes. Jacob was not a man of the outdoors. Summers made him sweat, winters made him shiver, cold rain made him miserable as well as blind. The Lord did not have human happiness in mind when He designed the world.

He peered through the rain, down the road leading to Red Lake. Marduk had to have come this way. The only other path from the citadel led south towards Edom. The southern path came to the field where the Yakashas had slaughtered the Yadish—according to pious legend. South was the way of death.

Jacob looked south. The rain and wind were at his back.

And there he saw Marduk, wrapped in that ridiculous shawl that passed for a priestly robe, soaking wet, walking stick in hand, and heading south.

Jacob felt panic ripple through his dense flesh. It had come to this. In order to serve the Almighty Lord he must endure the Way of Death. Then he remembered his theology. He, Jacob, had wrestled with the Lord. He was the new revelation. The Lord had marked him, set him off from the all the others—like Grand Duke Rudra who'd met the Lord face to face. Once he performed the sacrifice, the Lord would appear to him. His mind was racing, scattered ideas forming up like an Akkadean phalanx, spontaneously, (of themselves so.) He was not afraid, he told himself. "The Lord is with me," he said aloud.

The way was clear. Abruptly the rain began to taper off. A dark cloud of bugeaves appeared in the south. Such an impossible event had to be mistaken perception, Jacob told himself. He wondered if impure nature itself were trying to tempt him away from the holy task.

The road led him downward. Despite its antiquity, its muddy surface, the dismal light, the way was surprisingly well marked. It seemed to have been used recently. Perhaps the Lord Himself had prepared this path in the wilderness, Jacob prayed.

Pools of water, like tiny ponds, interrupted the way down. He tried to avoid them, but occasionally was forced to splash through. His red slippers were soon soaked. An odor seemed to arise from these ponds, the smell of decay, of death, of rotted flesh and vegetation—a dead marshland. The rain did not wash away the odor.

The road leveled. He saw Marduk directly ahead. The *sramana* had halted. A swarm of bugeaves flew towards them, coming in low and from the south. This had to be an illusion, Jacob knew, the evil temptation of a fallen world. He resolved to ignore what faith (and reason) told him should not exist.

EXALTED FATHER

BOOK OF PLAGUES
VERSE 3.4.4

The bizarre being could not be Marduk!

False Marduk wore nothing but a loincloth and his faded *sramana's* shawl. Soaking wet, it clung to his body, a body that belonged to someone, to *something* else. Here, in this place, Jacob perceived a wasted ascetic, a ruined ascetic, an ascetic for the ages, the prince of ascetics.

Marduk's stomach was so sunken that he might have been able to touch his backbone with his fingers. Sunken eyes staring from a skull, lank black hair falling past narrow shoulders, and there, covering his left breast, neck and shoulder was the blue-black sign of bugeave poisoning.

How could this be the same man? How could this be a living man?

The wraith said: "Greetings, oh priest." His voice crackled and broke. His eyes shone a dull green.

"Greetings, devil."

"What brings a well-fed, self-satisfied, pious and pure priest out of doors in such unwholesome weather?"

"It's been revealed that the ancient ritual of the Fall Sacrifice be revived this year."

The wraith danced a step on spindly legs. "*Such* does not answer my question. What brings *you* here?"

"Oh blaspheming blasphemer. The Lord has called me. A heavy burden has He burdened me with and placed upon my unworthy shoulders, He has"

"Ah ha, the Lord is silent, don't you know. Not even the Two Winds carry His thunderous voice, grown small, and smaller, so tiny as to vanish. Perhaps He died. Yes, that's it. Not perhaps. *He died.* Consequently, His blasphemers died with him."

"Speak to me no more of Suthralane and his riddles. You invent them as it suits your inventiveness."

"When did I say Suthralane?"

"He is arch-heretic, father of heretics."

"As Grand Duchess Miriam said of a certain Yad. What of the Grand Duke?"

Jacob gave a start. "What mean you, you devil?"

"Gaze upon thyself, priest. Why have you gone to fat so soon? Who would miss the resemblance? Did not the Grand Duke bestow upon you that blade? Why, poor child, did he sacrifice *you*?"

Jacob screamed and lunged at the wraith. He sought to slice the reedy neck, where the jugular stood out like a blue cord.

With a swift grace and impossibly fast, the wraith leaped back. Jacob cut an illusion, slicing through empty space where once stood a real man.

Suddenly a swarm of giant bugeaves descended upon the devil. Dark green and purple, they covered him head to toe in a cloak of the deepest night, embracing him in living darkness.

Jacob slashed madly at the loathsome creatures. They hovered above him, but they did not descend to embrace him in their slimy wings of death. Yet Jacob still cried out as though he were in terrible pain. His arm went numb, the knife slipped from his fingers. He could no longer see the devil. Silken wings encased the wicked monster like a cocoon.

And then like a rock falling from heaven, Jacob himself collapsed into the mud. Shock delivered the blow. His thoughts flew upwards as do sparks, prayers to the silent Lord of the Mountain. And the dark extinguished his awareness as Greater Wind would a fragile candle's flame.

EXALTED FATHER

BOOK OF PLAGUES
VERSE 3.4.5

How much time had passed? Jacob opened his eyes and saw bugeaves sailing south, carried along in the upper currents. Unconsciously he raised an arm. He extended his fingers as though to grab hold of the flimsy things. His eyes were open but he did not see, his ears did not hear.

He then fell into a deep sleep.

The devil stood there regarding him. He looked sad, his green eyes looked sad, his frown looked sad. The shawl had fallen from his body and it seemed that bugeave poisoning stained every inch of his exposed skin. In one hand he clutched sheaves of parchment, the other hand he placed over his heart.

"Ah good priest—and undertaker. Are not all priests undertakers? Do they not shoulder immense weights and undertake impossible quests? See how far they travel without walking out of the door."

(He smiled and the world seemed to spin.)

"What good is sacrifice? What sort of Lord finds pleasure in such a thing?"

He paused and glanced up at the last of the *kittim* as they flew south.

"Does sacrifice restore things? Return what is missing? Bring back what has been taken? Or is it a bribe? The Lord cares for me. I give gifts. The Lord receives gifts. *He will like me if I give Him gifts.* Naturally I give gifts I like. So, the Lord likes what I like. The Lord is like me. I am the Lord."

He laughed with pure delight. The wicked world laughed along with him.

He turned his face south. Now he spoke to the fleeing *kittim*.

"These many weeks have I've sampled the ways of indulgence. I am not my brother Jacob who sleeps in the mud. Who dreams of vengeance and would sacrifice others.

"The ways of denial have I practiced these many years. I am not my father the archbishop who sleeps suspended in his tower. Whose dreams flee with the morning light. His sacrifice is love."

The *kittim* seemed to leave luminous trails in the gray sky, heavy with rain. They were like shooting stars, and they sang. Yet, he could still not hear the music. It was in his ears but the hearer was absent.

"I am not *sramana*. I am not glutton. Thus do I renounce all belief. I renounce my renunciation." He threw away his walking stick.

He paused and laughed quite loudly. Far to the south, an army of Redfolk took his laughter for thunder.

"Oh, what of my great renunciation? Where will it take me?"

A break appeared in the clouds on the eastern horizon. The daystar opened its great eye. Greater Wind breathed its last and the world grew calm. Far away a bird, a purple morning-dove, ventured a few tentative notes. Closer by another answered. Silver and green swans flew overheard headed northwest to the Lake. No one had heard birdsong in the steppe for two Kalpas. Insects took up the melody. Tiny creatures scurried through the grasses. The steppe awoke.

A few *kittim* passed overhead. They'd changed course yet again and headed north.

He laughed. "The world is a great riddle. I will follow the path of Suthralane—"

That path led him south into Edom.

EXALTED FATHER

BOOK OF PLAGUES
VERSE 3.4.6

Jacob awoke. The sky was a yellow-blue patchwork of torn clouds and frail light. He shivered. His robes were soaked, by cold rain but not bugeaves—thank the Lord. A gentle breeze came from the north. It touched him lightly and he shivered again. He hated winds and breezes. The invisible movement of air betrayed a malevolent presence, he believed.

Autumn birds sang of the coming winter. There were rustlings in the grasses, insects still lingered in the chill air. Their music irritated him. He hated nature's songs.

The devil-wraith had vanished. A small pool of black water festered in the center of the path, like an open wound in the ground. He hated the clay, he hated the dumb clods of mud, the inert matter of his body formed from mere soil. The world was so poorly designed—a dangerous, unholy thought he suppressed the moment he thought it. *Corrupted,* rather. *He was not mud.*

Jacob struggled to his feet. He shook himself like a wet tarp hound.

He looked south down the path. Empty, deserted, unused for a Kalpa, it meandered off into the reddish haze of the desert. He hated deserts.

Marduk (the thing that had been Marduk) was dead. He liked that.

He raised his arms to the sky. "Oh Father, Father, I'm alive! Oh Father, my Lord, accept Thou my sacrifice."

A wind, neither Greater nor Lesser, stirred the pool that had once been the wicked *sramana*.

"The Lord breathes," Jacob said in ecstasy. "He is pleased with me."

At the moment of his greatest joy, a phantom rose from the disgusting puddle that had been Marduk.

Had Jacob been poisoned? Bugeave poisoning produced illusions, he knew.

This new thing of mud and water—and memory—took shape, *the shape of his old priest mentor Albert.*

Albert appeared to rise from the pool as the Runes once rose in the Lord's Pool. Slope-shouldered from long years of pouring over the scrolls, Albert was short and thick with a round face, beady eyes, and a smirking grin. The smirk might have been a grimace of pain, or hate, yet the grimace might have been a mocking smirk too. Either way he resembled an angry baby despite his bulk and great age.

The dead man reached for him as he'd done so many times in the past when Jacob was but a child. Dead, fleshy fingers reached for him—

They were back in the monastery. The old man was angry with him, as always.

"Dull ox!" he shouted at the cowering child. "It's a simple transliteration. An elementary thread of Runes."

He hit the boy with an old walking stick, hard. Jacob fell, covering his head with his arms. He was crying and pleading at the same time.

"Get up, lazy ox! Collapse for me these Runes."

Tears blurred his sight. His face stung hot.

"Get up, I say!" Albert gave him a vicious kick. Flecks of white appeared in his beard. His eyes were wide and shining. Perspiration formed on his broad forehead and he gasped for air.

"Why should I deserve such a novice? Look at Marduk, younger than you. Boy's a genius. Got more intelligence in a single tooth than you got in your fat head."

Jacob cried out in his child's voice: "Hit me again! Hit me, hit me, hit me—"

Albert raised his arm.

"I deserve it. I'm stupid. Dumb, wicked—I hate myself more than you ever will. Hit me. Please. Go ahead, do it—"

"You— you're not worth the effort!"

Jacob struggled to his feet. Then, with his open hand, he began slapping his own face, again and again, sobbing all the while. "Stupid, stupid, stupid—."

Albert frowned. The excitement instantly left him. "Fucking crazy."

"Yes, crazy, crazy, crazy—"

Albert grabbed his wrists. "Stop it, idiot!"

"Idiot, idiot, idiot—"

Albert let him go and backed away. He stepped into the pool—and dissolved.

Jacob stared at the black water. It was nearly gone, seeping into the soil. He remembered how the beatings had grown worse over the years. He remembered how father Albert had done other things to him, unspeakable things—and then he did not wish to remember.

The clouds departed and the daystar shone brightly. It warmed the autumn air. Jacob inhaled and his mind seemed to clear. Dead men could no longer harm him. Not Albert, not Marduk. The Lord had sent him another vision (blessed be the Lord!). Once again the Lord had shown him that personal experience far surpassed the testimony of any ancient text. He'd suffered terribly and still triumphed (with the help of the Lord). The Lord had struck down his enemies, first Albert and now Marduk. Blessed be the Lord.

What had the wicked *sramana* said before he died?

Miriam's son? *Rudra's son?*

Albert said Jacob came from the Ra'bim. Like that tribe he was short and prone to fat. Like Albert himself. He was twelve, maybe thirteen when he first saw the Grand Duke. Tall, dressed in a golden Yadish uniform, the Grand Duke ascended Upper Nalanda like the Lord on his Holy Mountain.

Jacob was still a child when he first gazed upon the golden colossus. His father? How could it be true? He had imagined in his child's mind that the Lord must look like this—like Rudra, stern, magnificent, a judge and protector who tolerated neither weakness, nor idleness, nor error.

In later years Rudra actually favored Jacob when he visited Nalanda, and poor, confused Jacob never knew why, why Rudra even noticed him. Jacob became like an obedient son. He revealed to his new father the secrets of Nalanda. He happily carried out the small tasks Rudra assigned him.

The Lord on High had called Rudra, had chosen Rudra to do His holy bidding. So, too, Jacob, Rudra's son. Could it be? He wanted it to be, therefore it was.

He turned and started back up the hill. He noticed Marduk's walking stick buried in the mud. Let it rot, he thought. Is it not the staff of evil? As he climbed, he saw that small rivers from the morning's rain still ran downhill carving out furrows in the dry ground. It seldom rained hard and long in this place. Another sign.

A glint of reflected light halted his progress. Here the rushing water seemed to dig deeper into the ground. The momentary flash of light had come from the bottom of an excavated miniature gorge.

He bent down to examine the source. At first he thought that it was a tiny broken piece of stone, perhaps white marble from the citadel. Then he saw that it was a tooth, a molar. He reached down and picked it up. There could be no doubt. It was human. And not very old.

(Thus came to pass the discovery of the holy relic.)

Jacob instantly knew that the tooth was a holy relic. The thought just popped into his head, and because of its spontaneous creation, which was surely not an effect of his frail brain—humble as he was,

Exalted Father

Jacob knew his own inventions (he could not call them creations, only the Lord created)—the relic had to come from the Lord. No man revealed it to Jacob.

The task remained to invent a saintly legend to go with it. Surely the Lord would grant him another vision. He trusted in the Lord.

Surely Jacob would become archbishop.

THE BOOKS OF MARDUK

BOOK OF PLAGUES
VERSE 3.4.7

That night, although thoroughly drunk, Jacob slept fitfully. Deeper theological thinking had deserted him and had gone west to haunt Nalanda. Sacred or not, legends of relics avoided his befuddled mind and also went their own mysterious way. He clutched the holy relic to his breast but it did him no good. A gallon of wine was not enough. Dreams would not come. Thoughts shattered into fragments as quickly as they arose. The fragments heated further and became steam, ascending like smoke from Stonehill.

Near morning as he tossed and turned in despair, a man entered the mansion. Jacob feared that it was yet another nightmare hallucination of Father Albert come to fondle him in the night—and worse. The form did indeed seem to be that of the long-dead priest, short, fat, grimacing—Jacob saw the smirk but not the face. The man's odor was stale, approaching putrid. Darkness concealed the man, or perhaps the dark was Jacob's own mind struggling to forget.

He wanted to spring off the divan and run, but his muscles failed to obey his will, and he lay there paralyzed and helpless, as in the past when the helpless child yielded to the superior power of the depraved adult.

And the man seized him, dragged him off the divan and wrestled him to the floor. He pinned his arms to his sides. Jacob tried to scream but could only manage a whimper. The smell of unwashed flesh was smothering.

And the man said to Jacob: *"Tell me your name!"*

Jacob said: "I am Jacob, son of Grand Duke Rudra, to whom the One Lord has revealed His Divine Self, He did."

The man grabbed his right wrist and yanked it up. *"What is this thing you clasp so lovingly to your breast?"*

Jacob told the truth. "It is a simple tooth. What's left of a false ascetic named Marduk turned devil."

"Ah," the man chuckled. *"Yet you dream of more."*

"I do," Jacob admitted. The man could not be Albert though he resembled him. Jacob never found it difficult to lie to Albert, although he often paid for his untruths with beatings, and worse. Something about this man compelled him to tell the truth.

"I dream of a holy relic that will make me archbishop. But I do not know the sacred legend attached to the relic."

And the man said to Jacob: *"I will tell this legend. Once there was a woman, beautiful and strong, dark as the alluvial soil that covers the river valley with the spring rains. She gave birth to a healthy boy who was the son of his father, alas, a rather common and dull man she'd married in the thoughtless passion of her youth.*

"The boy grew up moody and prone to violent outbursts. The fire of resentment burned in him and fatally hindered his every endeavor. You see, he sensed his mother's disappointment with him and her disdain for his true father. She longed for a king and instead gave birth to a clod of mud.

"And so she became an obnoxious old woman, loud, demanding, spiteful in the smallest of things.

"Somehow she acquired the art of potion making. It is whispered that a wandering sramana taught it to her. She became more adept than the greatest Ra'bim physicians. The years passed and she labored tirelessly. For you see, she sought a fertility potion by which she'd conceive another son, one who'd become a powerful Lord."

Jacob had relaxed and was listening intently. The man was no hallucination, no dream. He was too solid, too strong, too *present*. Illusions are odorless. This one smelled of the desert. The Lord had come to Rudra unexpected, and now to his only son. How fortunate Jacob, man of the fortune of the Lord.

The man said: *"And it came to pass that she became pregnant even at her great age. She conceived and gave birth to a healthy son, a princely child, a king. She laughed, saying: 'With the help of the Lord I gave birth to a real man.'*

"But who was the father? She would only say, *'with the help of the Lord.'*

"Many of her Tribe considered this blasphemy, for it seemed to them she was really saying that the One Lord, the Almighty, Lord of the Mountain, had come and pumped His holy seed into her aged flesh like any rutting swine. Therefore the old Prince of the Tribe ordered her and her bastard son exiled into the Yakashas Steppe. It is said they came to this very place where Yakashas devils attacked them and slew them. But the Yakashas devils were in fact assassins sent by the old man.

"Some of her Tribe whispered that her son was really the child of the old Prince himself. These slanderers the old Prince tortured and killed in the most gruesome manner. Others said the boy truly was the son of the Lord. And, they added, the Lord became so angry at mortal men for murdering His Only Son, that He cursed the Tribe with barrenness. And ultimately all the Tribes of men.

"Behold, man of the indoors, the Son's bones sleep in this very ground. Behold, priest, your relic.

"The dawn is breaking and I must depart this place. Now you have your legend. You must decide its conclusion."

Suddenly the man was standing in the archway leading to the portico, a vague shadow in the darkness. A dim light began to distinguish forms and shapes. The man wavered as do all shadows in the morning.

Jacob cried out: "Wait! Was he the Son of the Almighty? What was his name?"

At that moment Greater Wind began its hour-long visit. Its growing rumble drowned out the man's words. Yet Jacob thought he perceived a weak voice in the Wind. The Wind said:

Marduk.

THE BOOK OF PLAGUES

CHAPTER FIVE – Lower Nalanda

VERSE 3.5.1

Agni sat alone at the end of a long table. Unlike the gang of priests in the center of the spacious dining hall, drinking Banalis brandy and laughing with the two Ra'bim women, he sipped pure spring water from a pewter cup. He wasn't laughing, nor was he frowning. It was cold and he wore his blue military field jacket. The jacket's material was summer weave, of Min-vena make.

He shivered. The *kittim* wound tingled. It appeared to be spreading. This morning he discovered that it covered his entire left arm and had spread to his breast and rib cage. He knew that soon he'd suffer the death-dealing fever as had the Khan. His time was short and now he contemplated the course of his life, and though he knew how useless the exercise was, like grinding rotten grain, he indulged in self-pity and took pleasure from it.

He poured another cup of water and slowly brought his thoughts back to the present. Had *kittim* hallucinations begun? Was Nalanda a dream, its priesthood unreal? Were there really farvels in the world?

Laughter drifted across the room. Someone—half-blind Father Peter—had fallen off his chair. They were all half-blind of course, half-blind, old and overweight. Yet they all behaved like adolescent

THE BOOKS OF MARDUK

boys. They neglected their chores; they drank and ate—frantically—as though every meal was their last. Not a moment did they spare for any other occupation, not even to breathe, it seemed, and not a few dropped dead due to forgetfulness. Father Peter was the latest casualty.

Agni neither laughed nor frowned. For how many years had the Akkadeans, and many other Tribes, clamored for the annihilation of Nalanda? Here, right before his eyes, the long-desired event was coming to pass. Unexpectedly, the army of annihilation consisted of two rather simple Ra'bim women, Tera and Kera. He recalled their names well enough but was still unable to distinguish in the flesh between them.

Simple was too simple a word for their simplicity. Tera and Kera were profoundly empty. Agni grinned which was all he could manage. Or was it a grimace?[15] He actually felt more pity for the old foolish priests.

Tera and Kera called themselves *Washers of Souls*. They were devotees of a strange being they named *She-Who-Is*. This superior person had departed Nalanda a week before Agni had arrived. Agni pictured her as a common Ra'bim woman inflated by the worship of her foolish followers into a colossus of stunning beauty and magical powers. She would climb Elsseleron, Kera and Tera announced. She would test the Lord and He would deem her worthy. Worthy of what, they failed to mention. Or was it to tempt the Lord? Agni wasn't sure.

Tera and Kera proceeded to wash the souls of Nalanda—those that needed washing, which included almost the entire priesthood,

---

[15] Queeti poet-historians debated the authenticity of this passage: How can one possibly know that a mythical person has regrets or, more ridiculous yet, contemplates a fictional life? Modern scholars doubt the authenticity of this chapter, if not the entire content of Book III, which, they say, could not have come from the hand of Marduk.

Exalted Father

except for a few who were not up to the rigors of washing. The archbishop belonged to the latter category. He preferred to remain unclean. Those who believed that they were up for it, at the moment of reckoning, when the actual washing commenced, discovered that they were quite mistaken.

In fact, one might say that while all were called, many were found unworthy. There had been deaths. Alas, no births.

So, as poor Peter remained sprawled on the floor in the holy state of not-conscious, Kera (or was it Tera?) climbed onto the table and gave a sermon.

She seemed to be wearing a wig. Ra'bim females, like their male counterparts, were hairless. Kera sprouted a mantle of golden hair that for some strange reason made Agni think of his *farvel* hallucinations. She wore a tight-fitting gown manufactured from a shiny, light green material, with bellowing sleeves and embroidered Runes of gold, perhaps of Din-make, although the Din Tribe had not been heard from for a century. Most likely it came from the fabled treasure of Lower Nalanda, which Agni had yet to see.

Surprisingly, Kera appeared quite young. Her skin was not the cadaverous white of the Ra'bim. Her eyes were not yellow but brown and clear, her face round and youthful, her breasts large and firm. She had even gained in stature. Tera appeared even younger than Kera, or Kera than Tera, or both, or neither. The *kittim* hallucinations must have begun.

Kera spoke with a slight whine in her voice: "This is the Kalpa of cold. Lordpool is cold. The *Runehayana* is cold. Words are cold. Therefore we must take flight from this Kalpa to another. When things were warm, hot even. Like my teacher, *With-Us-She*."

With-Us-She. Now this was a new wrinkle, Agni thought.

"Tell us 'bout this teacher," a priest called out in the same voice he'd just used to call out for another cup of Banalis brandy.

Kera (or Tera) smiled. Agni noted that her teeth were white and perfect.

"Well now, the Lord was her father."

"How's that?"

"The One Lord, stupid. Do you think He does nothing all day but sit on His mountain?"

"What'd you saying?"

Another priest, bald and as round as a Banalis barrel, slapped his fellow inductee-into-the-mysteries-of-Kera on the back. "She's saying the Almighty came down and—*impregnated* a mortal woman."

"No—"

"Yup," Kera answered. "But not in a factual sense."

The barrel-like priest—Agni recognized him as Father Marcus—sounded mystified: "In what sense then does a woman get fucked?"

Another priest added: "Does the Lord have a pecker but not a factual one?"

The conclave of priests roared with laughter.

Brandy slurred the voice of the last speaker. Agni nonetheless knew that voice. How could he not? So smooth and poisonous, a snake sliding through the grass, it sounded like the old nasal insinuating tone—of Talib the Jester! Why hadn't Agni noticed him? He'd seen the black robe and looked no further. There sat Talib, bulging eyes and foolish grin.

Agni did not grimace, nor did he frown. Then neither did he smile.

Tera raised her arms, stretching the fine fabric. Not a few priests began to drool.

"Symbolically," she intoned, addressing the ancient rafters above. A family of finches that nested in the ceiling beams for the winter cocked their heads as if like the priests they too awaited further explanation.

"Symbolically," she repeated.

"Symbolically—fucked?" Talib gasped in mock surprise.

"Like—don't succumb to mere factuality," Tera answered him. "The obsession with factuality is a product of the Kalpa of Cold."

Exalted Father

Talib snickered. Agni guessed that inside he was seething. So many job applicants for the esteemed position of Court Jester in Nalanda must have had him worried sick.

"Our teacher came to the Ra'bim. And nobody 'cept me and Tera (this was Kera then) recognized her."

Kera blessed them with a self-satisfied smile.

"Cause we're like—genius—es. Everybody else's stupid. So we're here to tell you that all the books of the *Runehayana* are myths, also parabolas. Don't get hung up on factuality. That's why the Lord is silent."

"I like, like it," said Father Marcus.

Talib snorted.

"Well, He ain't silent no more. Nope. He gave to us our *She-With-Us*. She will take us back to the beginning of things, in the times of the Kingdoms of the Heavens. If we commit ourselves to her, truly, that's where we'll all go."

"Take me," Father Marcus pleaded. He drank a full cup of brandy without taking a breath.

"And me, and me—" sang the priestly choir.

Talib sighed. "Is this commitment also symbolic? Like fucking?"

Kera hesitated. The self-satisfied look faded. The look of superior beneficence faded as well. She no longer blessed them with such gazes. Many had hoped she'd bless them *factually*. But now it seemed there'd be no fact-blessing today. That damned Akkadean jester. Someone needed to bless him with a knife in the ribs—factually.

Kera said: "*We* decide what's a symbol and what's not. Me and Tera. Cause we're—*Washers of Souls*. On the banks of the Pearldew *she* called us—"

"I take it that the phrase *Washer of Souls* is symbolic?" Talib asked. Agni clearly heard the change of tone. He was enjoying himself again.

"Yup."

312

"Meaning?"

"It is a deep mystery that is far beyond the thoughts and language of men."

"Words are symbols, not so?"

"Why don't you shut up," said Father Marcus.

"There you go getting hung up on factuality," Tera added.

"Sorry. So you and Kera grasp this mystery, as you call it, that's beyond words?"

Kera answered: "Yup. That's why we're *Washers of Souls*. We'll wash factuality from your soul and you'll see everything clearly."

"How do I get to be a washer of souls?"

"By commitment—to us. Allow me to add that in your case there's a lot of committing to do."

"I'm committed, I'm committed," sang the choir. "You'll shut yourself up, Akkadean, if you know what's best for you. I'm committed, I'm committed—"

"Believe it!" said Kera in triumph.

"To believe it is to be-love—us," added Tera.

"Oh Kera! Oh Tera! We truly be-*love* you. Oh, we do—"

"And your beloved will be rewarded."

"Oh wash us—"

"Factually," Talib added.

The massive cedar door banged open. The archbishop dressed in his formal robes of red velvet, golden braid, golden embroidered Runes up and down the front panels, and golden frilled hems stood in the entrance. No one would have thought him powerful enough to open the doors. The robe hung on him as though it were draped over a scarecrow constructed of sticks and branches.

Lesser Wind blew in a few small *kittim*. No one, thank the Lord, was attacked. This had to be a sign from the Almighty.

"How busy you are," said the archbishop. "What profound discussions here. I certainly understand why there's no time for chores."

Exalted Father

"But Lesser Wind," Father Marcus protested.

"Oh have no fear. Didn't you know that bugeaves are blind—because they have no eyes." Theophilus laughed. "They can't see you, like sleeping Peter down there."

"He's dead—we believe—"

The archbishop grimaced. "No."

He raised his eyes to Kera. "Why not prove your teachings by a miracle, my girl. Wake 'em up."

"Miracles are symbolic."

"Too bad for poor Peter. Unfortunately monastery chores are only too real. There's some that really need to be done before nightfall. You know, chop wood, carry water, light the fires, clean the dinning-hall, wash the dishes—"

They hoisted Peter up and exited the commons into Lesser Wind. The moment they touched him he awoke and began to breathe. Then with a loud belch, he was back asleep. "Behold," someone whispered, "a factual miracle."

It is said that many died that night from *kittim* poisoning, including the recently resurrected Peter. The jester Talib was another. Some say that when the *kittim* took him he was already dead. Someone had lodged a factual knife in his ribs.

BOOK OF PLAGUES
VERSE 3.5.2

The archbishop sat down on a bench across from Agni.

"Brandy's over there," Agni said indicating the bottles scattered about the other tables.

"Haven't been drinking lately," Theophilus remarked casually. He tugged at his white beard. Not much of it remained to tug. His cheeks were hollow, his face more skull-like than ever, yet his sunken eyes glittered like tiny stars.

"Water then?" Agni poured him a cup from the pitcher. "I don't see any cooks about and the kitchen's cold. There's some hard bread and stale cheese over there—" Agni pointed again to the far tables.

"Two more cooks died yesterday," said the archbishop, watching Agni with a furrowed brow. "*Kittim* got 'em. This fall must be the deadliest of the Third Kalpa." He gave an exaggerated sigh. "At this rate you Akkadeans will see your dreams come true. By spring the priesthood will be nothing but memory, frail memory at that."

Agni shook his head. "Add the Yisskur and Banalis Tribes. We came here by the West Road. The Yisskur coastal towns are disserted. No fishing boats ply the Middle Sea. Sails, nets, tackle, boats under repair, boats under construction, all of it scattered about as though the people just decided one day to quit and leave, and dropped at the moment whatever they happened to be doing. No signs of battle, no bodies, not even a stray tarp hound. Gone, vanished. The White Cliffs—the lookout stations, lighthouses, all empty of life. Banalis too. Vineyards were overgrown with weeds, arbors rancid, vats dry, storehouses empty, breweries and distilleries cold. Good thing you've given up strong drink, archbishop. None will be arriving any time soon, I think."

"Even the dead disappear," the archbishop said heavily.

Exalted Father

"The living and the dead. Nothing—"

Agni hesitated. Should he tell Theophilus about the hordes of farvels? He'd seen them everywhere. They were on the White Cliffs at sundown. They popped up at dawn in the tall mustard grass of Banalis. He saw them in the late afternoon among the terebinths, red palms, and the sandstone mesas of the eastern Banalis plain. Farvels, thousands upon thousands of them, like the stars of the heavens. In the uncertain light of dawn, the late fall mists of dusk, they haunted him, always watching—the Silent Watchers—coats of shifting colors, knowing grins on cat-like faces, yet human eyes, round and intelligent.

He guessed it was due to the *kittim* poisoning. Maybe everything was illusion produced by *kittim* poisoning. Maybe he was dead already. He smiled. *Kittim* had washed his soul— He felt the tingling, deeper now, like a slow burning. He felt his lungs expand and contract, the inrush of air, the exhale, the surge of warm blood with every heart-beat, the cool water tasting faintly of old pewter. All symbols, dear Kera—

Theophilus was watching him carefully. "You've become awfully, well, I'd say dreamy these days. Not the hot tempered Agni I've heard so much about."

"What do you really want, archbishop?"

"You know the priest named Jacob, do you not? We call him ox."

"I know him. Whines and complains. He's an ox as you say, but he's stuffed with black bile—more an adder than an ox—like a Yad."

"Well yes. He's returned from the Yakashas Steppe with some tragic news." The archbishop drew a breath and his face looked unusually sad, the wry grin he usually wore erased. "You know the *sramana* Marduk?"

Agni blinked. "We met him on the road from Ai. I didn't recognize him until after he'd gone. Strange isn't it? He was heading south, I believe. I knew him from Akkad. He's changed. Poisoned by *kittim*. Completely mad, thinks he's Suthralane."

Jacob says that the *kittim* finally finished the job. Nothing left of him but a tooth, which the ox has in his possession. He refers to it as a relic."

"A relic?"

"A physical symbol. Oh yes, don't look so surprised. I've listened to those silly girls' teachings. Anything can be declared a symbol when it suits their purposes. So if symbols are as true as facts, then a fact that contradicts their stupid little stories is nothing but a symbol and can be dismissed. Pretty convenient, hey?"

Agni's face brightened slightly. "Maybe we're all nothing but symbols."

The archbishop grinned. "Pretty good, my boy. Maybe you should be the next archbishop. By the way, I think you know their *teacher*."

"I'm afraid I've never had the pleasure of meeting one of the Lord's holy bastards, male or female."

"Oh no. She's daughter of another lord, your Khan I think."

Agni leaped up, knocking over his bench. His hand went to the hilt of his scimitar.

Theophilus grinned. "Symbols are quick to anger. Not so?"

Agni stared at him. His *kittim* wound burned and he felt dizzy. Slowly, he set the bench on its legs and sat down.

"Devorah... She married Vishnu of the Ra'bim last spring..."

"That she did, my boy. But she's changed. I don't think you'd recognize her. She got away from old Vishnu and came here in the summer. Became a regular *priestess*. And don't ask me to explain her teachings. Now she's headed south, to the Lord's mountain I'd bet."

Agni put his head in his hands. "We were looking for her...until the *kittim*... How'd she get away from Vishnu?"

"Marduk," said Theophilus, the sadness returning to his voice.

Exalted Father

"A skinny unarmed *sramana* entered Tholos alone and took her from the Triumvir?"

"Well not exactly, according to Jacob."

Agni looked up. His eyes were puffy, red on the edges.

The archbishop's voice returned to its old teasing tone. "The Lord's suddenly become quite busy these days, or should I say, familiar."

"Familiar?"

"Well yes. He no longer speaks through His Runes that spontaneously appeared on the surface of Lordspool as in past Kalpas. These days he shows up *factually*. He's no vague symbol, no sir, no concept like the sacred energy of the universe or some such foolishness—no creative force, destructive force, mystery, sense of awe, or whatever empty phrases happen to appeal to people who never broke a sweat. Nope. Rudra meets a big white bear. Kera and Tera see Him on the banks of the Pearldew in the guise of a big white woman—your Devorah who saw Him in the guise of a confused *sramana*. And now there's Jacob."

"My Devorah," Agni sighed.

Theophilus watched him with curiosity. The Akkadean Orlok was easier to read than the simplest string of Runes.

"Jacob's got a relic."

Agni shook himself and drained the last of the water.

"A tooth? Marduk's tooth?"

"The Lord's tooth."

"I'm confused," said Agni putting his cup down.

"Well, Jacob's the new revelation of the Lord. The tooth verifies it. You see, according to Jacob, the Lord came down from His Mountain for a stroll one fine day, and found Himself in Akkad. Jacob naturally knows all the details. Conveniently, the Lord discovered a comely Akkadean woman who'd already given birth to one son but wasn't happy with the poor kid and wanted another, a more, uh, lordly son. So, the Lord, the essence of lordliness, obliged her, and out popped Marduk. The Lord rather boorishly returned to His Mountain, and the Khan got the blame. So, he exiled her and her whelp to the steppe. She gave the kid to the priesthood and you Akkadeans finally caught the little princely bastard and murdered him, although Jacob's none too careful with his chronology— All this happened some time ago."

"Time must be symbolic too," said Agni dryly.

The archbishop chuckled. "Who says Akkadeans don't have a sense of humor."

"I can tell you truly that no Akkadean killed Marduk!" Agni's voice rose. His wound burned. "None that I know."

"The Akkadeans hired a gang of Yakashas to do their dirty work."

"This just gets better—"

"Well my boy, the best part is that the Lord got very angry at what happened to his holy bastard and He's been blasting the Tribes with plagues ever since."

Agni laughed. "This story apparently confuses effect with cause. We are the effect of the curse, not its cause. And by the by, the Lord appeared to Rudra?"

"Don't know how Jacob works that in, if he can. But He's appeared to Jacob. The tooth's the proof. And Jacob says the Lord wants us all to follow Jacob to Starmirror. Jacob doesn't know why. It is a mystery."

"Marduk was the Son of the Lord on High?"

"Guess so."

"And part Akkadean?"

"Do you recall any stories of miraculous births from, say, your generation?"

Agni hesitated. The archbishop watched him carefully.

"No..." He sounded uncertain.

"Well now, there's a rule in the *Runehayana* declared by the Lord Himself at the founding of Nalanda. Only the archbishop knows from what Tribes the priests come. The archbishop is *never* to divulge this information. I'll not break this rule. We'll come at this from another angle. Let me ask you this: Did the Khan sell his only daughter to Vishnu?"

"Yes—" Agni's answer was barely audible.

"Well then—" The archbishop leaned back and brushed his robes. "And what might he have done with a bastard son?"

Agni sprang to his feet. His *kittim* tattoo was burning through skin and muscle into his very bones. His mind burned as fiercely as his arm and ribs. Mechanically his hand went to his scimitar. At this moment the old Agni was reborn.

"Assuming the Almighty does not go about impregnating mortal women," added Theophilus.

"All priests are bastards!" Agni said hotly. "Everything a priest believes is false."

He stomped out of the commons—and into a shower of *kittim*. The old Agni tried to slash at them with his blade, but the pain in his arm caused him to drop the weapon as quickly as he swung it.

Kittim flew at him like moths to a flame.

By the time the archbishop made his creaking way to the door Agni had disappeared into the night.

It is said, however, that he was not consumed. For the Lord had other tasks requiring his fire.

THE BOOKS OF MARDUK

BOOK OF PLAGUES
VERSE 3.5.3

Just as Greater Wind died and Dewdrop Moon set behind the northern hills, a man appeared on the northern crest of King Reuben's Road as it led down to Nalanda. He wore the desert brown battle fatigues of the Yadish Tribe and a simple breastplate of smooth silver. A helmet covered his head. It sprouted silver horns above each eye. His beard was dyed red and his face painted in swirls of black and red. In one hand he held a Yadish long-sword of ancient ancestry, and in the other a staff bearing the pennant of the Unified Kingdom, which was twelve golden runes arranged in a circle against a background of green. It was the pennant of King Joseph I.

Frightened priests summoned the archbishop. But Theophilus was already aware of the Yadish army approaching Nalanda's northern gate. He'd seen them from his tower. A man and woman dressed in what seemed to be silvery armor, not the usual chainmail but real old style plate armor, led them. Behind the two armored figures marched a motley assortment of Yadish nobles in various war costumes, mostly gold-dyed leather, a few wearing chainmail, and many wearing outlandish helms, mostly horned, many with single spikes on top. A hangdog gang of peasants reluctantly followed. Three of the nobles bore L-guns, as did the armored woman. The army probably numbered a hundred warriors, maybe more on account of the shadowy gang of peasants, reluctant reinforcements, fearful, no doubt, of priestly magic and the wrath of the Lord.

The northern gate was merely a name (*in these days*) of the Third Kalpa. The physical structure had rotted away a thousand years ago, although its image haunted Tribal memories. The gate marked the place where King Reuben's Road entered the large rectangle of barracks and libraries, and then shot straight as a L-gun's bolt to the Cathedral where it terminated.

Knees grinding, Theophilus descended from his tower and limped to the northern gate.

"Well now," he observed, "here at last is an example of a manifest symbol. I welcome you to our symbolic northern gate." He grinned at the towering stranger in Yadish gear.

"I speak for the Lord Regent," said the horned warrior.

His voice sounded like sand scrapping glass. Despite his magnificent sword, the banner, the army at his back, he sounded bored as though he wished he were someplace else doing something else—say, in bed sleeping.

"Does the Lord Regent's mouth have a name?" inquired the archbishop.

"I am the Marquis Baldwin—of the Yadish Tribe. I speak for the Lord Regent of the new King of Greenbottom and the Tribes of Men. Should someday the true King appear."

Jacob appeared instead. The ox rushed to the side of the archbishop. He also appeared out of breath.

Theophilus peered at him. "I don't recall, uh, calling for *sramana* Jacob."

Jacob stood up straight and looked terribly indignant. "I'm no *sramana*. I'm the new revelation of the Lord—which was revealed recently. I'm the mouth of the Lord Almighty and Keeper of the Holy Relic—"

Theophilus pretended to be startled. "Well, what a day we have here. The Lord, silent for so long, suddenly blesses us with *two* mouths."

"Impostor," growled the Marquis Baldwin, trying to locate Jacob. He seemed to be having trouble focusing on more than one priest at a time. "There are many false mouths and only one true one, as many false Lords, and many false heirs, and many—"

He stopped speaking and starting grumbling, looking from side to side as though he'd forgotten something.

Then he seemed to recover and said: "I bear a message from the Lord of the Yadish Hosts."

Theophilus wondered if he'd purposefully dropped the qualifier *regent* from his Lord or simply forgotten it. The day had become too entertaining for the archbishop to care.

"No! *I* bear a message from the Lord!" Jacob cried. "And I possess the Holy Relic to prove it, which the Lord gave to my possession—"

He drew a brownish object from the inside pocket of his priestly robe.

The archbishop stared at his open palm. "Looks like an animal tooth. A mosscat fang perhaps? Maybe the tooth of a farvel?"

"Old fool!" Jacob screamed. "It is the Holy Relic of the Lord's Son. Betrayed and murdered by the evil Akkadeans."

"Thought it was evil Yakashas—"

"So that's what really happened to him," Baldwin said. Now he was taking a great interest in the proceedings. "Damned Vishnu lied all along. I should be King."

"What's this 'bout Vishnu?" the archbishop asked. "Did he finally sire a child?"

The ox suddenly seemed to go berserk. "Blasphemer!" he shouted. "False blaspheming priest!"

With his free hand, the ox drew a finely made Yadish dagger.

"In the name of the Lord's Son!" he shouted.

He plunged the blade into the archbishop's left side just under his armpit where the seam of the ancient robe had separated. Theophilus would have never thought him capable of such an act, not that he lacked the physical strength but that he was deficient of will, of courage, of taking such a risk, of committing a crime.

The archbishop collapsed with a long sigh as though in some strange way he welcomed the thrust.

EXALTED FATHER

Jacob wrenched the blade free. A gush of blood and body fluids splashed his hand and his forearm.

He turned to face Baldwin.

"I'm archbishop!" he bellowed. "You will bow to me."

The Marquis had already started back down the road, longsword in one hand, flag of the Unified Kingdom in the other. At this moment he was far from bored. The scheming Grand Duchess knew all along that her one and only son had been slain years ago by Akkadeans. To be precise, Akkadean assassins.

The new archbishop decided that he did not like being ignored. Such was a grave insult to his dignity. The Lord would surely punish the offender, severely. He bent down and cleaned his blade with the former archbishop's robe. Too late did he reconsider that he might want those robes, as he was now the new archbishop according to his deeper theological thinking. Not an auspicious beginning, he thought, deeply. He experienced a deep resentment and anger at the former archbishop for dying so quickly, and for making such a mess of his robes.

Things being what they were, he was still the New Revelation of the Lord which certainly abrogated trivialities such as selection by the senior priests in secret conclave. Marduk was the Son of the Lord to be sure. But he was dead. The new archbishop was the Lord's spiritual son, so-to-speak, or better (he marveled at how easily he could spin theological subtleties in the middle of—impending—battle) *the manifestation of the Lord's will in the world*. He felt much better. Not he, Jacob the innocent, but the Lord had slain the old drunken (be sure to add that) archbishop for some divine reason which would probably remain a mystery until the end of the world.

Sheathing his dagger, he turned and started for Upper Nalanda. Then he realized that he far surpassed the old revelation in the defunct *Runehayana* (well, it had served a purpose, it had produced *him*). He was worthy of the Lord's Holy Mountain. Thus he decided to leave Nalanda to its fate.

The Books Of Marduk

Jacob turned and *ran* all the way across Lower Nalanda, and exited the monastery through the fictitious southern gate.

He decided that he would go to Elsseleron and speak with his true Father—truly.

EXALTED FATHER

BOOK OF PLAGUES
VERSE 3.5.4

Vishnu saw Baldwin coming. Drawing his own long-sword from the scabbard on his back, he waved it in the air and cried out: "Destroy Nalanda. Kill them all. Every priest and monk. The new Unified Kingdom has no need for such as these, for priests. It is written that the sorcerer should not be allowed to live."

The woman at his side also cried out in a fierce voice: "Kill them all. Burn everything. Burn every scrap of the Books." She waved her L-gun. Polished gray steel with a redwood stock, the weapon looked new, as though it came directly from a Nepptali machine shop.

Baldwin threw the banner in the dirt and stomped on it. Then, swinging his long-sword in a wide arc, he threw himself upon Vishnu.

Vishnu, the oldest living human being in all Greenbottom, moved as fast as thought. He stepped aside and swung his own long-sword. Sparks flew and Baldwin's blade snapped in half.

The Marquis staggered back and Vishnu followed, again with blinding speed. He slammed a white steel-clad fist into Baldwin's large midsection and then brought the pummel of his sword down upon his head. The horns snapped and the helm broke in half.

The Marquis went to his knees. Blood streamed down into his face and dyed his beard, painting it a deeper red. Peering out through a red mist he saw the woman. It was the Grand Duchess and she wore the armor of King Reuben the Conqueror, which was too tight in the wrong places and too loose in the important regions.

"Your son…is dead," he croaked.

"And thou shalt join him." She raised the barrel of the L-gun and pressed small button with her thumb. A blue bolt of lightning shot from the barrel and took him in the chest with a hundred times more force than Vishnu's fist. Flame erupted as the thin silver armor burned. The bolt knocked him backwards, passing clean through his torso. Beneath him the soil burned black.

Vishnu's armor came from King Joseph I and it fit him perfectly. This was odd since poet-histories said that the first Yadish King was a giant, at least seven feet tall.

The Viscount Donatien stepped forward.

He wore a suit of black plate armor he'd found in one of the lower levels of Green House. Much of the old metal, an alloy no one could identify, was rusted thin. Not a few pieces—especially the arm and leg panels—had fallen away. He'd immediately recognized the suit, he announced. It had belonged to the founder of his clan the Viscount Dominic. The black helm, sprouting bird-like wings where the ears ought to have been, bore a large dent on its crown. Dominic had taken an Akkadean blow meant for King Joseph I during the Great War of Unity. There on the spot Joseph had promised him the kingly title should the line of Josephites fail. At least this what Donatien had found in the hidden archives deep in the vaults of Green House—so he proclaimed.

He approached Vishnu warily. He was careful not to look upon Baldwin's smoking carcass.

"If it is true that there is no heir, then the title passes to me," he said as he approached. Out of the corner of his eye he saw Miriam swing her L-gun around and point it in his direction.

Vishnu removed his silver helmet. Long black hair spilled out and down to his shoulders. His skin was dark and healthy, his eyes no longer yellow but black with a tinge of red, as the Books described the bark of the whittling tree.

"There is an heir," Vishnu said. "He is with his father."

"His father is—"

The Grand Duchess stepped closer.

"No longer here."

Viscount Vladimir, veteran of the Battle of Misar, moved to Donatien's side. The three middle buttons of Vladimir's old leather fatigue jacket were open in order to accommodate his enormous belly.

He bowed stiffly. "Please forgive Donatien for questioning the obvious, oh glorious Lord Regent."

Donatien hesitated a moment, glanced at Vladimir, and then bowed to Vishnu and the Grand Duchess.

"The obvious," he repeated.

Vishnu smiled, perhaps for the first time in a hundred years.

"You have your orders. Destroy Nalanda. Suffer no priest to live."

The Books Of Marduk

BOOK OF PLAGUES
VERSE 3.5.5

(To this day, no queeti knows the true story of the destruction of Nalanda. To their credit, queeti poet-historians admitted this fact even as they sing songs of woe and dread.)

The poet-historians sing:
"Was it not the tenth day of the tenth month,
when the Lord of Hosts destroyed wicked Nalanda?
The Lord Who Is King,
The Woman Who Is Queen.
The army of the Lord, like a plague of locusts.

Priests tried to flee.
The Lord's hosts slaughtered them in the streets.
In their long houses,
In their Temple.
As tawny red lions of the steppe,
Famished, tear the flesh of lambs.
So the Hosts of the Lord.
So the evil priests, like lambs in the Temple.

One man fought them,
A warrior, not a priest.
An Akkadean.
Butterflies came,
And took him up into the air.
Was this not a fortunate thing?
A sign of the Lord's favor?

EXALTED FATHER

And the raging sea covered Nalanda,
By roaring waves was she destroyed.
And the sky red,
As the daystar turned its face, horrified.
That day the Winds came not.

Whores they spared,
Harlots, given to the Great Men among them.
Lifting their skirts over their heads,
And their backs flat on the ground.
By them children they sired,
The Great Men.
From such unions monsters came,
Not men, not queeti.
Despised and shunned by queeti and men,
They hid their faces,
Hideous, unspeakable, grotesque.
Like a plague they spread,
An army of scorpions,
Toads, worms, snakes, maggots, all that crawl in the slime,
Things that sting, bring blood, fire, corruption.

The Lord Who Is King,
Entered their Temple, and found there,
Abominations and idols.
A strange thing of glass and silver, gold and copper,
A pond, a pool, a cistern.
And taking an iron hammer he smashed it to bits,
Pieces of green glass, silver shards, bronze and polished steel,
Bands of iron, vines of copper, lamps and lights.
He smashed the statues, monuments, thrones and hanging lamps,
Golden altars and silver plates,

The Books Of Marduk

And carvings, Four Great Evils.
And libraries,
Such a burning He did make,
Of scrolls and books, stacks and pots and decorated jars.
And made an end of debauchery and idol worship.

The Lord of Hosts Who Is King,
Came to the mountain spire,
Of the Chief Priest.
And finding far worse,
Flew into a frenzy,
The work of destruction, like a great washing.
Washer of Souls he is named.
The spire He burned,
And the columns, of which there were ninety-six,
He smashed, causing the mountain to quake.
The Lord of Hosts Who Is King,
Did command the Blue Fire from the Heavens,
Not seen in this world for an Age (it is said).
And with the Blue Lightning made a cleansing,
Upper and Lower.
To make of it a fitting House of the Lord,
And His Queen.

Of this Queen we sing,
A cry from the North, a cry from the South,
A cry from the East, a cry from the West.
She found the Chief Priest of Corruption,
The Man of the Lie.
On King's Road she found him.
Old and drunk, half-mad, blind and lame,
Bloody hands and feet, a wound in his side,
Foolish man, asleep in the dirt.

EXALTED FATHER

And she put out his eyes,
She cut out his tongue,
She sliced away his manhood,
Gutted him like a fallow deer.
And the butterflies came and bore him away,
And where he's buried no man knew,
To this day no queeti knows.

Other poets sing,
Of one they spared.
And one alone.
A brown man,
They deemed him wise and made of him a satrap,
To the King.

So ends the Song of Nalanda's Fall, as the queeti poet-historians have it.

THE BOOKS OF MARDUK

BOOK OF PLAGUES
VERSE 3.5.6

Agni met Vishnu in the middle of the plaza of lower Nalanda. The heated air was thick with smoke, filled with cries and screams and all manner of horrifying sounds, many barely human.

"There is truly an Akkadean in Nalanda," Vishnu said. His eyes glowed red, like sparks from the flames that consumed the buildings around the plaza. "All priests lie, even under torture, so it is written. This day is the exception."

Agni raised his scimitar to the guard position. He took a short step forward, turned slightly and flexed his knees. A mocking grin twisted his mouth. His dark face glistened.

"Bring forth your Grand Duke, Yad, that I may instruct him in the fine art of the Akkadean sword."

"Oh foolish Akkadean, do you not recognize Vishnu the King?"

Agni blinked and his grin changed into a frown. "Indeed this is an exceptional day. Priests suddenly are telling the truth and Yads have become liars. You are no Ra'bim. Are you then the Grand Duke? Is that not his silver armor?"

Now Vishnu put on a mocking grin. "Come, my dear fellow. Am I old Rudra who is stooped and bald, sparse strands of hair in silly braids, old and big of belly?"

Agni looked doubtful. "It is as you say. Rudra is old and gone to fat, so I've heard. You seem young to me with your black hair and smooth face. You cannot be Vishnu, you cannot be Rudra. Are you Rudra's son?"

"Come, my powerful Akkadean warrior, and gaze upon the genius of Ra'bim herbmasters. White Soma and the bark of whittling—no wonder the Almighty forbade men the fruit of that tree. I would become the Almighty's equal. Behold, Vishnu reborn."

Agni sprang forward, swinging his blade in the underhand disemboweling stroke. The man, if it was a man, swung his long-sword down and out, easily deflecting the smaller scimitar. Agni spun around, flowing with the momentum of Vishnu's move, and danced past. He quickly squared himself and faced his opponent.

"Not Vishnu reborn, counterfeit Vishnu about to die."

He came in cautiously this time, marking the unprotected spots where the heavy armor left space for flexibility.

The giant leaped at him and struck an overhand blow meant to cleave Agni's skull.

Agni was just able to block the strike with his scimitar, but his blade snapped like a dead branch and his foe's sword cut through the Min-vena cloth into his bicep, slicing into his *kittim* stained flesh almost to the bone. The long-sword seemed to follow the stain down his rib cage, cutting through leather panels and flesh.

Agni gasped and staggered back. He did not cry out. He held his left arm against his side, as blood gushed out of the wound. Blood filled his mouth, gasping for air caused a painful gurgle that seemed to rise in his throat. Dropping his ruined blade, he went down to his knees.

"Oh very good. Kneel before you King."

"Finish it," Agni croaked. He coughed up more blood. Through a haze of blood and fire he saw the giant's eyes blazing red. This was no man but a frightful beast, a merciless predator from the steppe. Perhaps there really were Yakashas.

The monster laughed, a sound resembling lightning striking the ground. "Lesser Wind comes," he observed. The *kittim* will finish for me."

He strode past Agni. But then he turned as though he'd forgotten something.

"Duke Rudra had a spy in Nalanda. A Yad, I believe. Where is he? I must reward him. He will become the new archbishop."

Agni could not respond. The intense pain was the summary of his life. Only when the *kittim* finally did come and finish the job did he find liberation.

Vishnu shrugged, turned and continued on, following the road to the plaza's southern boundary at the Cathedral. The music of massacre drew him like an irresistible force.

The King discovered no Yadish priest among the dead or the living, and he made up for this disappointment by promoting the living to the dead. Neither on this day nor the days that followed did he promote a new archbishop.

When Nalanda fell.

EXALTED FATHER

BOOK OF PLAGUES
VERSE 3.5.7

The Reed Sea People say that a lone traveler in black robes and bearing a sacred relic crossed the Windward Straits in the winter. But this occurred many, many years past, and the Reed Sea People are no more.

So began the Second Unified Kingdom of which the queeti poet-historians sing. The reign of King Vishnu and Queen Miriam. Together they rebuilt Nalanda and made it into the most glorious city the world had seen. They leveled the ground for hundreds of miles, and filled the gorges and even the valleys. White stone walls fifteen feet high enclosed palaces, noble mansions, towers, glittering merchant piazzas beneath colorful canopies, and vast squares filled with splashing fountains and many statues.

They restored the priesthood. The new priesthood burned the old books of the *Runehayana*, those they could find. They composed a new version, sponsored by the King.

And Vishnu reborn abandoned his search for Devorah of Akkad. He had no need.

Miriam the Queen bore the Vishnu the King many sons. For he was truly the Lord of Hosts.

Then errupted the Great Northern War.

All these events occurred at the end of the first year of the first decade of the ninth Century of the Third Kalpa as reckoned by the Priests of Nalanda and recorded here.

THE BOOKS OF MARDUK

THE BOOK OF CONFESSIONS

EXALTED FATHER

PASSAGES FROM THE RUNEHAYANA

Sariraka (Cleansing) Book IV, Section III. *The Books of Starmirror* (The Wars of the Lord).

The following is a re-calculated, transliteration into Sandi, and translated by the *sramana* Marduk, former priest of Nalanda.

Verses From the Third Chapter:

6. Now the Almighty, He was a Singer of Songs. A musician and composer of music. The life-giving vibrations of the cosmos He sang.

7. Life-long is His Song in our ears. We hear it not, except those that hear.

8. [...] heaven-born Song, heavenly Singer.

Verses From the Fourth Chapter:

1. A Song for Her the Almighty sang.

2. Did She hear another? Some other voice, enticing, sweet, thick as honey in the fall, white as the milk of a banyan nut?

3. Had the Almighty *forgotten* the life-giving Song? That which He sang in the Heavens?

4. Did the Almighty sing a new Song? Of broken [...]? Dismembered harmony?

THE BOOKS OF MARDUK

10. His Song was the Cleansing Song, in the darkness. His Song [...] sound.

11. No meaning, no purpose, no goal, no pattern. Before the [...].

12. How could She hear? How, then, understand? For She was [...][16]

Narayana (The Purifying). Book V, Section II. *The Books of Starmirror).*

Verses From the Fifth Chapter:

17. She says: "I saw you in the afternoon, in the shadows of creeping dusk, among the leaves of the whittling tree. Are you for me?

18. A furry flat face, velvety and deep forest brown, long arms, coarse hands. I have no memory of you.

19. Are you for me? Did I forget?

20. Was this garden for me, or for another?

---

[16] Marduk's calculation of these strings of Runes gives multiple contradictory meanings, none of which make much sense. The entire Chapter is incomprehensible, let the reader understand. Marduk simply listed the possibilities. The List took up three papyrus pages. We will not reproduce it here entirely. A small sample should give the reader a sense (better, nonsense):
"She was: first and the last.
the wife and the virgin.
the mother and the daughter.
a woman of many weddings and no husbands.

The compassionate and the cruel.
The barren woman and mother of thousands."
On and on for three pages. (Note in the hand of the queeti Theophilus).

21. He squeaks and grunts, eyes like jewels, round and bright, flaring nostrils, lipless mouth.

22. She kisses his furry face, running her hands up his hairy legs, and [...].

30. No[t] or [w] Queen of Heaven.

31. *Him* she decides to kill.

THE BOOKS OF MARDUK

THE BOOK OF CONFESSIONS

CHAPTER ONE – From the Life of a Remarkable Woman

(In Her Own Hand)

VERSE 4.1.1

Many have said that I am a woman of striking beauty. Even the Yakashas acknowledge this fact.

So why did *he* turn his face from me? It matters little now.

Surely *he* who gave the gift of sight must himself be a seer. He must have seen us together in that house of infinite hallways. Our love. His sighs and exclamations, devotion and hymns of praise.

Why is it the *Runehayana* never speaks of an afterlife?

Am I a Seer too? At that moment, at the sound of his voice, in the crypt of the Ra'bim—but it faded with his passing, as say, the dull glow that lingers on the western horizon after the setting of the daystar. I felt it, knew it. I could not recapture it. Although I thought it genuine at the time, I have come to realize that my feeling is counterfeit, as say, the foolish Books.

A curse on such weakness. Am I not Akkadean? For such an insult he must die. I do not kill a man, I execute a gender. It is the true reason I went to Starmirror. *I confess it here.*

Exalted Father

Oh, but I digress. Such thoughts come from the distant past, and I have promised myself not to speak of *him*, not to speak of *his great refusal* except insofar as it pertains to the tragic story I tell here. This is difficult. He freed me from the chains of the Ra'bim. Once I tried to explain it to my queeti children. Dear ones, gentle forest souls, real freedom is liberation. Liberation is a breaking of thought-chains, as I did when I escaped the clutches of Vishnu. When you know that you are not serfs, although you remain serfs, you *are not* serfs. Alas, they stared blankly and blinked their forest-eyes.

Just now I made the whole thing up, I confess it. Past time does not vanish as easily as I made myself believe. Why then scratch away on this papyrus? Consign memory to the page. Take it away from behind my eyes, for good. Perhaps I'll be able to sleep.

I have observed men and not-men, and I know that I am special. What is special? I am not made as say anyone else, perhaps as no one else, but naturally I cannot assert such a thing because I can never know everyone. Yet I will assert it despite not-knowing. Did I not survive the Ra'bim somas? Am I not the only Akkadean warrior who is also a woman? I am special, and because I am special I will include all faults in this account, although I can truthfully say that they are not many.

I am beautiful—and humble. The queeti, dear ones, call me *She-With-Us*. *With-Us-Is* for short, they say in their primitive language of barks and grunts. In the end, they named me *whissling*, which I believe means something like *dreamer, or teacher*. The New-Men say it means mother of trees, but they are always mocking when they speak of the queeti, if they speak of them at all.

What I wish to record here in my perfect Sandi is an account of a special person, me, and the multifarious beings that inhabit Starmirror. I will save for later the lamentable tale of my becoming the Queen of the Great Lord Ra', King of the New-Men, White Lord of Starmirror.

THE BOOKS OF MARDUK

I do not speak of *him*. He is past-tense. I came south—I confess it here—to *kill him*. Let the reader judge.

I must confess, too, that my beauty (until recently) is due to my Ra'bim body-suit. It began its existence as a Ra'bim wedding dress. With my liberation it became something else. The Ra'bim poisons, forced upon me by the repulsive Vishnu's repulsive toadies, flowed out of my pores in gallons of repulsive sweat. My sweat soaked into the Min-vena gown, altering the finely spun fabric, transforming it as when the gray lumpy caterpillar transforms into the rainbow butterfly.

The saturated gown clung to my skin. It was an eerie yet not unpleasant feeling. At first I was able to shed the suit as bodily functions demanded. In time, the smooth and weightless material appeared to evaporate, leaving a brilliant white stain, not unlike *kittim* poisoning. The stain *covered my entire body*. I am no longer the brown girl who disappointed her father because she was not a boy. Was he my father?

I drink the light of the daystar. At night I outshine the moons Lotus and Dewdrop. Modesty forces me to conceal my light in the lovely gowns of the Queen of Starmirror, of which I've become very fond. I confess it, without them my life would be quite meaningless—these clothes that make me beautiful even as the years flee.

I've always sought the truth in all things. Such a habit, I must confess, is the source of my misfortunes. Moreover, I've always lived the truth and this habit too does not endear me to any creature, except my dear queeti children. Alas, they will think differently when they mature.

As long as I mentioned *him*, I admit to weak moments, though these are infrequent, as when I think of my so-called father, Khan Kuchem of Akkad. After these many years I've decided to forgive him. He knew me not. When he looked upon me he gazed through the lens of disappointment.

He loved Agni of Akkad as he would his own offspring. He regretted his decision to allow me to engage in martial training, for I bested Agni in everything, poor boy. It fatally crippled him. Agni became bitter and resentful. Bitterness became touchiness. Touchiness became mindlessness. Mindlessness became a self-consuming fire, which was loss of mind.

Instinctively, father knew that I should be the next Khan. Instead, he turned his face from me and refused to see. In later years he denied me. Someone else, he claimed, sired me upon my mother Hagar, his third wife. I was an abominable bastard, not his rightful heir. He did not often say these things, only when he'd been drinking. Yet I heard them in everything he said, and didn't say. I was a dark-skinned woman, but not as dark as my father, with black eyes, though my eyes sparkle, people say, with fire. They shoot sparks. I should have been Khan.

My mother was a foolish woman despite her great beauty. In later years, as that beauty slowly faded—she very nearly drained the Akkadean treasury spending extravagant sums on Yisskur silks and Ra'bim potions—she became shrewish, mean and prone to vicious displays of petty vindictiveness. The various somas turned her into a hideous creature. She began to resemble a painted doll. While the paint held only tenuously, flaking off in places, the wood beneath cracked and rotted distorting the symmetry of her face. Her body became as bloated as a white maggot after it has fed on blood. She only laughed at Talib the fool, who seldom neglected to heap ridiculous words of praise upon her. Talib, perhaps, bestowed more than words. He did have the balls, as they say.

So it came to pass that my father the Khan drugged and sold me to the Ra'bim. Where was his love? Another lie of my childhood. Why do we lie to our children? I promised myself I would not do so.

Now it appears that I shall never know if I am able to keep this promise.

Symenian merchants conducted the negotiations and drew up the contract. Everyone vouched for their integrity, which was probably why suspicious old Vishnu trusted them. Perhaps that trust also came from the fact that my stupid father paid an exorbitant fee for their services, from which Vishnu took a hefty cut. These so-called service fees reduced his profit considerably, some say completely. But this has never been verified.

Symenian merchants dress in gaudy clothes. They wear expensive Yisskur cotton tunics dyed in orange, red, pink, and green, fastened by silver clasps. Their pantaloons are generally yellow and they wear the most absurd headgear, a white silk scarf banded by flexible kerdofan. They are pasty white, as are the Ra'bim, except much taller. In fact, the two tribes may be related.

It is said that long ago a Symenian merchant Prince spied a Ra'bim girl bathing in the shallow waters of Lake Emerald. He approached her but she retreated further into the lake. Apparently Symenian tribesmen fear water, for he would only wade in up to his ankles.

The Prince called to her. "Come, lie with me," he said. She refused. He offered her riches beyond the imagination of the Almighty Himself. But she only shook her and pleaded with him to leave.

The sight of her naked, her breasts bobbing in the water, aroused him to such a height that he spilled his seed into the Lake. Shamed by his weakness and haste, he left her there and headed back over the hills to Symen.

As she was standing waist deep in the water, his seed entered her and she became pregnant. The Triumvirs heard her story—she came before them weeping, claiming she'd been raped—and sent her to the Symen Tribe for a huge wagon load of gold. It is said that she tried to kill herself. Eventually she gave birth to seven sons and seven daughters, all at once if that can be believed.

It is also told how, many generations later, a party of Ra'bim tribesmen secretly invaded Symen and raped as many women as they could find. This outrage had been carefully planned. A week before the raid, Ra'bim herb-masters had filled a Symenian order for dream soma with white soma, the sort that paralyzes its victim. So while they raped the women, who were conscious but could not move a muscle to resist the violation, they took advantage of the Lord's own gracious blessing (the potency of the white soma surpassed their wildest dreams) and castrated many of the men, except those who were descendants of the seven. Thus did the Symen tribe become a vassal to the Ra'bim.

My dear loving father surrendered me to such people. Have I said I've come to forgive him, if he still lives, which I doubt, given the many victories of the Yakashas and their devastation of Greenbottom?

Ah, I digress. Such, however, is the prerogative of the Queen.

The Books Of Marduk

BOOK OF CONFESSIONS
VERSE 4.1.2

Serrati, my guide on the road to Zell, was a rather common specimen of desert Yakashas. Oh yes, foolish scholars, priests, castrati, there truly are Yakashas, as you must know by now.

They call themselves *Redfolk*, sometimes *Redimp*, although the latter is considered demeaning and generally results in a bloody fight of tooth and claw. Their kind first inhabited Edom, but they'd spread into the steppe during the time of my father. Their language is similar to Sandi, though crude and primitive. I do not believe that the Lord in the fullness of His wisdom designed their tongues properly. They exhale their sibilants giving these the sound of a serpent sliding through sand. They tend to swallow their labials and therefore choke when they speak. Yet if you ask them, they say that their speech is perfect and even superior to that of men.

The Yakashas of Edom are somewhat different from those of Starmirror. The Starmirror kind are larger, nearly the size of a man, and stronger, although their bodies remain skeletal, as though they suffered from some kind of wasting disease. They come in two kinds: a dark gray color, almost black as, say, the mythical whittling tree. I call these *gray imps*, though they have a secret name for themselves which even the White Lords do not know.

Then there are those that have a yellowish tint to their hides and are quite large. These elite yellows form a kind of aristocracy. Yakashas of the south, both gray and yellow, possess longer tails, but many are born without genitals, as far as I can tell.

I recall the Yakashas creation myth as told to me by Serrati one night just after a light rain of *kittim*. We'd come to the Windward Straits. The rain of *kittim* so far south unnerved the poor creature and therefore his account was rambling and disjointed. I pressed him nonetheless. As I've mentioned, I'm a seeker of truth, a despiser of delusion, which I'm afraid to say, seems to be a habit among intelligent creatures. The queeti have just begun to learn it—alas.

At the start, everything was a vast desert, say the Redfolk. There was no water. No cloud above, nor well-spring below. No rivers, lakes, or seas. No creature lived.

Then one day the Lord came from the outside. He caused a hill to form in the ocean of sand. Over time the sand turned into rock. The rock turned into a mound. The mound turned into a mountain. The mountain became as glass.

The Lord said: "It is good that I've made me a mountain." Yet when He glanced down He saw that the rest of the world was still desert.

The Lord said: "Nothing grows. Nothing moves. Nothing happens. In the desert there are no distinctions. I'm bored."

Now, it was not good for the Holy One to be bored.

So the Lord caused it to rain. Then He struck the mountain with his fist and the mountain split bringing forth subterranean waters to fill the seas. The sweet rain filled the rivers and the lakes. Moss grew on rock, vegetation came to the land, the grasses to the steppe, and the trees to the forests. Wheat, rye, beans, barley, red onions (also called phalabulbs)—lemons, melons, apples, grapes, pomegranates, so too the whittling tree.

The Lord looked down from his mountain. The Lord said: "See what I have made."

But there was no one to see.

The Lord said: "Let there be sea monsters that dwell in the deep." And the gigantic beasts of the oceans came to be.

But the monsters arose from the turquoise waters and rampaged on the land. They devoured the grain, gobbled up the fruit, drank the rivers.

The Lord bellowed: "Where are my mighty warriors?"

The Books Of Marduk

So, the Lord made the White Lords (as Yakashas name the New-Men). How much they resembled the Lord Himself! Heroes as bright as the stars. They defeated the sea monsters and banished them back to the watery deep.

The Lord said: "The White Lords require servants. Lesser Ones."

So, Lesser Ones came to be.

The Lord said: "The land is devastated. It requires gardeners. Let there be tailless peasants."

Then the Tailless came to be.

The Lord congratulated Himself: "It is all very good."

Then came evening. The daystar dropped below the horizon. The time of darkness approached, the time of shadows, of shifting forms and uncertain boundaries.

The Lord grew sleepy. His great labors taxed Him. The only desert that remained was Edom. The Lord's head began to nod. A snore escaped His divine lips. Then another. The snores became regular, as one wave follows another.

The music of the Lord's snores drifted above the red dunes of Edom. The vibrations of the Lord's snores jiggled the fine granules of sand. Even asleep did the Lord create.

From the churning of the red sand came the first of the *Redfolk*. Therefore are Redfolk the last and the least of the Lord's making. They are neither a thought nor an afterthought in the mind of the Lord. They are made from the shadows of dusk and are of little substance.

Redfolk are divine no-thought become flesh.

"Thus I stand before you, oh Great Warrior," Serrati said. "I am a misshaped creature of red, bark-like skin, stringy, vine-like hair, of crooked limbs, a sharply curved backbone, hound-like face, wasted body and stunted tail. I am made to serve."

Exalted Father

He offered me a desert melon, which I gladly took from his clawed hand and ate. Edom may be a desert, it is true, yet it is not a barren waste. Frequently we came across large heaps of black rock unlike anything I'd ever seen in Akkad. It seemed to me that the smooth, almost glass-like rocks of black had been thrust into the ground from above, as a hunter might spear a red buck or fallow deer. Water seeped from the earth as, say, blood. Desert life clung to these wounds in the red soil. Melons, dates, species of tuber I had never seen, even small trees dripping with nuts and berries, and so much more. Edom was less a desert than a garden.

I took the fruit from Serrati as I listened to his tale. Dusk came on the wings of Lesser Wind. Surprisingly there were *kittim* in the air but they did not alight.

"Fear not, Mistress," Serrati said. "Maggots of the air touch Edom not."

He crouched beneath the rock outcropping where we'd taken shelter. His black, flesh-enclosed eyes seemed to smolder like tiny fires in the dying light. His lipless mouth twisted in a way I took for a grin, revealing his yellow fangs.

"It is...custom of Redfolk," he wheezed as though breathing was suddenly difficult. "I give fruit, you something give."

"That is?" I fingered the pummel of my scimitar.

Quite unexpectedly he raised his loincloth and exposed himself to me. His generative member was unusually thick and fleshy for one so frail. It measured roughly a third the size of his tail.

His eyes popped out of their protective sacks. His tail quivered, and spasms seemed to surge through it and his entire body. His member was erect, a disgusting curved thing purple at its tip. He stepped towards me. Deep in his throat he made a gurgling sound.

I am a stranger to fear. No danger intimidates me.

I killed him instantly.

I drew my scimitar and reversed the blade in one fluid stroke. Lightning is lethal from both ends, old Master Jebe taught me. I struck him in the temple with the rounded pummel. Yakashas are such frail creatures, formed as they are by the Lord's snores at dusk.

For his gift of a melon I returned death.

Disgust ignited my muscles, habit drove my hand, habit born of years of the greatest warrior training in the world. Yes, I felt some regret, maybe even pity. After all these years I still do. It is not something I should dwell upon, of course. My actions were justified, of course. Nonetheless, in the deep of night I sometimes awaken, usually from a dream I cannot recall, and my chest is tight, my throat constricted, and I wish it had been otherwise. Quickly I force myself to think of my own suffering, the many insults and pains life has heaped upon my own head. I have learned that vice often comes from frustrations, although killing Serrati was no vice. My misfortunes may have made me callous. If so, I have my reasons.

Later I would learn that the Lord had erred when He dreamed imp proportions (for are they not creatures of the Lord's dream, truth be told?). The female Redfolk are much smaller than the males. In fact, too small. They cannot accommodate the male member without their flesh tearing or their wombs punctured, as one might thrust a large spear into a small cotton purse. Mating is seldom successful. There are few births among them.

Still, the desert teems with them. Divine dreams must have flowed into the sands as water from a bottomless spring.

So I killed him. I was justified. They are misbegotten creatures, both red and gray imps. They are deceitful creatures. It would be best if the world is rid of them all. As it turns out I am their Queen. Such is not always the best way to govern a people, so I hear.

Would that I kill *him*. I am justified tenfold. Alas how the years have flown.

But I digress.

EXALTED FATHER

BOOK OF CONFESSIONS
VERSE 4.1.3

The day after I slew the disgusting creature—and that morning the *kittim* did indeed fall like snow—I sighted the Windward Straits.

Now, the Windward Straits are not really a body of water as the priests would have us believe. The place is a vermin-infested marshland. A foul kind of brown reed plant grows there. It rots in the southern winter and releases a most odious scent. Patches of evil-looking shrubbery with wide, spiky leaves form hedge-like barriers. The smallest cut from one of these causes fever and sometimes constriction in the lungs making it hard to breathe. The vermin are mostly insects: blood-sucking flies, gnats, mosquitoes, silverfish, a thousand kinds of beetles, and yellow-stripped roaches the size of a woman's hand. Fat brown snakes and red scorpions haunt the place and prey on travelers.

Gazing southeast, one sees on a shimmering horizon the silver spires of Zell. They are flaming spears in the white light of the daystar. Of Zell, Rekhmire's city, I will tell. It was not Emerald in the ages of Akkadean glory.

After three days in that awful marshland, I spied a roughly triangular peninsula of rock, stained green by many Kalpa of salty rain in the winter. Hundreds of feet high, rising from the marshland like a great wall of stone, the peninsula is a giant leap to the highlands of the south. Upon this jutting finger of rock stands Zell.

Zell is a fortress enclosed by mile-long brick walls some twenty feet high. The brick is made from marsh mud by queeti slaves. The queeti dip the brick in large heated vats of golden dye extracted from the noxious reeds. The cooking process releases poisonous fumes, and many queeti sicken and die.

Because of the punishing winds of winter, the walls are in need of constant repair. The hundreds of spires, serving no purpose as far as I could tell, were built during the First Kalpa, the New-Men say. None, however, know of the original builders, their purpose, or the kind of strange glass-like metal from which the spires are made.

The White Fathers, as the queeti name the New-Men, are obsessed with the art we translate as *geometry* in Sandi. This art seems to consist of figures in space, or rather figures *of* space. Zell is a model of such arrangements. The queeti say that the figures and the rules that govern them exist only in the heads of the White Fathers. When the queeti rebellion finally came, the queeti split open many of these heads in search of the rules and diagrams. They found only a sticky, grayish-green nest of worms and thick milky fluid. But they discovered no triangles, circles, squares, cubes, spheres, pyramids, or other figures.

Enough of Zell—of which I've little to say.

Although they are of His kind (according to the queeti), the White Fathers no longer pay much attention to the Lord on the Mountain. They almost seem to have forgotten the Lord. Let me say that the White Fathers, despite their own memory lapse, taught my honest queeti to the worship the Lord on His Holy Mountain. They taught the queeti His name: *Exalted Father*.

The queeti say that the White Fathers once served Exalted Father. They worshiped Him and obeyed His laws, especially the Law forbidding them to ascend Needleglass and gaze upon His Divine Person— "for on that day thou shalt die," as is written in the *Runehayana*. Surely this is a strange coincidence.

While I speak of coincidences, years later— and this will come as a shock to the priesthood, if any still live— I discovered that the White Fathers, the New-Men, seem to possess their own version of the Suthralane legend. I have often wondered if our Suthralane was

Exalted Father

really New-Men? Someday I may hear the truth from the lips of *He-With-Us*— before he dies beneath my blade.

The New-Men no longer believe in the Lord on the Mountain because of what Suthralane or his likeness discovered. Suthralane broke the Law and in so doing apparently discovered the truth, so they say.

The Lord, the New-Men claim, was not the Almighty at all but a minion of far greater Lords in the Heavens. In fact, He was an impostor.

The proof is this: The Lord on the Mountain was too fallible. He was sometimes gullible, ridiculous, susceptible to childish outbursts and adolescent moodiness. He could become irritable, also smug and self-righteous. He liked to blame others for his shortcomings and suffered from a crushingly inflated self-image. The Lords of the Heavens exiled him to our world. In the end, the New-Men say, he became old and bitter, and retreated behind a wall of silence. All this transpired many Kalpa ago.

They do not tell the poor queeti these things. I sometimes think that they really don't believe their own stories. Do they still fear the Lord? They refuse to climb His holy mountain to this day. Perhaps they are physically unable to do so. They have very little flexibility. They are large and ponderous (as I know all too well). When it is a matter of ruling the queeti, however, belief in the Lord is extremely useful. This is because the Lord on His Mountain created the New-Men in His own divine image. The poor queeti, no; they are children of the forest, of the plants, of the foul whittling tree, misbegotten and accursed. The doctrine says *only* the New-Men, of all other creatures, are the image and kind of the Lord. Loudly do the New-Men proclaim it—though they may not believe in the Lord.

King Ra' himself once told me an alternative story that he claimed was as old as the founding of Tharas Major. This was after a long agonizing night of fruitless wrestling. It did little to ease my suffering and nothing to relieve the pain of my abused flesh, even soma encased flesh. Yet to this day I can still remember every detail. It goes like this:

At the beginning of things, the daystar came to the New-Men in the form of a gigantic bull, like the kind the Gad once raised in Greenbottom. The Great Bull said to them:

"I am fire. I am life. I will live in you and you will bring me forth as you please."

"What must we do?" the New-Men inquired.

"Behold," the Bull answered them, "you must feed me."

"Feed you?" they scoffed. "You are fire."

"You must feed me. Your dead bodies. When you die you must burn your bodies. Then will you feed me. You will gain the Heavens. See how fire rises? All fire ultimately joins the daystar. So too, thou."

Well, the New-Men accepted the Great Bull's invitation. He entered them, all the males, for He was a bull not a cow. The fire burned inside them and they turned as white as the daystar—brilliant as living marble, as the two moons, as the luminous mist of morning that rises from the Pearldew.

When they came to mate with their females they burned them to ashes. *For there is no fiery cow, only a fiery Bull.* In a short time, perhaps a generation, there were no more female New-Men. So do they account for their present condition. Of the rest I cannot speak.

I did not climb to Zell, ruled by Lord Rekhmire. Rather, I went under, into the caves of the Reed Sea People.

This was after I killed the Yakashas Serrati.

EXALTED FATHER

BOOK OF CONFESSIONS
VERSE 4.1.4

I weep whenever I think back upon my dear queeti children. I weep especially on days such as this when the dark winter clouds roll overhead and the bitter winds penetrate the Queen's tower in Tharas Major. The cold is unusual for Starmirror. Perhaps there'll be *kittim*.

Smiles do not come easily these days. The brightest days seem dark to me. Gloom is my constant companion. I've suffered as no woman ought to suffer. I wish to cleanse myself of cursed memory. Into these pages I consign my memories, as if in a prison. I turn my back for good.

Am I not *whissling?* I'm not sure any longer what that title means. There was a moment, in *His* presence, when I seemed to fly above all solid existence. I was transparent. I was pure luminosity. In my mind I saw things that did not belong to me. Time became a quilted blanket spread out below and it did not bind me. I was—free. Perhaps there is life after death. Now I'm captive. A captive Queen in the Queen's tower, the wife of a monster. Of these circumstances I will not speak.

I had no brothers. No sisters. Such was the way of things among us back then. If a woman was fortunate enough to conceive, and even more fortunate to give birth, she almost always brought a single soul into the world. Afterwards her womb was sealed. That was the end of it. No one, not even the priesthood, knew why. But then what would priests know of such things, except as they dream them?

Some say that Agni's mother Livia birthed two boys, Agni and another, although I do not know the order of their birth. This *other boy* vanished, some say conveniently, for reasons I do not fully comprehend. It is probable that the Khan found him weak and sold him to the priesthood. My father was quite talented at selling Akkadean children. Why he took an interest in Livia's brat is something of a mystery to me, as was his love for Agni.

Agni was no prince. A great ball of hot gas, his famous fury, fiery and deadly, was in truth never more than vented hot air as, say, the screech of those old Nepptali boilers under too much pressure. I should know. I tested him many times. I wonder if he rules Akkad today. I know little of Greenbottom. The King's armies are always victorious, we are told. It will fall, and Agni too if he hasn't already. I can almost pity him.

I remember fragments, yet I still feel the pain as if it were today. The pain of yesterday merges with the pain of today.

On gloomy cold days, such as this, my mind wanders. Memories awaken, forgotten fragments come to life. Often they are memories I never knew I possessed. I know this sounds strange. If we are unaware of memories from the start, how do we know that awakened memories truly belong to us? I would be rid of them all!

This morning I awoke with a dream rattling around in my head. Too bad I fail to recall any of it. It did leave me with an odd mix of feelings, as does the after-taste of sour wine. I felt an undefined longing, a sense of opportunities lost, of sadness—and yet I felt a great mystery that was at once exhilarating and frightening.

For reasons just as mysterious, the dream awoke memories of my mother. Yes, in my youth I dismissed her as a vain and foolish woman, a companion to professional fools such as hawk-faced Talib. They said that I took after her, that I resembled my father the Khan not at all. Today I realize, after all these many years, she is still a blank page to me.

She was a third wife. My father the Khan never spoke of his first two wives, at least to me. I was given to understand that both died birthing children. The babes, of course, died too. Hagar was young enough to be his daughter. I am told that he pampered her outrageously. After giving birth to me she became barren as most

Exalted Father

Akkadean women (with the exception of Livia, as I've already mentioned—if the rumors were true).

While the Great Khan mostly ignored Hagar, there were exceptions. He would beat her upon occasion, either for her soaring vanity or her preoccupation with the fool Talib. In later years she became shrewish, contemptible in small things such as the vitriol she displayed when spoke about the Khan, or the little hurtful barbs she used in the most trivial conversations with people at court, even the servants.

Back when I studied for the priesthood in Nalanda, I came to believe her infertility really belonged to the Great Khan who was great in all things but one (or two). Such was the case in all the Tribes. Today it strikes me that if I was my father's greatest disappointment, she was a stinging rebuke of his pride. He grew fat, addicted to wine and bad poetry. It is still a mystery to me that while he wept inconsolably when Agni's mother died, he barely blinked at my mother's death.

It is her death the mysterious dream brought up this morning, a ghost from the dark underworld of groaning shades. But in the light of day, in vivid and precise detail, she appeared.

Maybe it was the absurdly expensive Ra'bim beauty potions, or maybe she caught a chill walking the shores of Emerald Lake in the winter. Perhaps she'd been poisoned by *kittim* as had the Khan, although I never glimpsed a stain on her flesh. Perhaps this was because she dressed in the most flamboyant silken gowns that covered her completely from neck to toe. She usually wore oversize clothes of gaudy color combinations and ridiculous cuts. If she hadn't been poisoned by a *kittim* she certainly resembled one who had.

She may have been ill for quite some time. Yet, one day in early spring at the High Table in the Khan's West Tower—the Khan drunk and reciting nonsense verses from the *Runehayana*—she suddenly became quite cheerful. This was unusual. Talib was nowhere in sight.

She rose from her chair and, as a hundred Orloks looked on, announced in a forceful voice: "I am not long for this world."

The crowd went deathly silent, as silent as the Lord on His Mountain. Even the befuddled Khan appeared surprised.

"What'd she say, that barren old woman?" He slurred his words.

"I said I'm not long for this world, oh Khan of wet dough. I might add that none of us is long for this world. We've never been *for this world.*"

Strange how her words come back to me exactly as she said them.

Deep lines appeared on my father's mottled forehead. His face became hard and stern, and his good green eye stared at her with cold malevolence. But he said nothing and soon went back to his reciting of poetic nonsense.

By mid-spring she'd taken to her bed. As the days grew bright and cheery, and as the wild flowers in the meadows released their fragrance, as if to perfume the cool air lingering from the retreating winter, a horrendous fever assaulted her. She burned from the inside. She soaked her clothes and bed coverings with foul smelling sweat. She seemed to be melting away, and daily she grew weaker. The fever was unrelenting.

She asked that they move her to a tiny stucco and brick bungalow near the lake where she could gaze upon its blue waters. At first my father pretended that her sudden illness was nothing more than a bad springtime cold. But when she began urinating blood and suffering from spasms of pain that shot up from her bowels, leaving her gasping and speechless, he called upon Ra'bim physicians. Now, that I look back upon it in such detail, I wonder if seeing me at her bedside gave them their happy idea of purchasing a black-eyed Akkadean wench for the disgusting pleasure of old Vishnu.

The Ra'bim experimented with a number of healing somas. These served only to increase my mother's misery. Her legs became swollen and the slightest exertion left her unable to breathe. I believe they hastened her death.

How could such memories exist in my head all these years without my knowing?

I am sitting with her one morning. To be honest, I avoided her and sat with her rarely. On this exceptionally cold morning after Greater Wind delivered an exceptionally large number of exceptionally multi-colored *kittim*, I come to visit her, perhaps out of guilt, probably more from curiosity. I'd heard the servants talking, how in her delirium she said weird, incredible things. She frightened them. The Ra'bim physicians nodded knowingly. Her time grows short, they concluded.

"She refuses her medicines, naughty girl," they scolded. They frowned and creases appeared in their otherwise smooth, pasty yellow skin. The shook fat fingers at me, "Naughty girl… The fever eats her brain."

Yet she looked upon me with clear eyes. She was propped up with pillows and gazing at the lake. I was dressed in my blue cloth fatigues, scimitar in my belt, hair cut soldier short. I'd just come from the training grounds.

"There are many lands," she said smiling. Her luxurious black hair had turned dingy gray. Beneath her hair her once full face had become hollow, her beautiful dark skin palsied. Still her voice was cheerful. "Many, many lands…entire realms beyond this one—"

I remembered thinking that she was dying and the shades were calling her.

(Strange how the *Runehayana* speaks not of our death. How silent is the Lord on His Mountain when it comes to the subject of death.)

"I see them," she continued, "in each drop of lake water. I see where I once lived. Not here. Not in this realm. You were there too, my daughter. You were not my daughter...in that place so long ago. You were my son, a child of my old age.

"We were a primitive people then. We wandered that alien land. We followed the ageless patterns, the great circles of the seasons drawn on the landscapes of that place, like the fixed stars in the heavens. We lived in crude tents and tended our flocks of rugged sheep.

"I was the wife of an old prince, thickset, black beard, balding...like Grand Duke Rudra of the Yads yearning to be a king. The Lord was there too. But he didn't isolate himself on some mountain. No, we glimpsed him at dusk, or in the early morning, usually strolling in the shade. He dressed in white back then, like a Rab. When he appeared close by, it was as if a patch of luminous mist detached itself from the horizon of that broad wilderness grassland and came walking in our direction.

"One day in the spring of my husband's seventy-fifth year the Lord appeared and spoke to him. Alas, the Lord spoke falsehoods. He made promises He did not keep—perhaps He could not keep."

"Such as?" I recall asking the mad woman who had once been my mother.

"Oh so many promises," she laughed. "He promised *you*, even in my old age. That one He made good. I birthed a son too. He forgot the others, or He simply lied. Perhaps He was merely boasting. He may have over-estimated His powers. He was a braggart, you know. He couldn't live with His weaknesses and blamed others for His failings."

"Tell me another."

She paused for a long moment. Then in an oddly scornful tone she said: "He promised us *immortality*. Stupid Lord that He was."

"Stupid?"

"Of course. What need have we of that, child? See the lake. The blue hills beyond, the Akkadean Stairs. Gaze upon the beauty of the yellow-blue sky, the glowing stars in black heaven's vault, the brilliance of the daystar. See the meadows, forests, orchards, arbors, fields of wheat and barley and rye, even the golden steppe and the red desert. What need have we of immortality when we possess so much at this moment?"

I shrugged. The Ra'bim physicians were right. Her feverish delirium had driven her insane.

"Did your old prince ever reproach the Lord for His broken promises?"

"Oh no. After your birth my prince believed everything the Lord told him. It would all come to pass, he thought, as long as he believed. Even when I died he *did not* doubt. When he died and returned to the soil he *could not* doubt."

"Yet here you are again, alive. You came back. In a sense the Lord did keep His promise." Like all those who suffer from mad visions, she'd wandered into a contradiction. Rudra had a proverb about contradictions, which I've forgotten.

My mother grew angry at my last words. "Oh no. This is not the doing of the Lord! He died too in that place. We didn't need Him. We grew up. We even forgot Him."

"Your ancestors you mean." She was becoming incoherent.

She glared at me, hard-eyed and severe, as if seeing me for the first time.

"Don't you remember? You were there. Your children, my children, their children's children. A thousand Kalpas ago. A thousand times a thousand Kalpas ago. At last they accomplished what the old stupid Lord Himself failed to do. It was—an abomination! Behold, *we* are that abomination."

This was all she ever said. She never uttered a single word again. To me, to my father, to anyone.

She died at the end of spring, on the very day of the Milrash festival when the last crops are planted, and the young men are brought to the Holy Shrine of Borassus. I recall that evening, how Lesser Wind brought a storm of *kittim*.

The Books Of Marduk

I am surprised how much I remember when I am in the mood. It frustrates me that I cannot recall *He-With-Us*, for *he* has faded from my mind as, say, a hopeful dream in which no matter how hard I try I cannot recall a single detail. So how can I kill *him* when *he* is already dead? Once I spill my memory into these pages my cup will be empty.

EXALTED FATHER

BOOK OF CONFESSIONS
VERSE 4.1.5

Zell sits a mile inland, built, as I've mentioned, upon a triangular peninsula of rock hundreds of Akkadean meters high. I've always felt a powerful urge to avoid the fortress-city. It's an old memory lacking form and substance yet filled with powerful emotions.

I recall feeling pain, loathing, hatred, inchoate feelings far worse than anything I'd experienced in the marshland. I did not go to Zell.

I wandered three days in the marsh of foul reeds. Each morning before the coming of Greater Wind (but Greater Wind did not come here, priests say), a strange, bread-like substance appeared on the narrow leaves of the reed plants. White as sugar, it tasted sweet and reminded me of Zub'lin figs. The queeti call it marsh-frosting but are quite unable to stomach the stuff. I ate my fill and grew stronger. It came to pass that during this time in that disgusting wilderness the Ra'bim body suit, my former wedding dress, finally dissolved into my skin like a *kittim* wound. Today I am as white as any New-Man, even my face and hair.

The village of the Reed Sea People is a nest of interconnected caves dug by an ancient sea into the sheer cliffs that form the Zell peninsula. Colonies of green lichen grow on the rocks, which the queeti find quite tasteful. It is poison to me. I tasted a tiny morsel from a queeti dish and found it beyond bitter. It gagged me and I experienced a violent seizure. It is strange that I have no buried memories of this place. Yet, a powerful force drew me to the Reed Sea People, a force opposite that of Zell.

The morning was cloudy. A light mist was in the air tasting of salt and fish. I'd slept fitfully the night before. Three times I awoke in the darkness. Faint cries drifted above the Reed Sea, non-human voices calling to one another in tones of distress and pain. I heard the screech of night birds, the slithering of thick bodies among the reeds, many other sounds I could not identify.

Grasping my scimitar with all my strength, I whispered into the darkness: "I am an Akkadean warrior, well-trained, hard of body and mind, blessed with the Lord's own endurance.

Am I not daughter of the Great Khan?

The Windward Straits are indeed a sea of reeds summer and winter. The winter of my coming to Starmirror the ground was unusually dry and hard. During spring and summer it is muddy and pocked by stagnant pools. The evil-looking poisonous reed plants seemed to wither in the dry salted wind of winter. Yet they still hindered me. Fortunately, a narrow road cut through the yellow maze. In those days I imagined that such was the road to Jambridvipa used by the great wisps (my queeti's name for the *grayfolk* of the south). This turned out to be a mistaken assumption, as I later learned.

There was nothing beautiful or appealing about the winter marshland, nothing to send me soaring into misty upper realms of blissful musings over the wonders of this world, as did my poor mother in her delirium. It stank of decaying vegetation. Nothing stirred. A putrid blanket of hazy air hung over the place. Neither the sea breeze nor the two Winds were able to penetrate its dense sea of reeds. The foul place nearly took my life.

The fat brown snakes turned out to be deadly vipers. They infested the marshland summer and winter. They would lie in the middle of the road gathering the warmth of the daystar. But this was a ruse. They mimicked logs of rotten driftwood and lulled their unsuspecting victims into a deadly trap.

I came upon one in the late afternoon of my third day crossing the straits. I was about to step over what I thought was an old tree trunk when it suddenly coiled up as though a fallen tree had come to life. It rose to nearly my full height and hissed like boiling water. Its mouth opened and retractable fangs appeared, dripping with venom. Instantly it struck, aiming for my face.

I had no time to toss off my bulky priestly cloak. Leaping to my right, I fumbled in the thick folds trying to draw my scimitar. The large triangular head darted past my left shoulder and buried its fangs in a reed plant. The deadly serpent coiled and spun around for a second strike.

I was helpless. It struck at me just as my fingers found the pummel of my sword. It sunk its fangs into my left shoulder, piercing the flimsy cotton of the black cloak as easily as a stick thrust into water.

The fangs did not break flesh. The Ra'bim body is no simple stain. Flesh turned to stone even though I'd not noticed it. My flesh became a very strange stone, however, flexible enough for normal body motion, sensitive to heat and cold, yet body armor that defeated fangs.

The force of the strike knocked me backwards. As I fell I tried to roll away, frantic to free my scimitar. The long cloak tangled and tore. The snake reared above me and struck again, three times more at various places on my body. Each time the armor-like skin turned its fangs.

It struck a fourth time aiming for my face. I was able to free my hands and catch the snake by the throat. Just inches from my face, hissing in frustration, venom dripping, burning through the rough cotton but unable to penetrate my Ra'bim armor, the yellow vertically slanted eyes pumped pure malevolence into mine, as though to paralyze me with fear. I squeezed with all my strength. The eyes seemed to bulge. The monster spit its venom. I twisted my head and white creamy fluid shot past my ear. I tightened my grip on its neck. I thought I saw a hint of fear in those wicked eyes.

While keeping my choke-hold, I tried to shimmy off my back. The torn garment made getting to my feet impossible. Damned priests and their silly attire! Allies of the serpent.

Seemingly aware of my difficultly, the hideous creature took advantage of my thrashing. Nearly ten feet of steel-like cord wrapped around my body and began to squeeze the air from my lungs.

We rolled about, crushing the reed plants, locked in our mutual embrace of death. The crushing strength of the serpent began to tell. My grip on its throat loosened ever so slightly. I began seeing black spots. With each painful gasp for a breath the serpent tightened its coils. The spots merged, ragged clouds coming together to blot out the sky. Those burning eyes shone through the shadow. The fear in them vanished, replaced by triumph.

What happened next is hard to say. Later, my dear queeti would fill in the gaps of memory.

From the corner of my fading vision I thought I saw a man holding a kind of bronze-bladed harpoon. But this could be no man. For while it stood upright, its arms were too long, and its oddly-shaped head jutted forward. It seemed to be wearing some short of hair shirt and trousers. Later I would discover that it wore nothing at all except a belt and genital cup made of sea-shell. It possessed a massive lower jaw filled with blunt teeth, not the sharp fangs of the Redfolk or the Gray. Flat nose, sharp cheekbones, the suggestion of a muzzle, protruding brow, a narrow forehead—yet the being's wide brown eyes seemed strangely human.

My strength ebbed away. My vision wavered and briefly I wondered if I'd imagined the brown-haired creature. As one squeezes the last drop from an empty water-skin, its image was the last drop of thought from a dying brain.

The snake broke my hold on its neck. Its hiss became one of victory. It reared and prepared one final strike at my unprotected face.

What occurred next came to me in fragments, as say, broken pieces of glass.

Something flashed in the fading light. The great triangular head flew past. The massive body flopped and coiled violently. The head fell like a rock, its mouth opened wide in a noiseless hiss. Black blood splayed over the nearby reeds, causing them to sizzle and turn to ash. Rough, callused hands grabbed me and lifted me upon broad hairy shoulders. And then starless night descended and the world went away.

THE BOOK OF CONFESSIONS

CHAPTER TWO – From the Life of a Remarkable Woman

(Of My First Encounter with the Reed Sea People)

VERSE 4.2.1

First Minister Leeander is exceptionally cruel and vindictive. I am witness to these qualities. It happened on the day he summoned me at the behest of an angry King. Leeander is the mouth of King Ra'. I know not his personal history. Nor do I know the personal history of any of them, including Ra' the King, my husband. It is as if they've always existed since the first coming of the Lord to His holy mountain. They have no history, but this seems impossible. Without a history how can they be alive?

Many years before the time of this writing, I've forgotten the number, a queeti village of the Blue Forest People failed to send its fall feudal rents to Tharas Major. The turnip and bean crops failed that season and the village faced a winter of starvation. The Blue Mother sent her Hetman, White-bark, to plead for leniency. Unlike the Reed Sea People, the tribes of the forests are ruled by Blue Mothers who select the Hetman. The Mother of the Reed Sea People is White.

Exalted Father

As First Minister of the King, it is Leeander's duty to deal with such trifles. The New-Men think of the queeti as animals, a tiny step up from dumb beasts. They are suited for only the most menial of tasks, such as supplying the White Fathers with produce and other raw materials, and providing menial labor. New-Men despise manual labor. As things stand, I do not believe them capable of it.

After nearly a half-century, I have yet to observe them engaged in anything remotely useful. They strut about and carry on, complaining of the most trivial things: it is too hot, too cold, too rainy, too cloudy, too bright—they hate the Two Winds. They act as though they are constantly busy, yet as far as I can tell they do nothing at all. They are marble statues. They mimic life with a kind of stony verisimilitude. Their only truly living organ is their tail, which whips about, wiggles and shudders as though they are constantly having a seizure in that region.

Hetman White-bark came before the First Minister in the *Grand Hall of Heavenly Peace, Prosperity, Freedom, and Brilliant Light*, which is the circular hub of the vast castle-fortress at the center of Tharas Major. It took him many minutes to shamble across the long white-tiled floor that separates Leeander's polished cedar dais and massive throne from the iron doors at the end of the Grand Hall.

The throne is two fused pyramids carved from an unknown crystalline material that captures the light of the daystar as it shines through a transparent dome overhead. The throne splits the light into an array of colors that makes the floor seem to alight as if it were a burning lake. The poor supplicant is blinded and generally unable to locate the throne's occupant. I am fairly certain that no New-Man including the King and His First Minister know the art of the throne's making, nor the material from which it is hewn. The New-Men know very little about how things work, as they know very little about the world outside their castles. Nor do they seem to possess the least curiosity.

Grayfolk guards stood on either side of the throne. They wore the purple tunics of Tharas Major and bore L-guns. These were palace grays and they lived outside the walls of Tharas Major in a vile village called Wooden City.

At the foot of the dais stood Ivan, a Yellow wisp, Leeander's Yellowfolk squire, who served as translator. Ivan spoke the queeti tongue, though quite poorly. New-Men never bothered to thoroughly learn the language of the serfs. It was beneath their dignity. How ridiculous that they should even attempt to mimic the barks and grunts of beasts.

During the year I lived among the Reed Sea People I learned to speak their language fluently. It seemed eerily familiar to me, as though I'd once spoke it long ago.

The old Hetman White-bark bowed stiffly. His arms hung at his sides and his large gnarled hands brushed the tiles. He squinted into the confusion of shifting colors, searching for the white-robed Lord seated upon the brilliant throne.

"Lower eyes, Hetman Bark-shit," Ivan snarled. "Look them to me. Dare not White Father. Seek thou thy death, bloated worm?"

"No, Great Lord." The Hetman bowed his shaggy head.

"Why come thou to the *Grand Hall of Heavenly Peace, Freedom, Prosperity, and Brilliant Light*? Stinking serf. See thou thy trail of hair behind thee? Look thou upon that stupid apron of bark that hides thy wrinkled worm-member. What need thee of such modesty when thy bulging belly hangs to thy knees?"

He proceeded to translate. The guards laughed, making the sound of serpents slithering through the reeds of the Windward Straits. I still shudder.

White-bark said: "A thousand pardons, Great King—"

"Lord Ivan, shit-head!"

"Lord Ivan shithead—"

"What do thou wants?" Ivan barked. I hid my smile.

"This old People this comes before…the Lord and His faithful servants… This one is begging a boom."

"A what?"

"A boom…uh…mercy…pity…feeling…"

Leeander spoke. His voice was filled with disgust and impatience. "What is this *thing* saying?"

Ivan turned and bowed. "It asks for a handout," he said.

"That's not what the queeti said." I stepped forward, dressed in the flowing purple gown of the Queen.

"Oh, my Queen, I'd almost forgotten," Leeander replied in a very different voice. It was sweet and soothing, dripping with honey, as the Yadish might have said.

"I've forgotten that you lived among these animals. What was it? A year? You truly amaze me. In so short a time you mastered the language of beasts. One might think that there is some bond…or…well, shall one venture to hypothesize a special *community* between your kind and, to be frank, these animals." He paused as though suddenly aware of the possible insult and afraid of how I might respond, although all this is conjecture for his face betrayed nothing, as is the case with every New-Man.

"Oh please do not be offended. I beg your forgiveness. It is a mere theory among us. Allow me to compliment you. Poor Ivan would be out of a job should you become translator. It would be back to the kitchens for him."

"Translators ought to translate," I observed. "Allow me—"

"Oh please, Mistress," Ivan begged. "Have mercy. Give this poor Yellow a chance. Please be patient with lesser ones such as Yellows. At least they're not Grays."

I ignored his foolishness. "When you speak to this Yellow wisp, speak simply," I said to the Hetman in his own tongue. "Speak simply for he is ignorant."

Ivan's sunken eyes shot sparks and his lipless mouth seemed to turn in a growling sneer. But he said: "Oh thank you, gracious Queen."

"A frost early came," said White-bark in a series of whines and shrill barks. "Sweet-bulbs died in hard ground, they. Alas, Great Ones, our gardens are graves."

"Frosts are rare on Starmirror, early or late," Ivan observed. "Of what concern is this to White Father?"

"No gifts for thee have thy faithful servants, they."

"What?"

"They can't pay their feudal dues," I said.

Ivan turned and bowed, and then translated for Leeander.

"These damned lazy serfs refuse to pay their dues. They're stupid and forgot to plant, or maybe they're too damned lazy to care for their gardens…or some such excuse. Now they think they can talk their way out."

"That's not the translation—"

"Please, my Queen, allow us to conduct our business. I'm simply doing my duty in the name of the King…as you ought to do yours." This time Leeander's silky voice bore a sharp barb. It lodged painfully in my abused flesh. *I had yet to do my duty.*

The First Minister said to Ivan: "Dispatch this animal back to his miserable pigsty with a little souvenir of his visit to civilization. If his garden is barren, then so be he."

Ivan understood. "Hold this thing," he said to the guards.

He drew a razor-sharp blade, the kind that I immediately identified as Nepptali steel. The New-Men never said how they acquired such weapons, or, for that matter, their L-guns, and every other manufactured instrument. They possessed no shops, no factories, not even tools. They relied on their serfs for the barest of essentials.

Ivan grasped White-bark's brown-furred paw in dirt-encrusted talons and with one smooth stroke sliced off two of his four fingers.

Exalted Father

Blood splattered on him and he licked it greedily. His tail whipped from side to side.

The Hetman's screeching was needles in my ears. He fainted away. The guards used old rags to stem the flow of blood, stuffing them into the wounds. They took the severed fingers, wrapped them in a rag, and tied the package around the Hetman's neck. Then they administered a draught of vinegar and wine which restored him, although he began to howl so loud that they were forced to bind his mouth with another rag. At last his howls became pathetic whimpering.

"Take him back to the Blue Forest Clan," Leeander ordered. He laughed softly. "See that those lazy peasants understand." He then addressed himself to the moaning Hetman. "Let this be a sign between your Lord King and you, wooly serf, so you keep the Lord's Laws. Obey or next time we'll slice away your *foreskin*. Break the Laws again and the whole pecker goes." His words were duly translated. Whether or not the old Hetman understood remains a mystery.

Ivan did as the First Minister ordered. But the old queeti died before they got to the village. Ivan flew into a rage. With his company of Grayfolk troops, he proceeded to slaughter the entire population, males, females, and cubs, experimenting with the most fiendish kinds of torture: mutilations, slow burning, various kinds of impalement...I cannot bring myself to enumerate the entire list, which Leeander took special pleasure in describing to me at a later date.

After his servants had washed the floor, Leeander stepped off his dais and bowed to me. He is smaller and weighs considerably less than my noble husband, yet he is identical in every other way, as they all are. Cold and dead, stone trying to imitate life, except for their grotesque tails, they are marble statues with serpents attached to their nether regions.

But I'm being redundant. My disgust is redundant.

Leeander sighed: "Oh, those lazy serfs. What foolishness possesses them? It is the same, in the Redrain Valley, along the Topartz. They refuse to work. Your own Reed Sea Clan has fled north, into Jambridvipa it is said. It's almost as if they yearn for punishment. As our Hetman here. They take perverse joy, it seems, in thinking themselves the victims of their Lords. If they think at all. It must be some sort of collective madness. How could they even conceive of rebelling against the White Lords? Their heads are full of straw. Well, we'll give them reason to feel aggrieved."

I stared at him and did not try to hide my disgust. As I've said, my honesty has always been the source of my misfortunes. So be it then, I live for truth. Vividly do I recall the terrible slaughter of my Reed Sea People. Their only flight was into death. I bear witness to this truth.

Therefore I gave him a lecture.

"Listen, Lord. Among my own Akkadeans are people who refuse to acknowledge their weaknesses, their blunders, more to the point, their blind stupidity. These people often tell themselves lies, mostly lies designed to avoid realities that bear witness against their inflated egos. When someone challenges them, usually by simply telling the truth, they take pleasure in acting aggrieved and hurt. How unfairly you have slandered us, they say. Why, it might not even be a truth that set them off. Merely a single word, an offhand gesture. They seize upon a word and invent the offense. It gives them great pleasure. It justifies hatred and violent acts."

One cannot read emotions in a stone face, but I am certain that Leeander frowned.

"You're saying that the stupid serfs seek punishment?"

"Was I speaking of the queeti?"

"Well, yes—"

Exalted Father

He was silent for a moment. "You know, my Queen," he said in that oily voice, "they're not lazy in one occupation. They breed like flies, like the foul *kittim* you love so much. Speaking of breeding and love, this reminds me of why I requested your presence today...my dear Queen."

"That is?" I asked sourly.

"The King wishes to know if his seed bears fruit?"

"Why doesn't the King himself ask me this question? Why hide behind a lackey?"

I imagined that Leeander's frown deepened.

"Our King is gracious and merciful. He is sensitive and compassionate, long suffering the faults of his people. It pains him much, as much as it does me his loyal *minister*, to make such, well, sensitive inquiries of his beloved Queen. Naturally, the Holy Father has explained to him the problem of *human* barrenness. This defect is due, he understands, to a flaw in the human male. A New-Man's seed burns with the fire of the daystar, and most especially the King's seed— Forget not he is Lord of the living ones and not the dead."

"Indeed, if the King actually possessed seed then it would burn like fire," I observed.

"Yes...well, a holy fire." Either he misunderstood or refused to understand.

"A very holy fire. Perhaps too scorching for his humble wifeling. If he had balls and something more than a tiny nub."

"Yes, well—"

"And?"

"Well, the serfs breed more and more each year, *and*, well, soon Starmirror will sink under their weight if we don't do something to, well, relieve the pressure. If you understand—"

Leeander shifted his considerable weight, although it was, as I've noted, quite less than the King's own.

"Are you finished?"

"Only to add that your health is utmost in the mind of my Lord."

"I'm sure it is. Are *we finished?*"

I sensed Leeander growing angry. "So am I to understand that you've not conceived?"

"You may understand what you wish to understand."

"In that case the King wishes to see you in his chambers this evening after Lesser Wind—to, well, discuss such matters."

"As the King commands." I did not bother to repress the shudder of loathing that spread through my bruised body.

EXALTED FATHER

BOOK OF CONFESSIONS
<u>VERSE 4.2.2</u>

I think back to my life with the Reed Sea People vanished from the world. I would banish those memories to these pages. Shortly I must go to him. This moment I choose to remember—in order to forget.

The cave chill revived me. My ribs and shoulders ached from the serpent's deadly embrace. Shortly, the initial shock of cold gave way to the warm and thick pungent odor of queeti bodies packed closely together. Half conscious, I wondered if this were a dream. Perhaps I'd died. Or, perhaps I'd truly become a priestess. Light surrounded me. Was it luminosity of mind?

No. A fire blazed in the center of a vast cave. I saw a huge fire pit, about ten meters in diameter and a meter deep. Later I would learn that each cave—a total of six interconnected caves matching the six villages of the highlands—cultivated its own sacred fire. The central fire was the heart of the cave, its life. Virgin queeti females served the fire. Their unending diligence kept it burning. Theirs was a sacred calling, for as long as the fires burned, the Reed Sea People lived.

This evening as I write, these pits are graves of cold ash.

My savior was a young bull not fully grown. I felt—dare I say it—shame. Have I not resolved to tell the truth about myself, with clear eyes, including my faults, although I must say that they are not many? Yes, I felt shame—rescued by a hairy beast. Am I not an Akkadean warrior, a remarkable woman?

The Books Of Marduk

He deposited me as say, a sack of grain near the lip of the fire-pit built with smooth white stones. Then he began barking and growling and shaking his spear.

The Reed Sea People emerged from cozy recesses along the walls of the cave. They were mostly females, cubs, an adolescent male here and there, and a few elderly males. There could have been no more than thirty although the cave was large enough for three times that many. I learned that this was true for the other five caves that comprised Lord Rekhmire's fief. Male adult bulls were plentiful everywhere except in the fiefs along the Windward Straits.

They approached cautiously. I saw that the females wore woven reed aprons although their bodies were covered by a thick pelt of hair, mostly brown, some black, in a few cases grey. Their breasts were small and smooth-skinned. This was the only attribute by which I could distinguish them from the males. Otherwise, they were just as tall and heavy, in fact in many cases larger.

A young female wearing a necklace of pink coral approached my rescuer. She held at her breast a tiny cub.

The female barked and whined and gestured with a six-digit paw. My bull replied with a series of grunts and clicks, and then a long rumble deep in his throat that sounded like words in Sandi.

She answered with a kind of shrill mewing and then a series of well-defined barks, quite loud and forceful.

The young bull lowered his head. Then he turned and lifted me from the stone floor and carried me away from the fire into one of the gloomy recesses.

I did not resist. Nor did I protest. I searched my mind, digging deep, past personal memory into other lives, those of dreams, from the time I was special, like *him* I'd sworn to kill...the sound of *his* voice as it vibrated through every cell in my body and past every cell, past physical being, when I could see.

But I digress.

Exalted Father

Seeking I did not find. I knew not of such creatures. The cave became darker and the damp chill returned.

These creatures are not of those other lives. They are not of the heavens. Their smell, their breath, their very being soaks these rocks, the black-soiled highlands, the forests and the southern jungles. They are of such places.

The young bull carried me into a narrow passage of stone walls polished smooth by millennia of running water. I knew not the passage of time in this place. We might have walked an hour, a day, or merely a few minutes.

Suddenly we were in a vast grotto of hanging stalactites. Yellow phosphorescent bulbs covered the slick walls. An elliptical pool of dark green water took up more than half the grotto's floor area. Its surface reminded me of the Lordpool in Upper Nalanda.

The bull set me down near the edge of the pool and pointed with his spear.

Only then did I see *the other.*

He squatted near the pool wearing the strangest coat I'd ever beheld. It seemed a few sizes too large for his body. A ragged patchwork of pieces of cloth cut haphazardly from diverse materials, a motley collection of odd fabrics sewn together in a mishmash of irregular shapes, the coat of many coats had billowy sleeves, a stiff high collar and frayed edges. Then I noticed that the colors were not random. They were the colors of the Twelve Tribes of Men.

It was the coat of the Unified Kingdom. The King's coat...which could only mean that this strange person was Grand Duke Rudra of the Yadish.

Although I'd never actually laid eyes upon the Grand Duke I knew him well from my father's descriptions.

It struck me: *This old man could not be Duke Rudra.*

At this moment he was preoccupied gutting the body of a fish. The creature still flopped about, and his small knife appeared dull and unsuited to his task. The fish suddenly squirmed out of his claw-like hands, blue-veined and covered with age spots. He cursed and scrambled after it. Wounded but apparently not mortally, the fish made its escape. It eluded him and splashed back into the pool.

He rose cursing, and laughing at the same time. A sparse grey beard partially covered his face. If it had once been full and black (as my father described him), it was now a motley joke. Patches of bare skin appeared as if to match the odd jumbled construction of his kingly coat. The dome of his head was hairless with stringy braids hanging down to his shoulders. The braids were in the style of the *sramanas*. I noticed then that he limped.

If this creature were truly Grand Duke Rudra, there had apparently been a bit of a slip from his once lofty position.

Like all Akkadeans, I despise the Yadish and their imperial pretensions. The Ra'bim I hate, of course. I've never really concerned myself with the other tribes. In a vague, off-hand way I'd sometimes wonder how they lived, what had become of them, whether they were still human. The Yadish, I came to believe, were the children of devils. I once heard it said that they interbred with the Yakashas, as did the people of Gad who also bordered the steppe. This incarnation of Grand Duke Rudra did nothing to challenge that belief.

He saw me and grinned hungrily as though I were another fish. I still wore the black priestly garb, now torn in many places.

"So— a priest," he exclaimed, and there was madness in his voice. It also seemed that he had trouble speaking, actually forming his words. "So, so—the, the monkeys caught a priest. Bet it was Log. He's a clever one, he is. Could be a priest himself. He, he, he…heh, heh…"

"Who are you?" I asked.

He danced a step, favoring his left leg. This threw him off-balance and caused him to teeter at the edge of the pool. A misstep and he'd follow his lost fish into the green water.

"Ha, ha...don't know a dead man when you sees 'em? So, so—who'er *you* is the question."

I remained silent. Who am I?

His dark eyes grew wide and he snorted. "So—how 'bout that. Ah ha, we sees it... White like the Rabs. Odd for Akkadeans, ain't so? By every asinine name that stupid stone monster of a Lord takes, I'd say you is a woman."

I drew myself to my full height. I did know why I answered him, the fool... "I am *She-With-Us*. Once they named me Devorah of Akkad."

"Oh yes, and so good for you. So—Wasn't it that scheming bastard Vishnu? I heard tell that the old Khan pimped his only daughter to the white bastard. And, and—some said she was the only fertile woman in Greenbottom. May be true, 'cept for the word *only*—"

I stared at him. He drooled and his head shook. His hands opened and closed, his eyes rolled. He appeared to shiver from the cold even beneath that ancient coat of the Unified Kingdom. I felt pity, a strange feeling for an Akkadean warrior. I must say that pity often comes too easily to me, as does love. It is true that my love is disinterested, not self-centered, so it is often mistaken for cold-heartedness. It is, however, the source of my pity.

"Vishnu's no more," I said flatly. I felt great joy.

"Oh no, no, no...don't be so quick to close the book on old Vishnu. Yes, yes, my priestess...someday you might add an entire Vishnu book to the *Runehayana*. Though, he'd probably rewrite it, I think."

"You know nothing of the poison soma Vishnu drank."

"Sure, sure, I do. I'm a dead man like him. Back from the dead too. Reborn, so to say. Call me man of the burial pit."

"You're Grand Duke, much diminished."

"Yes, yes, very much diminished, almost to a point, like a straight line that shrinks and shrinks. Buried in my grave. Resurrected by a monkey. Brought here to serve. To be served."

"What *are* these creatures?"

"Our saviors. Especially young Log. Killed Yakashas with his own paws, broke 'em in half, he did, like rotten wood. Sliced others with a harpoon. They was red Yakashas…don't know how he'd do against the grays or the yellows. He's quite a monkey, Log is."

"Log? You speak their language?"

Rudra's shoulders seemed to sag. His brow became furrowed as if he were in deep thought. "Not hard. Kind of takes you back to childhood, like when you made words up by clicking your tongue, smacking your lips, blowing air, coughing, groaning—noises. I seem to have a knack for it. Ah, I'm reborn, not so?"

Rudra was obviously howling mad, worse than I first thought. In the half century since then I've found nothing that compels me to change my mind.

"Your Log rescued me from the Sea of Reeds."

"So—so, what's an Akkadean priestess and Vishnu-lover doing in such a place, I wonder?"

I bristled. I spat at him: "Vishnu's vile, foul, failed and dead from his own foul and failed potions. *I know* about Ra'bim somas. If you must know, old fool, I'm on a …pilgrimage…the *Runehayana* names it. To the Lord on His Mountain."

"Oh no. The Lord on his chilly old rock? I know Him, I do. Don't you know I met Him in the steppe once long ago. I think it was once upon a time. Made me an Exalted Father, He did. Never a doubt 'bout it."

His face appeared hollow and skull-like, his sparse beard as dead moss covering ancient stone. But his eyes were alive, wild and crazed. Duke Rudra the Mad.

"How did you end up buried alive in your tomb?" I'd decided to play along.

EXALTED FATHER

"Why, your own Vishnu...also raised from the dead evidently. And his new wife. So, so—not really new. A Holy Mother she is."

The bull named Log entered the grotto. I had not noticed his leaving, but now he returned with the female wearing the pink coral necklace. She had exchanged her cub for a heavy club made from the branch of a black-barked banyan tree.

"What will these creatures do with us, Duke Rudra the Mad?

"Ah yes...so. They'll probably eat you."

BOOK OF CONFESSIONS
VERSE 4.2.3

The female growled deep in her throat. Next, she emitted a series of grunts and clicks. Log stared at me.

Rudra bowed clumsily favoring his left leg. He chattered and clicked in almost perfect imitation of the female. She responded, gesturing with a paw. Then she barred her fangs. Log turned to her and snarled.

Rudra suddenly began to whine. He hung his oversized head and appeared to cower.

The female glared at me. There was malevolence in her large brown eyes giving her a brutal, bestial air.

The young bull spoke again. He gestured with apparent urgency. I must say that since my awakening back in Tholos I've acquired something of a sensitivity to vibrations of sound and light. I am able to sense subtle things lesser folk do not. Am I not a remarkable woman? I knew that Log was asking a question.

Rudra kept his eyes lowered and did not respond.

"What are they saying?" I asked him.

"Foolish girl," Rudra hissed, "be quiet if you value your life."

The old man whined and clicked, and mewed like a cub.

Log barked. Rudra raised his head and lowered it just as quickly.

Then he muttered: "Hetman Log of the Reed Sea People demands that I inquire as to why you were spying upon his humble holdings—" He lowered his voice to a whisper. "Beware, foolish girl, the female believes you are a ghoul from the desert in the service of the red wisps."

"Red wisps?"

Exalted Father

"Yakashas. This is fortunate. Ghouls are inedible." He grinned up at me and smacked his lips. The queeti stared at him and seemed to grimace.

"And you?"

"Me? Oh, so, so, they don't know 'bout me." He grinned slyly.

A sharp exchange between the two creatures erupted suddenly. Log shook his spear and the female brandished her root-hammer. It went on for an hour, it seemed.

Finally, Log shrugged his massive shoulders.

The female growled at the former Grand Duke.

Rudra began mewing and moving his head up and down. He reminded me of the fool Talib. I had to repress the urge to laugh. The female glared at me and again barred her fangs.

Log padded over and grabbed me by the arm. He was not gentle.

"Don't resist," Rudra warned, still bobbing his head.

The bull dragged me through the narrow passage back to the main cave. The female followed, with Rudra in her wake. He shuffled along, favoring his left side—I noticed that his left shoulder seemed slightly lower than his right—muttering to himself and shaking his head. Froth formed at the corners of his mouth and dripped into his beard.

Laughing and muttering, "Farewell, wife of Vishnu, I hope the Reed Sea People serve you well."

The Laughing Duke I rename him.

THE BOOKS OF MARDUK

BOOK OF CONFESSIONS
VERSE 4.2.4

Over the years the steep staircase that winds up to my Queen's cell has become difficult to manage. It is not only due to the raw, burning pain between my legs. I know that I'm bleeding there at the moment. My body has become less agile, less flexible it seems, as though to somehow announce my barrenness. The Ra'bim white skin that once saved my life now threatens to take it. I'm becoming stiff, stone-like. It demands repayment. I'm becoming like the New-Men, a thing of creaking and grinding marble.

Who will rescue me from this body? Rather I should grow old and die—

My Grayfolk guards follow my uncertain steps. They bear plates of tarp hound liver, black bread, and that red, fleshy fruit they call peshapple. The New-Men find it delicious. In the past it gave me agonizing abdominal pains. These days it seems to agree with my constitution. I've developed a taste for it. Perhaps I'll grow a tail.

The wine is sour. It comes from the presses of Tharas Major. Southern wines no longer find their way north. Leeander tells me that an expedition is planned for the summer, to punish the lazy serfs of the Topartz, as was done to the Reed Sea serfs. As soon as we've concluded the Great Northern War and destroyed the Black One, he added.

Nonetheless I drink the wine and nibble the bread. The liver and peshapple I do not touch. When I'm finished, I drag myself to the narrow window and gaze down into the western courtyard, named *Thrice-blessed Yard of Orange Light and the Long Memories of Days End.* The daystar sets at a more southern angle. Winter is on the wane. A dreary day nears its end. Clouds chase the daystar over the rim of the world. Lesser Wind begins. There are *kittim* in the air, swirling down

Exalted Father

like snowflakes. They are large and colorful in the dull light of evening.

A hundred meters below, *kittim* catch three Grayfolk unawares. Unlike their lesser red brethren of the north, these servants of the New-Men have no fear of *kittim*. In the last year they've learned nothing. Stupid imps. The sound of their screaming bounces off the slick walls of stone and mortar. I can hardly see them in the gloom. In a few seconds they are pools of black liquid.

The King never says a word about the queeti rebellion in the south. Leeander is as reticent, although upon occasion he gives dark hints about wholesale disasters due to *kittim*. How can mindless *kittim* set traps and spring ambushes? The Great Northern War is a different matter.

The Holy Father merely laughs and indulges in long, convoluted discourses on legendary wars from a half-mythical past. It is the Lord's will, he will often conclude. No one, it seems to me, believes in any Lord on the Mountain, except for the drunken archbishop. Such pronouncements are for the queeti, those that remain attached to such hoary legends. Invisible causes do not defeat real armies.

Like all fathers, the Holy Father is an insane tyrant. I've considered killing him as soon as I can formulate a just reason, which is another reason for writing these *confessions*. Upon occasion he does exhibit a sense of humor, dark though it may be. Less frequently he indulges in spouting a proverb. Sometimes a thing exists and does not exist, at the same time in the same place, he will say—profoundly—which fucks with you, he adds with greater profundity.

The air is now thick with *kittim*. Perhaps I should put my new and improved body to the test. I will toss off these thick velvet robes, which they say are *kittim*-proof, and wander naked through the *Thrice-blessed* courtyard. New-Men are immune to *kittim* poisoning, they say. At least I've never heard of *kittim* taking a White Lord. They hide their vulnerabilities, I know. Yet, their ranks seem to be thinning. For how long this has been going on I cannot say. For what reason it is happening I do not know.

Wishful thinking and forlorn hope do nothing to relieve pain. Am I not one of them? Perhaps I'll grow a tail.

When I finally turn from the window and return to my desk I'm smiling.

Exalted Father

BOOK OF CONFESSIONS
VERSE 4.2.5

What remained of the population of the Reed Sea People gathered in the central cave. Log dragged me to its center where a fire burned in the pit of red bricks, bricks made by queeti slaves in the city of Zell. Far above our heads, light found its way into the cave through fissures in the rock.

All sorts of metal hooks and spikes hung from iron rods suspended above the fire from steel tripods. Other than Log's bronze spear, these were the first metal implements I'd seen among these creatures. The steel looked to be of Nepptali make. Briefly I wondered how these strange beings had acquired it.

I noticed that the female had taken my scimitar. Log eyed her warily. He pushed me forward and she raised the blade. She began to howl as does a tarp hound during a hunt.

The crowd howled with her. Up and down the scale, high and low, frenzied and gentle, they howled—now screeching, now rumbling as thunder over the horizon, or the grinding of rock deep in the ground.

She let out a series of barks and they stopped. Log bowed. She closed her eyes and began to moan. The moan gradually passed into a wail. The other females, and some cubs, took up the wail. The males, mostly stooped and old, began to listlessly beat their chests. Not a few suffered coughing fits.

Somewhere above, on ledges along the walls, drums began to beat. The smoke and gloom, pierced in places by daylight, revealed vague shaggy forms and barrel-like drums. I guessed these were older cubs, adolescents.

A young female approached the fire. Her brown pelt seemed more like finely combed hair than fur, and her lower jaw appeared smaller, more human-like. Her arms were shorter, her head bigger, her nose sharper, her ears rounded. Her eyes were brilliant green and she possessed six fingers on each hand.

She bowed daintily before the female who I learned was named Pink-coral, and who seemed to glare at her. She lowered my scimitar and barked a command.

Green-eyes (as I shall name her) carried a pouch made from animal skin—fallow deer, I'd guess. Hanging from a belt of sea shells that covered her genital area, the pouch bulged with some kind of dark purple bulb about the size of a human head.

She bowed again and began to peel away the plant skin, much as I recall Akkadean cooks peeling a purple onion. This bulb possessed an ominous look. It bled a red juice. She turned and tossed layers of skin into the fire.

The flames sizzled for a second and then leaped up. A pungent smoke began to spread about the cave.

I tried not to breathe the fumes. Naturally this was futile. When I finally did take a breath I could not help but fill my lungs.

The smoke did not burn. It hardly seemed like smoke. I felt as though I was back in Akkad sipping soothing milk from the vines of the sweetwater trees that grew in clusters by the shore of Emerald Lake. Sweetwater milk was good for sore throats and fever. The fumes from the purple bulb caused fever, but a bizarre fever not unlike the somas of the Ra'bim.

My body relaxed, became languid, then fluid, then gaseous, then…a field of living energy spreading out in space and time. Around me a profound stillness settled over the crowd. I experienced an indescribable serenity, a falling away, not unlike the effects of Marduk's voice—oh, I said *his name*—when he rescued me from the Ra'bim physicians. I laughed. I giggled. I flew out of the cave and into the dark sky without moving a muscle. Free.

Sensations… What is beyond time and space words cannot grasp, for they are born of space and time.

Exalted Father

Brilliant light, comforting warmth, the Reed Sea People there with me, of me, all in all.

I—they—*we* are standing in a clearing surrounded by a primordial jungle.

A mass appears, red, orange, white and yellow, yet it winks blue as the light moves, as its flanks soak in the light of the daystar. It pulsates, this mass, and light flows up and down its crystalline arteries. It is a mass of living rock reaching up past the clouds.

It draws us by invisible lines of force.

A Grey is with us. He is young. *I know him.* How? I cannot say. He is with us, small and furred, say, a field mouse. Grey is a male A White Mother—I see her too.

The great mountain of glass and rock and crystal and iron begins to rumble. It begins to smoke. Lightning flashes and splits the clouds that conceal its peak. Thunder rolls over our heads and we tremble. Then we begin to wail. I've never felt such fear, *never*.

Black clouds billow down the mountain's sheer flanks. They seem to coalesce and form a barrier, a wall. Grey steps forward. We cry out in dismay. The cloud-wall expands, gobbles him up. He vanishes.

We stand wailing, sick at heart. In a moment we will panic and scurry back to our jungle home.

We give a collective gasp. The wall splits. Grey emerges. His fur is white as snow, his eyes glowing as do embers from the evening campfires, but his body seems broken. He has aged suddenly.

"Behold," he cries in a voice as loud as the thunder that rolls through the mountain peaks. *I understand his language. I grasp the language of the queeti.*

"Behold, I've seen the Lord face to face, I have. Behold, I still live. He is a consuming fire. He is a black cloud. He is the presence of a raging storm—"

Grey began to weep. He cried as if in real pain. He beat his chest and tore his fur.

"Alas," he howled, "and the Lord said to me: *You are not of my kind. You are not in my image. You are destined to serve and obey."*

"How may we serve you, oh Lord, Exalted Father?"

"I am not your Father, but I am Exalted. You will serve me nevertheless. Wherever you are, whatever you are doing, whenever you are doing it, you must stop and sacrifice to me. Blood must you pour out at my feet. Blood and more blood. Then you serve the Lord who is not of your kind—"

We came back to the cave. I was there beside Pink-coral. She raised the scimitar. Her eyes were clear and fierce, blazing red in the firelight.

"Have we served Exalter Father?"

"NO," the people shouted in unison.

"Why not?"

"Grey forbade it," Log growled. The people nodded.

What had the purple bulb done to me? I could still understand their grunts, barks, clicks, snorts and growls.

"Grey forbade the shedding of blood, he. Grey and the other Greys before him. Another came between he and his Lord."

The crowd repeated these words like a chant: "Another came between we and our Lord—"

"*I don't forbid it!* Exalted Father has punished us, he has. He took my mate, the greatest Hetman of the Reed Sea People. He has sent red wisps to rape my sisters, to kill our brothers, fathers, uncles, husbands, sons. Why?

"Exalted Father have we failed. Grey was wrong. To water the soil with blood. To sacrifice."

She grasped my arm and pulled me to her. Her grip was iron.

"*Blood!*" she screeched.

"*Blood,*" they answered, even Log.

She tore the soiled priestly cloak from my body. She brought the sharp blade to my throat.

EXALTED FATHER

THE BOOK OF CONFESSIONS

CHAPTER THREE – From the Life of a Remarkable Woman

(How I Became a White Mother)

VERSE 4.3.1

I confess it here.

I participated freely in the rituals of our Tribe of Akkad. I mouthed the formulas. I sang the sacred litanies of the Milresh Festival. I stood for the three days and two nights in the Plaza of the Borassus and braved the *kittim* of the fall. I fasted the week of Vernal in the Spring. I danced the Twelve Days of Frutose and wept the dark days of Motsol.

Though I did all that was expected, I never believed. As I've said, I sought the truth in all things. There was no divine Lord on Elsseleron. No revelation in the *Runehayana*. All priests were liars. I knew these things with unshakable certainty. Especially after my Protector deserted me, for he too was a lie.

I laughed at the stories of Suthralane. The *Runehayana* I never read (then). If I had, it would have bored me, for I despise uncertainty and grow weary of probabilities. I knew I was more intelligent than any priest. Even in Nalanda, even during my struggles with the Runes, I knew.

It is a hard thing when life itself forces surrender, when certainties die long before their time. These are dark days indeed. Yet I still refuse. I detest the whole gang of Fathers, Protectors and Seers and all other dung-filled shit-bags. I cling to my refusal and will continue to cling even if the Lord Himself should thunder into my cell and shit in my privy.

Lesser Wind has ceased. The night air grows cold, strange for this continent named Starmirror.

The King taunts me. Even his servants taunt me: "Why so sad? Why are you weeping? Why don't you eat?"

I am wretched. I want no child. I am not of *his* kind—despite my Ra'bim metamorphosis. I am not of his kind.

Such thoughts oppress me as I stagger back to my writing table. Another memory forms, some slimy thing from the bottom of Lake Emerald.

By chance I met the Holy Father newly crowned, coming from the Presence Room. My hate burned, for I hate all Fathers, be they Khans, Great, Exalted, or Holy.

"Ah, Rudra, the Laughing Duke," I addressed him with contempt in my voice, refusing to use his new title, "once Grand Duke, Grand Liar, Betrayer, Pimp and Prophet, now *Holy*. How's that?"

"My Queen," he answered grave and slow, groping for his words, and limping. "You are—so unjust. Are you not.... Queen? What a fine gown. Did you know it takes the Topartz serfs a year of labor to sew such a garment? And what's this? Wool from the silver ram to wear over it? So much toil for such privilege."

I hugged the silver woolen cloak about my body. "I'm cold, even in the thickest coats, even in the southern summer."

"A shame it is. Perhaps...one should refuse the red onion."

"Ah, Rudra, have you not forbidden the queeti their herb of visions? I've heard tell that you've ordered the Topartz gardens burned and uprooted."

"So, so…yes, it breeds disorder…and illness. I see its effects on you. And, my dear Queen, it is the source of terrible illusions. Lord Illusion, I name it."

"As the Lord on His Mountain. On this we may agree."

The Holy Father bowed his head, which despite the vast and bulky robes of his office still appeared overlarge for his body. "The Lord is no illusion… for serfs…yet the herb produces them."

"Perhaps you fear what they might see? Perhaps you fear another Grey? A Blue perhaps?"

"They are children. They will never understand. We must guide them."

"Ah, you and your drunken archbishop."

"Do not abuse us, my Queen. We do the King your husband's holy work. We are not New-Men. We still believe in the Lord."

"I know the red onion of the soul, Rudra Betrayer. It was very much like another experience from long ago, which has faded but which I believe was quite real."

Rudra gave a faint smile. His teeth were yellow and two were missing. His beard had turned a dingy white. "Oh, my dear, speak not of crazy Marduk. Forget not we have his tooth in our Cathedral. It is all that remains of his foolishness."

"The archbishop doesn't think him a fool."

"Oh, the dear archbishop. He drinks too much. But we need not worry. The ignorant serfs will never comprehend a single spider-hair of his tangled theology. As long as they believe in the Lord of the Mountain and His Holy Laws—"

"As long as they serve the White Fathers?"

"And the dear archbishop is the Exalted Father's mouth…and the tooth came from the mouth of His Son."

"Which you do not believe? As I do not believe."

The new Holy Father bowed his huge head. His long black braids dangled like thick friff vines. "No, I believe—"

"Ha! Duke Rudra the Mad, Laughing Duke turned madman, liar turned saint, the dead return."

"Holy Father."

"Yes, of course. Tell me, then, *Holy Father*, did an illusion produce the sacrifice?"

"What do you mean?"

"Do false visions caused by jungle plants produce rituals that cause people to spill blood? Is it not evident that the vision comes from their own heads, though they swim in smoke? The plant opens the door but does create the monster that waits within. Don't forget, Rudra Betrayer, I know the Ra'bim somas."

He shook his head. "It is rather the ritual that they create to give meaning to the visions."

"That merely pushes my question a step back. What, then, is the origin of the ritual itself?"

Rudra gave a shrug and adjusted his colorful robes. "An off chance observation. A serf cow sees a slaughtered animal. Perhaps a mosscat takes down a fallow deer. How much blood there is. And soon afterwards she finds herself pregnant. 'Spilled blood gives life' says a Grey, his head soaking in the smoke of the red onion. Then he has another vision, a red lion tears apart a serf from the village. You know how the Greys think: his vision is more real than the cow's. So, he orders a serf be sacrificed. But nothing happens. Not a single cow turns up pregnant. That season the crops wither. Such failures do not deter a Grey. Oh no. He orders another sacrifice, and another. And then it happens: a cow is with child. And so the red onion founds the ritual of sacrifice. Only later do stories told around campfires anchor the ritual to reality."

I recall Rudra's self-satisfied look.

"Of course," he added, "there is another way. We-who-know create the ritual and claim that it descends from the Lord's Holy

EXALTED FATHER

Mountain. We package it in rules and stories, dim history filled with mysterious meanings, mysterious at least in their furry ears. It is probably easier that way. Prevents any misunderstanding."

"So they remain serfs."

"Oh, they're born to it. We give them explanations."

"Rudra, I was mistaken. You really are a Holy Father."

He bowed. It was difficult for him.

I remember just how it went. I hate the whole gang of fathers. I will consign this memory with the others, and be rid of them.

THE BOOKS OF MARDUK

BOOK OF CONFESSIONS
VERSE 4.3.2

She held the scimitar to my throat. The cold Nepptali steel cut into my soma-coated skin causing the warm blood to flow.

"Blood, blood..." the crowd howled.

I had but one chance. My tough Ra'bim skin could not defeat fine Nepptali steel and it retarded my reflexes. But I had to try. One chance. Am I not an Akkadean warrior?

I exhaled. Pressing back against her, I drew into myself, and then tried to fall away.

Her claws tightened, nearly breaking my bones. I could not clear the blade. She hissed into my ears. Once more I was in the embrace of a deadly serpent.

Log suddenly snarled and barked a string of words. I could barely comprehend their meaning—the red onion was wearing off. In a moment I'd be dead.

Pink-coral hesitated. Log barked at her. "See, she is no ghoul—" He grasped what remained of the priest rags and tore them from my body.

Pink-coral inhaled sharply. She dropped the scimitar and pushed me away.

Snarls, growls, howls, high-pitched whines, sounds I'd never thought possible filled the cavern. My white Ra'bim skin blazed as if the daystar itself had come to dwell underground.

"A White Mother!"

They dropped to their knees, even Pink-coral, although somewhat reluctantly.

"White Mother."

"Whissling."

"Queen."

EXALTED FATHER

Thus did I become the White Mother of the Reed Sea People. Pink-coral hated me but was powerless. Log and the elder males acknowledged the fact. She could not sway them. That I never claimed the titles they bestowed upon me, that I never encouraged their beliefs, matters not a grain of sand. Once their minds were fixed there was no argument, no fact, which contained the force to budge them. Their faith was a mountain that refused to move.

How they came to this conclusion baffles me to this day. I was White Mother of the Reed Sea People—as though I'd been so since the day of my birth. They suddenly perceived what was always there. *In those days* they were children, of course. They judged immediately. Their minds had yet to mature.

THE BOOKS OF MARDUK

BOOK OF CONFESSIONS
VERSE 4.3.3

By mid-winter I'd managed to acquire a reasonable grasp of their language. Rudra the Betrayer at least told the truth in this: it was like a return to childhood. Not a childhood I'd known personally, rather I seemed to enter a deeper childhood not unlike those memories of other places and different times when I knew *him*. The language caused seeds to sprout. Vague, without meaningful form, random weeds that suggest real things in the world, I sensed memories that were not mine. Somewhere, sometime, some*thing* had once spoken such a language. I could not say its name.

Lord Rekhmire did not return to Zell. None of the White Fathers come north in the winter. *Kittim* crossed the Windward Straits, air-born armies of locusts, and the Winds blew steadily. The Reed Sea People loved *kittim*. They laughed at their beautiful colors and aimless cavorting in the winds. If one should dissolve into their fur, they'd lick the spot as though it were dew.

Along with their language, I learned of the Reed Sea People's war against the red wisps of the Edom Desert. Log described how the wisps had abducted females, even Pink-coral herself. He told of the Great War, how Hetman Green-eyes (a common name among the queeti, as was Pink-coral) dared to lead them across the desert and into the steppe, and won a tremendous battle. Spear-toe, so old that two young cubs supported him, one under each arm wherever he went, told of the heroic Shaman Grey (all Shamans are Grey). Grey gave his life as a diversion.

"Behold, and there stood Grey amid grasses tall," croaked the ancient bull, "seen of the wisps, and they seen not Hetman's army, they. It closed circle around 'em. Yes. And Hetman Green-eyes kilt them all and ate them all, he. One red wisp escape and betray Green-

Exalted Father

eyes to gray wisps that serves the White Fathers. Grey wisps in fire drown them, they. Pink-coral escape—"

Pink-coral *said* she'd escaped the steppe wisps. She refused to speak of it, and she refused to speak to me. To her I was invisible. I thought it probable that she still believed I was a ghoul. In this I was mistaken.

Spear-toe had a habit of dozing off in the middle of a discourse. Sitting in the late afternoon sun, the warmth soaking his old bones, the wind gently stroking his fur, he gazed off to the Reed Sea and soon his words fluttered above the winter brown marsh like *kittim*. They left him at last, and he'd grunt softly, which I took for slumber. Language seemed new to these creatures. Their grasp on it was easily broken.

I learned to wait patiently. I'd grown quite fond of the old bull. Eventually the discourse would continue, but not always where it left off.

"She say Grey made her a White..." He paused and glanced back into the cave. Then he winked at me and whispered: "Thinks she likes phalabulb too much, she. Wisps only capture her in her dream. Never in steppe, her. Hid away to avoid work. Green-eyes believed her captured and died 'cause of it. With her, phalasmoke fills the cave but we never go to joyful places as with Grey. No, bad, dangerous places, like Exalted Father's mountain, dark jungles of the Topartz, twin-mountains of White Fathers. And *he* is never there—"

"*He-who-is-never-there?*"

"Wanderer who is lame. Who loves poor serfs of Zell, him."

Naturally (and not for the first time) his language puzzled me. Before I could think of something to ask, Spear-toe grunted with contempt.

"She thinks herself a White. Young Six-fingers, she say, is sign of Exalted Father's blessings upon her, Him.

"Log come back with Many-colors. He laugh in her face, Log did. I Hetman, says Log. Challenge if you dare, you. She didn't, yes.

Log then throw Many-colors into Pool Cave. Many Reed Sea People think him a ghoul."

I laughed. "My dear old Spear-toe, he's no ghoul."

Spear-toe gazed at me for a long time. His eyes were milky, nearly all white, yet he said that he saw perfectly with the help of the phalabulb which he often mixed with his morning tea. "Many-colors say that White Mother is a ghoul, she. I know she no ghoul."

"No—" I gently patted the top of his large head. "No ghoul."

I was about to add that neither was I a mother, white or brown, yet something stopped me. A memory perhaps. I remembered my foolish speech (*these days* it sounds foolish) before the drunken archbishop and his deceitful ox back in Nalanda. Yes, how foolish. Perhaps even now. Yet, why should I change? To these simple ones I am White Mother.

Spear-toe let out a long sigh. "That is good. Many-colors is a ghoul, so says Pink-coral. She also say that tomorrow we put him to the test."

EXALTED FATHER

BOOK OF CONFESSIONS
VERSE 4.3.4

I find it difficult reading queeti expressions. They still elude me.

Pink-coral, it seemed to me, was fuming. She surely resented my abrupt ascendency among the Reed Sea People. She hated Log, I think. For sure she despised Spear-toe with his self-professed knowledge of arcane customs. She had no patience for his incomprehensible lectures on those customs. Yet, his stumbling rhetorical nonsense was empty of arrogance and pride as much as it was empty of sense.

A stiff, rain-filled wind blew cold salt air from a distant sea, as though the weather was impatient for the arrival of Lesser Wind in the evening. Perhaps there'd be no spring for Starmirror this year. The *kittim,* no doubt, had decided to remain sailing serenely above the heavy clouds this day.

Rain-water hanging in huge drops from their fur, a forlorn gang of queeti stood huddled together in the open on the sandy shore of the Reed Sea, only because Spear-toe insisted that the trial of a suspected ghoul be held in the open, "near water."

"For if he be a ghoul butterflies will take him," Spear-toe observed searching the dark skies with his milky eyes.

Rudra Yadish stood with his back to the sea facing the tight knot of queeti. He smirked. He appeared to be enjoying himself. "Do ghouls dissolve in the rain, my dear scholar?" he asked Spear-toe.

"No—"

"What do Spear-toe know 'bout ghouls that none else know? Is he a Grey?" Pink-coral barked.

Spear-toe looked in her direction but I could not be certain if he actually saw her.

"He's no Grey, I am," Spear-toe answered her.

"Then how know you he's a ghoul?"

"From past."

"What past? Father? Grandfather?"

He appeared stumped. Shaking off the water as does a tarp hound, he said: "Grandfather—"

"Grandfather no Grey. Did he meet a ghoul?"

"No…but his grandfather did, who told him, who told his father, who told…father, then me."

Pink-coral gave a sharp whistle, which I think meant she was scoffing and mocking and laughing at the same time.

"We know not what this grandfather saw. Perhaps he saw a White Father from far away and thought it wore many-colors like this ghoul.

Spear-toe seemed puzzled. "Others saw it—"

"And who heard these others tell of this seeing?"

"Others heard."

"And those others? Who heard them?"

"Others. Lots of others *in those days*, them."

"Enough." Log growled. "What do we actually know for sure 'bout ghouls?"

"Big are they," Spear-toe continued doggedly. "Not as big as White Fathers. They've no tails, and are many colored, some gold like fire, fire are they. And—" He glanced at Rudra, or at Rudra's wavering outline— "they steals tiny cubs in the night, and eats 'em."

The crowd emitted a collective howl.

"Take this thing to Lord Rekhmire," an old male bellowed, one they named Black-tooth. Actually, his teeth *had been* black at one time but were now mostly missing. His long face and heavy lower jaw gave him the look of one in constant pain. He was missing a left ear.

"Lord Rekhmire is not in Zell," Log barked, "and…I decide, not you."

Exalted Father

"You are not Hetman," Pink-coral reminded him. "My mate is Hetman. Till he returns, my cub Six-fingers. I speak for cub!"

I had not yet learned to read queeti faces as I've said (I'm not certain I can read them now). Pink-coral seemed determined. Her wide nostrils flared and her thin lips curled, exposing yellow fangs. What little she had of a forehead appeared furrowed and pushed down on her protruding eye sockets.

Log glared back at her with an almost identical determined—and dangerous—look. "Your mate is dead," he declared, "and you are not Mother."

Pink-coral snarled: "Not true, not true. Saw I did. Green-eyes. He was hiding in the weeds that grow along the shore. He was fishing. I ran to him."

Log gave a grunting laugh. "He is dead and you were dreaming. Why no other People see him?"

Pink-coral refused to yield an inch of ground. "Is because he only appears to me. Yes! Exalted Father raised him from the dead. And you must believe this before he appears to you."

Black-tooth appeared to brighten and the rain no longer seemed to fail on him. "Green-eyes dead but now alive?"

"Yes," Pink-coral acknowledged. "Although once dead, Exalted Father raised him up. I White Mother, better than any Grey. Better than a Blue am I. I see things others don't. Believe in him. Believe in me."

"What 'bout this White Mother?" Log tried to sound genuinely curious, but even I could tell that he goaded her. "She *White*."

Pink-coral exploded. Her growls came deep and dangerous, her fangs fully exposed. She gathered herself and prepared to spring on me.

Black-tooth stepped between us. "Gives her to Lord Rekhmire, I say, when he is back in Zell."

"No!" Log barked again. He shook his spear. Black-tooth backed away and although Pink-coral still growled she shrank back too. Log was a massive young bull, an imposing match even for a resurrected Hetman.

"I Hetman."

"Cub is Hetman." Pink-coral was obstinate. "Until father return."

Spear-toe suddenly spoke up. "Tradition say that Hetman is chosen...by Lord Rekhmire instead of Mother as in times past. Who choose Green-eyes? Not Rekhmire. Reed Sea People choose Green-eyes, as told to by Exalted Father who spoke to Grey. Exalted Father only speak to White Fathers, who speak to serfs, which is us poor ones. Until Grey. He dead, he. White Father not here, Him. Exalted Father does not speak to us...and, Reed Sea People cannot be without Hetman..."

Spear-toe was breathing hard. It amazed me that he was able to keep his *fathers* in order.

"*...therefore, Log is Hetman.*"

"Then we proceed," Log announced not giving Pink-coral a chance to respond.

Booming laughter suddenly filled the wet air. Rudra was laughing so hard that he nearly collapsed. His braided locks jerked like serpents. I thought his oversized head might break his skinny neck.

"Oh, I like this," he gasped, fixing his eyes on Pink-coral and Black-tooth. "I died too, you know...yes, yes, dead and buried. Yet, here am I." He paused and glanced in my direction. "So, so, many possibilities are possible, even the most improbable."

"Ghoul mocks us," a young female said. I knew her as Bird-breast. She was much thinner than the others; her fur seemed finer and in some places I could see bare skin. She seemed less...well, bestial than the others.

"Not a ghoul until trial," Pink-coral snarled.

"Then, trial," Bird-breast said.

Log looked at Spear-toe. "What is trial?"

"Don't know—"

EXALTED FATHER

"He is Rudra," I interrupted in my halting queeti, "a Yad."

Rudra lifted his arms and flapped like a bird. His patched coat, threadbare and soiled, added an abstract splash of changing color to the drab wet scene. He was a hundred *kittim* come together.

"I am Rudra, I am Rudra..." He laughed and danced, and reminded me of Talib.

"...I am Rudra, a Rudra, more powerful than any stupid ghoul. Aye, aye, more dangerous too. I'm back from the dead..."

He danced up to Log, who despite having an advantage in weight and weaponry (his forgotten spear) looked startled if not frightened (if I read queeti emotions correctly).

"You know me, Log."

"I know you." Log seemed to mew like a cub.

"I am a Rudra, wind from the desert. Exalted Father raised me from my tomb. You, Log, are a witness. You, Log, His instrument."

"Yes, great one." Log appeared to be in a trance.

"So, my dear, dear Log, the *Lord* names you Hetman."

I wondered if by using the word Lord, Rudra was referring to himself

Pink-coral whined.

"White Mother I name *Blue*."

I assumed he meant me.

Pink-coral choked.

"To Pink-coral I say, damsel, arise and return to your cave. Forget thy vain hopes."

Black-tooth rumbled: "He a Rudra, no ghoul." He looked forlorn again.

Spear-toe looked confused.

Log breathed: "Oh *Lord*, what is a Rudra?"

"A Yad," I said, but I didn't have the words to explain to them what a Yad was.

"A wind from the desert, a voice in the wind, the mouth of the Exalted Father on His Mountain, Law-giver...death-dealer, a father...a Holy Father," Rudra cried.

"He is...jokes you..." I said, but they ignored me. Like Greys, Blues spoke in riddles, they said. I was *onion-addled*.

Pink-coral shook and drooled. The others dropped to their knees and put their heads face-down in the mud.

"He is Rudra. Holy Father."

Rudra waved his arms in a blessing. He glanced at me and grinned.

"Behold the beginnings of my kingdom, White Mother-now-Blue. Behold the creation of a Holy Father."

"Rudra," I groaned in Sandi, "Who would ever believe such foolishness? Except the Laughing Duke—"

Rudra laughed.

"The trial is concluded. It is settled."

"It is settled," Log agreed.

The great majority grunted their approval. Spear-toe still looked confused. Pink-coral seemed shocked.

So it *was* settled. Rudra was no ghoul. He was a Holy Father, raised from the dead by the Exalted Father of the Mountain, in whom neither Rudra nor the White Fathers believed. Oh, all those damned fathers! Did I say that I hated the whole gang of them?

EXALTED FATHER

BOOK OF CONFESSIONS
<u>VERSE 4.3.5</u>

We lived among the Reed Sea People for a year. Rudra directed the young bulls to construct a throne, the seat, the *see* as he called it, of the Holy Father. He seemed less obsessed with his death and rebirth. He appeared more vital, although life still seemed to be something he observed at a distance, as though from the top of a mountain or even one of the nearer stars. His appetite improved and he gained weight, which was something of a miracle given that, as I've remarked elsewhere, queeti delicacies were like poison to us. Yet his head still appeared overlarge, and something within him still appeared to be missing.

The queeti built a magnificent throne of acacia wood harvested from the forests south of Zell. As Log explained it to me, the Holy Father taught them that the acacia wood, the terebinths, olive trees, the vineyards, yellow meadows, all belonged to the peasants. The White Fathers, he added, cannot claim as their own the natural world, for they were not eternal, though they may seem like it (or think themselves it—I still had difficulties with the language despite its simplicity).

Log said: "We are gardeners. Even White Fathers, though they do not garden for they have not the tools. Cut trees, take wood. All belongs to all. Belonging to all, all belongs to no one."

Because Zell appeared deserted, Rudra declared that its wealth (the queeti word he used was *stuff*) "belonged to everyone and no one." Fortunately for Rudra, this wealth included many large casks of wheat beer, which also belonged to everyone, especially the Holy Father.

When they liberated Zell from the burden of its *stuff*, they discovered a few Grayfolk lingering in the empty city. Almost all of these lingers did their lingering in bed since they'd been poisoned by *kittim*. Based upon the principle that "those who do not work are eaten" (again it became evident that queeti language was ill-equipped to express the profound thoughts of the Holy Father), they were slaughtered immediately. I don't know if the queeti ate them. Log scowled when I asked the question and looked at me as if I'd understood nothing. He did call them possessors…or was it possessed?

"Holy Father say we must dispossess the possessed. So we did. They are possessed no more."

I learned later (from Spear-toe) that they first dispossessed the possessed of their weapons: a few bronze swords, two blades of good Nepptali steel, and a working L-gun. The Grayfolk spoke Sandi, which surprised the Holy Father greatly. He interrogated the captain of the Grayfolk for a long time (the length of a piss, Spear-toe said, by which he meant the time between two consecutive urinations—I believe). In the end he honored the gray wisp (as the queeti named them) with a death at the hands of the Holy Father—to which no queeti was witness. Rudra told them about it later. "I disemboweled the bastard," he said, and everyone approved, although no one had witnessed the act, for they trusted the Holy Father's truth implicitly.

Rudra's acacia throne was quite large and finely made. The queeti proved to be masters of the wood, as they said proudly. Rudra placed the throne at the east end of the main cave and set it upon a dais of rocks. The throne resembled a crude rectangular box the arm rests carved to look like bird wings.

It became the habit of the Holy Father to spend his entire day sitting on the throne and dispensing what he labeled "the Lord's Justice," while drinking wheat beer.

Log became his Grand Vizier (a term the queeti found hard to pronounce—they said something like "Grand Wizz"). Rudra convinced Log that this office was far greater than a mere Hetman, for it carried a certain dignity and splendor, and could never be bestowed by a White Mother or a Blue (which, I've come to learn, means something like "Great White Mother" though the precise meaning is uncertain), but the Lord-on-the-Mountain alone. Log recruited a dozen adolescent bulls as guards and armed them with dispossessed weapons, though he made sure to explain that this was perfectly in keeping with the Holy Father's teachings since they were not "of the possessed by weapons," or something to that effect.

Female queeti tended the fishing nets and worked the gardens outside the walls of Zell. Each day they braved the hazards of the marsh or made the exhausting climb to the city. The Holy Father graciously awarded them the honor of providing the necessities of life, for which they were especially well suited, he said. Theirs was the holy life of labor.

Tragically, fortune (or the Great Lord on High) did not always smile upon these happy female queeti. Two drowned, three became marsh serpents' dinner, and two fell to their deaths on the moss-covered stone of the slippery staircase cut into the plateau.

Not a few females suggested that perhaps it would please the Holy Father, and the Lord on High, if his holy guard assisted them in this holy labor. Rudra was quick to point out that the Lord on High, the Lord-on-the-Mountain, had destined the male-folk for other occupations. Serving in these other occupations meant serving the Lord. Of course, the Holy Father added, all occupations were of equal value in the eyes of the Lord.

The Books Of Marduk

BOOK OF CONFESSIONS
VERSE 4.3.6

One day I asked Spear-toe about the origins of the Reed Sea People. He blinked and pondered the question for a long time.

At last he said: "We are like all queeti. We come we from the south, where the River Topartz flows from Exalted Father's mountain and waters the land. There did a garden grow—"

"A jungle?" I said the word in Sandi.

He stared at me with those milky eyes. He looked but did he see? I could not be sure if he saw me or was gazing back in time.

"Yes, White Mother Blue, as you say, you. We were free then, not peasants. Then White Fathers came. Our Tribe fled north, we did. Others stayed and became peasants then. White Fathers do not like the north, you know."

"I know. How often does Lord Rekhmire come to Zell?"

"Sometimes in the summers."

"Last summer?"

"Last, last summer, I think. Gray wisps are always there."

"Yes, I know. Tell me more. Why only your Tribe?"

"Our Grey us led."

"This Grey…why did he lead you from the …garden?"

Spear-toe frowned. Or he grimaced. I find it less difficult reading queeti faces, yet Spear-toe was always a problem.

"Our Grey discovered the mystery of the red onion of the soul. Was the first time he visited Exalted Father's mountain, before coming of Exalted Father. Then this Grey named it Flat Cake Mountain."

"Are you saying there was a time when Exalted Father did not live on His Mountain?"

EXALTED FATHER

"Yes. Grey found him not there at that time, he did. *There was then a time when He was not.*"

I took a deep breath and experienced once again the binding of my Ra'bim skin—a soft flexible metal, a protective prison. "I once learned of this back *then*...in Nalanda (I said the words in Sandi) from *Isa*, the first Book of the *Runehayana*."

Spear-toe shrugged. "Does White Mother Blue speak of White Fathers?" he inquired.

"No. Of Exalted Father. Of the *then* before Exalted Father."

"No Exalted Father then," Spear-toe repeated, sounding irritated. "No White Fathers or White Mothers. Not white, not black. Neither not-white nor not-black."

"What did Grey find."

"Not one, not two. One and two. Neither one and two. Neither not-one and not-two... Only goats."

He paused and now I was certain that he looked beyond me to that *then*, when there was only the garden of the queeti.

"We did not work the land then, we had no need then. Nor did we fish the rivers then. The queeti of old, neither did they speak. They had no need, they. Then they possessed no things, no names, no words, and they were happy. When hungry they ate. When tired they slept. They were like the birds of the air. They were like the butterflies—"

"How did they live? I mean, was there a Hetman?"

"No Hetman, only a Grey and a Blue. One Grey for many tribes. Blue too. Our Grey dug the red onion, as I've said."

"Before Spear-toe said? Who said before?"

"Others. Others before them. They make a shoreline longer than the Topartz on both sides. They are all Spear-toe, they. Those who remember."

"Your Grey climbed Flat Cake Mountain?"

"As I've said." Spear-toe stared at me. His look might have been one of impatience.

"And found nothing?"

"No thing, no Exalted Father, only goats. Is White Mother Blue deaf?" Impatience turned into bemusement.

"Why, then, did Grey lead the Tribe north?"

"*Then* he saw—"

"Saw what?"

"It was his work to see, and so then he saw."

"What?"

"What…do you say?"

"What he saw on Flat Cake Mountain?"

"As I say, he then saw no-thing there."

"Yet some-*thing* caused him to lead the Tribe north."

This time Spear-toe seemed to laugh, which was like a choking sound deep in his throat. "*On* Flat Cake Mountain he saw no-thing. *From* Flat Cake Mountain he saw a star with hair, with a mane like red lion. It was a sign from heaven. To north go."

His milky eyes suddenly seemed to melt and run down his cheeks, down the hollow places where his cheeks had once been. "It did no good. White Lords came north later. All the way to the Reed Sea. So we became peasants, we. Who will rescue us from our curse?"

"What about Exalted Father?"

"White Fathers taught us about Exalted Father. He ruled the mountain, then. No more goats. There were others too, much older. Of those ones we know no-thing. Grey knew."

It had become clear to me that Spear-toe confused his Greys, and I doubted that he was aware of his shuffling a Grey from one period of time to another. For him, while each Grey was distinct and unique, all of them were One Grey. I don't think he was even capable of making the distinction between an individual Grey and the category Grey.

"Grey knew because Grey climbed the mountain—"

Suddenly a thought flashed through my mind: *Spear-toe in a very crude manner had just related the Legend of Suthralane.*

"We from the north—the hairless—have our own Grey," I said to him.

He nodded. "All have a Grey, yes."

"Our Grey was named Suthralane."

"Funny name. He not a Grey then?"

"No, he *was*, only with a different name."

"Then how could he be a Grey, he?"

"Different name…but the same…" (I had trouble finding a word) "…*stuff*," I concluded lamely.

"Only Grey can be Grey. White Mother Blue is very confused."

He hoisted himself up and waddled out of the cave to soak in the afternoon daystar. It was his way of dismissing me. To Spear-toe of prodigious and shining memory, I may have been a White Mother Blue, but I was surely a poor student of queeti lore. As it turned out, he never again attempted to give me instruction in such obtuse and cryptic teachings, although I begged him frequently.

Every time I asked, he would say: "Oh no, no, the rolling wheel confuses our White Mother—Blue."

THE BOOKS OF MARDUK

BOOK OF CONFESSIONS
VERSE 4.3.7

One-day Pink-coral refused to work the nets. Apparently, she'd given up on the return of Green-eyes, and so she believed that little Six-fingers the rightful Hetman. She was the rightful Blue. A Blue does not fish.

She planted herself before Rudra and bellowed her frustration. She bellowed, growled, barked, spit and hissed, but she did not whine. I could not understand her. I was not certain that the noises she made were language. It was quite clear, though, that she had had enough of the Holy Father—the White Fathers, the Father on High— Fathers in general. Although she hated me and was always doing petty, mean-spirited things to make me miserable, I found myself in sympathy with her. As I've said many times, I, too, despise the whole gang of Fathers.

When she'd finally exhausted herself hurling abuse at the Holy Father, Rudra rose stiffly and descended the dais. He'd gained weight, as I've said before. I noticed that his coat of many colors split at the seams in the region of his belly. He also appeared pale and unhealthy. In this he resembled the albino fish that swam in the underground pool. He was nearly as white as any Ra'bim, but there was something sickly and unnatural about his color, or better, lack of color.

He shook his oiled braids and graced Pink-coral with a benevolent smile.

"My dear girl, fishing, tending nets, gathering, uh, tasty seaweed serves the tribe, as it does the Father of us all. Fishing is...how would a Grey say...*wonderful making the nest of the Lord.*"

She responded with a long and deep growl. Once more I failed to grasp her language.

Exalted Father

"Oh, surely not," Rudra chuckled. "I know my ancestors better than that!" He paused and I could see that he, too, was having problems formulating his thoughts in queeti although he was fluent as any native speaker. In fact, he was quite inventive. In only a few months he'd expanded the language adding many new words and phrases. He even talked of writing it. Now he seemed to flounder.

"...maybe that *one*..." He pointed in my direction. "She...who embraces serpents."

Cuddled and asleep in his mother's powerful arms, little Six-fingers suddenly awoke and began to whine."

"Oh, is your cub ill? Fever has him perhaps? Root—" he addressed a large young bull standing next to the throne. "Take you Pink-coral's cub to the green pool and cool it—off."

Root was large for his age. His arms were thick as oak branches. His shoulders were broad, his chest deep, legs as strong as the roots of the papal tree. His black eyes seemed lifeless, however, hidden in the dark recesses of overhanging brows. His face was flat and brutal.

Root reached for the cub. With her free paw, Pink-coral grabbed his forearm. She yanked it away from little Green-eyes and then sank her fangs into his fur.

He yowled and clubbed her on the top of the head with a huge fist. The blow staggered her, but she shook herself and went for his throat. Instantly, the other guards swarmed in biting and clawing. They tore young Six-fingers from her grasp. Thrown off balance, she missed her attempt to tear at Root's jugular. Screeching, she fought them as would a wild mosscat.

The fight was too fast to follow: a maelstrom of snapping, barking, screeching, howling, and blood flying in all directions. One of the guards stumbled back like a broken doll, blood spurting from his torn throat.

A harpoon blade flashed. Pink-coral fell to the floor and rolled at Rudra's feet. Blood splattered his highly prized coat of many colors. She remained still and silent, a pool of blood expanding beneath her.

Root was bleeding in a half dozen places. He stepped back, gasping, and dangling little Six-fingers by one leg. He looked at Rudra with dead eyes. The Holy Father nodded. He was frowning. Yet even his frown was benevolent.

"Oh, this is terrible. I didn't want anything like this to happen. Oh no. Dear children you must love one another. I tried to teach my own dear Tribe this lesson, but, alas, they ignored me, even my own dear wife the Grand Duchess. They betrayed me, even my own dear wife. She and her evil, uh, ghoul, executed me for my honest teaching of love-ethic. They buried me. Yet, I've returned to you, my dear children. Will you not listen? Will you reject me like my native Tribe?"

Root loped off to green pool. Moments later I heard a splash.

Rudra emitted a grace-filled sigh. "Dear White Mother Blue, let us partake of the red onion this evening and you'll take us on a heavenly journey. It is fitting that we accompany dear Six-fingers on his way to the realm of his beloved father. Oh, how we loved him."

EXALTED FATHER

THE BOOK OF CONFESSIONS

CHAPTER FOUR – An Epilogue to the Life of a Remarkable Woman

(And Two Hymns)

VERSE 4.4.1

How passive I've become. Things happen to me. I cannot stomach the rich and heavy fare of the King's table. Yet my body continues to gain mass, not really in size but in density, so that it seems my flesh has become as granite. I subsist on pure grains and rice, which is the diet of the serfs. It makes no difference. I might as well try living on a grain a day.

My heavy body drains my spirit. Lethargy rules my will. Nothing appears worth the effort.

I am as white as any of them. I've become nearly their size. Perhaps I'll sprout a tail. I am a White Mother, and a Blue.

On the evening of Pink-coral's death, and the unfortunate drowning of little Six-fingers in his bath (according to Root), the Reed Sea People gathered around the central fire. In time I learned the queeti word for this fire, *athanor* they named it, which literally meant womb. They say that it is the original fire, beyond the flow of time, the same fire that burns in the daystar and the nighttime skies.

The queeti say that it flows underground. It begins as a black liquid deep in the foundations of the Lord's Mountain. It ignites as it rises and appears only in special places, such as the *athanor* of the Reed Sea People.

They burn the red onion in the Lord's fire. Only then do the fumes arise pure and strong to fill the cave. There is no need for pipes. One breathes and instantly passes beyond time, into freedom—they say.

Grey had been their guide. The Grey of this age had gone into the steppe and perished. Pink-coral was no Blue, and she was no more. As White Mother I am a Blue. Thus, that very night I exchanged my torn black scholar rags for the blue seal cloak of the Reed Sea People. The cloak's long billowing sleeves contained inner pockets, designed Spear-toe said, to carry the herbs of a Blue, as well as hooks and fish knives. Fish bone reinforced a high collar and was sown into the cloak all the way down the back giving it a spine. A Blue sat straight as a board.

Log brought the red onion and tossed it into the *athanor*. The red-purple bulb, the largest phalabulb I'd ever seen, popped with a loud thunderous clap. Thick yellow-red smoke filled the cave.

"You are guide, White Mother," Log chanted, "Lost we a Grey, gained we a Blue."

The Reed Sea People chanted along: "Lost we a Grey, gained we a Blue—"

Seated upon his throne on the other side of the fire, Rudra grinned behind his beard. He wore his coat of many colors, one of which was now the dark rust color of queeti blood. "You are guide," I heard him say.

Beyond the closely huddled forms of the People, vast shadows crowd seemed to fill the cave. They took form in the smoke, say, shadows that congeal at the dusk as the light fades and the boundaries disappear. A crowd of smoky ghosts.

EXALTED FATHER

I inhaled deeply. The People inhaled, the shadows did also. I could not say if Rudra the Holy Father inhaled the fumes of the red onion, perhaps Holy Fathers have no need of such.

I am no Blue, I thought.

Together, we climbed out of the cave. The air was salty wet and freezing, sleet, mist and rain intermingled, swirling with a wind that came from the sea.

We traveled through space and time, through jungles, steppes, and meadows. We climbed the Lord's Mountain Elsseleron, once called Flat Cake. We continued climbing, from the Mountain into the starry heavens.

We journeyed to Elsewhere. It was hot in Elsewhere, this Somewhere Else. A new daystar blazed overhead in a dark blue sky. Its fire was of the *athanor*.

Heads hanging, tongues lolling, and panting, they followed me. We walked through a white desert. Poor creatures of thick pelts and dense muscle. This world was too bright for them, too hot. Its air seared their lungs. The sand was hot coals on the soft pads of their feet. The world seemed *too small*. Why, I cannot say.

We trudged on towards a shining horizon. Despite their suffering, the Reed Sea People followed. Only the Holy Father was missing.

We walked for days…a month…a year. The days seemed too long, the nights too brief, the night stars all confused, their patterns strange, their rising and setting chaotic. In the desert there are no sign posts, no distinctions. Nothing moved except us. We aimed for that place on the horizon where the daystar was born.

Then the desert gave way to a garden, a land not unlike my old Akkad of lakes, green hills, and lush valleys. Flowers of red, yellow, white and lavender populated green meadows; sunflowers, lilies, purple bush, lemon and fig, and so many unknown to me, they spoke to us in the language of the plants. Whispering, laughing, singing, they divulged their secrets. We could not understand. Then we came to a pure happy brook at the base of a small waterfall. The Reed Sea People drank their fill and were refreshed. But only for a short time.

Even here in this welcoming garden, we experienced a powerful feeling that we did not belong. Our bodies were all wrong, our ears failed to translate the subtle vibrations that filled the thick air, our lungs burned, eyes became bleary, and in the end the pure water did not satisfy.

We came to a gentle rise. There on a shimmering horizon we saw a great walled city built upon a mountain plateau. It was not unlike Zell which overlooks the Windward Straits. Not a few of the Reed Sea People noticed the resemblance, for they howled at the image of their serfdom. Yet this was not Zell, it was of the absolute Elsewhere.

Tall buildings of blue glass soared upwards and seemed to disappear into the brilliant sky. Thousands of towers enclosed by walls of some silver-like metal, the buildings rectangular, some like pyramids, others elliptical and seemingly balanced on a point, the city was a wondrous sight. It was a thousand times more beautiful than Emerald.

The queeti howled in dismay. They cowed behind me, whining and averting their gentle brown eyes. They refused to take another step forward. I am not a Grey. They howled and whined and gnashed their teeth.

"A frightful thing," moaned Log. Even Root shook with fear.

But worse was yet to come.

EXALTED FATHER

BOOK OF CONFESSIONS
VERSE 4.4.2

Only a vision, a dream, an illusion conjured by a mysterious queeti herb, an onion, named red but of purple hue, not unlike the somas of the disgusting Ra'bim...

We remain seated on the stone floor of the cave, as if dead, buried in a cave at the foot of the plateau upon which sits the real Zell in the real world. Even as I write this account so many years later, I still feel the need to remind myself that nothing of that long-ago horror was real. What I write is not real. So why do I write it? Is not the darkness of my true life enough? To banish memory, I say. Once on papyrus I need no longer remember, and I may choose whether or not to read.

A dream, a vision, not real.

The phalabulb that causes the vision is very real. My brain too, my mind. Are they the same? Is it not a mechanical thing, a Nepptali time piece, or one of their other more complicated engineering feats, the secrets of which they jealously guarded until the gray imps stole them and gave them to the New-Men?

How may the unreal come from the real? If my mind is a Nepptali machine of the natural world, then how could its visions *not* also be natural, as real as this time and place? Does not the world produce the red onion of the soul? If the red onion births visions, does not the world birth visions?

Once more I digress.

That place was not *this* world. It was like that all-too-brief moment in time when *his* voice freed me from the Ra'bim. The vibrations changed. I feel them in the other light, the other air, the other water, the other garden. Despite all this I know it was a vision and unreal. Yet it is *more* real to me than this dismal tower in which I sit and write. And yet...

I noticed a small man standing ahead, his back turned, gazing at the city. Why had I not seen him? He wore a black priest's robe, not unlike the battered and patched garment I still owned.

He began walking towards the city. Without conscious decision (it seemed), not of my own volition, I followed in his steps. "You remain here," I ordered the Reed Sea People.

"Oh White Mother Blue, do not follow this thing," Log pleaded. "It is a black ghoul."

"The black ghoul and I will go up there, to the Lord, and I will return to you with the Word of the Lord."

They howled and whined and growled and moaned, but did not move. They shielded their eyes from the glare of the brilliant spire of the Lord. Even Root's dead eyes seemed to come to life, and they appeared to be filled with awe and wonder—and most of all fear.

"Is the Exalted Father's forbidden mountain," howled a young male named Black-bark. "It is death. Who will save us from death?"

The small priest—black ghoul, if you will—marched to the city-mountain of the Lord, Almighty and Singular. I followed, trying to catch him. For every step I took, no matter how quickly, he also took a step, and no matter how small a step or how slow a pace he still remained a step ahead. I got closer and closer—he was always a step beyond me. I became frustrated, irritated, angry, enraged. Then I noticed that the city-mountain appeared to recede as well, always a step ahead. No, two. Every step forward that we took the city took two steps back.

The dwarf priest stopped and lowered his head. Thus did I catch up to him, though it took me quite a bit longer than I expected; the distance was greater than I perceived, for such was the effect of the red onion.

He was no man. He was a young boy, dark-skinned with long black braided hair, perhaps just barely in his teens. How could I know his age? I'd never beheld a living human being younger than myself and Agni—and *him* I came south to kill.

The boy turned and looked up at me, and there were tears in his eyes, and his eyes were bright green, wet grass after a spring rain. And I knew *him* instantly.

Here in my dream, my red onion illusion, a youthful version of the *sramnana* Marduk, he that I loved and hated and had sworn to kill, *He-who-denied-me.*

"See you the Lord's Mountain," he sobbed softly, "from which everything is born. Where is the gate? Where is the key? In all worlds I've never been able to reach it. It flees from me. How can a mountain walk?"

I reached for my scimitar. Instead I drew forth a queeti knife of flint. Nepptali steel prevails against Ra'bim somas and, so it seems, resists red onion dreams. No matter. Queeti flint was sharp enough to accomplish my task.

He looked at me again, raising his black eyebrows. "You are White Mother? I know you, don't I? What are you doing here? This is not your world. You are not a part of this Legend." His voice sounded childish, piping and excited, yet his words and the thoughts behind them seemed older.

"The Lord will have His due," said I, not understanding my own words. It was at that moment I believed I heard a voice coming from the mountain. The voice was in my head, and it spoke not in words but—how do I say this— in the language of desires, intuitions, emotions. Something powerful invaded my mind, like a slap that stings the cheeks and brings tears to the eyes. It said: *Behold, here is the sacrifice, the Lord's due.*

"The Lord's due? Where is the sacrifice?" asked the boy. He must have heard the same language. How may two individuals experience the exact same hallucination?

"Surely the Lord will provide," I answered.

The boy sniffed and turned. "He does not provide a way to His Holy Mountain."

"Why not take a vow?"

"Vows? Do they move mountains—as do dreams in which mountains walk?"

"Vows are dreams. Come, boy, what do you want with such tyrant Lords squatting on top unholy mountains?"

The boy said as if talking to himself: "Then I must *invent* the Legend?"

"Legend?"

"Suthralane."

"Suthralane? Why invent such a monstrous lie?"

"It makes me happy. Makes people happy. I'll invent it, but not all inventions are lies."

"Lies make people happy?"

"Well yes, when the Lord is too far away. Lies are necessary, but the original liar must be sacrificed."

Then I knew why I'd come to this alien place. I knew what was required. I reminded myself that this was a drug-induced dream, and so what did it matter the crimes I committed in this place? I reasoned further, that it is no crime, rather, a moral obligation, when one obeys the will of the Lord. *It was perfectly clear to me that the Lord demanded I kill—sacrifice—the boy.* Should I disobey, I would be guilty of rebellious willfulness against the Almighty. It is impossible that the Almighty, that Being of which no greater being can be conceived, order me to perform an immoral act. Thus it stands proved.

Am I not a remarkable woman? An Akkadean warrior? Am I not a stranger to fear? Intrepid? What did it matter? How can there be right and wrong in a dream, a vision produced by a simple plant of

EXALTED FATHER

nature? Had I not sworn to kill *him* and *his* ridiculous vows? Yes, it is true that this boy had not yet offended me so grievously. Well, I'd kill him preemptively.

But what sort of monster demands the death of a child?

The Lord Almighty ordered his sacrifice, blessed be the Lord. There must be some mysterious reason, and some good must come of it. Of course this was a vision, a dream, better, a nightmare.

Gentle reader, avert thou thine eyes. Read not further…

I grasped the knife and brought it to his throat. He did not resist. A trickle of blood—

I did not fail the Lord. My hatred failed. I nicked his throat. My hand would obey my will. It knew better. I could not do this thing. I could not…

The Lord could. The Lord did the rest. With my hand, the Lord sliced deep into innocent flesh.

Who is to say that this reality, this strange, eerie, sinister, familiar world is not as real as the one in the cave beneath the fortress city of Zell? Perhaps the red onion does not give us dreams but awakens us?

Well then, if a dream I committed no crime, for there is not right or wrong in an illusion. If real and I awaken to a dream, then I sacrificed a child at the command of the One Lord, the Almighty. How can an omnipotent, morally perfect Being order an immoral act? If such a Being did so that Being could not be morally perfect, which the Lord must be by definition. Therefore, an apparent wickedness is goodness when demanded by the Lord. Thus it stands proved.

Therefore I am good, dream or no.

The boy's eyes grew wide and their sweet green faded as if beneath a passing cloud. He touched his neck and felt the blood. The life seemed to drain out of him although he was still alive. It took an eternity for him to die.

I wept. But wasn't my weeping, my pain, my feelings of guilt unpleasing to the Lord and themselves deserving of punishment?

In this world, I knew, there'd be no legends of Suthralane.

EXALTED FATHER

BOOK OF CONFESSIONS
VERSE 4.4.3

A Hymn:
I had a vision of the Lord.

The Lord is a woman.

Time here does not pass, it stays where it is. I see it as passing but this is incorrect. It remains next to me, this absolute Elsewhere, even now, like a single sheet of parchment, but upon which I can no longer write. In the now is no time, so the past never was and the future will never be. Only I am moving.

But I digress.

The Lord is a woman.

She sits upon a heap of cushions. The cushions are of many colors as is Rudra's coat. She is gray-eyed, white-haired, and very beautiful. Her skin is very dark and velvety as the skin of most Akkadeans, except for me. Large of body, she wears a gown of the finest silks, with an embroidered scarf of gold over her shoulders—the designs appear rune-like—and she smiles down on me.

I felt—I feel in this cold gray world of my torment—the power of her presence. Power, magnificence, compassion, healing, beauty, and mystery, she lives in a place where I flounder, a tiny boat that has lost sight of the horizon.

I cannot record her exact words. What I am able to present is a vague and garbled reading. Her language is not of my world, or any world.

She speaks in a voice soft as a spring rain, as perfect as the mathematics the old archbishop once tried to stuff into my poor skull. Perhaps only *he* might understand. But *he* I've killed. Oh, I grow confused.

She says, and I hear: "Daughter, many times blessed—" Tears come to my eyes. "How you disappoint me."

I hear: "You are like nothing else in *that world.*

"Your life is in my mind before your birth.

"Your face is in my mind before your birth. Do you know it?

"Your many lives do I know like pages in a book.

"In that world, the moment you are born, I am there smiling.

"I make you many times."

"Yes, Lord," I hear myself say. I call her Lord. Should it not be Lady? What does it matter? Words fail, as I say. Yes, Lord…the same words I say to the King when he summons me, when He brings pain.

"Yes, Lord." What can be said to overwhelming power? I wanted to ask her about the boy but the question died on my lips.

She smiled and the universe wept with joy.

"You are born in that world, my daughter, in my image. Surely you must know *that world* is not your final home. You are made for much better. For the stars, I make you again, again and again.

"Surely you know that world is temporary. A step in that world is a step beyond that world. Do you not feel it? In your disappointments? In your pains, both great and small? Especially your longing for something else, for somewhere else, for Elsewhere?"

"Yes, Lord."

"Gaze upon thyself."

I do it, there is no resisting her. I see my body coarse and brown, before the Ra'bim skin. Tufts of hair, beast-like, eyes, mouth, teeth…how different am I from the queeti? But I am, I know it…a remarkable woman. Finally I see my hands. Why don't I ask Her about the boy?

"See thou *that world*? See how it rejects my gifts?"

"Oh Lord—"

"Am I ever-loving?"

EXALTED FATHER

A million voices cried: "Yes Lord!"
"Behold. You brought them My gift.
"They reject it.
"You taught them.
"They did not listen.
"See what becomes of them."
She raises her hand and beckons…

THE BOOKS OF MARDUK

BOOK OF CONFESSIONS
VERSE 4.4.4

Screams and howls fill the cave. Smoke is everywhere and I can barely see. It is not the smoke of the red onion. Brilliant flashes of blue light cut through the dense fog as do hot knives through butter. The pungent odor of burning fur, the sizzle of melting flesh, blood bubbling—slaughter and the queeti die.

Why continue in the eternal present? The red onion has lost its hold. Once more I am a prisoner and this is no vision.

A horde of Grays attacked the Reed Sea People. I don't know how many, maybe a few hundred. Suddenly they were everywhere, slashing and stabbing. It was my fault really. I trusted the Holy Father. My quest for knowledge by means of the red onion made us vulnerable. In a collective trance we failed to detect the long line of Gray Yakashas as they climbed down the hidden rock stairs from Zell. We did not hear (or smell) them as they invaded the cave. We did not see them raise their L-guns, draw their Nepptali swords, until it was too late.

Log shook himself and barked a warning. For a brief moment I felt relief. But then a Gray, nearly the size of a man and wearing the white tunic of King Ra', stabbed him in the back with a bright sword. Log screamed. The point emerged from his chest. He clawed at the blade and tried to twist around. His sudden movement and the weight behind it wrenched the sword out of the Gray's claws.

Log fell upon his enemy, biting and tearing at the wisp's throat. They both went down in a blur of fangs and claws, Log on top.

I tried scrambling to Log's aid, but four or five Grays—I wasn't counting at the moment—seized me. Later I learned that they had orders to take me alive. Although I was without my scimitar (in the real world weapons do not appear as though from nothing, in *this* world from nothing, nothing comes), and despite the binding of my Ra'bim skin, I killed two with my bare hands. I snapped their necks like rotten branches.

By the sheer weight of numbers they subdued me, but only after suffering more broken bones. They pinned my arms and bound my legs. They endured more bone-cracking blows. Am I not an Akkadean warrior?

One of the cowardly creatures hit me from behind on the head with what was probably the pummel of a sword. I went down. Tails and fists pounded me until the darkness came.

Cold salt air revived me. We were outside the cave on hard packed sand. A gang of Grays, each one dressed in the white tunic of King Ra', dragged me, a piece of driftwood. They seemed frantic to reach the spiraling path leading up the plateau to Zell. It was still night yet the sky had begun to change from black to yellow-gray. The stars were dimming for the daystar was on the way. Soon Lesser Wind would begin. Oh how I yearned for a rain of *kitim* (as I do now).

The scenes on the beach can hardly be described. After all these years language still seems to fail and I weep at the memory. May it be consigned to these pages and forgotten.

The Grays massacred the Reed Sea People in the most fiendish ways. They seemed to take pleasure from it. The few queeti males who survived they impaled on sharp wooden stakes from groin to the base of the skull. The wicked monsters mocked these wretched creatures. They made horrible faces and tried to mimic their impossibly high-pitched screams and yelps.

I spied Spear-toe among the crucified. He refused to scream or beg. He stared at his murders in silence. This defiant behavior caused the Grays to fly into frenzy. They slashed at him with knives and swords, slicing off bloody slabs of fur and flesh. They gouged out his eyes, cut off his fingers and toes, then his arms and legs, his tongue, his ears, and still he surrendered not a whimper. They dropped their trousers—those that were wearing trousers, unlike their red cousins they go not naked—and urinated on him.

He died in silence.

Babies they ripped from their mothers' arms and smashed their little heads against the rocks. They attempted to rape the females, but failed. While they were nearly the same size as the queeti, their diminutive members were disproportionally tiny and weak. Even the arousal of battle failed to harden them to the task. The females fought them as viciously as any queeti male, breaking their bodies, snapping their necks, smashing them as if they hammered sandstone.

I yelled at them, threatened them, ordered them to stop, but they smashed me in the face, although they could not bruise my Ra'bim armor. One, a human-sized Gray in a white tunic, pushed the others away from me. He bit a fellow Gray in the neck. The wisp dropped like a stone, went into convulsions, and died on the spot. After that, no one touched me again and I was free to shout and curse and threaten them with all sorts of revenge. Alas, mere words do not sever bonds (except once), nor could they stop the slaughter on the beach.

Smoke poured out of the caves. They turned their L-guns on the crucified and burned them. The wretched queeti burned like the torches.

Lesser Wind suddenly began to blow. It came from the north like an avenging army

The *kittim* came, but we made the rock stairs in time.

EXALTED FATHER

BOOK OF CONFESSIONS
VERSE 4.4.5

Lord Rekhmire stood beneath a polished copula which had been carved out of some sort of hard black wood from a species of tree I'd never seen. It glistened as do the smooth scales of a serpent. The supporting columns were of the same strange wood. Symbols that reminded me of runes were carved into them. I knew that these could not be the Runes of the *Runehayana*. They might have been failed copies of the Runes, however, like the failed scratching of a fledgling priest. Only later would I learn that the New-Men are unable to read *any* script.

Lord Rekhmire stood on a dais of white marble. His tail whipped back and forth in agitation. He did not sit in the throne. None of the New-Men sat comfortably.

Grays packed the vast domed temple of Zell, named the Green Sea Temple of the Blessed Ones of Heaven.

Rudra and I stood before the Overseer of the Straits. The so-called Holy Father wore his tattered coat of many colors. I wrapped myself in the blue seal robe. I was White Mother Blue, defiant to the end.

Rekhmire spoke in a mechanical voice: "This is the foolish northern woman of the fish serfs?"

That is when I first saw the archbishop. Draped in heavy, glittering robes of red and gold, he stepped out from the crowd of Grays and mounted the dais. His movements were slow and careful as though he were afraid of falling. I saw that he'd lost weight since our last meeting long ago in Nalanda, so much so, in fact, that I barely recognized him at first glance. Yet this was the same priest, puffy face drawn into a frown, long braided hair, small weasel eyes filled with contempt and deep mistrust, black as the copula's strange wood.

Jacob, Priest of Nalanda.

Perhaps I said the name aloud.

He bowed to Rekhmire and curled his lips, which I took to be a smile. He concentrated on me and studiously avoided looking at Rudra.

"Devorah of Akkad," he announced in a soft lilting voice, "wife of Vishnu, later Seer, a *Blue* the primitives name her, I believe."

"Seer? Explain this, archbishop," Rekhmire said.

"Archbishop?" I exclaimed. "What would Theophilus say, I wonder?"

"Not much, I fear. He no longer has the breath for it." He smiled and his smile—or grimace—required some effort.

Jacob turned to Rekhmire. "She is simply a foolish woman as you say. Once long ago she had the good fortune to meet the Lord-On-High's Son in the flesh. Of course being a female, she couldn't grasp his teachings. I must say that few among us were capable of it, even our late archbishop who was of weak mind though he thought himself clever. Of course Men of the Tribes are all clever animals. As I was saying, she did indeed encounter the Lord-On-High's Son, although that single meeting unhinged her frail mind, that is, caused it to be far more unhinged than it would normally be, as she is only a *female*...Man of the Tribes. She came to believe that she could see into the past, and into other worlds besides this one. Of course these are dreams *in* her own head which she takes as worlds *outside* her head."

"Such is preposterous," Rekhmire observed. "If she dreams as you've said, archbishop, then this proves her guilt. It is well known by all that only animals dream."

I interrupted. "The only dreamer here is Jacob who imagines he's the archbishop." I expected him to grow agitated as I remembered, but he kept his composure.

EXALTED FATHER

"Do you see, Lord Overseer, she consorts with beasts of the caves. She's become like them, eating as they eat, speaking the language of the plants. She drinks their soma and wears their primitive garb. She's no longer in the image of the Lord-On-High, though outwardly she may resemble such. And more than this, she is from the wicked Tribe that *murdered* our High Lord's blessed Son, who was of the Lord's own essence without division."

That was true. I murdered him. In a drug-induced nightmare. In the pages of these Confessions.

If this bit of news enraged Rekhmire his flat metal voice did not reveal it. His words, however, were of a different stuff. Later I learned that all New-Men were like this, including my dear husband the King. Their voices are cold and changeless, only the meaning of their words carried emotion. Meaning is disputable.

"Then she must die. As her entire Tribe must die. We will exterminate them. We will blot them out with such a burning as this world has never seen."

Scornfully I asked (what had I to fear now?): "Who is this *Son*, Priest Jacob? What do you know of sons? Perhaps you have confused your vows."

Jacob forced himself to smile. "We have his bones," he answered in triumph. "Preserved in Thrice-Blessed White Cathedral at the foot of Needleglass."

These bones I would learn later amounted to a single tooth of dubious ancestry.

"Your advice, then, archbishop?"

"She must die for the sake of *He-With-Us*," Jacob declared.

The title, *He-With-Us,* startled me. I inhaled sharply, and then cursed myself for allowing them to see my surprise.

"This death will not please the King," Rudra observed.

He limped forward and fixed his eyes on Jacob. The self-named archbishop seemed to shrink in his presence. A large Gray with a hint of yellow in his skin, one named Bhut-ton, followed him and took up a position on his right.

"What is this creature?" Rekhmire directed his question at the Gray.

"Behold," Bhut-ton announced trying to sound important and dignified despite the nasal whine of his voice. "This is the *Chosen* of our King Ra'. He has fulfilled the task given to him years ago by our King. He has delivered to us a *fertile woman* who will be the wife of the King Ra'. He was once named Exalted Father. He died and has risen. Now he is Holy Father."

"The King failed to inform me of such a thing." The nervous twitching of his tail betrayed an irritation that lurked neither in his voice nor in his changeless facial expression.

"The King our Lord goes where he will," said Bhut-ton. The Gray appeared insolent and bold, and so became careless.

"She must die!" Jacob howled. "It is written in the *Runehayana* that one should not suffer a priestess to live. Her kind murdered the Son of the Lord."

Rekhmire appeared to ignore him. He fixed his black eyes on me. Like his face, they were unreadable. But his tail twitched furiously.

"Fertile, you say? You know this to be true?"

The Gray smiled, exposing his formidable fangs. "It is certain, Lord Overseer. Our Exalted Father, Chosen of the King, now Holy Father, revealed this knowledge to us. To doubt it would be a terrible sin."

Rudra smiled behind his beard.

Jacob was about to say something but Rekhmire raised an arm. The motion resembled a column of stone being rising from a great edifice. I could almost hear the grinding.

Exalted Father

"Perhaps if what you say is true we should keep her for ourselves."

Bhut-ton frowned and glanced at Rudra. The so-called Holy Father gave a slight shrug and remained silent.

"The King would not be pleased," the Gray said with just the right amount of menace in his voice.

"Oh, but I jest. Am I not known among the Reed Sea People as the jesting White Father Overseer?"

"There is no longer a Reed Sea People to know you," Bhut-ton said.

"Yes, that is true. In the end they proved quite impossible to train. We will require new serfs, of course—to serve Zell and its jesting Overseer, of course."

"Oh, they breed so quickly," said one of Rekhmire's lieutenants, a Gray nearly the size of Bhut-ton wearing the turquoise tunic of the Straits Overseer. He glared at Bhut-ton who happened to be dressed in the King's white.

"Yes, very true. It is as good Lab-el says," Rekhmire agreed. If he were happy to see the subject drifting away from me (his tail seemed less agitated), he unexpectedly changed course as does a drunken sailor who turns his boat into the teeth of an oncoming storm. "I yet wonder why we should not keep her here in Zell? At least for a season. I'm willing to share with the King."

It was this statement that sealed Overseer Rekhmire's fate.

"Such an arrangement would not please the King," Bhut-ton repeated. He appeared to snarl.

Lab-el glared at him. His right claw went to the pummel of a steel sword he wore in a leather belt. The steel, I guessed, was of Nepptali make. The leather belt—runes had been engraved into the leather—I'd seen among the wares of Din merchants.

I do not see the King's White in the audience Hall of Zell. I notice a sea of turquoise, however."

Bhut-ton looked at Rudra.

The Holy Father spoke: "It is as my son the archbishop says. That wicked Tribe we name Akkadeans murdered the Son of the Lord-On-High. They must pay for their crime, the greatest crime this world has ever seen. All the Tribes of Men must pay. Annihilate them all. And you, my Lord Rekhmire…the King will no doubt call upon you to lead the campaign against these greatest murders of all time. Behold—" He pointed to me with a nod of his huge head—"this female is from that Tribe. *But she did not participate in the Son's murder, for at that time she studied in Nalanda.* Yes, it is an absurd thing, a female priest, a priestess. I cannot fathom why they allowed it. I do know that the old archbishop was a hopeless drunk. Perhaps this is the reason. Theology and wine come from the same vineyard—a proverb of mine, for which I'm famous." He grinned and glanced at Jacob, who turned his head away.

"Nonetheless, she is Akkadean. She is fertile. Many are there like her in Akkad. You, O' Lord Overseer, will have your pick from among them. Perhaps more than one? Take up your banners and cross the straits. Do this service for your Lord and King. You will be rewarded."

I contend to this day that at that moment, with those words, Rudra really did become the Holy Father. They sealed his elevation.

He shifted his attention to Jacob. "Is this not so, my son?"
Jacob looked shocked. He had difficulty speaking, yet he said: "Yes, my father."

At that moment Jacob truly became the archbishop.

Rekhmire's tail went limp. Lab-el seethed but said nothing. Bhut-ton showed his fangs in a smile or a smirk, or both.
The Straits Overseer declared: "She shall be the wife of our King and Lord. Behold, the Queen."

EXALTED FATHER

The words *behold the Queen* spread through the Hall as would a gigantic and irresistible wave. Even the archbishop joined in. Led by Rekhmire, all heads turned and bowed to me, even the Holy Father. Rekhmire of course couldn't bend, rather he leaned slightly forward, a tower about to fall over.

At that instant—I still wonder today if it is truly so—came another awakening. Can one awaken more than once?

It was as though for an instant lightning flashed inside my skull, a brief, total illumination in which I saw everything as it truly is. Words are mere threads of smoke that abruptly evaporate in the heat of reality. As I've said, the source of all my misfortunes is that I've always sought the truth in all things. I saw it for a moment, so clear as to make me weep. Then it vanished and left me in sadness.

Daughter of the Khan, Akkadean warrior, wife of Vishnu, Blue-Seer, White Mother, *murderer,* and now Queen of Starmirror, remarkable it is true, my entire identity rests upon these titles. See how frail that identity is. See how it changes, alters, transforms and passes away. When I try to grasp it through my fingers it slips, as though I tried to grasp empty space.

Oh my former selves, how I loved you! Each was a hope and a future. Oh how quickly you died. What was I doing when they took you from me? Where is the seer who watches the one who sees? How can that seer be the woman seen?

I am a special woman in this world. It cannot be otherwise. I am *whissling*. I am White Mother, a Blue. I am an object and an instrument. I am a means to an end. I am the future generations. I stand between the dimensions of time. Yet I am more, but it does not count. Nor would *they* understand it. Alas, I behold this truth and despair.

Who is there to rescue me from this prison?

THE BOOKS OF MARDUK

BOOK OF CONFESSIONS
<u>VERSE 4.4.6</u>

Perhaps there are other worlds in which the Lord Almighty is a woman. Perhaps the phalabulb is the key to unlock their passage. Or, perhaps on these days of despair, when the clouds gather and my vision becomes narrow, perhaps the red onion of the soul causes the sprouting of impossible hopes. It brings on the delusion of optimism, which is not only a delusion but is wickedness.

I do not know.

A Hymn to Clothes:

Recently, I've become concerned with clothes. These days it matters to me how I look. I am deeply concerned that my royal status is properly acknowledged, that my subjects pay me the proper respect.

I love the velvet-like material of purple royal gowns, the fine lace, soft collars of gold, embroidered designs. I barely feel such things against my flesh, but somehow the mere possession of them sooths my mind. I welcome the warm summers of the south, for I am able to exchange the heavy materials of the winter for silken dresses, diaphanous shawls, and soft golden slippers. In the cool summer evenings I sometimes imagine myself a *kittim*, perhaps I'll leap from my high tower and fly with Lesser Wind.

I often find myself staring into my mirror. I admire the pure white of my body, so solid and changeless. Even my hair is pure white. It falls past my shoulders these days and I braid it in imitation of the Holy Father and his son the archbishop.

I think of myself as holy and gracious. I try not to think of the Reed Sea People. Of the young boy I killed in a vision. Now that I've recorded it all here, I will close that book and hopefully forget. Once down on papyrus, what need of memory? Let the book remember, I wish to forget.

I remain barren.

THE BOOKS OF MARDUK

BOOK OF CONFESSIONS
VERSE 4.4.7

This morning Greater Wind brought a swarm of *kittim*. I was out for a stroll in the northern courtyard, the one named Blue Yard of Wind-swept Memory Cloud, when they came spiraling down from a cloudless spring sky.

None among the New-Men believed it possible. Even the King expressed surprise. A small number of Grays—maybe five—were caught out in the open. The *kittim* appeared to seek them out. Their deaths were especially agonizing. They became puddles of foul smelling black ooze—poor creatures.

I hurried for cover. Alas, my beautiful white body is no longer capable of its old Akkadean speed and agility. My limbs move as though they are encased in thick armor.

Kittim fell around me. They soaked into stonework and masonry. They left black stains as they melted in the heat of a spring daystar.

A large blue-green *kittim* of five interconnecting triangles appeared to swerve from its straight downward free fall. It came for me.

I *ran* for the cover of the red-tiled copula that covers the portico leading into the North Tower. The *kittim* was quicker. The flimsy kite-like thing was inches from my body when it began to fold its panels, as if to embrace me as one does a lover.

I perceived that my death had finally arrived. I welcomed it. Perhaps I'd be reborn in one of those other worlds, in the Kingdoms of the Heavens where women are Lords Almighty, and where the Reed Sea People live in joy and freedom, and fly on the wings of the red onion of the soul. Where children are not sacrificed.

It fully embraced me now. It dissolved into the green silk gown I was wearing, changing the gown's color into the dark green of the

Exalted Father

northern Akkadean forest. Then it soaked through into my skin. There was no burning pain, no stinging, no biting. It felt as does a soothing bath, a warm mixture of salts and water that relaxes tired muscles, eases tension, and calms the mind.

It must be obvious by now that I didn't die. It is true that I suffered a high fever for many days. The King's physicians did fear for my life.

I sweat and dreamed.

What dreams. What sweats, yellow and thick as salted butter. When I came out of my delirium the change that illness wrought in my physical body was astonishing…

I did not die. How may one write their own death?

This evening, as Lesser Wind whispered into my cell, I looked out and saw perched on a nearby turret a smiling farvel. A farvel just as the *Runehayana* described them, but somehow this farvel reminded me of the old archbishop Theophilus.

These codices of papyrus are transcribed and translated as they have come down to us, in all probability with few editorial changes. Unlike the other four books which by tradition come from the pen of the sramana Marduk, but which archaeologists believe to be comprised of many sources, redacted many times, having suffered many scribal alterations (and there is no knowing how many), this "Confession of Devorah" appears to have come to us unblemished. From internal evidence it most likely comes from the end of the ninth century of the Third Kalpa.

It goes without saying that the "queeti" described herein cannot be considered anything else but slanderous caricatures. Why the book was ever included in "The Books of Marduk" remains something of a puzzle. We include it here.

THE BOOKS OF MARDUK

THE BOOK OF
RUNES

EXALTED FATHER

PASSAGES FROM THE RUNEHAYANA

Muttaka (Last Words), Book V, Section 34, (*The Books of Jambridvipa*)

Verses From the First Chapter:

1. These are the (last) words that the Lord spoke to the Tribes of Men on the [...] banks of the Pearldew River.

2. The [...] year of the [...] decade of the [...] century of the Second Kalpa.

6. And the Lord said to Suthralane: *this, my Holy Mountain, is forbidden to the Tribes of Men* [...] *back* [...].

7. And the Lord became angry with Suthralane (of an evil generation).

Verses From the Fourth Chapter:

1. Obey the Lord and [...] and [...] set above the stars. The Kingdoms of the Heavens, in the Ark, which the Lord has given to you.[17]

---

[17] In the hand of the queeti poet-historian calling himself Theophilus: This is the first mention in the *Runehayana* of something called the Ark. Many of us believe that it is some kind of vessel, like a boat, but one that sails in the heavens. The *sramana* Marduk claims that the old Nepptali knew quite a bit about it but that their knowledge was very technical and hard to understand. During the Third Kalpa of Silence they lost the expertise to decipher their own books.

THE BOOKS OF MARDUK

2. For the Lord gave you hands, not tails (if) you [...].

Verses From the Ten Chapter:

16. The Lord on His Holy Mountain is holy.

17. You will fear and obey in all things, and observe His [...].

18. And to you He will dispense fame and renown, and set you above, and destroy those that you [...].

58. [...] inflicting extraordinary (plagues?) and all manner of evil cling to you will.

59. The *kittim*.

60. And scatter.

61. Not the land Greenbottom, not the Land Sea of Reeds, not the land Star [...] [...] of the Heavens.

Verses From the Twelve Chapter:

1. Of your Exalted Father remember. From the Kingdoms [...] to the Kingdoms.

2. In Edom too.

3. Those of the twilight.

4. Grew fat, grew rude, grew coarse [...].

```
Of course, Marduk is notoriously unreliable when it
comes to technical matters.
```

EXALTED FATHER

5. [...].

6. [...]. face to face.

7. [...]. one?

8. [...].

9. [...].

10. [...] displayed before all, none know where [...].[18]

---

[18] In the hand of Theophilus: And so ends the *Runehayana.* The Runes ceased to appear on the surface of Lordpool. By tradition, however, every Sandi copy of the *Runehayana* concludes with three blank pages, which are meant to represent the Lord's silence. Only Marduk challenged the tradition and composed verses to fill the three pages. For this outrageous heresy many consider him another Suthralane.

Scholarly Note: *The old historians accepted Theophilus's conclusions for reasons which will become apparent. Modern scientific historians tend to think of it as part of the myth. No extant copy has ever been discovered containing three blank pages, and many lack all of Section 34 which must have been written much later.*

THE BOOK OF RUNES

CHAPTER ONE – Thrice-Blessed Cathedral of the White Mountain

VERSE 5.1.1

He felt the bone-penetrating chill of a rainy dawn even within the great Cathedral called White Mountain (for short). Spring had arrived unusually cold for the south.

The Holy Father of the Universal Church of the Two Continents hugged his thick red robe tightly about his aged body. Embroidered golden roses and pistilli of the south graced the heavy fabric, interspersed with large silver triangles containing tiny silver moons. About his neck was a string of Reed Sea pearls. Golden bracelets encircled each wrist, each finger bore a ring that held a different precious gem, and each foot was clad in a red slipper, light and airy, and cold on the marble floor. A skull cap of white silk covered his bald head, which was also cold, and the remaining strands of his black beard were tied with silver threads which were meant to give the impression of tiny shooting stars in the deep vault of space.

The Holy Father of the Universal Church of the Two Continents was quite imposing especially in the eyes of the poor queeti peasants, although most of the time their poor eyes were averted.

The Holy Father's gait, however, was rather graceless. He'd acquired a great deal of weight in forty years, nearly multiplying himself by two. Not bad for an exhumed corpse, he often jested, referring to his resurrection and subsequent elevation to nearly divine status (the poor peasants generally dropped the word *nearly*).

He was quite old now, older than any Yad who'd ever lived, older even than Vishnu, he claimed, although he'd heard it said that Vishnu still lived, albeit a different Vishnu who went by a different name. He'd heard this last bit of news from Gray Yakashas veterans of the Northern War. But Gray Yakashas were notorious liars, so he was not obliged to consider their war stories as factual, or even probable (of course anything was possible).

Slowly, so as to preserve his holy dignity by not stumbling, or falling flat on his holy face, he issued from a side door near the High Altar. With dignified caution he mounted the nine steps of the marble dais and carefully lowered his dignified bulk into one of the thrones that flanked the Altar. This particular piece of furniture had been manufactured by queeti artisans. It was a rough-hewn oaken chair that might have passed for a vertical boat carved from a tree trunk.

The Altar was also of queeti make, an irregular block of white marble, cracked down the middle. Upon its roughly flat surface lay the Holy Relic and fifteen leather-clad books. These were of course the Sandi *Runehayana,* three stacks of five books, rescued by the King's army from the ruins of Lower Nalanda. Every page of every book suffered various degrees of destruction by burning.

The Holy Father noted the small number of shaggy heads sprinkled throughout the vast Cathedral, mostly red-brown queeti from the southern Topartz villages. A few Redfolk veterans sat among them. The Holy Father still thought of these as Yakashas and still doubted their existence even though their Gray and Yellow brethren comprised his honor guard.

He also noted that these southern queeti were quite large, nearly the size of a man, and nearly all of them walked on two legs. Entire families journeyed to the base of White Mountain (which he still thought of as Elsseleron), an arduous trek with a horde of pups in tow. In the past, Topartz queeti were the most fanatical and loyal, yet even their dedication to the Church had begun to decline *these days*, as the faith throughout villages of the Redrain. The Holy Father would have to take this up with the archbishop, when the archbishop was sober.

This morning the Holy Father wore a frown, and it was not because of the cold or queeti lack of faith.

One of the White Lords approached the dais. The Holy Father knew him by his signets and military uniform. He came before the throne and leaned slightly forward, a vague gesture that passed for a bow.

The White Lord spoke with an emotionless mechanical voice: "Greetings, Holy Father, from the King and his Once-Queen."

The Holy Father sounded bored: "How does the royal couple, O Strong Protector?"

The White Lord struggled to inject sadness into his tone: "Alas, not as we would wish. The Once-Queen remains barren and has been dismissed from the King's service. There are no New-Men young and so Starmirror has no heir."

"Yon queeti seem fruitful," the Holy Father observed.

"Indeed," the Strong Protector agreed, trying to force reluctance into his voice. "We fail to understand the amazing fertility of these animals. Has it not—accelerated—year after year? What of you—the Tribes of Men? Were you not so in the past?"

The Holy Father studied the White Lord. They were all identical. Only the signets on their sleeves, and the white military uniforms, told them apart. And the distinction between New-Man and the specific garment was—seamless. They were all male, yet how could he be certain? Would he recognize a female New-Man, a New-Woman, White Lord?

"Quite potent. In the past."

"The King, alas, despairs. Has His experiment succeeded?"

He fixed the Holy Father with those black changeless eyes set in a changeless porcelain face mounted upon a changeless body of marble. Only his tail showed signs of life.

"We are afraid, no," said the Holy Father. "We are very sorry. You may assure the King we did not fail for not trying."

In truth she nauseated him. They all did. Fornication under command of the King is how the Holy Father thought of it. The *experiment* was as much a failure as the attempt to mate Yakashas and queeti, as well as the Tribes of Men and New-Man. None bore fruit. The archbishop had howled like a tarp hound when the Holy Father ordered him to take a queeti female. He'd actually tried to kill her with his ceremonial dagger, ending what he termed a non-repeatable experiment.

The Holy Father's own experiment had fared no better. She actually bit him. Scratched him, beat him, yowled—but it was all pretense, poor beast, since he'd been incapable of that peculiar sport for a century, as were all males of the Tribes of Men thanks to Suthralane (and why not blame some mythical event to account for the unexplained?).

"Is the Holy Father also aware of the increase in the flocks of poison bugs? A fortnight ago, a swarm attempted to infest the Fortress-city."

"No—" The word escaped him.

The Strong Protector's face remained frozen, as hard and cold as the marble upon which he stood. Sanakht—the Holy Father remembered his personal name. Sanakht was Strong Protector of the Cosmos, Lord of the Armies of the King, and a hundred other titles which, fortunately, the Holy Father did not remember.

"Know, thou, Holy Father, the King is—concerned. Extremely so. New-Men remain without heirs. All the females from the Tribes of Men, but one, captured during the Great Northern War died. The queeti beasts prosper and experiments fail. Does the Black One send poisonous bugs against us? But is *this one* not defeated? What says the Lord-on-the-Mountain?"

The Holy Father bowed his head. "The Lord Almighty is silent. He has been silent. He will be silent. *He does not speak to us.*"

"The Holy Father is unworthy perhaps?"

"Perhaps. We've not heard the words of the Lord. The archbishop heard them many years ago. He met the Lord. He wrestled with the Lord—he says. You know, Sanakht, the archbishop was the Prince of Disciples, for he walked with the Lord's own Son. His Holy Relic we preserve here. Of course the archbishop's stories change with the weather and it is said that the New-Men do not believe in the Lord-on-the-Mountain."

"Enough," Sanakht ordered, and if he were capable of it he would have groaned—at least the Holy Father thought so. "We will believe what we will believe when we wish to believe it. We have heard in Tharas Major the teachings of the archbishop. The King knows of the *Runehayana*, more perhaps than the Holy Father himself. *The King wishes to know what has been added.*"

Sanakht (and the King) appeared rather confused. How could a non-existent Lord have added anything? The Holy Father fervently hoped that the archbishop had not been blabbering about Marduk's verses. He made a note to remind the archbishop not to give sermons when he was drunk, which probably meant that the world would hear no more sermons. He decided to change the subject.

"How goes the construction of the Ark, O Strong Protector of the Cosmos? We've heard that much was salvaged from the Nepptali workshops."

"Nothing was salvaged," answered Sanakht, and he might have sounded suspicious.

Exalted Father

"How unfortunate," said the Holy Father who knew better. Not only did his canaries nest in the courtyards of Tharas Major, but they flew in the north with the armies of the King—and they sang in the ears of the Holy Father.

"The stupid queeti make poor artisans. They're too dull besides being lazy. They're fit only for tilling the fields, if that. They cannot follow the simplest instructions. Everything they construct fails."

The Holy Father wondered just how the New-Men gave instructions, given that the White Lords themselves could not decipher the simplest Sandi, which meant that the Nepptali volumes of diagrams and long technical texts would be closed to them. Like the Lord-on-the-Mountain, he chose silence (in regard to such doubts) and with an aloof air replied: "Perhaps the King should reconsider this—Ark?"

"The Ark will take us to the Kingdoms of the Heavens. He is King of the Two Continents, north and south. What remains is—up."

The Holy Father rearranged his considerable bulk. He'd never been able to grasp this business about the Ark. The true reason for this visit had yet to be revealed, and the Holy Father's holy patience was wearing thin.

"What else?"

"What else?"

"Why does the Strong Protector of the Cosmos fresh from his great victory in the Great Northern War waste his greatly valued time by coming all the way to Thrice-Blessed Cathedral of the White Mountain?"

"The King has revealed to me what I now reveal to you: Behold, he is coming here, and he will scale yonder forbidden mountain. Nothing is forbidden King Ra', White Lord of the North and South, and all that lives."

The Books Of Marduk

BOOK OF RUNES
VERSE 5.1.2

I don't believe in the existence of the Yakashas, Rudra said beneath his breath. *We* don't believe in the existence of the Yakashas. And *we* are not Rudra, not since our return from the grave.

He watched the stooped Yellow warily navigate the vast space from the red cedar doors to his desk at the far end of his personal chambers. It was one of the elite, a Yellow Yakashas, but of course it could not be there because he refused to believe it existed. But he thirsted for the information it brought, so for the present and however long the present should last, he would put aside its non-existence and pretend it existed. He was the Holy Father and what he said existed, existed.

Burdened by the excessive weight of the Nepptali great-coat, the non-existent Yakashas found walking at any pace a struggle. All of them, red, gray, yellow, appeared to be suffering from some wasting disease, growing weaker, smaller, more emaciated with the passage of time. He thought of it as reverting back to their true state, non-existence, which only reinforced his initial belief.

The Holy Father permitted himself a brief smile. Having once died and tasted the grave, the nothingness of death, the presence of *nothing* was familiar, if not banal.

Outside his west window *kittim* fell in a steady shower as Lesser Wind swept down from the north. These bugs were even larger and more colorful than last year's crop, and, he guessed, more deadly. That the Yellow had apparently survived them on her journey from White Mountain Cathedral impressed him. Nepptali great-coats seemed as impenetrable as Nepptali steel was sharp. He found himself, despite his craving for news of the War, a tiny bit disappointed that she'd not been poisoned. She knew too many of his

Exalted Father

secrets. Fortunately, no one—except his drunken son, the archbishop—knew the terrible secret of Elsseleron. He meant for things to remain that way, despite the designs of the foolish King.

She removed her hood and bowed. She looked no different from the other Yellows, from the Reds and the Grays for that matter—with her sunken eyes covered by folds of leathery skin, her moss-like hair, her fangs and claws, tail, spindly bow-legs and stick-like arms. There was no telling that she was female unless one removed her loincloth. The Holy Father alone knew *her secret*.

"Holy Father blesses me," she inhaled the words. She bowed and deposited an armful of codices on his desk. Most were in Sandi, a few were written in Runes.

"You have our blessings, child."

"Why's it, Holy Father, I'm called in the time of Short-time Wind?"

"O, dear child, dear *girl*, we are very sorry. But we felt it necessary. For these." He gestured at the books.

With immense satisfaction he noticed that she glanced around quickly, and although he couldn't see directly into those black eyes he was sure that they were wide with fear. Ah, but it gave him such pleasure to perceive fear in others, mild apprehension for that matter, how much power he wielded over them. If only the New-Men were able to show fear.

He grunted and rose from his chair. Dressed in simple white linen, he moved with greater ease than when he wore his formal robes. He still wore his red slippers.

She took a step back. He was as tall as the largest Yellow but far more massive and threatening. Again it pleased him.

"My dear little canary," he rumbled and he stepped around the desk, "let us retire to that bench lest the *kittim* learn to break Nepptali glass." He pointed to the east wall.

She followed his lead, although it seemed to him, reluctantly. This interview had begun splendidly.

"So, our trusted canary." He spoke as soon as they were seated. "Were you not present at the sack of Bethsham?"

"Yes, Holy Father. Black One used Nepptali L-guns, destroyed Redfolk before we got there. Black One, he fought with much...death...to hold Bethsham."

"Yes, yes, so we've heard."

"Redfolk, they're no smarter than marmots. *We* took Bethsham—" She let out a hiss followed by a clicking sound, which he took for a laugh. "Creaking warriors of old legends do not defeat Yellowfolk—"

"Yes, yes, we know," he said impatiently. For a brief moment he considered asking her about the white-haired Witch-woman who fought beside the infernal Black One and was said to be more deadly than any warrior. But she came from the time before his death and so mattered nothing to him now, as did everything else but for the *One Thing*—

"Tell us, little *canary*—" He kept using the word because he knew how much she hated it. Canary meant *young maiden* among the Yellows, and would surely prove deadly to her if other Yellows heard it, making the game he played with her all the more pleasing. How long, however, before she realized that a single knife-thrust would end her torture? Would she also realize that it was futile to kill a dead man?

"—tell us of books?"

"As many as the sands of Edom."

"Yes, yes, we know—look there." He pointed to the vast nest of shelving behind his desk. "We own many Nepptali texts, graciously bestowed upon the humble Holy Father by the King himself. Alas, what a pity, our gracious Lord does not seem to understand Sandi."

"Yes, yes—" she mimicked him. The Yellows were addicted to the habit of mimcry.

"Yes, well, we wish to know of those the Holy Father does not possess? Of Runes? What of the books you've brought this evening?"

Exalted Father

She again hissed and this time seemed to gurgle deep in her throat. "The Holy Father, he refers to the ones the White Lord King bestowed upon the archbishop, may he be blessed. Those White Lord King kept for his own blessed self. These come from the trash."

"Yes…those. How were they divided?"

"There were many such. Day-ra' knows not. Knows not why he gave those and kept those. He knows not Sandi. Perhaps he knows Runes. Some were Runes. I thinked he consulted the Holy Father."

"No, no—" She'd startled him with this bit of Yakashas speculation. Yellows could not be that smart, especially creatures that he stubbornly told himself did not exist. He and the archbishop had long suspected that while Ra' knew no Sandi, *he knew his Runes*.

"Yes, well, it is a puzzle. Yet, tell us, little canary, as a Yellow among so many Reds and Grays, surely *you* had a say how the books were distributed. We've heard that many were burned. *Someone* must have chosen—"

"This canary—" she pronounced the word with distaste and, though she tried to hide it, fear "—does not know Sandi, does not know Runes."

"Come, child, it is a wicked thing to lie to the Holy Father."

Reluctantly, hesitating, glancing around, she drew a deep breath. "Strong Protector ordered us to look for certain strings of Runes—" She bent down and sketched two lines of Runes in the dust.

$$\text{XXX VVI IV}\wedge \text{ TFI } \wedge\wedge\text{X TI}\wedge$$
$$\text{TFI } \wedge\wedge\text{X X}\wedge\text{V XXX VVI XXV}$$

The Holy Father's weak eyes were barely up to the task and it took many minutes for him to even identify the symbols. The knowledge he needed to assign fractions, calculate words, and transliterate the string into Sandi came to him in broken fragments, shades of memory from a former life. It was impossible. So, in the end he guessed.

"Something 'bout the *Ark*?"

"Yes, yes, Holy Father, but I don't know *something*—"

"Ah—"

He bent down and using his Nepptali dagger scratched a long series of fractions on the surface of the smooth rock floor. Then he formed Sandi letters. He crossed out many and started over a number of times. Again and again. But the possible fractions were endless and he had to stop sometime.

"Did my trusted canary see these?"

She studied the letters and emitted a small moan.

"His canary should answer her Holy Father."

"Yes, yes, Holy Father."

"Ah—"

"Does his canary understand them?"

"No, no, Holy Father."

"How does His canary know that this is 'bout the Ark?"

"Heard the Strong Protector."

"White Lords know not their Runes?"

She moaned again but did not reply.

"You serve Sanakht. Tomorrow you will return with him to Tharas Major. You will report back all he says to the King."

"*All*, Holy Father? Your canary cannot hear all. And forget not, *he serves the Strong Protector*. This Yellow Day-ra' must report the Holy Father's words to the Strong Protector."

"Yes, yes, and Day-ra' ought to pray that her gender remains a secret...*he*."

"Yes, yes, Holy Father." Her words were barely audible.

"Well yes, and we see that Lesser Wind has ceased. Return to your master. Should he inquire about your visit here, you will say that you came seeking absolution as all creatures ought to do, even the Strong Protector of the Cosmos—and the King."

EXALTED FATHER

"What is this... *absolution?*"

"Don't worry your head 'bout it. The archbishop may be the only one who really knows. He was the first announce it. But remember it is very significant and all creatures require it—and it comes exclusively from the Holy Father."

"Yes, yes—" She rose quickly snapping her tail.

"And dear canary, remain ever vigilant—in the name of the Lord Almighty who lives upon White Mountain Elsseleron, and never sleeps."

THE BOOKS OF MARDUK

BOOK OF RUNES
<u>VERSE 5.1.3</u>

The quartz lamps flickered. He heard them hiss. Soon they'd fail and there were no Nepptali left to repair them. Soon he, the Holy Father, would, like the rest of them, become a slave of the daystar. Without the Nepptali, everyone, even the King, was a slave.

The Sandi letters danced and squirmed on the brown, creased and torn papyrus pages. He cursed the non-existent Lord-on-the-Mountain for designing his eyes so ineptly that they should not see in the night, or in the realms of the infinitely small. Such was the nature of reconstruction.

"Now who might have written this?" The Holy Father asked aloud. He imagined that he was interrogating the cloud covered mountain and the horror that inhabited its plateau, which he'd seen with his own eyes—I have looked upon the Lord and lived—which was nothing to brag about.

The author calls herself Queen of the Heavens. She pretends to be an eye-witness. Yet she also claims that she is writing *before* the siege of Bethsham, years before. She describes a historical event before it happens.

The problem made his head ache. Had time ceased to flow from past to present to future? If time is abolished must not cause and effect also disappear? Anything that could happen would happen?

He liked that. For it would seem that his old self, the Grand Duke, had been resurrected before he was buried, or he'd been resurrected and simply invented the buried part. Take away the tragedy and skip right to the comedy. He really liked that.

The Sandi was corrupted. It was similar (but not identical) to the vulgar Sandi of the south, invented a few years ago by the archbishop for the purposes of converting the queeti. And suddenly, as if to add to his confusion, he realized that if this were true then the whole thing, which pretended to be an eyewitness account of the final destruction of Bethsham, had been written *in a language invented four, maybe five decades after the event.*

"Well now," he repeated aloud, "the account must have written on Starmirror, and quite recently too. It could not have come from the libraries of Bethsham. But who is the author? Why invent some ridiculous Queen of Heaven in order to hide a forgery?"

The uncertain light, his poorly designed eyes, his skepticism, all resisted his efforts, yet he read:

And the Lord said to the Queen (of Heaven):
Your people are stupid,
They heed me not.
Like foolish children,
They think me a jester.
Like your Akkadean father,
They are clever in their stupidity.
Old as they are,
They remain rebellious—like children.

Old and rebellious made him think of his former Tribe, indeed all the Tribes of Men. The Queen of Heaven made him think of Devorah.

He puzzled over the next few lines:
Disaster overtakes disaster,
Ascend like clouds, red and gray and yellow,
And all-conquering white.
Calamity they bring,
And Tribe after Tribe is annihilated.
For all the lands are ravaged,
From the south, the east.
A whirlwind of fire, blue-burning,
Woe to us—

Except mighty Bethsham where we stand.
And all around is waste and welter.
No-thing lives,
Birds of the sky flee,
The towns and cities in ruin,
Mighty Haran too.
Edom has come to Greenbottom.

The Holy Father rose stiffly and limped to the western window, favoring an old wound in his left leg. It was dark and lights of Thrice-blessed Cathedral twinkled like stars against the backdrop of the Lord's Holy Mountain. Between the Cathedral and the mountain lay shadowed gorges, small ravines and the secret paths of the Lord. Unyielding darkness covered the plateau of the Holy Mountain. Thick clouds blanketed the place day and night. The Lord preferred His holy peace enveloped by holy secrecy, the Holy Father liked to say. Of course he knew the awful truth.

The Holy Father's memory drifted back through the years. Giving thanks to the horror on the mountain that his thrice-blessed memory still functioned tolerably, he found that he did recall, if only vaguely, the Strong Protector's triumphant report to the King. Bethsham was taken, he'd announced. No one, neither man nor woman (there were no children) survived. King Ra' sighed (he simply exhaled air; a sigh would require at least a spark of emotion) and inquired after the capture of any human females as if he'd not heard the Strong Protector correctly.

None, none—even the *Queen of Heaven* is no more…

"Ah," the Holy Father said smiling. So he'd heard the title. How fortunate he remembered. So, there'd been such a person, and it couldn't have Queen Devorah—or, because she'd failed to conceive for so many years and was now too advanced in age, the Once-Queen.

Exalted Father

He returned to his desk and read further. Now the verses became repetitive: ignorant Tribesmen, wicked leaders, base councilors, feeble and greedy populace. Then he came to the following passage:

The Lord's punishment, they say,
For crimes and wickedness,
Cast into the pit,
No water, only mud,
No food, only kittim.
Sank into the mud, and died.
But the Lord speaks, not as in Nalanda.
And spared the Queen of Heaven,
Thrice-blessed and fertile
[...].
Retreated to the north, yet the flood
Of Reds, Grays, Yellows...destroyed the wicked.
The Queen of Heaven, thrice-blessed and fertile,
The Ark [...]
Mountain of the Lord.

"Well now," exclaimed the Holy Father aloud, "our little canary surpasses herself. What a gift she brings her Holy Father." He laughed loudly.

The battle for Bethsham had been the bloodiest day of the war, when the King's own legions had been decimated. The Black One (the name Sanakht gave to the King of the Tribes) had rebuilt the city after its first sack at the hands (claws) the Redfolk before the death of the Grand Duke. For over forty years this Black One (the Holy Father guessed his true identity) fought with working L-guns, and the poor Yakashas died in droves. Under the command of the Strong Protector of the Cosmos, the Grays and the Yellows finally prevailed, yet they too suffered dreadful destruction.

Oh, that lying Sanakht! The Holy Father glimpsed his convoluted plotting, like the shortest distance between two points on a rolling surface of hills. Ah, *Miriam*, after all these years.

The Holy Father remembered how the Strong Protector had described the victory. He'd almost choked laughing when Sanakht had told of the *farvel army* that fought for Black One.

"The Holy Father has rightly heard," Sanakht snapped at him, if such a word as *snapped* could be said of a marble statue. "Fought they with tooth and claw, O King, yet the Strong Protector prevailed—mightily."

"When was it," the Holy Father asked innocently, "that the Strong Protector passed from the real cosmos in order to protect an imaginary one? Did he climb a ladder? Take a boat? Did he learn to fly?"

"We do no such things, Holy Father. We have our courage, our skill, and our devotion to our King."

"Yes, yes—" Amusing that a block of lifeless marble should be a literalist.

"Today the Great Northern War has come to an end. But Ra' still does not have his woman."

So, that's what this stupid Queen of Heaven is saying. Now *she* comes to him like *kittim* riding the Winds. And despite her great age she's fertile. Nothing is too great a miracle for no-thing to accomplish.

"Ah, our dear canary, this fulfills your service to your Holy Father," he said aloud, closing the leather-bound codex. He'd have to remember to burn it later.

What of the Runes? What of the Ark?

How clever the Neptalli. How did they ever guess that there really was an Ark on the Lord's Holy Mountain?

EXALTED FATHER

BOOK OF RUNES
VERSE 5.1.4

The archbishop teetered as he walked. A few times he nearly fell. Maintaining his balance appeared difficult given the immense amount of weight he'd added to what was already considerable bulk. He existed almost exclusively on loads of bread and sweet cakes, and copious amounts of spiced beer his most devoted queeti followers brought as offerings. When he spoke, it always seemed that bits of food jetted from his mouth—but this was surely the case of one or two such events being multiplied a thousand times with the passage of time.

The archbishop tried to teach his queeti followers the rudimentary Sandi that he'd invented for their edification, and they in turn instructed him in the primitive queeti tongue of barks, snarls, growls, sighs, whines, gurgles, gasps and whistles, all accompanied by various body movements. These days, along with bread, cakes, and beer, bits of queeti jetted from his mouth when he gave sermons in his vulgar Sandi.

The Holy Father remarked that his new habits of speech improved his theology immensely.

The archbishop mounted a wooden platform erected on large wine barrels. Dewdrop moon had set, driven out of the sky by the daystar. Greater Wind became a whisper and the rain of *kittim* ended. This morning there'd been a downpour.

The queeti audience, no more than several dozen, failed to notice that the archbishop occupied the stage. They busily groomed one another, licking up the syrupy moisture of dissolved *kittim* that glistened on red-brown pelts.

The archbishop noted that three Yellow Yakashas had been caught in the morning's shower and had died in agony. Their screams, he thought, were eerily similar to those of the queeti he himself burned at the stake for various heresies and blasphemies in this same Thrice-blessed Plaza of Thrice-blessed Cathedral of the White Mountain…and so on.

Dressed in his crimson robes and red slippers, the archbishop gazed over the plaza hoping to see at least a few new-comers, maybe some of the larger queeti from the villages along the Topartz. Alas, the flock that gathered here was the usual gang of forest serfs who served the Cathedral.

He sighed and emitted a short whine. His escort of three brown bulls emitted low growls in response. Generally, a sigh and whine denoted the presence of a blasphemer. When *he* growled, a heretic.

The archbishop inhaled and pursed his lips. Crimson blotches sprouted on his cheeks and spread upwards to his bald plate. When calm, his skin reverted to a pasty white. The Holy Father said that he looked more like a Ra'bim every day. He accepted the compliment as teasing rather than what he really knew it to be. For all his brilliance and accomplishments in the way of theology—his immensely long book of theology graced the High Altar—he knew that he deeply disappointed his father.

"Harken thy ears to me," he cried out, vainly striving to pack more authority into his whining voice than it would bear—like pouring good Banalis wine into old leaky cups, he said to himself, but only when he was sober and before he'd drained said leaky cup.

"Harken, listen, though thou ist dull and dim, and thus harkening will hear—" The word harken began to slide into a barking sound… "listen, hark, hark…bark, bark…"

The serfs harkened, and many secretly hoped they'd not have to harken too long, for the morning was growing warm and there were many tasks that also required their harkening. The Grayfolk overseers were none too patient with either harkening or non-harkening serfs.

"Your own, thy archbishop will now commence to discourse on the glorious and one-alone creation of the *uni-verse*. The *uni-verse* is a word that can be found in your-thy archbishop's great book, which is named *The Lord's Revelation Revealed to Jacob Gold-tongue on Stone Hill, Which Came to Gold-tongue, Chosen of the Lord, From the Lord*, or for short, *The Revealed that Was Revealed to Jacob Gold-tongue*—"

He paused and smoothed his robes, sighed, grunted, and puffed his red cheeks.

"Now, thou dull but dear ones, close eyes and think about not-a-thing. Now, how does a queeti think about not-a-thing?"

A young female in the front row lifted her paw and waved as he'd instructed her. "I think 'bout not-a-thing all the time," she said.

The majority of shaggy heads nodded vigorously in agreement.

"No, no, stupids—" The archbishop tried to growl but coughed instead. "We mean...no-thought, no-thing, nothing—"

They remained silent sensing his anger.

"No, no...imagine...close queeti eyes...a garden plot before it became a garden plot. What does a queeti see?"

"Angry overseer!" an old graybeard cried.

"Why so angry?"

"Because of no-work, lazy fur-balls."

"Yes, yes, think of no-work."

"No-work is beatings, no-supper, no-rest, no-joy—"

"No-garden!" the archbishop shouted. "No-work means no-garden, and no-garden means no-queeti. So and therefore, queeti are here, now, in this plaza of learning, hearing archbishop, so and therefore there must be a garden, otherwise no-queeti, but there are queeti—"

His listeners nodded vigorously. All agreed that this was true and was certainly easier to grasp than the mysterious not-a-thing from which every-thing began.

"So—" the archbishop intoned, "no-garden means no-queeti. Then, who is it who plots, plants, waters and digs the garden?"

"Queeti," they answered in unison. The answer was ridiculously obvious. The archbishop had to be joking with them—or he'd been in his beer already. No-queeti, no-gardens were obvious. It was this *nothing* that didn't make sense.

"No, no, dim-witted children, dullards. Before queeti, before Grayfolk, Redfolk, before even White Lords."

They frowned and drooled and furrowed their heavy brows. They wished the sermon would be over. If no-work, the overseers would see to it that there'd be no-queeti.

Suddenly the young female laughed and cried out: "A jest! Archbishop has become jester for his queeti. Make us happy."

"What's so funny?" asked the archbishop sourly.

"Before has no-before. Gold-tongued says not-a-thing but really means not-a-before."

"What?"

The rest of the crowd nodded their heads sagely as though they'd been following these fine points quite closely. Everyone knew that Soft-eye, which was the young female's name, wasn't soft at all when it came to argument. And she was always right.

"Not-a-thing means no-before. If no-before, then Gold Tongue's question is funny joke. Gardens come *after* work, and work comes *after* queeti arrive to do work, and queeti work *after* queeti arrive to garden. So and therefore..." She pronounced the Sandi perfectly "...there can be no before *before* no-before, and no after before no-after, and that is funny joke."

The archbishop's round face twisted into an elongated howl of anger. "The Lord-on-the-Mountain comes before everything because everything comes from the Lord-on-the-Mountain, because everything cannot come from not-a-thing, and so must come from the Lord!"

Soft-eye seemed to shrink in height and width at once. Her shoulders slumped, her head sank into the gap between them, her barrel chest and round belly deflated. She did not, however, step back or cower like the typical serf.

"This before of the archbishop is not a queeti before," she replied quietly yet firmly. "Or might be that poor dullards queeti don't know high holy language of archbishop."

The archbishop attempted a smile but had to settle for a smirk. "Yes, yes, poor dull serfs. Such as they know not from whence they came. Not-knowing from whence they came, such as they know not where they're going."

"We'd better be going to work," growled a young bull serf standing directly behind Soft-eye. He made certain that the archbishop couldn't fully see him.

"Yes, yes," agreed the rest, nodding their large heads.

Except Soft-eye who was up for this challenge too.

"South, on the Topartz, high in fire trees named Copper Jungle, there live small creatures we call—" she emitted a series of barks and whistles far too quickly for the archbishop to follow, although he thought he heard the word *whittling*, but that was impossible since whittling referred to a kind of tree (cursed in the *Runehayana*) and not animals living in the tree— "who have black fur, tails, teeth and paws like a miniature queeti. Yet these do not speak, they chatter. Blue taught that some of these ones came down from the trees and lived a different life, and many, many seasons of the daystar later became like us—"

Soft-eye abruptly stopped speaking (or chattering like her creatures that the archbishop had never seen and were not mentioned in the *Runehayana*—as far as he could remember). A few of the younger queeti had begun to mew and moan, for they suddenly recalled smoke and fire arising from the great dome of the Cathedral (Thrice-blessed) accompanied by the smell of burning fur. Had not the archbishop done his best to exterminate every Blue within his reach, and had condemned to death those beyond his reach?

Obviously the archbishop had seriously misjudged the intelligence of his audience. They were not merely dull and dim; they were positively stupid and dark. No-thing—why, they were negations of no-thing.

"How can anything become something else?" the archbishop asked peevishly. When he spoke in such a manner, the queeti heard threats.

"Just as chosen queeti become farvels," Soft-eye answered.

The crowd's moaning increased in volume, mixed now with a few nervous whines and simpers.

"Farvels?" roared the archbishop, wondering if he were drunk without being aware of the fact. "Farvels are no-things—incarnated."

On the archbishop's left hand, a young bull named Mustard bellowed: "No, no...see farvels all the time, queeti do, all around. More farvels nowadays then when Mustard was a cub."

The archbishop had heard enough. "The Lord Almighty made everything," he howled, "and made everything the way it is now. And later some things He made did not please the Lord, and these he blotted out. Graciously did the Lord give *some* queeti a mind, and if it is working properly, this mind comes to the truth which is the Lord. But if this mind only serves the purpose of breathing, eating, and—fucking—then it serves no-truth. So and therefore, mind of queeti cannot know truth of queeti, or farvels, or whittling, the daystar or the *Lord*, and so and therefore *itself*, if it serves only queeti—fucking."

Soft-eye said: "But queeti changed since those times. Now queeti *speak*...and speak *truth*."

Lo, not only are they stupid and dark, but they know not their stupidity and darkness. The archbishop would have to reconsider how far the queeti could be trained to speak and think properly.

"Dim and dark ones, harken closely. The Lord Almighty gave some queeti the ability to speak, it is true. Since they value not this ability, demeaning it, saying it came from nonexistent small furry tree rats chattering to one another in trees, the Lord, though He ought to strike those queeti dead, instructs them to speak no more and abuse His gift. So, be silent and work! So and therefore, *get to work.*"

They howled and scurried away as fast as their bow-legs would carry them.

"I must speak to the Holy Father," said the archbishop to his Grayfolk retainers. Grays, thank the Lord, never argued with him and did without question everything he demanded.

First some spice beer, he said to himself and naturally did not get an argument.

Of all the gifts the Lord bestowed upon His archbishop, spice beer surely had to be the happiest—except for the sad fact that it required queeti brewers. Just as there could be no Banalis brandy without the Banalis Tribe, there could be no spice beer without the queeti. Well then, the Lord must have created the queeti in order that there should be spice beer for the archbishop.

The archbishop smiled for the first time this morning. After all these years he had to admit that he was still a brilliant theologian whether his father recognized his talent or no.

The Books Of Marduk

BOOK OF RUNES
VERSE 5.1.5

The archbishop's bleary eyes were fixed on the High Altar as he muttered curses.

"My dear archbishop, does it rain still?" asked the Holy Father.

"Rain isn't still, it drops," the archbishop snapped. "It rains eternally on this damned mountain."

Queeti heads turned and ears flared. It was an oddity about the archbishop that they'd learned to accept as a great mystery—how he often uttered blasphemy within Thrice-blessed Cathedral.

"Eternal rain does not fall in time," the Holy Father observed, keeping his temper. "Tell me, archbishop, *my son*—" he emphasized the word *son* "—do you *still* cohabit with a queeti female?"

The archbishop was incensed. "I've never done such a thing!"

The Holy Father raised a finger to his lips. "Careful, my son. The King expects all of us to fulfill our duty."

"Ain't your bastard son, Rudra."

"Ah, but you know the truth of it. You're no bastard."

Jacob chose to ignore this truth. "Don't screw no monkeys either."

The Holy Father grinned, exposing broken teeth that had turned dull yellow from age. "Ah, monkeys? I see you've been at the ancient texts."

"Don't need 'em no more. Jus' listen to queeti jabber away—"

"You're still a priest then? You have your vows?"

"What'd you want, Holy Father?"

"The King grows desperate for children. He's come to accept the Nepptali manuscripts as genuine. He believes every word, and takes every word literally."

EXALTED FATHER

The archbishop spat. "Don't he know Nepptali forged it all? Wanted to rule Greenbottom like every other damned Tribe. Like you, my Grand Duke. But when they realized that the Tribes of Men were coming to an end, they gave it all up. They abandoned the future."

"That may be, my son. Ra', however, believes it is all true. It is impossible for him not to believe. All the New-Men are like this. They believe in the future. Oh, they make a big show of their skepticism and suspicion. Yet in their hearts—if stone statues have hearts—they cling to belief. They only wish to appear that they do not believe. Probably because belief reveals their weaknesses—and their fears. *To believe is to fear—that there is nothing to believe, which is probably true. On the other hand, tyrants cannot not believe and remain tyrants.* Ah, my proverbs get better with age."[19]

"So what," said the archbishop. The Holy Father had begun to irritate him—he was the one who gave the sermons around here.

The Holy Father slumped back into his throne and smoothed his thick robes. He noticed that Jacob was wearing red slippers. Only the Holy Father ought to be wearing red slippers. He forgot the precise text in which this was stated, so many had become available since the discovery of the Nepptali archives. He considered chiding the archbishop, yet Jacob's level of drunkenness—if such a level could be even measured—was quite high.

---

[19] It should be obvious by now that such proverbs, when they come from Rudra in Book V (the queeti are the source for Jacob's sermons) are the forgeries of scribes. The disparaging remarks about ancient queeti seem to indicate the existence of an ancient queeti community that for reasons we will never know suffered some kind of self-loathing, or guilt, or deep seated resentment, perhaps because these scribes and their community perceived themselves through the grid of their own literary creations. For example, no modern queeti believes (and it is an unsubstantiated belief) that we arose from some lower or primitive form.

The Holy Father sighed. "Our Strong Protector of the Cosmos presented to his King a manuscript that speaks of something named the Ark, which we think is something like a large boat that travels in the air. He returns to Tharas Major bearing more."

"I know all about the stupid Nepptali Ark. What's it got to do with fertility?"

Maybe Jacob wasn't as drunk as Rudra first thought. "Well nothing. But in the King's sluggish, uh, let us say straight line of thought—you know none of the tailed are able to change course quickly—there seems to be some connection between the Ark and the future survival of the New-Men. Anyway, the Nepptali writer said something about the Lord's Mountain, that it was an Ark, you know, probably a symbol, perhaps part of an allegory. Taking it all literally, the King decided that he's coming here and will attempt to climb Elsseleron upon which, he thinks, rests the Ark."

"Howling mad!"

The Holy Father frowned but maintained his dignified holy composure. He stared past the archbishop into the shadows of the vast Cathedral. Late afternoon light filtered through the massive stained-glass windows, populating the smooth marble floor with strange wavering forms of stranger transparent beings. Such eerie scenes were born of some mysterious artistry that filled the windows with an alien world, and only the light of the real world brought this imaginary world to life. Spires and turrets, mountains and green rolling hills, oceans and stark deserts materialized as if from nothing. Strange beings occupied themselves with even stranger tasks. There was something unsettling about the art, something that caused the Holy Father a great unease and forced him to avert his eyes. He knew, however, that it all had something to do with the horror on the mountain.

"Should they actually climb the mountain—which may well be beyond their physical abilities—we both know what they'll find." The

EXALTED FATHER

Holy Father sounded desperate. "We need something to divert them. A new revelation perhaps? Is there a still small voice in the Winds?"

The archbishop snickered and peered owlishly at him. "We both know the Winds speak to no one, and never have." He spoke softly so as not to disturb the queeti pilgrims.

"We need something. We cannot allow them on that plateau."

"They don't believe in the Lord Almighty. So what if they know?"

"Weren't you listening to our homily on belief?"

The archbishop gave a bitter laugh. "Look at us. We who know. How I believed... When I lecture the queeti it all comes back and I believe it all over again, and feel good and powerful. I met the Lord Himself, don't forget. I wrestled with him. To me was given the revelation of Marduk. Yet like you I know what's on the mountain."

The Holy Father waved his claw-like hand. "All these are purely scholastic issues. Once they've scaled the mountain, no matter what they still believe or don't believe, *they'll no longer have any use for us.*"

"Ha, another Suthralane, huh? Well then, we can finally quit this chilly tomb and get drunk."

"Think so. Look upon yon queeti."

He turned and studied the scattered lumps of fur, many on their paws and knees, protruding foreheads pressed to the cold marble. Today, many were red-brown. These were true pilgrims, not the Cathedral serfs. He thought he saw some trembling. Perhaps they'd heard bits and pieces of the conversation. Naturally they could barely comprehend Sandi, if at all, and even if they had understood something of the exchange, the mysteries of theology lay far beyond their feeble grasp—as he'd experienced this very morning.

"What 'bout 'em?"

"Think you they'll remain docile servants? They'll find another Lord as quickly as they forget our Lord-on-the-Mountain. And their Lord 'ill probably be some kind of super-queeti, and mark this, my son, their new Lord will be our mortal enemy. Beneath His banner they'll seek to destroy us utterly."

In a surprisingly sober tone, the archbishop said: "I see the point, my father."

The Holy Father bowed his head as though in prayer. A few queeti, mostly Cathedral serfs, arose, genuflected, and exited the great Church. The working day had finally concluded. Outside, Lesser Wind began. Only the very old—those who could no longer serve—and the pilgrims remained. Sometimes the old ones chose to die in the Cathedral. Suicide by pilgrimage, the Holy Father called it. Usually their corpses began to smell before anyone realized what had happened. *Piety is nauseating, especially after it dies*, the Holy Father remarked, adding this bit of profundity to his collected sayings of sacred wisdom, his proverbs.

He raised his eyes and watched the queeti shuffle out. "We'll require something new," he said thoughtfully. "A miracle, a wondrous event, something extraordinary, an act, not mere words—something they can see. Perhaps we should remind them how the Holy Father came back from the dead. Our mere presence—"

"The queeti might be impressed but the New-Men will laugh."

"Ah— after all this time, we still don't know them."

"The Holy Father appears forgetful. They're fearful, he said. But of what? Have you seen one become ill? They don't seem to age. Have you ever seen one die, except when caught in a *kittim* storm?"

"No, but we think they hide their weaknesses."

"All creatures that can imagine into the future must ultimately see their death."

"Perhaps not."

"What then, my *father*?"

"Ah, mocking us? Well, perhaps my *son* is right. They think of themselves as immortal. A resurrection would not impress an immortal."

The archbishop spat again.

Exalted Father

"How 'bout your Marduk tooth? It could be of use in some way?"

"A fraud, my *father*, a convenient lie, phantoms leaking out of a drunken mind. I wrestled with the Lord, don't you remember?"

"*You did,*" said the Holy Father forcefully. "*You, my son,* met the Lord and prevailed."

"I did."

"*And Marduk is the Lord's true name.* And you, my dear archbishop, are His true disciple. You need to somehow *show* them. Marduk is Lord. That He's back from the dead."

"Where? What? A miserable tooth?"

"In *you*, my son."

Jacob found that he liked this. "Yes, yes, in me. Marduk reveals Himself *in* me."

"You shall preach these things, *my son*. Naturally you'll be sure to add that Marduk has forbidden the Holy Mountain to all beings. Which is why we preserve His Holy Relic here—and He speaks through His archbishop."

"What about the King and his Nepptali Ark?"

The Holy Father frowned. "Ah, that will require some very subtle and fine tuning."

"What means the Holy Father?"

"We must convince them all that a true reading of the Nepptali scribbling, a deeper reading, demonstrates that the Ark is merely a symbol."

"A symbol for what?"

"Nothing! You're good at *nothing*, are you not, my son? Let the symbol stand alone. Pretend that it points to something, very, very mysterious."

"But no-thing."

"Exactly."

"Are they stupid?"

"Don't know. Do rocks think?"

"Do they fuck?"

"Better ask the Once-Queen that one."

They both roared with laughter, sounding quite alike, and frightening the remaining queeti—and accelerating, perhaps, the deaths of the older ones.

"By the way, my dear archbishop, please inform that Yellow bastard, uh, Persaah we think he is named, that the Holy Father has a message for the King in Tharas Major. And, oh son, watch out for *kittim*, even after the Wind's let up. They've become quite dangerous these days."

So and therefore, with these final words, the Holy Father bestowed his blessings upon his child the archbishop, and dismissed him.

Exalted Father

BOOK OF RUNES
VERSE 5.1.6

At dawn, as Greater Wind swept away the lingering morning fog, the spectacular fortress-city of Tharas Major emerged from the mist like a copper mountain forged to resemble a peninsular-like arrow pointing west. Soaring fired-brick walls built upon a massive layered rectangle of iron-rich rock some hundred meters in height, the walls added another twenty meters. A forest of towers rose above the walls. Thousands of golden spires caught the first light of the daystar making it appear that the walled forest burned fiercely.

A great golden dome dominated the center of the fortress-city, as though the daystar itself had settled there. This was the Grand Hall of Heavenly Peace, Prosperity, Freedom, and Brilliant Light—the Dome of Ra', of which it was written that there cannot be two daystars in the sky and there cannot be two Ra's in the world. East of the dome the fortress-city's rectangular mountain base widened and became an asymmetrical plateau of courtyards, minor palaces, towers, as well as single-storied brick buildings that served as living quarters for the servant class of Grayfolk.

Tharas Major was a miracle of architecture, an engineering marvel in its sheer size and construction. No one, not even the New-Men, the White Fathers as they were known to the queeti and Redfolk, nor of course the Grays and Yellows, knew who built it—or when.

The Sacred Way was a single roadway that connected the Cathedral to Tharas Major. It crossed the Redrain River at the Bridge of the Celestials, about two days by foot from the fortress-city. All told, the journey from Thrice-blessed Cathedral to Tharas Major took seven days, although in these times this had become less predictable due to the increasing frequency of *kittim* showers. Although travelers, mostly Grays and Yellows, trusted the efficiency of Nepptali greatcoats, they didn't trust the ability of queeti seamstresses to follow Nepptali diagrams and so preferred to travel between the Winds.

The Holy Father had instructed his servant Persaah that only the King, and the King alone, was to receive his message.

"Behold great Ra', a Church offering," The Holy Father instructed the Yellow to whisper into the kingly ear of stone. "Here is your Ark. The Nepptali always spoke in symbols and allegories, strange but true for a Tribe of engineers. The Ark stands for the fertility of the female, all females from all species that inhabit the lands of the Two Continents. Only males are sterile. Until now. Until *you, O King*. This is a great mystery. Your children shall be more numerous than the stars of the heavens. Behold, O King, this fertile Ark is *your own belief*. Believe in the Church and live."

This should be enough until the Holy Father and his drunken archbishop thought up something believable, say, a miracle or two, the resurrection of Marduk—*in* the archbishop.

The Holy Father dearly wanted to add that the weak-minded took the Ark as some sort of vessel, a ferry, one might say, for crossing to the stars, although this is how the Nepptali seemed to understand it. Of course he knew what it really was, having climbed Elsseleron—and like Suthralane, encountered the Lord face to face. He thought of it as something of an irony that Suthralane turned out to be a real man, Grand Duke Rudra, a Yad returned from the dead. How the priests would have loved this jest of fate. It was only because he had died that he had not gone insane like the ancient Suthralane, if such a Yad ever existed.

The Holy Father instructed his Yellow to conclude his message with: "Behold, glorious King, so and therefore, your august presence need not come to Elsseleron, for Elsseleron manifests in your presence."

"Be sure to say these words exactly as we've said them to you—" The Holy Father then caused the Yellow Yakashas Persaah to repeat them three times.

Later, he instructed Day-ra to tag along and keep an eye on Persaah.

Now Persaah was one of the more intelligent and dependable Yakashas who served the Thrice-blessed Cathedral. Nearly the size of a man, his face was flat and long, lacking a protruding muzzle; his ears were round, his hair silky, his eyes light brown and his tail was stunted. With him, it seemed, nature had tried to form a man from an imp. He might have been part queeti, but the Holy Father was of the opinion that cross-mating produced monsters that died quickly.

No matter how tall he stood, or how splendid he looked, Persaah remained a Yellow to the end. The secret knowledge his Holy Father had imparted to him festered in his mind and worked to unravel the binding rules of his long training as servant of the Cathedral.

He knew the secret of canaries.

On the night before they crossed the Bridge of the Celestials, he surprised Day-ra inside her *kittim*-proof shelter, which was in fact an abandoned queeti hut. The Strong Protector's word made it *kittim*-proof.

"No male art thou," he said using Cathedral language, which the Holy Father had taught him and which, the Holy Father said, was the original language of the Lord Almighty.

"What nonsense is this?" growled Day-ra.

"To his trusted servant has our Father revealed the truth." He shook off his greatcoat and lunged for her.

She fought him with agility and speed, but he was too strong and clever. He managed to tear off her greatcoat and strip away her linen shirt and trousers. Her breasts were tiny and shriveled, no larger than his, but they were still the breasts of a female Yakashas. Knowing nothing about female anatomy, Persaah 's first thought was that she was missing a penis, yet something drove him to force her legs apart.

His own penis was stunted and withered, and he barely achieved a suitable erection. Driven by instinct, he forced himself on her, whining and growling at once, beating her with his fists and vainly striving to penetrate the folds between her legs.

"Please, pleassseee… I love thee… eee…"

A long banging on the rotted wooden door suddenly shook the hut. Imp voices from outside cried: "What's the ruckus in there? That you, Persaah? Who's in there?"

"No one," Persaah gasped.

"What's that panting we hear?"

"Fear."

"No. Is love-panting. Have you a female in there? Bring her out so we may know her."

"No one…lives here."

"Bring her out, Persaah, or it'll go badly for you."

Persaah pushed Day-ra out of the hut. They saw that Day-ra was neither queeti nor male but a female Yakshas. Maddened by need and desperation, they tried to rape her. Like Persaah, they failed, and so they beat and abused her for the rest of the night. With the coming of Greater Wind she died. And then they seized Persaah and tried to rape him. Failing that, they tortured him with knives and lances. As many were naked, having cast off their greatcoats, a sudden shower of *kittim* caught them unprotected. They perished in agony, every one.

So, when the Strong Protector gathered his servants for the final leg of their journey to Tharas Major, he discovered not a single Yellow Yakashas except for black puddles of oily water.

His tail jerked violently, swinging from side to side like a fish out of water. Whether he was shocked or angry, or dumb-founded or frightened, could not be told from the inertia of his emotionless face.

Exalted Father

No Yakashas, Red, Gray or Yellow, understood the meaning of a White Lord's thrashing tail.

The Strong Protector proceeded on to Tharas Major, but the Holy Father's message never reached the ears of the King.

THE BOOKS OF MARDUK

THE BOOK OF RUNES

CHAPTER TWO – Olive

VERSE 5.2.1

This particular queeti hamlet of roughly a thousand souls slumbered beside a small tributary of the Redrain River. The stream would often shrink to a trickle during the summer months, and usually flooded in the early spring. Once, a decade ago, it destroyed the hamlet causing those residents who survived to question the beneficence and loving-kindness of the Lord-the-Mountain.

If not for its hardy olive trees, the hamlet might have never recovered. Quite by accident, a small contingent of refugees fleeing south from the Reed Sea massacre settled in Olive and revived its mainstay crop. They built its first olive presses. Soon, they expanded into other crops, spices and especially the red onion (which they kept secret from the White Lords of Thraras Major).

So the hamlet began to prosper, although because of the erratic river it still suffered setbacks. The olive presses helped, but soon the serfs learned to nurture different crops.

Upstream, where the valley became wide and open, the poor peasants planted barely and wheat. Their hamlets prospered. As might be expected, the Lords of Tharas Major took notice and levied a yearly tax quota, not only on the new produce but also the olive oil which flowed from the hamlet like the river itself. Besides feudal dues, they also paid a tithe to Thrice-blessed Cathedral. Thankfully, the Cathedral had yet to require a yearly draft of young bulls to fulfill its insatiable labor needs. The hamlet, though growing in wealth, still required every available paw.

On this particular morning in mid-summer, the sturdy peasants trudged out to the fields for another of those endlessly identical days of exhausting labor. Olive had succumbed to the age-old rhythm of agricultural life that revolved with deadening regularity. So, it was something totally unexpected and frightfully exceptional when the young field-hands came fleeing back to the hamlet with a strange tale.

An excited crowd gathered around the main olive press to hear them. Voices were raised, fights erupted, and general mayhem ensued. Worst of all, work came to a complete halt.

Finally, an older buck suggested they call a council. The elders came, even the Blue, although she was extremely old and from the original Reed Sea People. The hamlet's Hetman for this year was a shaggy, tall, and powerful bull named Six-fingers. He was second generation Reed Sea, and like many from that vanished tribe, bore an extra digit on each paw. Reed Sea bloodlines, it was said, produced not only six-finger bulls (and almost all females bore the trait) but giants. Six-fingers was nearly the size of a White Lord.

It took all of his size and exceptional ferocity to bring order to the council. He was forced to administer a few powerful cuffs, smash two noses, and twist a number of ears. He also awarded a vicious bite, drawing blood.

The Hetman took a long time untangling the main cause of hysteria. It made no sense. Nothing like this had ever happened in any hamlet along the river. He did vaguely remember a few tales of the Reed Sea People from his youth, but these were obviously stories for impressionable cubs. He was tempted to thrash the lot of them for laziness and send them back to work. Naturally, he dared not reveal his own perplexity, and so confusion stopped him from acting instantaneously.

As far as Six-fingers could make any sense of it, the peasants had gone out into the fields as usual and there discovered the strangest living being anyone could imagine, and possibly stranger than anyone was capable of imagining. From their nearly incomprehensible jabbering (how could anyone even *describe* a thing they could not even imagine?), he gathered that this creature was not a queeti. Other than this fact, they were talking nonsense.

At last they calmed down. The creature was indeed odd but not incomprehensible. Its hair was black and braided, its face flat and beardless, and it constantly showed its teeth. It had the color of a copper owl and wore a black garment that fully covered its body, and despite being black nonetheless shimmered in the light like the pelt of a farvel.

"Now this thing is...where?" Six-fingers asked.

"Where we left it," said a large peasant buck.

"Idiots," Six-gingers bellowed. "You left no watcher, to watch it?"

"No. Don't know what it is—"

"Stupids—" A powerful blow felled the speaker. The others cowered and chattered excitedly. Behind them, the females and cubs began to wail.

"Cease this racket," the hetman barked.

A female shrieked: "A *ghoul*. A ghoul out of the forest. Will steal and eat cubs—" Said cubs wailed louder.

Others took up the cry: "A ghoul, a ghoul—"

Although he struggled not to show it, Six-fingers experienced a churning in the pit of his large belly as if a nest of brown snakes from the straits had taken up residence there.

"Ain't no ghouls in the forest that comes out in the daylight," he said, not very convincingly.

The female cried out: "A daytime ghoul!"

EXALTED FATHER

"A daytime ghoul," took up the chorus.

A young buck yelped: "Call for the Blue."

"Call for the Blue—"

Six-fingers seized the fellow who unfortunately stood close by. Grabbing him by the rough of his back where the fur was most thick, the Hetman shook him violently as a mosscat would shake a squirrel in its jaws. The youngster shrieked and went limp.

"I Hetman," Six-fingers growled, "and I decides what we does." With a mighty blow he sent his would-be councilor sprawling.

Immediately he felt better. "Where is that lazy old woman," he asked.

An ancient wizened queeti female, all gray and white, immeasurably fat, nearly blind, teetered forward and peered up at the Hetman.

"Well, Blue Mother, you heard?"

"I have—" Her voice crackled like a fire on dry wood.

Six-fingers declared with all the authority he could muster: "It cannot be a ghoul—"

"I know that. Ghouls have not-a-hair and they is white as death...like White Lords."

Blue Mother shut her eyes for many minutes. The tension of the crowd began to grow again. Six-fingers felt it too, a palatable fear like a heaviness in the air before a monsoon. He watched the Blue. *The old female had fallen asleep.* He gave her a vicious kick in the ribs. "Wake-up, lazy bones."

The old one drooled and stared back dumbly.

"I asked you—"

"Asked me what?"

"What is this being."

Six-fingers barred his fangs and let out a warning growl. The Blue looked confused. They always seemed confused.

"Been dreaming, I have. Hetman, what is this damned creature?"

"Asking *you*. You the Blue."

"Oooo..." The Blue began to wail like the other females, like the cubs. "Gather all Olive. Choose a bouncing female. Need we a *sacrifice*."

Six-fingers felt his fear return in a rush; it threatened to pass into hysteria. Only anger blocked this disastrous plunge.

"A what—?" he managed to squeeze out.

"A *sacrifice*. Gives it a female. A naked hairless thing, flat faced, black-haired, can only be one...thing. Worse than any forest ghoul."

Hetman Six-fingers was not about to sacrifice a juicy young female no matter how terrible the creature proved to be.

"What then?"

"A mountain-demon. Come down from the Lord's own mountain to mate. Sacrifice a female, Hetman!"

He'd never heard of a mountain-demon, but he knew that ghouls stole females and tried to mate with them. The stupid old Blue was confused. This had to be nothing more than a forest ghoul.

He barked out orders reinforced by a few well-placed kicks and blows, a nip here and there that punctured ears, and one bite that took a fingertip. In short order, he cobbled together a bristling war party that exhibited plenty of bravado, and uncertain determination.

"Ain't no such things as mountain-demons. Ain't nothing but onion-soaked stories toll by senile old Blues to frighten cubs.

Such talk unnerved them. Seldom, if ever, had they heard a Hetman contradict a Blue. Blues generally had the last word. Of course Six-fingers was different, a Reed Sea queeti. They looked to the Blue for some sort of rebuttal. Not a few, however, felt a sudden thrill, a giddiness, as they perceived the challenge in the Hetman's voice.

"Are too mountain-demons," the Blue complained. She sounded fearful, which did not further her case among the young bulls who had for the first time felt pride in their Hetman and hence in themselves.

Six-fingers snorted: "Ain't never seen no mountain-demon. Ain't never seen no ghoul neither. Don't give a green olive what a stupid ole Blue say. White Lordses say nothing 'bout 'em. Neither does the Church."

"Oooo... Mountain-demons want to seed our females. Come at night they do, which is why Hetman sees them not. Usually drunk he is. They *know* females, but nothing comes of it 'cept terrible monsters that die quickly."

"Then why should we *give it a female?*"

"So it goes away. Better than hanging around here and *knowing* us every night."

"Oooo..." some of the females echoed. It takes us in the night— "In the night it comes—and penetrates us, and burns us, but nothing comes of it— Oooo..."

Six-fingers roared like a gold lion of the steppe. "Ridiculous! We goes and kills this creature."

Blue shook her head. "Only White Lords can kill such a thing."

"Whatever a White Lord can do a queeti can do."

Many of the young bulls roared their approval.

BOOK OF RUNES
VERSE 5.2.2

They found the thing sitting on a small rise on the river bank where the valley widened into tilled fields. It sat as straight-backed as a young whittling sapling, its legs folded in a manner that no bow-legged queeti would have ever been capable of. Covered by a torn old black cloak, its eyes were closed and its breathing was deep and regular. At first glance, the creature appeared to be dozing in the warmth of the newly risen daystar.

Six-fingers grunted and gave a signal with his paw. The war-party surrounded the monster and slowly began to creep forward, slowly closing the circle.

Suddenly, nearly too fast for queeti eyes to follow, the creature stood and faced the Hetman. Its open eyes were a startling green, like the fields in late spring after a drenching shower. The creature seemed to be smiling.

Six-fingers froze, stifling a yelp. Two study bucks threw aside their staves and bolted, howling like frightened tarp hounds. Three more scrambled up a nearby tree.

The Hetman held his ground. So did the former Grey renamed Silver, another descendent of the Reed Sea People. In Olive, Greys became Silvers. In the past, Greys had been subservient to Blues. No longer. A Silver was greater. He hoped that this one had the testicles.

The monster took a step towards them. Six-fingers emitted a warning growl. Silver wet himself. Not a good sign.

"Do not be afraid, do not," the creature said, speaking in the barking tongue of the queeti. Silver recognized the nearly forgotten Reed Sea dialect. The creature's voice, however, was soft and musical, comforting in a strange way.

Exalted Father

Silver clapped his paws over his ears and shut his eyes. "Do not hear the ghoul," he moaned, "it casts a spell, it does."

The creature laughed, sounding like the happy splashing of a waterfall. "Ah, a Silver—Silver is the word, is it not? Once Grey?"

Silver howled shrilly. "Ghoul-spell, don't hear, Hetman—"

"Shut-up, fool," Six-fingers growled.

Addressing the monster, he said: "I mighty Six-fingers, Hetman of Olive, vassal to Lord of Tharas Major. What're you?"

The creature let out another musical laugh. "There is a wanderer, there is, from another shore, come here with good news."

Silver let out a pain-filled yelp as if he'd been stabbed.

The Hetman swung around and cuffed him, and then turned back to the creature. "Who does thou serve? Who is thy Lord." He decided on the language of the Church—the little that he knew—just in case the stupid Blue and Silver were right and this was a ghoul.

"Are no Lords."

The Hetman decided that this creature, ghoul or not, was quite mad. All creatures were slaves of the White Lords—who themselves were slaves of the Lord-on-the-Mountain, the Lord the Reed Sea People also named Exalted Father. Then the Hetman noticed that Silver was staring open-mouthed at the thing, no longer terrified, a look of rapture on his blunt face.

"You there, you are free in the world?"

"You have said it."

Six-fingers hooted: "Impossible! Lord Almighty on His Mountain. White Lords bow to Him, we to them, wisps bow to them too, crops to us bow— Who you bow to?"

"Have you seen the Mountain Lord? Heard Him? Seen His footprint perhaps? Smelled his scent?"

The Hetman's ears flared like open flowers and his soft brown eyes grew wide. He glanced at Silver who was drooling and looking sillier than usual. He could think of...*no-thing*...so he repeated: "We vassals of Tharas Major." Saying this gave him comfort and eased his fear. This creature spoke dangerous things. It frightened him.

The thing smiled, and the sky became dazzling—and from far away the Hetman could hear the river bubbling in song—and the air became perfume. Six-fingers felt intoxicated as if he'd consumed a barrel of fall spice-beer.

"Take away the Lord and you take away His servants, and you also take away your masters who speak in His stead. Lord of Mountain rules such things and such things rule you. See you butterflies in the air? Your masters say they are Lord-make. You are Lord-make. White Lords, wisps, farvels—all manner of beings are Lord-make, they say. So, Lord is on Mountain, then come others, then come queeti on the bottom. Queeti on bottom must work, not so?"

"Are Winds Lord-make?" asked Silver.

"Shut-up, fool," Six-fingers said, but he no longer seemed angry at Silver.

The ghoul sighed and looked southwest, in the direction of brooding Elsseleron. "Now listen, dear ones, you. The Lord is not important. The Lord is a word, a sound. Words do not exist. Sounds are just sounds. A queeti sees something that has never been seen. What does this queeti say? How does this queeti tell another queeti who has not seen this some-thing-never-seen-before?"

The ghoul closed its eyes. "No queeti has seen the Lord-on-the-Mountain. Now, one day a Silver sees something strange and knows not what to call it. Say he sees a shadow in the light of the daystar, or a light in a black night, or he hears singing in a forest grove. So, this Silver says *Lord*, a word he learned as a cub. Now, this Silver tells another queeti about the Lord, and he says the Lord is *like* this strange something. He says the Lord is like the Two Winds. So when the Winds blow the other queeti hears the Lord. Maybe this Silver says the Lord is *like* a giant Silver, and so the word Lord conjures a giant Silver. These are things any queeti sees. How does this one know what every queeti sees is *like* that which no queeti has seen?"

"No queeti knows," Silver breathed.

"Shut-up, fool," said Six-fingers automatically.

The ghoul paused again and brought its verdant eyes back to the two queeti. The rest of the war-party had wandered off to find shade and steal a mid-morning nap.

"Yon river twists and coils like a serpent. Its waters rush past. They are held captive by steep banks. A queeti comes upon this river, having never before seen a river. Does this queeti know a *river* until this queeti steps into the swirling waters? Perhaps it is crystal? Perhaps shiny rock? How does it taste? Smell? Like what? So this queeti comes upon another. 'I've seen a strange thing,' says he. 'Flowing crystal…' So, there now is such a thing as flowing crystal. But this is not the river. *An infinity of words cannot say what is invisible.*"

The ghoul studied them. His smile disappeared. Six-fingers gazed back in perplexity. He fidgeted, but the melodious voice still held him.

The creature said: "So words do not matter. Things formed by words do not matter. Memory brings names to the lips. A queeti pronounces these names and thinks, yes, this is the thing. Therefore, that queeti easily becomes confused—because names do not matter.

"Behold, a queeti must forget names. Remember rather the no-named. Reality is the no-named. So, forget the Lord. Forget all Lords and Exalted Fathers. Think rather of the river, the sky, these fields, yon forest. Names are empty. Whatever *is* is not-named. Forget even these words which I have said here. Remember the meadows. Cease talk of no-things. Cease talk of Lords. When you become quiet you will understand. Then you will not be slaves. Forget, thou, what this one has said. It is not important. Names are not important—"

"What is your name?" Six-fingers asked.

"Split a melon. What have you?"

"Sweet and watery guts," said Silver.

"And then what?"

"Seeds."

"And?"

"What?" Six-fingers growled.

"Split a seed."

"Pieces of seed."

"And?"

"No-thing," breathed Silver.

"No-thing, yet a great plant grows from it," the creature murmured. "Names do not matter."

The creature closed its eyes again. Only the gentle rise and fall of its breathing indicated life.

Silver glanced at the Hetman. "Kill the ghoul?" he asked.

Six-fingers stared at the ghoul. "You serve no Lord? No Lord stands above you?"

The creature opened its eyes. "We are free in the world. This is our way—"

"Show me this way."

"You know it."

"The Hetman does not understand."

The creature closed its eyes and spoke no more.

Exalted Father

BOOK OF RUNES
VERSE 5.2.3

The Hetman and his Silver watched warily, their eyes wide and bright, their ears flared, their nostrils quivered. The Hetman noted again that the creature emitted a rather pleasing odor, like summer wild flowers in the meadows south of Olive. No living thing that walked and spoke smelled quite like this—

Then Six-fingers recalled his cub-hood. Memories of the stories of the flight from Zell arose from that dark place in his mind he avoided at all costs. This time the memory wasn't an evil one. During their flight, Greater Wind brought a rare shower of butterflies (for those days), and though the exiles howled in fear—Lord Rekhmire had taught them to fear the poison butterflies and flee into their caves—they discovered that the pretty things actually dissolved into their fur and tasted sweet when they licked the wet spots. Since then they'd not feared the touch of butterflies. He recalled the taste. *Smelling this creature brought back the taste of the butterflies,* so vividly that his tongue tingled.

The Hetman frowned and glanced at Silver. "Do you understand this ghoul?"

Silver experienced a change of heart. The ghoul's strange speech frightened him. He could not imagine living without the Lord-on-the-Mountain. He could not imagine living without any Lord.

"Kill this thing. It a ghoul, wants Olive females. Kill it now. The Lord of Tharas Major will reward His Hetman."

Six-fingers growled.

"Kill this ghoul."

"*NO.*"

"Why not?"

"Because—" Six-fingers stared hard at the creature. "It not a ghoul."

The wanderer watched them with a bemused smile. He saw that the fledgling priest sensed the truth of it. That the wanderer was worse than a ghoul—he was a resurrection.

Fragmented images passed before his eyes and he watched them fade as quickly as they arose: images of what he'd once been, of his death, the cave which was his tomb, where the *kittim* brought him back. He'd struggled against the attraction of rebirth. Within the dank cave of the Reed Sea People, cold inertia doused his flickering existence, a gentle process that brought soothing release as his particles slowly dispersed. He welcomed it, this dispersal into other things. It was beautiful, harmonious and peaceful. Yet, the *kittim* compelled him. The secret of his rebirth, which was no secret, belonged with the *kittim,* and he could not fully grasp it. He wished to remain here, in the cave of inertia, cold and dead. The *kittim* would not allow it. He was reborn within their filmy embrace. And while he knew not the technique of the process, he understood its purpose.

He was Suthralane. He would climb the mountain and face the Lord Almighty.

Alive once more, he yearned to join the others, especially the old archbishop. This yearning, he knew, was the gift of Lord Illusion. The cold stone had whispered to him during his repose, as the molecules departed to build other existences. Lord Illusion, he knew from the *kittim*, was the Lord-on-the-Mountain. But he could not fully grasp this identity. Indeed, he wondered if any identity truly existed outside his cave. He saw it in the soft eyes of the innocents. *Was he wrong to interfere?*

Exalted Father

BOOK OF RUNES
VERSE 5.2.4

The ghoul and the two queeti sat staring at one another. Afternoon came. What remained of the war party decided to take the day off, to go home and fill their round bellies with spice beer. Early evening arrived and Lesser Wind commenced to blow. Swirling down from the north, a drizzle of *kittim* descended. The drizzle soon became a shower.

Gaily-colored butterflies, larger than any they'd ever seen, seemed to head directly for them. Silver began to howl. He jumped up and ran in the direction of Olive, waving his arms frantically, swatting futilely at the silken moth-like beings.

The Hetman yelled at him to stop, that the butterflies would not harm him. Despite all evidence to the contrary, many queeti believed without question that the butterflies were deadly, since such was the teaching of the Church. The White Lords made it dangerous to believe otherwise. Alone in their unbelief, the Reed Sea People had doubted this truth. Thus they'd perished. Exalted Father had destroyed them. Six-fingers, it seemed, had inherited this doubt, along with his extra digits.

Nonetheless, Silver's panic affected Six-fingers. The other's fear caused a palpable wave of mindless terror to wash over him like the rain of butterflies. The panic of the other overcame his doubt. He, too, prepared to flee. But something pushed him to turn around and gaze once more at the ghoul.

The creature had not moved. It gazed back at him with that eerie smile. The butterflies acted as though they were drawn to the thing. They flew above its head, swirled down, and actually came to settle on the creature's head. And then—they dissolved into it like frost melting in the midmorning heat of the daystar.

Six-fingers gave a yelp, not of pain but of surprise. Silver stopped and turned around.

Butterflies covered the creature. They whirled about him reminding Silver of the daystar when it broke through a heavy overcast. Silver had heard that the White Lords looked like this, like the daystar among us, as Blue often taught the cubs, but Silver had never seen a White Lord and neither had Blue.

The creature absorbed the butterflies and began to glow as if it had been transformed into a dazzling fire of changing colors. Motion and color joined together, yet the thing sat immobile, seemingly unaffected, smiling. The changing colors made Silver think of a farvel, and he'd seen plenty of farvels.

The brightness became so intense that the two queeti were forced to look away. They actually felt the heat on their fur. And now the creature lost all semblance of solidity. It became a burning column of pure white, without smoke, like a cold star, so it appeared to Six-fingers and Silver.

They feel to their knees. They were sobbing in the way of the queeti—long broken wails broken by inconsolable whining.

Abruptly the fire went out. The butterflies departed into the air and disappeared. The creature lived.

Six-fingers cried out: *"The Lord Almighty has come among us."*

EXALTED FATHER

BOOK OF RUNES
VERSE 5.2.5

And so in the fullness of time it came to pass that Hetman Six-fingers, he of Reed Sea People descent, along with his Silver, witnessed the miracle of the Wanderer of the Pure Light, who, they were convinced, was the Lord-on-the-Mountain come among the queeti. They bore the news of this miracle to the inhabitants of the hamlet called Olive. In short time, it spread to other queeti hamlets, and, eventually, to the larger villages up and down the Redrain River.

Six-fingers and Silver—although Silver still entertained the possibility that the Wanderer of the Pure Light was actually a clever ghoul—agreed to keep the details of this appearance secret. They wondered if they'd been too rash when they decided—actually Six-fingers decided and Silver went along with his Hetman—that this had been the Lord Almighty. Rather, they'd say that they'd encountered the Captain of the Lord.

After several months of careful thought, Silver, though still skeptical (we don't know the powers of ghouls he warned the Hetman) suggested that the Captain of the Lord was in fact His first born son.

Now it was Six-finger's turn to be skeptical. "Then who's his *mother*?' he asked. "Must be of the Lord's own kind, except the Lord's got no kind 'cause He's One and Only as the Church say. He don't have no kind, say the Cathedral queeti who hear the golden words of the golden-tongued archbishop. So, if He had son, and thereof, the Lord must've come down and—" He made an obscene gesture which meant masturbation— "since ain't no kind others. There's no female White Lords, or wisps, or yellow and gray wisps, or ghouls that we know."

Silver looked downcast. Maybe the Wanderer of the Pure Light was a ghoul after all.

"What's this, Silver? No-thing to say? Maybe consult spice beer?" Six-fingers roared at his own joke.

"Maybe I will, I," Silver answered defiantly. "Will work it out, I will. Because I'm a—" he searched for the word the Cathedral queeti used— "*priest.*"

So he began to call himself Silver the priest, a title which he said made him superior to any Blue of any village. Once he adopted the title, he solved the puzzle. Many would find it difficult to believe that the Lord Almighty had come among them. But why worry about the stupid Lord? The Wanderer of the Pure Light was *greater* than the Lord of Rocks. The thought had come to him in a dream. Silver liked that. No one had told it to him. Forget the dumb rock Lord. They'd claim that *a liberator queeti had appeared to Hetman Six-fingers and his Silver, in simple Olive, near the Redrain, on the continent of Starmirror.*

A Liberator, greater than any Lord.

EXALTED FATHER

BOOK OF RUNES
VERSE 5.2.6

"The Lord Almighty once spoke to the ghouls," Silver said to the crowd gathered about the central olive press. To his satisfaction he saw many had come from other villages much larger than Olive. The size of the crowd and its enthusiasm gave him courage and he began to improvise.

"Thus have I, Silver the Priest, heard from old ones who once lived near the White Hive."

"White Hive?"

"White Hive on the Northern Continent."

Some began to laugh and jeer. "Ain't no such place—"

"Stop this noise," barked Six-fingers. "Sound like animals. No more animals now that Liberator is come to the queeti."

"It true," Silver said dismissively. "Heard from a White Mother who once lived among the Reed Sea People."

This brought forth a stunned silence. Everyone had heard legends of the great and noble Reed Sea People.

"And Lord Almighty cursed the ghouls. And cursed every creature, even the innocent."

Many began to whine and moan. "Why this? Why this. Even innocent queeti? Why—"

"Because ghouls sought His *face*," Silver declared.

"Whose face?"

"The Lord's face, stupids."

"But every White Lord looks like every other White Lord—"

"No, no, silly stupids, animals. The One Lord. Exalted Father."

"Shut up!" howled Six-fingers.

The crowd quieted, not so much because of the Hetman but because it took some time for all this to sink in. A whole gang of Lords was confusing.

"Why this so bad?" a young buck finally asked.

"Because—" Silver hesitated, he'd lost his way in a jungle of twisting mental vines. "Well, so and thereof…a very terrible ghoul climbed the Lord's glass mountain."

"Why that bad?"

"So…because of the Lord's face."

"His *face*?"

"Yes. The ghoul looked at His face. You see, the Lord is so ugly He don't want to be looked at. So he cursed ghouls, White Lords, wisps, and last of all *us*."

Silver stood as straight as he was able. "And in the fullness of time a Liberator has come to the queeti, and *he will defeat the Lord Almighty and free us…and we must begin by freeing ourselves from the White Lords.*"

Silver liked this little addition, as did the Hetman. They both agreed that this would be their story of the wandering ghoul, the *Liberator*, a creature that burned but was not consumed.

They named the addition: *revolution*.

EXALTED FATHER

THE BOOK OF RUNES

CHAPTER THREE – Tharas Major

VERSE 5.3.1

The great fortress-city of Tharas Major swarmed with newly arrived Redfolk who came directly from the battlefields of Greenbottom. As the summer wore on, company after company of Redfolk warriors streamed into the fortress-city until even limitless Tharas Major became over-populated. They were like a plague of red ants.

The brown woman who'd once been Ra'bim white watched them as they flowed through the western gate into the vast courtyard named Blue-yard of Wind-swept Memory.

She was also the Once-Queen. *Kittim* poisoning had restored her to her original Akkadian morphology. But now she was like a shadow, and the King had put her aside, more from physical necessity than bareness, at least so she told herself. Now she simply waited to die. Her mind had become as frail as her body. Sometimes she read the *Confessions* and laughed. Sometimes she cried. Sometimes she became angry. She knew she suffered delusions. She heard voices.

The Yakashas—old word—were no delusion. She should hate them, they were Yakshas after all, vicious desert imps. Things being what they were, she no longer possessed the strength to hate. She'd disengaged, the priests might have said. She hardly found them interesting.

She did like to stand high on the west tower in the early morning hours. Observation was, despite what old priests might have said, a kind of engagement. This morning she engaged in memories of Marduk. She once hoped that she'd abolished those memories by burying them in the papyrus leaves of her book. But far too often on such mornings, as Greater Wind dusted the fortress-city with poison *kittim,* her memory— cursed thing— conjured up Marduk as some magician might raise a ghost.

This was her delusion. Like the Yakashas, she no longer hated him, no longer wished to kill him—how does one murder a dead thing? If the archbishop could be believed. Anyhow, she'd killed him in another world, which was another delusion.

Kittim poison spread through her cells, and very soon she'd walk the dark path. She was free from the Ra'bim—finally. Resurrected. Only to die again.

She remembered something Rudra had told her many years ago. After his resurrection, he said to her in an off-handed way, one would think that he'd be grateful to be alive, that having first-hand knowledge of life's sufferings, how fragile it was, one should have come to realize how precious life truly is. And, knowing this, such a one would feel a great current of empathy for all living things, and from this deep stream, like the circulation of the blood, one would know compassion, which then would infuse every act, every word, every breath.

But then Rudra snorted. "Isn't it so, Devorah? Should not the Holy Father embody such things? *Well, I'm not grateful. I'm hateful and I have no excuses. It feels good. It's the way I am.*

"*I do not live, I hate. I died and was resurrected, but not really. My awakening was merely apparent—a dream, a pause, another dream. So I hate. It feels good. No excuses.*"

Exalted Father

She had good cause to hate Rudra. "Hate is another Ra'bim soma," a voice whispered in her ear, "and so a prison." She was alone. Whose voice? She sighed. Did it matter?

She looked down.

Year after year, news of tremendous victories reached Tharas Major. The smashing of armies, the annihilation of opponents, the inevitable conquest of the Tribes of Men—and still the Great Northern War wore on and never seemed to come to a conclusion, to a *final* victory.

Always there was the Black One, as the Yakashas named him. The Black One suffered epic defeats but still managed to thwart (somehow) the overwhelming forces of the King. Descriptions of the exact geographical sites of these smashing victories, the literal tactical unfolding of the conflict, the singular clash of armies, seemed to Devorah confused and contradictory. She wondered if those who reported the victories—actually only Sanakht, Strong Protector of the Cosmos reported the victories—knew anything of the actual geography of Greenbottom. The Nepptali had fallen, he claimed, then the Ra'bim, then the Yadish (Nalanda wasn't on the list). The way he described this chain of conquests made one think that the invasion came down from the north, and that these tribes still existed. It was something of an inconvenience that they'd disappeared many years ago, long *before* the Great Northern War.

The identity of the Black One remained a mystery. Perhaps he was a priest like that sniveling ox Jacob...but all the priests were dead and Jacob was the archbishop. Perhaps he was an Akkadean (she hoped he was), maybe Agni himself.

It was said that even wild beasts fought for him. He led an army of farvels, the hysterical Yakashas declared. Farvels armed with L-guns. That made her laugh. Farvels bearing weapons, next we'll hear of mosscats fighting with scimitars. Sure enough, with their own eyes the crazy Redfolk witnessed armies of armed mosscats on the attack.

All had been crushed, the Strong Protector announced, defeated a thousand times. And still the Black One survived and the resistance continued. The King was not amused. Devorah, the Once-Queen, laughed.

Farvels? Creatures of delusion, dream-creatures haunting her waking hours, emergent monsters from her feverish, *kittim*-poisoned mind. Her deluded senses had conjured them like the old court fool. One even reminded her of Agni, except the Agni-farvel was smiling.

But something had happened. The Redfolk had begun to flee Greenbottom in a panic.

She turned away from the window and in the process lost her balance. These days she seemed to be losing the sense of her physical body, its orientation in space, as though the normal dimensions of height, width and depth were becoming foreign to her. It was, she believed, yet another sign of her gradual exit from the world, borne away on the gossamer wings of *kittim*.

Exalted Father

BOOK OF RUNES
VERSE 5.3.2

Someone stood at her open door. Tall, skin like white pearl, rigid, expressionless face, a marble statue granted the semblance of life, yet beautiful, perfect, and boring—she could not identify him in the semi-dark of her tower. Nor could she have in the clear light of the daystar, they all looked alike.

"The King requests the Once-Queen's presence in the...Dome, Grand Hall, Glorious Axis of the Universe...of Brilliant Light."

"For what purpose?" She scrutinized the White Lord. He seemed especially lifeless and inert, both in movement and speech. His tail dragged on the stone floor like a dead tree limb.

"The King did not say."

Many Redfolk resembled living corpses, some Grays and Yellows did too. A corpse was once alive. This White Lord appeared beyond corpse-like, a thing that had never lived. If she had to guess she would say that this was Leeander, and she wondered at her inability to recognize him, one she knew quite well, who had not changed at all and yet seemed totally different.

"I'll be along," she said in a sullen voice.

"Pardon me, Once-Queen, but the King gave orders that you come *immediately*." The voice sounded strange, the words seemed to fade like a soft sound carried away by the Two Winds.

She grimaced. Her very cells seemed to preserve the memory of sharp pain. Yet, that too was slowly wearing away as the *kittim* poisoning claimed her body. Now that the King no longer had any use for her, she'd become the Once-Queen. For what reason did he want her today? His tiny nob, a mere swelling of stone, could no longer penetrate her. He'd gradually lost the flexibility required to obtain an erection. From stone to stone... In frustration he beat her.

That was the extent of their love-making. She would never conceive. The King appeared less alive every day, even his tail. Like all of them, he'd become a victim of some strange creeping inertia—

"I'll be along—"

Leeander did not reply. With an audible grinding of stone upon stone, he moved to the side and halted, and froze, like a piece of fortress masonry.

She went to her desk and locked her book away, sliding it into a secret compartment that one of her trusted queeti carpenters had constructed at her bidding. How strange to her now that remarkable woman incarnated within those papyrus pages.

She entered the Grand Hall from a side passage, through a small inconspicuous door about a hundred meters from the massive throne. The great domed Hall was crowded with Reds, Grays, and a handful of Yellows. Somehow Leeander had preceded her to the Hall, although she couldn't imagine how he'd done it, how he'd negotiated the thousands of steps, the twisting turns, the transit through vast courtyards. Yet there he stood—a petrified ornamental statue, indistinguishable from the four marble columns that held up the red painted copula above the dais, from which the paint had begun to fade and peel off.

The King leaned forward and studied her. His face never changed, neither in anger nor in passion, not a single crease, not a wrinkle, and still he seemed ancient, older than her faded memory of Vishnu. The King's black eyes swallowed the light and gave nothing back. His unwieldy body resisted the life energy of his *soul* (for some strange reason priestly language suddenly popped into her mind—symptoms of poisoning, no doubt). All of them seemed to be gradually crumbling away, she decided, like eroding rock.

"Once...the Once-Queen appears rag-ged," he said in a toneless voice.

She bowed her head. "My apologies, O King," she said.

"Once-Queen is no—"

"*Kittim* poisoning."

"Most distressing."

The King sat back. The Grand Hall had become silent, which was something of a miracle for so many Yakashas brought together in one place. Generally they'd have been tearing each other's throats by now. Perhaps the sheer size of the place allowed for enough separation.

The King said: "Queeti multiply like maggots."

She shrugged. "Means more serfs for your fields and workshops, O King."

"They...Sanakht attacked at the Bridge of Celestials...his own queeti peasants."

She was having trouble following him. That the gentle and dull queeti of Starmirror should prove aggressive seemed impossible to her. The tribes here were quite unlike her Reed Sea People.

"You, queeti tongue do know? Who else know?"

"The Holy Father for sure. The archbishop perhaps."

He may have sighed, or spoke in anger, or simply declared a fact. There was no way of knowing.

"The Holy Father... We've summoned *you, Devorah of Akkad.*"

"That one no longer exists," she said sharply.

"Once-Queen remembers?"

She looked startled. Someone had to be feeding him this information. Who else knew about the Tribes of Men?

"Memories of the one named Ru-dra? Of one named Jacob? We, too, have memories of Ru-dra."

"Yes—"

"We know these. Have you memories of the one named Marduk?"

A shiver passed through her body. *He-With-Us. He, the woman in the book wished to kill. Murdered—sacrificed.* She dared not utter these thoughts.

"Marduk?"

"Mar-duk—"

He turned his body and seemed to glare at Leeander. Suddenly from behind Leeander, the Strong Protector of the Cosmos stepped forth. Until this moment she'd not seen him hiding behind the New-Man column.

Sanakht spoke: "The Holy Father and his archbishop ferment rebellion among the queeti."

"I'd say the White Lords have done their best to ferment all sorts of things among the queeti," she said bitterly. She glanced at Leeander. He seemed to have stopped breathing (if any of them had ever drawn a breath). "Why would the Holy Father do such a foolish thing?"

"To destroy us—"

"He *is us*...you."

"He *knows* 'bout *something*...not, not..." Sanakht began to stutter.

The King said: "We go to the mountain Elsseleron and find his *something*."

She doubted that. Climbing the dais was a major test of the King's flexibility and stamina. She wondered if they'd heard the Legend of Suthralane, but she was more interested in how they knew of Marduk, long dead.

"What *are* Marduk's powers?" Sanakht asked.

She gave a sarcastic laugh. "The Strong Protector means what *were Marduk's powers*. He's been dead for many decades. He had no powers when he lived. Only deception, the power of persuasion...his voice."

"Ah," said Sanakht, "but we have it that you loved this...priest."

"No," she shot back quickly. "Why these questions. He's dead. The Holy Father and his archbishop lie—"

"The archbishop *seed* him. He is from the dead risen. The Holy Father *seed* him, then five hundred peasants all *seed* him at one time.

EXALTED FATHER

They stir rebellion in his name. They say he is son of the Lord-on-the-Mountain, and he forbids us the mountain, for he is Lord alone."

Rocking back and forth, like a stone child in anger, the King declared: "*We are the Lord alone. We are displeased.*"

Sanakht said: "The archbishop comes north, teaching the dirty peasants about this Mar-duk. This Son of the Lord is liberation of serfs, light to peasants all over. They *resist*. They breed like garbage flies. They are confused. They confuse archbishop with this Son."

"Once-Queen will tell us the truth about this Mar-duk," said the King.

"He was a big talker," she said, "very persuasive. He ensnared people with his voice—there was something about his voice, that's all. He came from the priesthood. But he was no monk. He liked to wander among the Tribes of Men, telling stories. He was a—*sramana.*"

"We are not familiar with this word."

"Let it pass. Marduk got people to do things they would not think of doing otherwise, against their will."

She paused and bowed her head. "He was a fraud, a liar, as were all priests—it was a rule among us that whatever a priest believed the opposite must be true. Marduk was exceptional, he made you want to believe him." Her tone had gone from sad to bitter.

"You, Once-Queen, *knew* him," Sanakht declared. "The Holy Father has said it."

"He freed Once-Queen from the Ra'bim Tribe," the King added.

She stiffened. "The Holy Father exaggerates. He is a Yad. All Yads are liars."

"He has said the same about Akkadeans. Did any of your Tribes even know what it means to tell the truth?"

"It matters not," said Sanakht. "They're gone now, vanished. We are victorious."

"Yet the Northern War continues," Devorah observed.

Sanakht twisted his dense body in order to glance at the King. What passed between the two of them, if anything, remained hidden from her.

Sanakht turned back to face her. Movement seemed difficult. "The archbishop—he saw this Marduk die. He brought that one's tooth to the Cathedral. If this Marduk has returned from the dead, he must be missing a tooth. So, if this Marduk is not missing a tooth he must be a fraud—the fraud of a fraud."

"None of the dirty peasants say liberator is a tooth less," said a Yellow standing nearby.

"The tooth itself may be a fraud," said Sanakht.

"Which means you need to find the body of a *sramana* who's been dead for forty, maybe fifty decades, maybe more, and see if he's missing a tooth," said Devorah. She was beginning to enjoy the absurdity of the whole thing. Dead men do not return, less a tooth or not. And if by chance he did, Rudra'd send him back to his grave.

"Behold, the Once-Queen has said it," The King agreed.

The Strong Protector studied her. "Your *kittim* poisoning appears very grave, Once-Queen."

"It grows worse by the day."

"Indeed."

"Perhaps it eats your memory."

"Perhaps."

"Your memory, too, has become barren."

She did not reply.

"Go then," said the King, "we have no need of such—"

EXALTED FATHER

BOOK OF RUNES
VERSE 5.3.3

"She is a dead thing," Sanakht said to the King as they watched her walk unsteadily out of the Grand Hall.

She passed row after row of Redfolk and their noble Grayfolk captains and subalterns, and their Yellow over-group commanders, glancing neither right nor left. She walked as if in a trance.

The Strong Protector spoke loudly so that his words carried to the far end of the vast hall: "We fear that the Holy Father and his archbishop spin foul plots against thee, oh King and Lord Alone." He appeared to be speaking from a prepared script.

The King responded just as loudly (and from the same script): "They conspire with the dirty peasants, even the fortress serfs. We would wish some terrible accident befall them." He paused.

"But of course such a wish would be a sin against the Universal Church."

"First Minister, dismiss the assembly," the King added almost as an afterthought.

The column that was once Leeander stared straight ahead. He didn't seem to have heard.

"Leeander is fallen asleep," Sanakht observed.

The Strong Protector turned and faced the crowd. They were his troops. Like them, he wore the *kittim*-proof Nepptali great coats, which, when hoods were drawn, made them all indistinguishable one from the other.

"Clear the Grand Hall," he shouted.

The massive doors creaked open and the hordes silently exited, some still in great fear. These Redfolk had survived the monster *kittim* of Jambridvipa. They'd witnessed the terrible destruction of the

King's armies. Some claimed that the *kittim* fought for the Black One. Hideous mythical creatures such as farvels rose up against them.

"The First Minister sleeps," the King agreed. "Many have fallen asleep. They speak not, nor do they move They live not, nor are they dead. They are…emptied."

Sanakht ignored him and went on with the script. "Harken, Lord King Ra', our Lord King Ra' the Victorious. The Great Northern War is at an end. The Black One is defeated. We bring to thee the spoils."

"What are the spoils?"

"The spoils are—singular."

"What are the spoil?"

"Behold, oh King Ra' the Victorious."

A side door opened, the very same Devorah had used. And indeed, another woman entered the Grand Hall of Heavenly Peace, Prosperity, Freedom, and Brilliant Light, and placed herself before the King. She wore a long golden gown spun from the finest Yasshur silk, embroidered with Runes that—as she'd explained to the Redfolk Captain, one Menes, who'd captured her—spelled the words: "Unified Kingdom." Her hair was a pure white mass of coarse tangles and knots, her eyes soulless black, her nose beak-like, her teeth fang-like, her mouth a sneer, Redfolk-like. She was whiter than the King or any of the New-Men, short but just as massive in the density of her body. The only thing missing was a tail.

She bowed stiffly and attempted—painfully it appeared—to twist her sneer into a smile, which because of her teeth turned into a threatening snarl.

The Strong Protector intoned: "Behold, King Ra', the fruits of your great victory."

The King gazed at her. He appeared unable to speak.

The old woman with the wild hair and beak-nose boldly looked at him. "I am the Queen of Jambridvipa," she announced, "Exalted

Exalted Father

Mother of many offspring, more than the grains of sand of the Edom Desert, more than the stars in the night sky. I give myself to you, Lord King, of my own free will."

King Ra' seemed paralyzed, not unlike Leeander.

"She surrendered to us," said Sanakht, "after we defeated her husband the Black One. I personally struck him down on the shores of the Lake once named Emerald."

The King awoke. "Where is the Black One? We see him not in our presence."

"He is defeated and cast out."

"Where?"

"No one knows where he is buried."

Exalted Mother interrupted: "Forget the Black One, O King. He was, after all, merely a Ra'bim. He succumbed to his own somas. Never was he truly worthy of his Queen."

"Where is the Black One?"

"He is not here, but I am. The victory is yours, O Lord King. I am yours."

"Where?"

"I am here."

Sanakht said: "She is fertile, O King. She is the one you've been seeking since the day so long ago when you journeyed to the north and met the Holy Father. Before the Black One, she was the Holy Father's wife, and a son they had. That son lives. He is proof."

"Now I am yours," she said. Exalted Mother, White Mother. Take me. Give me children or I shall die."

THE BOOKS OF MARDUK

BOOK OF RUNES
VERSE 5.3.4

"...because with my own eyes!"

The archbishop's voice became shrill and his fragile hold on the queeti language began to slip. Usually when he was moderately drunk—as he was now—his queeti was passible. Today, however, he stammered and had to dig for the proper sounds and gestures, the barks, grunts, clicks, whines, growls—all accompanied by various shakings, twitches, and eye-rollings.

"He done it, bringed a dead—ghoul—back to life, and lives himself, he does. Truth is it—"

The queeti mob jabbered excitedly. He caught a few words here and there. They were *mocking* him. He would have hardly believed it possible. The vermin dared to ridicule the archbishop.

It had been like this, one bleak village to the next, up and down the Redrain valley: disbelief, obscenities, resistance, mockery—and a crazy tale about a liberator of the queeti. The further north he went the worse it got, as now he approached the core of the infection, a most miserable hamlet called Olive.

"I witness his miracles—"

A huge queeti, nearly the size of a White Father, standing as straight as a man, strode up to the archbishop and waved a six-digit paw in his face. It spoke Sandi far better than the archbishop spoke queeti. It spoke persuasively too, as though Sandi was its native tongue. It used the language of the Church.

"You are deceived, Prince of the Church. Are not your promises cries of our oppression? The moans of the world's suffering? Are not your absurd doctrines escape from intolerable conditions? Did not your beliefs enforce our servitude, reinforce our lowly state, and reduce us to beasts? Are not your lies the spirit of a spiritless world?

Exalted Father

The red onion of queeti everywhere? Behold, the bonds are broken. The liberator is come among the queeti. And we alone are given to know His name, which none may utter."

"No! No, no, no…"

The queeti lifted its head, which must have been extremely difficult, if not painful, given the mound of muscle that anchored its head to its shoulders. It gazed in the direction of Elsseleron.

"There is no Almighty Lord on the Mountain, *therefore there are no Lords*. All must work equally. The fields, meadows, hills, forests, rivers, lakes and mountains belong to all alike. There are no fiefs, no rents, no service. No Lords, no serfs. All must share the bounty and the burdens equally. The Liberator has abolished many words, and so many false ideas. They are no longer useful. They are positively poisonous. They produced many harmful illusions."

Desperation proved more inebriating than spice-beer and the archbishop's queeti ignited as if he'd been struck by language-lightning.

"The queeti must *serve*, that is their definition," he bellowed. "They are created to work. So the Lord created…those ones. The proof is found in White Cathedral. There are great books. There resides the holy relic, remains of the One the Lord has resurrected. It is a great mystery, known only to the Holy Father and his archbishop. For they are witness to his miracle. And this—*stuff*—you must believe."

The giant queeti climbed a few steps up the hill upon which the archbishop stood. He turned and addressed the growing throng of serfs who'd come from the fields to listen to the debate.

"A liberator has come. And I know His true name."

He waved a paw at the archbishop who seemed to shrink in his presence. "How convenient that *your holy one* should suddenly arise after all this time. Tell us if you dare the *forbidden name*."

"Such as you are not worthy," the archbishop snapped.

"See you how they use us. Make of us slaves and beasts, less than the meadows, the rivers, the fields. Persevere in your misery, they say smugly, so that after you die you'll become like the Lords. After your death will you achieve peace and rest from your endless labors. For now, however, in this world, you must serve. Listen, brothers and sisters, are these not lies and fables?"

"No," the archbishop sputtered. He saw the females and the little ones sprinkled among the young bulls. Their wide-eyed devotion demonstrated how badly he was losing this argument—and them.

The queeti preacher laughed. Spreading his thickly-muscled arms, he roared: "Why wouldn't the Lord-on-the-Mountain speak to me, or to him" —he pointed— "or to her, or even to a cub? Why shouldn't this liberator come to us who are in need of liberation? I will tell you, brothers and sisters, *there is no Lord-on-the-Mountain.* There is the wanderer who is come to us. So come you, lazy one of the red cheeks, who-does-not-work, come and tell us his true name."

The crowd howled its approval. Shaggy heads bobbed up and down. "Why not a queeti?"

"Come, pronounce his holy name."

The crowd began growling menacingly. "Why not a queeti?"

The Holy Father's canaries had not exaggerated. If anything, they'd woefully underestimated the madness. Like Red and Gray, Yellow Yakashas could not be trusted.

The archbishop told himself that he didn't want to do this thing. But they were beyond hope. They'd gone collectively insane and there was no longer any reasoning with them. Perhaps it was foolhardy to think that one could reason with animals.

Down the hill, across a lovely meadow, the river flowed through a wide ravine. The archbishop turned in that direction and gave a signal. From this ravine sprang a company of Redfolk, red Yakashas, armed with L-guns. They advanced upon the peasant mob. The queeti had not caught their scent until this moment. The Redfolk quickly crossed the meadow and the surrounded them. Another company headed towards Olive.

"Recant this nonsense," the archbishop shouted.

"Say the name," the six-fingered bull shot back. "Give us the name."

He gave another signal.

The Redfolk formed a ragged line and began to discharge bolts of blue lightning into the crowd. Some, however, couldn't recall the Nepptali firing diagrams their Yellow captains had shown them. Reversing the sequence, they caused the guns to explode. Redfolk standing close by instantly jumped to the conclusion that their comrades were firing on them, and they fired back into their own ranks... and the ranks fired back, and soon as many Redfolk became fiery torches as queeti.

The queeti offered no resistance. They gathered around the giant bull as if to protect him, and *they sang as they died.*

He is our strength,
Is our hope.
A mighty fortress is He,
His name abiding—

Dumbfounded, the archbishop backed away. The stench of burning fur was overpowering, and the smoke stung his eyes. The battle had become a chaotic whirlwind of blue lightning, red flames and black smoke. He stumbled down the hill and sought the cool meadow.

The meadow burned too, but with a different fire.

Memories of so long ago...when he was a priest in Nalanda...from the *Runehayana*, stories of the First Kalpa before the triumph of the Tribes of Men.

He rubbed his eyes and stared. He searched the memories. As drunk as he was, he still was able to retrieve them. What he'd seen through a curtain of smoke and a fog of tears he now saw clearly.

Farvels.

Turning the meadow into a sea of gold, an army of farvels. Silent Watchers.

His mind seemed to snap like a rotten branch and he began to weep.

Farvels, farvels...

The queeti sang joyously, and died.

Exalted Father

BOOK OF RUNES
<u>VERSE 5.3.5</u>

She came to King Ra'. None were permitted in the King's private chambers, but she entered unchallenged. Past the Yellow guards, through the double doors. None dared oppose her. Dressed in a gown of silver spider-web, purposeful, powerful, fertile and dangerous, she came to the King.

She glanced about the chamber. "Such magnificence," she cooed as she wandered through the vast, empty spaces.

She lumbered across the magnificence to the canopied bed upon which he lay, very still, in his white robes and on silken sheets. His black eyes were opened yet unfocused.

Shedding her spider-web gown, she straddled him and began kissing his cold lips. She grunted her declaration of love— "I love thee, O King. Only a King is worthy of me—"

None-too-gently, her claws tore at his outer garments. "Where is *it*, O King? Give me children or I shall die."

He stared past her as though hardly conscious of her immense weight, her enormous breasts swaying out over him, her tree-thick thighs, her bloated stomach.

"Where? Here?"

She tried to tear away his robes but it was like scratching at polished stone. And all the time he stared past her and lay as if dead.

"O King, have some purple soma. It always worked for old Vishnu."

She extracted a small vial from a golden medallion that hung on a chain around her neck. She then poured the contents of the vial into his mouth, which was partly open and from which he breathed, and which was the only indication he lived.

He swallowed. His eyes focused. Like the creaking branches of a knotted old oak, his arms moved, his hands grasped, and he pulled her down by her shoulders.

"Ah, ah—" She redoubled her efforts, gasping for air, her wild hair flying.

"Yes, yes… More soma, O King—"

"Yes, yes."

"More soma—"

And then Ra' came to life. He grasped her again and flipped her as though she weighed no more than a drifting *kittim*. His tail whipped with frenzy and he was not gentle.

"Yes, yes…oh, oh, burning…ice, ice…. oh, oh— *No,*" she abruptly screamed. "Nothing —"

"Yes," he declared like pronouncing a doom. *"You are she. The Holy Father has delivered."*

And the Lord Almighty, had He been awake just then, would have heard her screams of rage from the summit of far-away Elsseleron.

EXALTED FATHER

BOOK OF RUNES
VERSE 5.3.6

L-guns burned wide swathes through the mass of queeti bodies, but then the L-guns began to fizzle and many failed outright. The Redfolk, only a moment ago gloating over the carnage, suddenly perceived a deadly look in the eyes of former serfs, and they trembled.

The few remaining queeti roared as if with one voice and threw themselves at the Redfolk, breaking their frail dry bodies like rotten twigs. If not for their overwhelming numbers, it might have gone ill for the Redfolk army. As it was, many broke and ran. Screaming threats backed by blows and the sharp edge of his sword, Captain Menes stiffened the ranks and directed the slaughter that was less a slaughter of the queeti and more a destruction of his own troops.

The archbishop had fallen to his knees and covered his face. "No, no—" he cried, "no farvels, no farvels, not a one, not a one, none—" He repeated the words until they ran together and became long gasps of wailing cries.

The wailing denial brought a refutation. The farvel army grew in numbers. The more he howled his denial the stronger it became, until, eyes still closed, his hands over his face, he *knew* that farvels could not exist and therefore he'd imagined them, and this made them a delusion, and his deduction was irrefutable and therefore true.

When he regained his courage, what little remained to regain, he looked up, opened his eyes and found that the army of farvels had vanished. There had never been an army of fravels in the first place. Then did he find his voice and shouted loudly: "No more!"

The Yakashas ceased their slaughter and looked around. They saw the archbishop standing on his hill waving his arms as though he were swatting *kittim*.

Captain Menes lowered his dripping sword and bowed. "There are a *few more*, my archbishop."

The archbishop shook his head. "There are no more. Were never—more." He appeared bewildered.

"His Lordship's ill perhaps?"

"No more," muttered the archbishop. He gazed down upon the smoking queeti bodies. One queeti remained standing. He glared defiantly at the archbishop.

"You—"

The Yakashas swarmed over him, beating him with their fists, biting, kicking him, but he offered no resistance.

"Bind its arms," Captain Menes barked. He glanced at the archbishop. "Kill this thing?"

"No more—"

The archbishop's had too much spice beer," said a large, bloodied Yakakshas standing next to Menes. "I say we kill this animal—"

Menes glared at him. "No more."

"Perhaps our Captain's had too much spice beer."

Menes shook his sword in the Red's face. "Perhaps you die."

The Yakashas backed away.

Menes straightened his back as best he could. "We are soldiers of the White Lords," he said. "We take this animal to the King."

"No, no," said the archbishop.

"We take this beast to King Ra'. Him we serve, not the Church. No more talk. Perhaps we bind *you*, archbishop."

They bound the bull queeti, formed ranks, and started north at a loping, tongue-waging trot.

The archbishop didn't seem to notice that they'd quit the battlefield. He muttered. Now he whined. Then back to muttering.

Lesser Wind came and there were many *kittim*. A large kite-like thing of intersecting triangles—red, orange, yellow and green—dove for him. He quickly pulled up the hood of his Nepptali great coat and crouched down. The large *kittim,* nearly the size of a man, enveloped the archbishop, Nepptali coat and all. The metallic material appeared to resist its poisonous embrace. But he'd forgotten that his red slippers had not come from Nepptali workshops.

THE BOOKS OF MARDUK

THE BOOK OF RUNES

CHAPTER FOUR – Wooden City

VERSE 5.4.1

The Strong Protector of the Cosmos rarely visited Wooden City. A small detachment of Grayfolk accompanied him for this most rare event. (In these later days) every detachment of Grayfolk was small, and *(in these later, later days)* even the Strong Protector himself found it difficult assembling a detachment.

Set in a narrow valley between the plateaus of Tharas Major and Tharas Minor, Wooden City was a foul smelling maze of crooked streets, dilapidated workshops, trash-filled courtyards, and stone fountains covered with evil-looking moss and filled with brown water brought into the city by rusted plumbing from another age. Wooden City had once been the abode of the Grayfolk and their queeti servants, but *(in these last days)* it swarmed with the Redfolk of Edom.[20]

Sanakht knew them. They were a defeated army, fleeing from the north, from Jambridvipa, seeking refuge with the White Lords.

---

[20] According to modern scholars, it is obvious that the phrases "in these later, later days", and "these last days" were inserted into the text by a later scribe since they indicate events that the writer (Marduk?) could not have known at the time of the writing.

Sanakht knew the truth of the war. He knew many things and more, for like the Holy Father he too had his canaries. Yet he came to the Wooden City, for there was a thing he did not know.

He picked his way through the labyrinth of lanes and streets, headed—so he believed—towards Dew Drop Courtyard. But in a particularly narrow intersection a gang of Redfolk ambushed them. The Redfolk poured out of hidden doors, dropped from open windows—they appeared to materialize from the street itself, springing up from cracks in the street like instantaneous weeds.

In spite of fine Nepptali steel, and the skill required to wield it effectively in battle, the guards' unit was overwhelmed and forced to fall back. Maddened Redfolk climbed over their own slaughtered companions to offer their own frail and twisted bodies to fine steel. They bit, and tore, and beat upon the guards even after taking horrendous wounds. They came on as though they eagerly sought death.

The Strong Protector stood unfazed amid the swirling maelstrom. He seemed unconcerned, even numb. Silently erect, dignified, he stood as if patiently waiting for the interruption to end so he could continue his mission, whatever that mission happened to be. The *purpose* of the attack—why his own army sought his life—didn't seem to concern him.

At last, they tore the last blade from the claws of the last guard and struck off the last head. Only then did their murderous, suicidal frenzy subside. They surrounded the Strong Protector of the Cosmos.

"All-mighty White Father comes wid us," snarled a particular ugly Red. His parchment face was black and twisted, deformed either by a battle wound or birth, probably the former. He lacked a nose, his teeth were broken, and the folds of skin were so thick around his eyes that one would have thought him blind.

"Great Captain Menes will pass judgment on this one."

The horde of Redfolk howled their assent to this proposition.

"It is Menes I've come to see," said Sanakht. "If indeed this Menes of yours is the Menes I seek. There are so many Menes among Redfolk. More Reds than names it seems—"

The black-faced one growled. "Let this Father follow. If not for Captain's orders, we'd kill it now, here, as we did the Grays and Yellows, traitors all—if children pay for the crimes of Father why not Father pay for crimes of children?"

Under Redfolk guard the Strong Protector resumed his mission. He studied the streets and noted the telltale signs of bug feeding, those dark stains on the surface of the road that had once been bodies of flesh and blood.

They came at last to Dewdrop Courtyard. A large Red stood in the center of the courtyard, the largest the Strong Protector had ever seen, wielding a Nepptali blade and wearing a smirking mask of disdain and hatred.

"So, Strong Protector of the Cosmos. Come to inspect the troops, huh?"

Sanakht stared at him.

"No-thing to say? No-troops to inspect that need inspecting. Blowflies got 'em."

Sanakht continued to stare at him, his black eyes dull, lifeless.

Menes growled and spat at his feet. Black rotting flesh covering one side of his face indicated bug poisoning. Almost every Red bore similar wounds. Sanakht didn't seem surprised.

"Gets worse up north, Great Lord. Does King All-mighty know? Does King All-mighty know that blowflies fight for the Black One? That legions of gold tigers prowl the valleys and the hills? That they feed on his loyal servants? All-mighty must know. How could he not and remain All-mighty?"

Finally Sanakht spoke. "The Black One defeats his enemies? Is this not so?"

The Redfolk howled as if from one throat, like the wind howling through the deserted streets.

Exalted Father

"No! *We triumph*—"

"Yet you flee."

"What is it to you?" Menes asked. "You no longer command in the north. And King All-mighty has his woman."

"What of the Black One, her previous King?"

More screeching and gnashing of teeth.

"What is it to you?"

"How was she taken?" The Strong Protector's voice was metallic, like an old Nepptali recording.

"She to us came—willingly."

"And still—"

Menes stared back.

"If Black One lives, then why did his queen surrender herself to the likes of you?" He gazed up at the hazy forest of spires and towers that comprised Tharas Major, once a fortress city now a tomb. *Kittim* played among the towers, and only *kittim* occupied the battlements.

"Therefore Black One must be dead," Menes declared. "So must be by necessity."

"*By necessity*," the Redfolk responded, repeating the liturgy.

"And where did the woman surrender herself?"

"In Bethsham of the Nepptali."

"And you discovered—palm-leaves there? Leaves covered by much scratching?"

"We brought many such back. Gave 'em to a Yellow of the Holy Father."

"Ah—"

"We were betrayed," Menes howled, shaking his sword and clutching his chest. "Blow flies larger than any Redfolk ambushed us—"

"Where?"

"Red Lake. They flew over lake and took us on flank. Gray captains laughed to see us die. But some escaped. Those ones made a vow: No more White Fathers. No more White Lords."

"No more White Lords," sang the Redfolk choir.

"No more Strong Protector."

Sanakht's glacial serenity did not melt. His tail hung limp, his eyes appeared fixed on the distant spires of Tharas Major. His voice became no more than the wind blowing through a gutted, empty courtyard.

"Poison bugs do not serve anyone. Mindless things, they rise and fall like the moons. Not even the Lord All-mighty on the mountain plans them. They have no direction. They are—without purpose."

Menes gave a rasping laugh. "So and therefore, the Black One must be more powerful than Lord All-mighty on the mountain. *We follow him.*"

"Having no direction— Without purpose— No— commanded— Un—"

"White Fool. *He commands.* Him we follow— Him we saw."

"Saw—what?"

"Him. We saw Him riding them. They bound together and formed a great boat of the air, of the water, upon which He lay, on Red Lake. On Emerald Lake too. He sleeps and he dreams, and he commands them still. He sleeps and yet is victorious. He does not act and all is accomplished. Such a one is superior to all All-Fathers in all-places."

"And how does a dreamer conjure?"

"How?"

Sanakht went silent.

"Poor Redfolk. Betrayed by White Lords. So and therefore, there are no White Lords," Menes said. So saying, he plunged his blade into the chest of the Strong Protector of the Cosmos...or, attempted to plunge his blade, for he found that the white folds of the Strong Protector's robe were impenetrable and that his blade was turned aside.

The rest of the red army fell upon the Strong Protector, biting, clawing, beating him with fists and rocks torn up from the road. A thousand wounds they caused, or tried to cause, for no wound

EXALTED FATHER

appeared, and they cried in frustration, and some even expired right there.

The Strong Protector did not move, nor did he speak. His gaze remained fixed on the *kittim* frolicking among the towers of Tharas Major.

Menes barked at his troops to cease their attack, for how can one kill what is already dead.

(They abandoned him there, a stone pillar, where he stands to this day according to travelers in those devastated parts. They say that the millennia have erased the sharps edges and deleted identifiable marks, so that a featureless and boring slab of rock stands in its place, like many in this mountainous region, rather an artifact of climate and time.)[21]

"The King must die," Menes declared. "All must die, for all are dead."

Then came Lesser Wind. It blasted the Redfolk with a deluge of *kittim*, such a rain of bugs as none had ever experienced, even in the north. No Red had seen so many at a single time, so large, so purposeful, not even when commanded by the Black One. They soaked the thickest Nepptali greatcoat and burned into flesh like acid.

Menes was among the last to perish.

---

[21] Yet another case of scribal insertion. At last such insertions become too numerous to mention.

THE BOOKS OF MARDUK

BOOK OF RUNES
VERSE 5.4.2

Under full Lotus Moon, the archbishop painfully mounted a ramp of smashed stone that led to the domed Grand Hall of the King. A unit of Redfolk trailed him like a pack of whipped tarp hounds, looking about fearfully. They guarded a prisoner who required no guarding. The archbishop favored his left foot, dragging it and grimacing. Feverish and perspiring, his only wish was for some strong drink and a soft bed, and maybe some food, although his generally voracious appetite had left him.

Each member of the guards' unit had been infected. They wailed and moaned, and two died right there on the spot. Had he so desired, the prisoner could have escaped easily. But he did not. He strode forward as though he'd just returned triumphant from a battle. His dark fur glistened in many places yet he did not suffer. Nor did he appear exhausted. He seemed stronger than ever, larger too, for he walked completely upright and straight-backed, no longer with the bow-legged slouch of the typical queeti.

Save for the frozen statue of the one once named Leeander that stood at the foot of the throne like a pillar of polished stone, the Dome appeared deserted. The throne stood vacant.

Then the archbishop saw that the Dome did have at least one occupant. A woman. Initially he guessed that it was Devorah, the Once-Queen. He realized that he was mistaken.

The woman was white like a New-Man, yet her hue was sickly white as a lack of color and health, not an addition of colors as in the spectrum of white light, but an emptying of them. She was not tall, she was wide. Beneath a hooked nose, a mocking smile greeted the archbishop.

EXALTED FATHER

He knew her. He became aware of the burning pain in his feet and he began to tremble. He knew her—Miriam, the Grand Duchess, much changed, it was true, yet he knew her. How could he not know her?

The conflicting emotions were like *kittim* stings, sobering and painful at once. Was she not Vishnu's whore? Had not she and her Ra'bim lover dispatched his Father, his Holy Father, into a premature grave? A live burial?

In a scornful voice she said: "Who is this that dares disturb the King's peace?"

From somewhere out of his sight a Gray cried: "It is the archbishop, White Mother."

"White Mother *and Queen*," she angrily corrected him.

"Queen?"

"Dare you question me, foolish Yakashas? Have you not heard that the King has taken a new Queen, one who will most certainly provide him with an heir, with many sons, more than the stars in the sky, the sands of your red desert—"

She stopped speaking and gazed for some minutes at the archbishop.

"Come closer," she ordered.

He limped to the foot of the dais.

"Ah, so another lame priest. They proliferate like *kittim* in the winter."

He raised his face. Despite the *kittim* poisoning soaking his poor feet, his face was still round and jowly, his eyes still small and suspicious and empty like an ox, and his voice was still dismissive and condescending.

"Don't you know me, mother?"

"Queen, lame priest. Queen."

"Queen—but once Grand Duchess."

She frowned and her eyes became narrow slits.

"You had a son—"

"I did," she admitted, "and his father took him from me and sacrificed him to the miserable Lord-on-the-Mountain, 'cause he thought the cruel Lord Almighty would make 'em King of Greenbottom. Turns out my dear husband wasn't king material. Too bad for him. Too bad for our son."

The archbishop shook his head. "That son lives still. The Grand Duke sacrificed that son, it is true, but to the priesthood. Perhaps, someday, that son would become archbishop and declare the Grand Duke King. The Church, you must know, can do what the Lord-on-the-Mountain is unable to do, given His Divine Non-existence. Here, in your presence, under your eyes, that which the Grand Duke sought has come to pass."

She stared at him, closely examining him. At last she grunted a scornful laugh.

"What? *You?* My son would have been tall and strong, keen of mind, virile, sleek of limb, not a slug, not a dumb ox."

"I am he."

"*He is dead.*"

A tear rolled down his cheek, followed by another. He was a novice the last time he cried.

"Who told you this nonsense?"

He mumbled: "The Holy Father."

"What is that?"

"Holy Father—"

"Holy Father?"

"Once entombed, but reborn to a new life."

"Does the Holy Father have a limp also?"

"Yes—"

She grinned, showing broken and black teeth, some sharp like fangs. For a moment she resembled a Yakashas.

"—and bald with a black beard, probably grey by now."

"Once Rudra, Grand Duke, and I am his son, the archbishop. Only the son knows the Holy Father."

Exalted Father

"Ach! That bastard still lives? Holy Father, you say? Still up to his old tricks. His exaggerated delusions. Well, we'll have to pay him a visit."

"Mother..." the archbishop whispered.

"Don't be a fool. My son would have been a prince."

He felt his feet burning, especially his left one, and he whimpered like a queeti cub.

"We are Queen of Tharas Major," she continued. "To hear us is to hear the King. To see us is to see the King. Enough of your blubbering, archbishop. We know *thee*, and we know the Holy Father."

She pointed a sausage-like finger at the bull queeti. "So, foolish ox, tell us and do not lie. What is this creature?"

Listening to them intently, as if it understood every word, the bull suddenly spoke. His deep voice sounded like a bell in Thrice-blessed Cathedral. It, queeti and bell, spoke perfect Sandi.

"See how the butterflies of heaven come with *Him*?" the six-fingered bull declared. "The powers of our world rise up to defend *He-With-Us*. They are His shield and His avenging army. The righteous ones fear them not. They are poison to unbelievers. They are the rain of heaven upon the Blessed.

"What is this *him*?" the Queen asked sounding irritated.

The queeti raised his arms: "The Liberator. I have heard His teachings. He declares that the fields, the meadows, the rivers and the forests belong to all alike. Their bounty is to be shared by all alike. For the Lords, nothing. For their slaves, nothing. For the wisps and ghouls, nothing. The world rises up against them and they will be cast out into the outer darkness. I am witness to His miracles. The greatest miracle is called *revolution*."

"What trash is this?" growled the Queen, directing her question to the archbishop. "What does the Holy Father teach these vermin?"

The archbishop gazed past her and said nothing.

The queeti laughed. "Their Church teaches ignorance and lies. To us, the poor ones, the destitute yet pure ones, has the Almighty revealed Himself in the form of His Liberator. He has chosen us to be His people, and to us has He spoken His true name."

"And what might that name be?"

"The Wanderer, Liberator. The name above all names."

The archbishop let out a laugh, followed by another, and another… "I know, I know—"

The bull rumbled deep in its chest.

"What nonsense is this?" asked the Queen.

"Profane not the name."

"Ha, ha, ha…I know, ha, ha, ha…"

The huge bull suddenly broke loose from its captors and set upon the archbishop. Biting, clawing, he tore at the Nepptali cloak seeking the archbishop's throat.

The Yakashas guards recovered quickly and threw themselves at the bull. A whirlwind of claws and tails, teeth and fists exploded too fast for the eye to follow. Broken bodies stumbled back, spurting black blood and dangling smashed limbs.

By sheer force of numbers, the sickly Grays and Reds managed to separate the maddened queeti from his clerical victim. But they paid dearly for the privilege of saving the archbishop, suffering nearly half their numbers lost in less than several minutes.

Not a few veterans of previous similar engagements recalled the battles of the Great Northern War in which death-rates were even higher. They'd saved the archbishop, but with this victory their responsibilities ceased, or so they reasoned, especially these veterans. Therefore they backed away from the murderous queeti.

Six-fingers broke free and loped to the doors at the far end of Hall. He pushed the doors open. Outside, airborne regiments of *kittim* drifted lazily in the calm evening air. Six-fingers paused, turned around and raised one long hairy arm, extending the thick digits of his paw as the Holy Father often did when he blessed queeti pilgrims.

EXALTED FATHER

"Speak not the unutterable name," he bellowed, "for His wrath will be swift. He rides the clouds of heaven and bends the storms to suit His will."

With these words he vanished into a thick curtain of *kittim*, his reddish-brown fur glistening in the soft evening light. None dared oppose his leaving.

The archbishop's laugh broke and faded into a low sobbing and whimpering. He muttered and sobbed, and whined, and his words were slurred and indistinct. He kept repeating a name, but no one could understand him.

Many Yakashas began to whine and howl like a startled pack of tarp hounds of Edom.

The Queen shook her head. "My son, my son...such a spineless thing." Then a smile turned her lips, and her eyes became like narrow creases in her heavy face. Her laugh sounded sardonic as though she took pleasure in the archbishop's painful insanity.

"We feel the fine hand of Rudra the Holy Father in this. How easily we see it." she said. "Yakashas!" she snarled, "stop this yammering and gather the armies. *We march upon Elsseleron.*"

They saluted and exited the great chamber. It seemed better to take their chances with the *kittim*. Especially the veterans of the North who were done with all wars. No one dared tell the Queen that there were no more armies left to march.

The Books Of Marduk

BOOK OF RUNES
VERSE 5.4.3

She'd heard the name whispered in the courtyards, cursed in the towers, praised in the queeti workshops, until there were no longer any queeti to work the shops, no whispering Yellows in the courtyards, nor any White Lords to prowl the towers. She remembered her vow, how she'd come south so long ago to kill *him*. She remembered the dream-world of the red onion, how she fulfilled that vow.... She sighed.

She refused to pronounce the name, to whisper it, even within the cold stone corridors that were deaf to all whispers. The *name* itself, unspoken yet vibrating in her mind, contributed to her perpetual inner chill that grew like a slow wasting disease.

She reread parts of her *Confessions*. It did her little good. She was not that person. Yet, the vow would not leave her mind. It would not rest quietly in the grave of her book. What should she do about the vow *in the real world*?

These cool mornings brought back memories of Akkad, of Emerald Lake, the green rolling hills of the Akkadean Stairs. She admired the swirling clouds of *kittim*, although it was probably their poison that caused her inner cold and would ultimately bring her death. The poison seemed to work in strange ways. She didn't die, her Ra'bim skin died. She was no longer Queen, no longer White Mother, and for this she was thankful.

One such brilliant morning, she took a stroll to the far northern precincts of the immense fortress-city and happened upon the archbishop himself in all his glory, robed and jeweled and prepared for a morning sermon. Unfortunately, none remained to listen and admire the words of golden-tongued, except perhaps a stray *kittim*, and who knew if they even had ears to listen.

Exalted Father

At one time this vast complex of workshops and barracks swarmed with queeti labor-gangs, coming and going throughout a workday that never ended. Working in three consecutive shifts, they were building something the King referred to as the Great Ark. She had no idea what the words meant, nor what the thing was supposed to do. The Great Ark lay scattered in a million pieces, a vast wreckage of twisted metal sections, wires, crystal-like substances of various shapes and colors, and many other objects incomprehensible to her. All about the streets and workshops Nepptali papyrus leaves blew in the winds like *kittim*.

Since the rebellion (the New Queen forbade the use of the word *revolution*), the queeti work crews had melted away like the winter's last frost. The White Lords had been unable to stop them. Redfolk units sent to bring them back never returned.

Every desertion was accompanied by an act (or acts) of sabotage. Although they appeared random at first, such acts were hardly haphazard. Their randomness was cleverly planned, as though there were a master-mind behind what seemed on the surface pure anarchy. The New Queen, of course, refused to acknowledge any pattern in the chaotic destruction. The Once-Queen perceived a carefully designed campaign of slow destruction, a gradual but purposeful dismantling of the Great Ark, whatever it was.

No one had seen the King all winter. The New Queen gave her commands in his name. She dismissed the Once-Queen with contempt. 'First Vishnu and now King Ra'" she laughed scornfully. "We see that nothing comes of it. Youth apparently is no cure for a barren womb."

"I see no young ones here," answered the Once-Queen.

"Oh, there will be, Akkadean slut. Didn't the King tell you? Lord Vishnu was the father of many sons, an Exalted Father many times over."

"Well then, where is he? Where are they? I've heard they were defeated."

"He sleeps," the New Queen answered quickly. "His many labors exhausted him. We were too much. Our sons have gone elsewhere, to conquer other lands beyond the Two Continents. We seek a real King, and you shall witness his progeny like the stars of the heavens."

The Once-Queen shook her head. "Forgive me, Miriam, but it seems too easy. Perhaps there is a betrayal in this story."

Waving her arms, the New Queen shouted: "We were taken while he slept! But it matters little. We are Queen, there, here, everywhere. To see us is to see King Ra'"

"Is King Ra' also exhausted from his labors?"

The New Queen either ignored her question or failed to hear it.

"We are the presence of King Ra'. He has little time for trifles, such as mere physical presence. He plans. He guides. He directs and bends all things according to his purpose. Even this foolish rebellion is according to his will. It will serve his most secret purposes, as you'll soon see. His mighty hand pulls the levers of the fate of all creatures. His mighty will cannot be gainsaid."

"He is invisible, then?" asked Devoah, mocking her.

"We are his visible presence."

The Once-Queen bowed to the New Queen. "Pardon our obtuseness, oh Queen."

The New Queen visibly relaxed. "Pardon is granted. After all, thou art our predecessor even if a failed one. Poor barren woman of Akkad."

She perceived the planned anarchy of queeti destruction and the carefully executed dismantling of the Great Ark. She remembered the New Queen's boast.

And she nearly collided with the bejeweled archbishop golden-tongued, limping along and searching for an audience.

EXALTED FATHER

BOOK OF RUNES
VERSE 5.4.4

"May the Almighty's blessings be unto you, oh Once-Queen," he said.

"So now it's back to the Almighty? By this I suppose you mean the Lord-on-the-Mountain?"

The archbishop grinned foolishly. A clipped laugh followed each word as if he believed nothing of what he'd just said.

"Yes, yes, but He-on-the-Mountain has a son."

"The queeti think *Him* Lord—"

"They are confused, of course, ha, ha. The finer points of theology elude them. *He* is the Lord's mouthpiece, the Lord's mouth...ha, ha..."

"*He's dead.* You have a molar to prove it. Or is it a canine?"

"Yes, yes, *He* is spirit. *His* spirit lives. *It* is with us."

"And you, my dear archbishop?"

He drew himself up and smoothed his robes. "I'm archbishop...ha, ha, ha...of the Universal Church—"

"What service did you render Rudra Betrayer for such an honor?"

His heavy face twisted into a frown. "Rudra, Rudra, once dead now returned...but Rudra lost his mind. He's shown signs...of insanity for years. But oh, ha, ha, ha, poor archbishop, yes, yes, poor, so very poor. Did not this poor one see them? Did this poor one fail to see what was before his very eyes?"

She sighed. "He is your father, Jacob, holy or not, and Miriam, the Queen, is your mother."

He glared at her. "Never say that! No. Fathers do not sacrifice their children. Not for the best of reasons. Such a thing is…disgusting, yuk, yuk, it sickens the soul…the very stench of it, simply saying it, is…" He began to bark like a queeti.

She knew the language. He made the sounds of an abandoned cub.

"I'm quite aware of these things," she said.

"Are you now? Ha, ha, ha… Are you? Sold *you*, the ole Khan, 'cause you weren't a boy. Oh yes, yes, yes, your archbishop knows the tale. The Holy Father knows. The Nepptali knew too. *They knew everything…* And they knew he wasn't really your father." He sounded gleeful.

"The Nepptali?"

"Yes, yes, ha, ha, they *knew everything*, oh daughter of a fool—"

She watched him closely. His head jerked from side to side. White foamy saliva dripped down his diminished chins, and his eyes rolled. He limped, favoring his left foot, and he grimaced in pain. The laughter seemed mad and forced at the same time. She remembered Agni's conviction that all priests were liars. If a priest claimed something to be true, you could be certain of the opposite.

"The archbishop's father was no fool. No, no, no… Quite clever, him. Gave the archbishop to the priesthood. Called it a sacrifice. What did we say about such things? But not really a sacrifice. We're archbishop! Well, well, well, he got his wish. In time there'd be a Yadish King, anointed by the Lord through His most holy archbishop."

He began to weep. "You know. How politics decides morality. The deeds of the fathers are visited upon the sons—"

"So you betrayed your father Rudra to Ra'? Long ago, when he passed through Nalanda?"

"Not *my* father!" he howled. "Not, not, not…but yes, yes, yes…"

He dropped his voice so that his words were barely audible, as if the Lord Himself were listening.

Exalted Father

"Deeds of the fathers are also signs for the sons—and daughters too. The Holy Father, not Rudra, *sent me here to kill the King.*"

"*You?* Why?"

"Doesn't want the King comin' to Elsseleron—"

"Why?"

"Because— Holy Father stirs rebellion. He invented the whole Liberator thing to rouse the queeti. The archbishop supplied the theology. Yes, yes, don't look so skeptical. *He is dead as you said.* But there's worse than dead, oh, oh, oh—"

"You know that you're a bad actor, Jacob. We both *know* the King cannot be killed. Now tell me, what's worse?"

"My Holy Father. He grows whittlings, he does. Yes, yes, yes, and whittlings grow *kittim* in thousands of Lordpools, and that's the great mystery—"

It was her turn to laugh. "Ridiculous—"

"Do you know how great a priest Jacob was? How great a mind. What a taste for theology, why it melted in Jacob's mouth. Jacob was always greater than *him.* He's just a tooth."

He giggled. "Only a tooth now, but he can't bite. Saw him die, Jacob did. The dead are dead. How can you grasp such things? Stupid woman who tried to learn her Runes. Never teach Runes to a woman, Jacob used to say."

The old Devorah might have killed him right there. The new one sighed.

"You loved 'em, didn't you?"

"Who?"

"The tooth. Everybody knew. At Nalanda. You couldn't stop talking about him—"

"I sought his life—" she whispered.

"Too bad. *Kittim* got 'em first."

"But *he's* returned."

"Foolish woman, daughter of a fool. We explained it to you. Our father brought him back. Your *He-With-Us* became our *He-Who-Has-Come-Back*... We ought to thank you for the inspiration."

She hung her head.

"Stupid Akkadean—"

She reached for the Nepptali dagger hidden in the Nepptali belt that bound her plain green Nepptali *kittim*-proof smock. But she moved slowly, with hesitation, and when she looked up he'd disappeared into the shadows.

She heard the barks and mews of the abandoned queeti cub.

EXALTED FATHER

BOOK OF RUNES
VERSE 5.4.5

Like *kittim* poison, rumors flowed into Tharas Major that spring. The rumors arrived embodied in those whose bodies flowed with poison.

The rumors told of terrible defeats, of the practical extermination of Grays and Yellows. Crazy, jumbled accounts, told by maddened Redfolk on the edge of death, screaming in agony, the rumors flooded a nearly empty fortress-city as air-born legions of *kittim* fell from the skies like a perpetual blizzard.

L-guns failed, sometimes they blew up in a Redfolk's face. Nepptali steel broke, Nepptali cloaks leaked, and the Yakasshas cursed Nepptali ghouls as they died.

The queeti used new weapons: bronze-tipped spears, short swords and even scimitars that resembled the old Akkadean make. They were organized. Well-designed strategies governed their battle tactics. A Supreme Hetman emerged and united the tribes from the forest to the Redrain valley, from as far away as the Topartz.

This Supreme Hetman, so the stories said, had been captured and taken to Tharas Major where the wicked King Ra' tortured him. The evil King sought to extract from his lips the sacred name. This Hetman, described as having six fingers like the martyrs of the Reed Sea, remained steadfast and refused to blaspheme no matter how brutal the torture.

And the Lord on His Holy Mountain, whose Son bore the unutterable name, gave ear to the cries of this Hetman. The evil wisps had placed him in a tower cell abutting a wall of the main palace. In the early morning hours, this six-fingered hero, perhaps in despair, but probably out of a heroic desire to deny the King the pleasure of torture, threw himself out a window. Immediately, a mighty wind blew from Elsseleron, neither Greater nor Lesser, and a-thousand-times-a-thousand *kittim* came flying from that direction. And they fused together like an impenetrable cloud and they bore him to safety. So and therefore, the Lord blessed the Hetman.

The Lord Himself has chosen Hetman Six-fingers to lead the queeti to victory.

The Supreme Hetman lived most simply, sleeping on the bare ground beneath the open sky, unafraid of rain or *kittim*. He ate little and distributed captured wealth among the queeti poor. The fields, he taught, belonged to those who worked them. Wealth should be shared by all, and none should live so far above others that he or she did no work. No one, especially a queeti, should exist solely for eating, drinking, and fornicating. No one ought to dedicate his or her life to the mindless pursuit of pleasure, or power. Animals did that. Such a life was beneath queeti dignity.

The age of servitude had passed. The Lord's Day had come, an age in which all these marvelous changes would be realized.

In Tharas Major, no one believed the rumors—except the Redfolk, but they soon died of the poison soaking their frail bodies…poor creatures, after-thoughts of the dusk.

Some died of starvation, others of insane, murderous melees that erupted randomly throughout the fortress-city. Grain shipments had ceased in the middle of winter and storehouses were soon emptied.

In the middle of spring the Queen announced a great banquet of victory to be held in The Thrice-graced Hall of Overflowing, Plenty and Great Joy.

EXALTED FATHER

BOOK OF RUNES
VERSE 5.4.6

The Queen occupied the King's place at the High Table. King Ra', she explained, had been up all night planning the summer campaign against the upstart queeti and their ridiculous up-rising. Presently he was laying down, resting, sleeping soundly in fact—such a satisfying sleep—unlike any sleep he'd had in many a year.

Three White Lords attended the banquet. They appeared listless and apathetic. They'd arrived from Tharas Minor by way the Wooden City. They did not speak, nor did they eat. They simply sat and stared straight ahead. Everyone ignored them.

The Once-Queen attended. She sat at the far end of the long table and, with a slight smile, observed the Redfolk squabbling and fighting. She noted how as a species they'd seemed to have degenerated in the last year. They cared little for rank, had almost forgotten how to speak properly, and almost all of them now went naked. There was much screeching, clawing and biting. At least five died right there, either from bites or more likely—she guessed—*kittim* poisoning. None dared approach the Once-Queen, although a few might have entertained dreams as evidenced by their suddenly erect penises.

The archbishop had disappeared, she noticed. No one else seemed to notice.

She noticed a scattered remnant of Grays and Yellows. They seemed to die quickly. The mere brush of a *kittim* and they were screaming in agony. They died in seconds.

Amid the din and mayhem, the Queen rose from her chair. Awkwardly, although it might have been an attempt to illustrate her authority, she ceremoniously raised a large goblet. She wore a long white billowing dress that looked as though it had been through a number of dinners, perhaps once in service of a table cloth. It was lined with gold trim painted on the dress by a rather shaky hand.

She waited for the noise to cease and the fighting to stop. This was like asking time itself to quit flowing. The starving Redfolk were preoccupied with more pressing matters. The Grays and Yellows were apathetic. She raised the goblet to her lips and took a long drink. She held it up again, this time a bit wobbly.

"We wish to speak—"

"So speak," howled a Yakashas near her. Others began hooting and cursing.

"Thank you, thank you, our dear subjects. Listen now to your Queen."

More hooting and curses greeted these words along with some rancorous laughter.

"We march on Elsseleron."

More laughter.

"Far more important is news of a great miracle—"

"You're still breathing?"

"Your Queen is pregnant."

Silence.

"Is there anything too wondrous for the Lord-on-the-Mountain?"

The Redfolk looked at each other. "How'd that happen?" one asked. "The Lord…? Did He come down from his Mountain? What'd the King say 'bout that? The Lord Himself done fucked our Queen…"

The Hall erupted into a cacophony of barking, howling, whistling, and an enormous variety of animal sounds as wondrous as any strange carnal escapades of the Lord.

"Foolish Yakashas!" the Queen bellowed. "Shut your foul mouths. Such mysteries are beyond your kind. Go prepare the armies."

Exalted Father

"So, the Lord ain't fucked our Queen? But got her pregnant all the same?" another Yakashas asked the fellow next to him. "Then how's *that* a miracle of the Lord?"

"Tis Lord Ra' she means."

"The King? Did he climb the mountain?"

This brought a hoot of laughter. "Sure did. He done seeded it too."

"I heard the White Lords got no peckers. They does it with their tails."

Many Redfolk heard this last statement and began laughing.

"Enough!" the Queen shouted. "Go now, on your way. The next one who laughs burns."

The Redfolk ceased their yammering and headed for the doors.

The Once-Queen *laughed*. It was the first time she'd laughed so hard in half a century. She laughed and laughed, but she never burned. The same could not be said for the many Yakashas who died that day, taken by storms of *kittim*.

THE BOOKS OF MARDUK

THE BOOK OF RUNES

CHAPTER FIVE – Topartz

VERSE 5.5.1

A tidal wave of excitement flooded the queeti villages along the Topartz River valley that spring. A new strength, a new sense of freedom sprouted within the houses and common lodges like fresh wheat in the fields. Many queeti raised their faces, straightened their backs, and walked as would a White Lord.

Messengers came from the north. They were large, powerful bulls who walked erect, and with with dignity. In confident voices, they spoke a new queeti language which adopted a new sophisticated vocabulary using fully formed words in place of gestures and grunts. They spoke Church language.

They declared that the Day of Queeti Liberation was at hand.

"Look you to the holy martyrs, your brothers and sisters, who spilled their blood for you. They died so that you might be free from tyranny and slavery. They went to the White Lords. They went to the Holy Father and the Universal Church. The old ones, the young ones, the males and the females, they went. They begged peacefully. They pleaded for justice, for equality, for a share in the wealth that they themselves produced.

"And how did the White Lords answer them?

Exalted Father

"Peasants, see it happen in your mind. The White Lords did not even listen. They struck them down and burned them with the blue fire. The White Lords and the Church watered the fields with innocent blood.

"Peasants! This is how the White Lords answer their serfs.

"They say the queeti are animals, and less than animals. Perhaps the queeti have a language, they admit, but animals have nothing to say.

"We say the Day of the Queeti is at hand.

"One has come to the queeti. Liberator, Wanderer, he bids the queeti to seize their scythes, their pitchforks, and their hoes, and water the fields with the blood of the wicked White Lords.

"Let a new fire burn in your hearts, brothers and sisters. A fire hotter than the Lords could even imagine. Such a fire has a name. It is called revolution."

So spoke the messengers to the crowds, from village to village, all along the steamy Topartz river valley. And the queeti rose up and did the messenger's biding. They slaughtered Grayfolk and Yellow. They devastated the lands of the Church, burning everything and everyone until the very river turned black, choked with ash. The fury of their revolution could be seen from as far away as the great Cathedral.

Everywhere the queeti whispered to one another *the name*.

Tremendous storms of *kittim* came with the Winds, and there was much talk of the Supreme Hetman Six-fingers and of how he commanded the butterflies, even the Winds. Every queeti swore an oath to the Supreme Hetman. A few refused. Those who balked at swearing such an oath—of total obedience—were accused of rebelling against the revolution. These few were brutally tortured and in due time such fools repented their madness. They were forgiven before they were executed. Their villages were utterly destroyed. The villages were also forgiven. The Hetman was compassionate, the messengers said.

The Books Of Marduk

In order to clarify his unique status as Hetman of many villages, Six-fingers replaced the appellation *Supreme Hetman* with the title *August*, which was a word he learned from Silver who'd heard the archbishop use the word in reference to himself.

August…yet this title seemed too abrupt, too short. So, Six-fingers and Silver gave it more thought, and Silver decided to add the sound of *eee*…to the end, spelling it in the Sandi, *Augustii*. Six-fingers happily adopted the title. Wailing voices in the Winds—voices of the martyrs—begged him to do so, he said.

Exalted Father

BOOK OF RUNES
VERSE 5.5.2

At the end of spring a beggar appeared in the south. Queeti who encountered him could not identify the beggar's kind. He was not a White Lord, nor was he a Red, Gray or Yellow, and he certainly was no ghoul. He begged in the hamlets and only rarely in the larger villages. Some said he was the Liberator (one or two used the forbidden name and were instantly struck down by their fellows). But this was quickly disproven since he walked with a limp and wore a black thread-bare traveler's cloak. His hair was long and braided, his face smooth (like a ghoul), but his skin was dark and he seemed quite young (unlike a ghoul). Everyone knew that the Liberator was a giant creature, bearded and dignified, powerful and sound of body, and, as Silver described him, walked in a luminous cloud, difficult for an average queeti to perceive, except for the Silver and the Augustii who perceived him clearly.

Passing through the larger villages like a shadow, he favored the poorest hamlets. For despite their abysmal poverty, the inhabitants filled his begging bowl with food, but also gold, pieces of machinery taken from abandoned work-sheds, jewels, and papyrus leaves brought from the north, perhaps the Cathedral itself. The food and other items of wealth he gave back to the poorest families, the papyrus leaves he kept.

No one quite understood the invisible power he radiated, although he cut a miserable figure limping down the dusty roads. The poor felt an odd kind of reverence for him, the sort they used to feel in the presence of a White Lord (which was seldom), or when a representative of the Holy Father visited their hamlets, even if it was only to collect donations.

THE BOOKS OF MARDUK

The beggar rarely spoke. When he did utter a few words, he spoke in the new queeti language of the Augustii. His accent was odd, and no two queeti could agree on exactly what he said. Still, there was something very captivating about the beggar's voice. They could feel powerful vibrations in the air and in their very bodies, as though the Winds, Greater and Lesser, were speaking to them, but from the inside. They were compelled to listen.

For all of that, the beggar's voice seemed to calm them. Their rebellious blood flowed less hotly, their furious hearts beat less madly, and their hatred was dampened. They became quiet and thoughtful. Listening to the beggar, they suddenly perceived an unanticipated beauty in their own dismal existence. They noticed things that until now had been invisible to them. They heard the grain growing, the dew evaporating, the daystar shinning. They tasted the Winds and saw once-invisible spirits cavorting in the upper currents.

Afterwards, after the beggar had departed and they contemplated the experience, they found themselves lost and confused. Skeptics spoke of mass hallucinations. Not a few queeti agreed. Many complained that if they followed the beggar's advice (and don't forget, they added, he begged and did not work), they'd become numb and drooling, mindless beasts who know nothing except endless toil…the very life they revolted against. Such brutes live only for those brief moments of respite when their instinctual needs are partially fulfilled.

(Years later, after the Wars of Liberation had remade the world, a few ancient ones who claimed to have heard the beggar's words wrote down what they could recall. Very little of this survived the devastation.)[22]

---

[22] Whether or not these old ones actually *heard* the beggar's words *as he spoke these words* remains in dispute. Therefore, according to modern scholarship, nothing

EXALTED FATHER

The beggar instructed the poor serfs that before they sought justice they needed to know truth. False words, he explained, no matter how *eloquent* (a word no one quite understood, but probably meant something like *well-spun,* such as the web of the green jungle spider) will not lead you to the truth. That is a path you yourselves must walk. It is found in the streets of your hamlets and villages, in the fields of you labor, in the trivial tasks of your everyday existence. You must walk these streets, plant these fields, dig these wells and see the truth in the most mundane things. Stand you on the streets and see.

The beggar told them little homilies, mostly about animals, plants, and the rhythms of nature. Stories for cubs.

He cautioned them against obstacles to the path, such as greed, envy, anger and hatred. But when he moved on and the magical effect of his voice wore off, his homilies seemed hollow and his admonishments silly, even to queeti, poor and ignorant. After he'd departed their hamlets and villages, their lives reverted to the dull, drab, and boring—and hard.

In time, the sayings and stories of the beggar spread from hamlet to village, village to larger village, yet always among the poorest of the Topartz valley. The revolution had not come to these places. The great tides of change had yet to wash out the rot and grim of superstition, as Silver might have said.

A persistent if obviously false rumor had it that usually a day or two after the beggar had moved on, someone experienced a *healing.* Generally, a chronic illness abruptly left the benighted serf's body. Rarely—if at all—was it something life-threatening.

```
can be said for certain about the teachings that
follow here. Most likely, such reminiscences are
garbled and fragmented. We'll never know what the
poor superstitious creatures heard, or even if they
comprehended the beggar's language. The sheer
impracticality of these teachings counts against
their authenticity.
```

THE BOOKS OF MARDUK

At first, the Augustii and Silver let it be known that the beggar's appearance was a divine sign from the Lord-on-the-Mountain that their cause was a just one.

When Silver actually heard a version of the beggar's teaching from a serf who'd mocked the Augustii (and was about to be burned), he decided that the beggar was ghoul who'd lost its mind. Insane ghouls such as this one, Silver cautioned, were fit to be ignored. The Augustii declared that even foolish ghouls might be dangerous.

Silver explained that if handled correctly, fools, be they ghoul, wisp or queeti, added a bit of levity, and hence brief but welcome diversion, to the deadly seriousness of the revolution. It was the handling of fools that presented problems. Silent fools are the most well-handled of all, the Augustii observed.

EXALTED FATHER

BOOK OF RUNES
VERSE 5.5.3

The beggar abandoned the dusty southern road and entered the wooded remnant of a forest that once covered the entire eastern half of Starmirror. He judged by the elevation of the daystar that Lesser Wind would shortly sweep down from the north. He did not enter the forest to avoid *kittim*. Of them he had no fear.

He seated himself at the base of an ancient oak. In a short time three farvels came to the tree and sat upon their haunches like huge mosscats. They watched him with large green eyes. One of them was completely white. They resembled statues of ancient golden lions guarding a long-forgotten temple.

At last, the oldest of them, the white one, wearing a silver muzzle and thin-haired silver mane, raised a paw and motioned over the beggar's head towards the north.

"So, my good *sramana*, have you not made things worse? First Suthralane and now you. You Akkadeans should never have been priests. Or didn't you know?"

The second farvel, also quite old and missing an eye, let out a short laugh that sounded surprisingly human for such a creature. "Of course he knows. This one too." He indicated the third farvel. "Brothers they were, sons of Livia. One inherited her temper, the other her brains. One we gave to Nalanda, the other we kept in Akkad." Again he laughed. "Akkad had no need of this one. Priests make poor orloks."

"You've made things worse," the elder farvel repeated. "Account for yourself."

The beggar knit his brows and his green eyes were downcast.

"I awoke in the cave of Zell. Do you understand what it is like? Yes, surely you must. My body was still cold and rigid, my eyes fixed, and it was horribly painful when I took my first breath. I wished to remain in that state, immune to desire, to pain, to delusions and truths—the frightful weight was removed as was the poison. The dead fear not poison. I wished to share the inertia of stone and soil, and remain in that dark place, in the cave of Zell, where once lived the innocent clods of mud in the innocent honesty of their innocent poverty."

The elder farvel whistled: "A touching sermon, my boy. But not touching enough for the *kittim*, huh? So they played you a jest and brought you back like us, yet not like us. Why complain? Always complaining—I see *that* hasn't changed. Still cold too. Now you're a child of this-worldly mud. All the better. No more vows."

"My vows died with me," the beggar agreed.

"Your death broke them. So why still seek the Lord?"

The beggar shook his head. "I don't know."

"Oh, my boy, I'd think you know."

"Oh, Theophilus-who-knows-everything, do *you* know?"

The farvel laughed. "We know that we tend the whittling grove from which the lovely *kittim* are born."

Briefly, the beggar shared the creature's laughter. "Hardly trees, wouldn't you say? If not trees, hardly groves either. More like bubbling pools of water. Another joke on the priests and their precious books."

"Yes, yes, poor priests. But not water either. Empty space itself bubbles. We tend the surrounding garden."

"Poor priest. From tending books to tending gardens."

"What about poor *sramanas*? So you wanted to stay planted in the mud. Your wish was granted. Do you know why?"

The beggar stared at the farvel.

"You hurt *her*, you must know. Deeply."

"Who?"

"Don't be stupid," said the one-eyed farvel. "She was a child of a fool, not you."

EXALTED FATHER

"Fifty years it took to dissolve your vows, foolish one," said the ancient farvel, "and yet I see that they haunt you still, making you cold and aloof. Begging, poverty, wandering, teaching, celibacy—what pride."

"I renounced pride," the beggar protested.

"And you're proud of it. You think yourself free from all entanglements? But this is not freedom. It is *fear*. You shouted a resounding *no* to life. *No* to her. What pain your *no* caused. Monstrous. And do you know any more about the world? Serene ignorance remains ignorance. Do you know why you beg?"

The beggar hung his head.

The gray-bearded white farvel continued relentlessly. "Fear of life, yes. Also laziness. Who works the fields, tell me? Who then produces, creates, gives birth? Oh, oh, I've taken a vow of poverty. So, the rest of you clods of mud must work hard to keep me in poverty—"

The three farvels laughed.

The youngest farvel said: "What pain you caused! She was for you. Would that she'd been for me."

The beggar gazed at him and asked: "Brother, do you have memories of other places, other times?"

The farvel gave a disconcertingly human shrug. "Some of us do, others not. We're *kittim*-make now and those memories glow faint as do embers from a once-roaring fire."

The beggar sat beneath the ancient oak and contemplated these things for a long time. Lesser Wind arose and *kittim* rained down gently, swirling as tree spores swirl in an autumn breeze. The beggar pulled his black cloak tighter about his frail body. The farvels glowed with a golden light.

"You don't fully grasp it, do you?" asked the old farvel. "What *they* are. They're words, sentences, paragraphs, composed in a language none of us are able to fully grasp. Perhaps the Nepptali did once. That tribe knew more than the priesthood. The *kittim* are composed in the deep pools of this world, like the Runes we mistakenly believed came from the mind of the Lord. The *kittim* translate this world's formulas, and these translations compose living things, as a pendulum swings back and forth."

The beggar watched them. "It's the colors, isn't it?"

"Ah, you understand—"

He sighed. "I was wrong to reject the mud and dirt. I never appreciated it. I never acknowledged it. My vows were an averting of the eyes. A kind of blindness. All vows are such—"

"Of course, fool. Arising from fear they must be."

"I will go to her, after—"

"After you confront the Lord Almighty? Come, come, my boy, you must know that there never was a Suthralane."

"Yes, father. I know that there never was a Suthralane. But there will be."

The beggar got to his feet and limped back to the road.

The elder farvel purred in resignation. "He was the greatest scholar of us all. But he's always been obstinate and rebellious. You could never tell him anything. He never listened to anyone."

The third farvel, larger and darker than the other two, nodded and shook his thick mane. "Yes, he, my brother… He too is fearful and impatient. From such things comes anger, which I know well. His anger smoldered where mine blazed—"

The one-eyed farvel rumbled deep in his throat. "Livia, your mother, was like that."

"You knew her, father," said the third farvel.

"In another life," said one-eye.

"Still, acts come from desire and bear fruit, strange fruits that none are able to anticipate," said the white farvel.

The third farvel growled. "Always the priest, huh? Always a sermon. He goes to Elsseleron to speak face to face with the Lord. Should we have told him?"

Exalted Father

"You do not know him as I did. Even after his resurrection he would not have believed us. He must experience the monstrous Lord for himself. It's his old obsession with Suthralane. Deep in his heart he always knew that there was no such person. He lacked the strength for what he knew. He would will it into existence."

The third farvel sighed. "My brother cannot not will."

The Books Of Marduk

BOOK OF RUNES
VERSE 5.5.4

The daystar broke through the green haze of early morning and ignited the walls of Tharas Major, causing them to burn with a white heat that did not seem borrowed. Greater Wind brought its quota of *kittim*. Dewdrop Moon emerged, silver, bright and full. A small number of Redfolk were caught lingering in open courtyards. *Kittim* sought them out, propelled by a force other than the Wind, drawn, perhaps, like bees to pollen. They were large and constructed from complex interlocking geometric membranes. They were mostly blue and green and orange. They wrapped the victim within the folds of these impossible geometric shapes and burned as bright as the daystar until the Yakashas was fully consumed. Their light was not borrowed.

She made her way through the narrow avenues. She tried to run in the open courtyards, but her body was shriveled and brown, and her muscles had dissolved. For many, many years now, her body no longer contained the coiled energy of an Akkadean warrior. She guessed that another poisoning would probably kill her. Yet, the prospect didn't seem as awful as it may have once seemed so long ago, if it had frightened her even then, times which she failed to recall. When she considered the matter, she recognized that her ridiculous running was more an act of reflex than conscious fear. After all, the *kittim* had liberated her from Ra'bim corruption. Her life was stored away in her *Confessions* (the title she finally decided upon). Her existence here and now was an appendix, an afterthought. It was hardly an existence at all.

Despite all these years, the maze of the fortress-city still confused her. After she'd become Once-Queen, her reassigned personal apartments overlooked the Blue Yard of Wind-swept

Exalted Father

Memory. This courtyard was on the rim of the great wheel of high walls and farthest from the center Dome, the Grand Hall of Heavenly Peace, Prosperity, Freedom, and Brilliant Light, which was the hub of Tharas Major. The courtyards and their connectors were intricate spokes of the wheel which, so she'd heard, all returned to Dome. She'd never in all the years as Queen been able to verify this claim.

She believed that the King's private apartments were located within a jumble of government buildings west of the Grand Hall. King Ra' had never granted her the privilege of an official or unofficial visit. All her service as Queen, her fornication under command of the King, occurred in the Grand Hall, usually in the presence of White Lord witnesses. She'd heard it said that the government complex numbered ten thousand halls, and she could well believe it.

She stopped at the edge of a small, summer-green courtyard near the center of the complex. Here she faced an ugly square building with few windows that for some reason, perhaps the materials of its construction, seemed out of place. It was built from red brick which reminded her of Zell.

Funny how *those memories* were still so vivid. The Reed Sea Folk were more real to her now than the King himself and all those years of fruitless rape. Funny how distant memories suddenly pop up as though called forth by hints from the present. Seldom, however, were there any glimpses of the future. For the aged, the future is short and dark.

She sighed. Her mind was becoming as frail as her body. *Kittim* poisoning was slowly consuming her, rising from her withered body into her brain, slicing her thought-stream into separate pieces so that what was once a steady stream of images, feelings, sounds, ideas, loves, hates and infinitely more, became a broken road of brief spaces, mostly in the past, separated by dark chasms. One of those spaces belonged to *him*. Although she resisted, she still remembered *him* as vividly as ever, indeed more so. At times it seemed that *he* was alive, as *he* had been the first time she saw him. Only now she recognized that her hate, and her vow to kill *him*, oddly intertwined with love, as the early light of the daystar mingled with the green haze of morning before the coming of Greater Wind.

Suddenly she noticed something else. For the first time this morning she realized that she'd been carrying the leather-bound papyrus sheaves of her *Confessions* under her arm.

BOOK OF RUNES
VERSE 5.5.5

A farvel had come to her the previous night—at dusk, with Lesser Wind, as if the Wind had swept the creature into existence, rushing down from Edom and gathering the necessary elements to make a farvel. It padded out of the forest and stood at the base of the wall, gazing up at her as she leaned out of the window to gaze down at it. The farvel's fur rippled with many colors, reminding her of Rudra's old coat. It sat on its haunches, contemplating her with wide-eyes, gold-flecked black and disconcertingly child-like, a child from the Tribes of Men. The farvel seemed young to her, yet she had no means of truly judging its age. It might have quite ancient for all she knew.

"Devorah," it purred.

"Here I am," she replied automatically, not the least bit surprised that a farvel could speak Sandi. *Kittim* poisoning was in this way similar to Ra'bim somas. It caused delusions, but such beautiful delusions, so lovely, so serene, peaceful, and comforting… Why not believe?

"How odd you should've loved a *sramana* so long ago. Knew you nothing of their silly vows?"

"My love became hate," she said, perhaps for the first time acknowledging the terrible transformation, the truth of it. "I knew of their vows yet I thought such things were no more than their priestly garments. I learned otherwise. I would have killed him *in this world* had not the *kittim* accomplished a preemptive murder."

"Ah yes, the *kittim*. They restored him, you know, minus a tooth of course."

She laughed, for the second time. Her delusion was quite entertaining, which was one more justification for substituting it for reality.

The farvel shook its head from side to side as if it'd caught a squirming marmot in its jaws.

"You love him still."

She didn't answer.

"How odd an Akkadean warrior woman should fall in love with a *sramana*. But not so odd, for he was born Akkadean."

That a farvel should know something about the Tribes of Men, and the great secret of a priest's birth (which was known only by the archbishop) should have shocked her. It would be as if a mosscat understood the inner workings of an L-gun, or a fish could read the most difficult Runes. Yet she hardly raised an eyebrow.

Farvel: "The other brother loved you in his own way. You treated him very badly, you know. You perceived him as a rival."

She did not speak.

Farvel: "That's the problem with death. There's always more to say. What requires clarification, correction, simple apology, must forever be suspended in the air, never reaching the ground."

"It is very sad," she sighed.

"Yes, it is."

She had no memory of these things. She accepted it as truth nevertheless since she'd already surrendered herself to the delusion.

The farvel grinned, showing sharp fangs. "I knew his brother, I did. Quite intimately if I may say so. Alas, no better than you know yourself."

"What do you mean?"

The farvel gave a very human shrug. "To know yourself is to forget yourself, and to forget yourself is to know all things."

"How very cryptic," she laughed, "even for a mythical beast such as *yourself*."

The farvel's large triangular ears popped up and flared. "Do you wish to see him? Speak with him perhaps? You, an empty soul whose memories are confined to a book?"

"Why yes," she breathed.

"Then take you your book and present it to the King, and take a pilgrimage to Thrice-blessed Cathedral at the base of White Mountain."

"Why give my book to the King?"

The farvel shrugged again. "Who else is there? The Queen? The satraps? The Redfolk, the Grays, the Yellows? But for the Queen, all have departed. Perhaps you would present it to the Holy Father or his archbishop?"

"No— to the King," she agreed. "The others? All dead?"

It was the farvel's turn to laugh. "The *kittim* are brilliant engineers like your Nepptali. They act quite spontaneously and unpredictably. The old archbishop says randomly, yet I think they have a hidden purpose. Naturally he laughs at me. He argues that a hidden purpose is effectively no purpose at all, and therefore equivalent to randomness. Who can argue with the archbishop?"

"You sound like a priest," she said.

"When a priest tells you something you know immediately that the opposite is true."

She stared at the creature. "That phrase—"

"You remember."

"There're no priests in the world."

The farvel laughed and vanished as the first rays of the daystar ignited the wall.

THE BOOKS OF MARDUK

BOOK OF RUNES
VERSE 5.5.6

She walked slowly across the courtyard, savoring the morning air, careless of a *kittim* attack, in fact desiring one. Perhaps with one more poisoning she'd no longer be able to distinguish between delusion and the disillusion of the real world.

The *kittim* ignored her. They flew above the highest turrets of the fortress-city, passing south towards the Lord's mountain.

The entrance to the King's private dwelling was a huge triangular vestibule, which led to another, and a third, each a bit smaller and less perfectly triangular than the last. The doors were thrown open and the building appeared deserted.

She passed through the three vestibules and entered the main chamber. Here, not a single ray of the daystar entered; the windows were actually plates of polished silver. There was a luminance nonetheless. An eerie greenish light rose from the floor itself. For a moment she thought she'd come to the shore of a shining green pool that glowed with phosphorescent sea-life, like Lake Emerald at the dawn, or better, more like the pool inside the caves of the Reed Sea People. She realized, however, that the floor itself gave off the light and its water-like appearance was due to an unknown material as smooth as glass but hard as Nepptali steel.

She stared at it and then laughed. Except for its green color, the floor was identical to the crystalline Lordpool of Nalanda. Who was to say that this was a copy and the Lordpool was the original? Perhaps this was the original.

"What would the priests say?" she exclaimed aloud.

As she studied the surface of the green pool she perceived faint scratching...but not scratching, rather script...*Runes*. Runes of the *Runehayana*. She knew enough to be able to identify them as such.

Exalted Father

Strings of Runes forming words, and words forming sentences, transliterated into Sandi if one could compute the crazy mathematical formulas, which she could not.

And then she looked up and saw row upon row of stone seats. She stood in the pit of an amphitheater as in Nalanda.

The chamber was absolutely silent.

She took a step and froze. An imposing giant sat in the middle of the bottom row, a White Lord. It seemed asleep, slumped over in an awkward position.

Slowly she crossed the green floor, stepping lightly upon the Runes of the *Runehayana*. The sleeper didn't stir. She held her own book in front of her as she would hold a weapon, the old Akkadean training which apparently her wasted muscles remembered although her mind had forgotten.

The sleeper was King Ra' himself. As she came close, prepared to offer up her *Confessions*, she saw that he wasn't asleep at all. *He was dead.* She knew it from the smell of him, for nothing had changed in the statue of stone except his tail which hung limply from his seat like a dead serpent. Otherwise his features were set as they'd always been. The odor of death was that of ancient stone baking in the heat of the daystar, like stale bread reheated, like plants at the end of autumn, wine turned to vinegar, rotting wood, the canals of Tholos.

The King was most certainly dead. Had it been *kittim*, she wondered? But there were no silken *kittim* here. Had he been poisoned? The body bore no sign of wounds or struggle.

Someone must have administered poison—

Suddenly she knew, but she didn't know how she knew. She knew.

The archbishop.

(And so she placed her *Confessions* on the lap of dead stone, and she turned and fled the tomb. And thus in the course of millennia

The Books Of Marduk

this most significant codex was discovered by archaeologists excavating the ruins)[23]

---

[23] This is obviously an interpolation, and is marked as such, although a few scholars believe it authentic, albeit an expansion done by translators who favored the target language.

EXALTED FATHER

BOOK OF RUNES
VERSE 5.5.7

She searched Tharas Major, as much as she was able to cover in a day. By late afternoon she'd given up. It was highly probable that she'd visited less than half of the fortress-city, this walled paradise of infinite delights as some of the Redfolk referred to it. She could not imagine from where the Yakashas got the concept of infinity. A wandering *sramana* perhaps? Was death also one of those delights? The city reeked of it.

She stumbled upon the Dome, the Axis of the Universe, and found its massive double doors closed and sealed. She thought that she heard voice coming from inside, perhaps the sounds of the Queen shouting orders. How could she be certain? Devorah of Delusions had only recently encountered a mythical beast and— if this delusion were not enough—had spoken to it.

She put her ear to the crack between the doors. The imagined voice belonged to the imagined Queen, and since she'd decided that the voice and Queen were imagined, and yet she heard, well then there was no difference between an imagined Queen and a real one. She decided not to concern herself any further. What was real was imagined, what was imagined was real. A new proverb for Rudra, if she ever saw him again.

The Queen seemed to be giving orders to a crowd of soldiers. She was discussing colossal military campaigns over vast land masses, against super-powerful enemies, for the greater glory of an eternal dynasty. They'd go south and slaughter the rebellious tribes of the Topartz—after they'd massacred the tribes along the Redrain, captured and tortured the upstart Augustii. Then they'd move on White Mountain Cathedral and put the Holy Father on trial. After that, Elsseleron itself where the Queen would confront the Lord

Almighty Himself (His Divine Self, rather), and challenge Him for supremacy of the World of Two Continents. For she was the Queen. And *she was pregnant*. And He was sterile...like all men.

Devorah of Delusions failed to grasp the rest of it. The Queen's voice became louder, more intense and excited; her words seemed to overflow their banks as the Pearldew often flooded farmlands in Greenbottom valley, causing chaos and destruction.

Devorah felt a great weariness. Something flashed through her head like a tiny bolt of inner lightning. Somewhere, sometime, not this where and not this time, she'd heard similar schemes, but she'd heard them in different languages and with very different names. Did present delusions cause deluded memories too? And if delusional experiences were obviously false, then what of delusional memories? How could a person know? Where was the inner reality to provide a measure of comparison?

She shrank away from the doors and teetered down the marble steps that led to the Grand Hall Dome. She crossed the courtyard and entered a wide avenue which, if she remembered, in reality or otherwise, led to the great gates of Tharas Major. The two guard towers that formed the entrance looked deserted. The massive doors made from cedar a foot thick hung ajar from their iron hinges.

A wide ramp of crushed rock and stone led down from the plateau of the fortress-city. In the hazy distance she thought she saw the light of daystar reflecting off the glistening waters of the Redrain. Delusion.

Somewhere south sat the Sacred Way that led to the Bridge of the Celestials over the river and on east to Thrice-blessed Cathedral, and the Holy Father.

Rudra... She could almost feel him plotting from far away, yet she felt no fear. Whatever could be done to her had been done. Perhaps there was a world in which women were not passive objects, a world in which they determined their own destiny, forged and wielded their own purpose. Perhaps. The queeti with their

Exalted Father

matriarchy—as she'd experienced it among the Reed Sea People—might well usher in such a world. At the moment it mattered little. Poisoned, delusional, old, Devorah of Akkad today at least chose freely to leave Tharas Major.

She caught a sliver of movement on the road. A speck, like a tiny bird, fluttered in the shimmering heat of the daystar. Even at this distance she knew. It was no delusion—at least this is what she decided. The bird on the road was the murderous archbishop hopping on one foot.

THE BOOKS OF MARDUK

BOOK OF RUNES
VERSE 5.5.8

She found Jacob in the late afternoon, a little before summer dusk and the commencement of Lesser Wind. He'd stepped off the Sacred Way into an orchard of young apple trees.

Apparently he'd eaten an unripe apple, perhaps more than one, for he lay curled up beneath a tree, groaning and hugging himself, and sporadically launching into convoluted theological dissertations about good and evil, death and rebirth, farvels and their ways, along with learned discussions on the virtues of Banalis brandy as opposed to queeti spice-beer, especially in reference to what he called its "intoxication acceleration function," which counted as a new theological principle he himself had invented, most humbly. Or had it been revealed to him? He wasn't sure. Before he weighed in on this obtuse question, he emitted several more groans. A bloated stomach was quite painful, true enough, but he had to admit that indigestion could give rise to theological breakthroughs.

She crept silently around the tree. She visualized the act: grab the braided hair and yank the head back, twisting, and then deliver the blow with the palm of her hand, all in one fluid motion. She concentrated, gathering herself—

Something distracted her. At the periphery of her vision, beyond the grove in the shadows of the deeper forest that bordered the Sacred Way, something moved.

She hesitated. A number of heads suddenly popped up out of the gloom, golden fur, large ears, human-like eyes in a mosscat face. They watched her silently.

Again it had come to her, this delusion of mythical beings brought on by *kittim* poisoning. Creatures born in the heated imaginations of long-dead priests had come to haunt her final days.

Exalted Father

"*Farvels,*" she said the word aloud.

Jacob stirred. "What—?" He shifted his once-considerable bulk in order to see around the tree. Then he let out a yowl and tried to scramble away on all fours like a plump cockroach suddenly startled by light. He dug into the moist ground, thrashing about and howling, and threw dirt and small stones at her. "You're alive—" he screamed.

She wasn't listening to him. She gazed into the shadows of the forest. He stopped his hysterical antics and followed her line of sight.

"What'd you see—?"

"Farvels," she whispered.

"Impossible."

"An Akkadean trick," he howled. "When I turn you'll shove a knife in my back."

Yet he couldn't resist.

"Nothing," he groaned. "Play of light and shadows—"

"They were there," she answered, knowing at the same time that he'd confirmed her suspicions, that the poison produced hallucinations, and to believe in hallucinations was delusional. She felt a deep sadness.

"You, murderer, join the shadows—" But she could hardly move. The sadness penetrated into her muscles and sinews like a Ra'bim soma. She really did wish there were Farvels in the world.

"No, no... You must join us. You're one of us, from the Tribes of Men, chosen of the Lord, in *His* image."

"Not in *his* image, as you can surely see."

"A simple turn of speech...a metaphor perhaps...a word, sound...nothing to upset you, nothing to get you excited, no, nothing..." He eyed her warily.

"Nothing? Nothing but a priestly nightmare, all of it?"

"No, no," he wailed, holding his head in his hands. "Nothing, nothing...yes, yes. No, no, something... Oh, oh, it was so clear, so sharp, persuasive, comforting. Did you know I was the greatest theologian of the age? Greater than Marduk. Yes, yes. Until... *We* climbed that mountain, scaled its sheer flanks, like spiders we did. What we found... What did we find? The Lord Almighty? Are we Suthralane? No, no—"

"What'd you find?"

"Oh, oh, how mystical, how spiritual, how moving. What an experience. Words are like straw, the *Runehayana* is like straw. Dung, ash, clods of mud."

"You met the Lord on High?"

"Oh no, no, no. We saw—" He peered at her and whispered as though afraid the forest would overhear.

"*You are in His image; I am in His image. We are, the Tribes of Men, in His image, male and female, doesn't matter. But the others...the Yakashas, the White Lords—the others—no, no, no...*"

She recalled the rule: When a priest speaks, the opposite of what the priest says must be the truth.

She sighed. "Get thee home to the Holy Father," she said, mimicking the speech patterns of the Church.

"Ah," his lips curled in a calculating sneer, "but the sacrifice?"

"You killed King Ra'."

"No, no..." He sounded hurt and offended. "We didn't slay the King. We've no knowledge of poisons. Unlike, say, the wife of the Ra'bim Vishnu."

"So, you know he's dead? That he was poisoned?"

"Ach, caught, we are like a fish in a net. Yes, yes, we know. But knowing is not causing."

"Then who did?"

"Who did what?"

"Killed King Ra'?"

"You know then? Maybe your knowing is causing."

"Fool. He was dead when I found him."

"Ha. Daughter of a fool knows a fool, huh?"

She didn't answer.

"He was poisoned."

EXALTED FATHER

"Indeed."

"Can't go drinking soma all day long."

She laughed. "Playing the fool, huh? Better to play the priest. When a priest speaks the opposite is true. Did the Holy Father order it? Sure he did. Wouldn't the sacrifice of a King please the Almighty? Why not try again? Why not a Once-Queen?"

"Devorah," he said sounding suddenly very serious and sober, "tell us if thou believe in Marduk's resurrection?"

The question took her by surprise. "I..." she hesitated.

"Tell us, Devorah of Akkad. What is the difference between resurrection and *reconstruction?*"

She saw that he was diverting her. But the question hung in the air like a heavy dark cloud.

"I...don't know."

He grinned. "Neither do we know who poisoned the King. We are a bit surprised that the White Lords could be poisoned at all. But then we know very little of the more potent Ra'bim somas."

"What does this have to do with—" She couldn't say *his* name. Jacob apparently understood.

"Come, daughter, we will reveal a great mystery. Why are you in the Lord's image?"

She stared at him and shook her head.

"Because you too are reconstructed."

She groaned. "More priestly nonsense."

"Remember Suthralane?"

"You are Suthralane."

"No, no, the myth, not some pale imitation. Perhaps Marduk told it to thee? The version in which Suthralane is puzzled by the term *Kingdoms of the Heavens,* those cryptic verses in the *Runehayana.* And the Kingdoms fell, went out one by one—"

"The whole damned thing is cryptic. Maybe cryptic is just another word for nonsense, huh? Maybe it's nothing more than shooting stars."

"Ah ha, a true scholar. We've forgotten thine studies in Nalanda. Are the Kingdoms just stars? Do stars fall?"

She shook her head.

"The great mystery...the star fell *on the mountain.*"

"More nonsense."

"We fell, my daughter. Our fall was with the Lord. The Fall of us both, men and the Lord. Our Fall is called creation."

"Created in Greenbottom? The Tribes of Men?"

"Oh, what a scholar. What a priest. Priestess. Yes, yes Greenbottom. Fell from the Heavens. The Lord on His Mountain, we in Greenbottom. The Nepptali knew. How ironic that they knew. Not to the priests was the revelation first given, but to the Nepptali."

"Rambling gibberish," she moaned holding her head.

"There's a deeper mystery the Nepptali did not know. Only Suthralane knew. In Greenbottom. The Kingdoms of the Heavens. The Fall. *All reconstructed.* RECONSTRUCTED as would a Nepptali mechanic. But not Marduk. *Marduk is a resurrection.*"

"Please stop," she begged, still holding her head.

"The Tribes of Men are reconstructed. From the Kingdoms of the Heavens. But Greenbottom is not the Kingdoms of the Heavens. The whole thing was doomed from the start. The Lord Almighty is insane. The *Runehayana* is insane. We're crazy—"

"Crazy?" she repeated, looking up. "Well, that's true. Maybe priests do stumble upon the truth every so often."

"Marduk was a reconstruction once. From *there* to *here.* Now he's a reconstruction from *here* to *here.* So he's a resurrection."

He hung his head. "We are like straw tarphounds—"

She saw his hand moving, reaching into the thick folds of his archbishop's robe. She knew that she ought to respond, but she was too weary, too confused, and her hatred had died. The *kittim* wound burned and itched. She actually felt the venom surging through her veins.

He drew a long thin blade, sharp and bright, of Nepptali make.

Her only resistance was a sad smile.

"Will you join us then? Now that you know the truth?"

He struggled to his feet. She saw that one foot had turned black and was twice the size of the other. Both were partially wrapped in dirty cloth taken from the Yakashas.

"Join you, archbishop?"

"The Holy Father graciously excluded you from the sacrifice. You ought to be thankful."

"Too late," she laughed.

"Let's see if you'll be resurrected, Devorah, daughter of the fool."

He took a step, then another, and brought the blade to her throat.

THE BOOKS OF MARDUK

BOOK OF RUNES
VERSE 5.5.9

At that instant Lesser Wind began. He staggered back yelling at her, but the sudden gust of Lesser Wind carried his words away.

Suddenly the space all around them was filled with *kittim*. These were the largest bugs she'd ever seen, nearly twice the size of a White Lord. They came in every possible geometric shape, and some that were impossible, and they seemed to fly purposefully, as if by their own free will.

Entranced, she watched them alight in the apple trees. The branches and leaves instantly appeared glistening wet as if covered in ice. The forest shadows came alive with color and motion, and the late afternoon curtain of gloom was ripped apart by the scythe-like radiance of thousands upon thousands of these strange beings, blue, green, yellow, purple, and their infinite combinations, merging, disappearing, and re-emerging like boiling water.

She no longer feared them, if she ever had. They were too beautiful, too dainty and frail with their silken wings and odd shapes, so soft and fragile. They glided to her. Then the *woman of the book* remembered how *he* had loved them, and how she had hated *him*— but now both women loved them, and both women had always loved *him*. The hate had died and the love remained.

A giant bug came down upon her. In wide, spiraling circles it lazily dropped from the sky. It reminded her of two giant hoops of silk, blue and gold, joined together by crimson tendrils.

She laughed and clapped her hands like a child. The *kittim* instantly ceased its haphazard spiraling and came straight for her like an arrow. Smiling, she closed her eyes.

The *kittim* flew right over her head and went for the archbishop. He threw up his hands and gave a wordless cry. The creature had him in a second. Wrapping around him, it completely covered his body with its silken hoops.

He screamed once.

Everything became luminous. A sudden blinding flash filled the apple grove. The brilliance intensified until it seemed that the daystar itself had come down from the heavens and burned among the trees—but did not consume them.

He burned like a torch. Briefly she wondered if there'd be an archbishop resurrection.

In a moment she felt a soft wing brush her face. Then another, and another. She experienced no terrible pain, no burning skin, but rather a gentle caress, like a kiss.

Kittim covered Devorah head to toe. Her last thought was how lovely they were. She felt clean as if she'd bathed in cold spring water and washed away the last remains of Ra'bim corruption.

Farvels filled the wood. They were watching her, silently.

The Books Of Marduk

THE BOOK OF RUNES

CHAPTER SIX – The Whittling Pool

VERSE 5.6.1

A grove of black elms grew in the foothills of the Holy Mountain. They encircled a green pool. Young immature *kittim* floated on the surface of the pool like lotus plants. Once every few days a *kittim* broke free from the surface and ascended into the sky. The rate had been slowly rising for perhaps a century. The Lord Almighty, if he cared to look, would have been able to see the green pool from his lofty plateau.

In the fresh light of the morning, the shimmering face of Elsseleron reflected the daystar like a colossal mirror. The pool swallowed the light and burned with a green fire. Green pools such as this one were special and rare. *In these later days* black elms almost always grew about their banks. The elms were stunted forms of another species of tree that grew about the pools before the coming of the Lord to His Holy Mountain. The ancient priests of the *Runehayana* knew these trees as whittlings.

Stepping off the ancient road that wound its way through the foothills of the mountain, a hobbling traveler came to the pool. He seated himself on its bank and discarded his weather-stained cloak. It was hot here beneath the glare of the Lord.

Exalted Father

The wander's shriveled nut-brown body was covered by darker blotches of *kittim* poisoning. His age was indeterminate, but his green eyes were sunken and his long-braided hair was matted and dirty.

He sat very still and upright. His eyes may have open. He didn't flinch even when a couple of noisy dragon-flies came to inspect him.

He remained here for the entire morning.

Farvels came and went. Some tended the black elms, carefully examining the tender bark, watering, weeding with their claws, stopping every so often to gaze into the green waters of the *kittim* pool.

Naturally the farvels saw the wanderer. They refrained from disturbing him until at last the wanderer exhaled a long sighing breath.

A very old farvel, all silver and white, flashing a hint of gold as he moved, seated himself beside the wanderer. Its eyes were large and green and its voice was as soothing as a fresh breeze on this hot day.

"What'll you do now?" it asked gently.

"Go on. The goal is in sight."

"No more preaching, then?"

The wanderer shook his head sadly. "No, maybe I'll return to composing poetry. Parables perhaps, like Rudra, confusing enough that no one'll understand. Useless occupations. Meaningless. Poetry and parables. No more sermons."

"Come boy, admit your folly."

A faint smile creased the wanderer's face. "Is it not *their* folly, my dear archbishop? Why am I not a farvel? Why was I resurrected in this form? Am I Suthralane?"

The old farvel shook his head.

The other's smile turned into a frown.

"Do you know that the queeti are now at war with one another?" asked the farvel, abruptly changing the subject.

The wanderer looked surprised. "Why no."

"Once they'd defeated the Yakashas they commenced to bicker over exactly what *you* taught them. Worse, they also began to argue over *who you are*. Soon they passed from argument to war. It's terrible, worse than the Yakashas. Worse even than that fraud Vishnu. They say that those on the opposing side are eternally damned. Opponents are not queeti, not us, they say, but wholly other, not-queeti. They slaughter without guilt. In fact, destruction is a moral good."

The wanderer hung his head. "Moral good? *That* is all I wanted—"

"Good?" The farvel emitted a short deep rumble which passed for a laugh. "What's this monster? There's good weather. But all weather's good. There's good sleep, but all sleep is good. Good food, but it's always good to eat. Perhaps even death, especially with the *kittim* around. Good something, even the queeti understand this. You might not think queeti food is good, but nourishment is. Too much is not. So, the is-not is also good. And, what is good today may not be good tomorrow. Does your good not float above our heads like a tree without roots, a field without crops, clouds without a sky? By the way, have you ever seen a poorly designed cloud? What is this monster you call *good*?"

"I saw the suffering of the queeti, the gruesome cruelty of the Lords, random violence, underserved and without purpose. I could not become a Silent Watcher," said the wanderer.

"So act you did?"

"Yes."

"Do you presume to know the destiny of every creature? Can you calculate every tiny whisper of wind? You know only the big ones, the Two Winds. Like us, then, you must watch carefully and not interfere. Watch silently the unfolding. The rains come of themselves without you. Watch, wait, let not thoughts of *good* cloud your mind. Be subtle as the summer breeze. When the queeti are free they will say, we did it ourselves."

"Then why'd they bring me back?"

The farvel gave a very human-like shrug. "For amusement? To see which way a counter-current would go?"

"You don't know, do you?"

"Maybe the Lord knows. Or perhaps He does not. He's very *bad* at giving straight answers, *you know*."

The wanderer studied the farvel. Suddenly he laughed. "I know *you*, mythical beast. I know all about you."

The farvel growled. It sounded identical to the growl of a golden lion. "You know nothing about *me* except those episodes from my story that amused you."

"You climbed Elsseleron and the Lord maimed you for your presumption and arrogance."

"I never climbed yon mountain," the farvel snarled, showing its formidable fangs."

"How can you be such a blatant liar? All the legends agree on this point."

"Ah, see the *kittim*. They're like Nepptali machines, but they're living things. They can build anything. Wanderers and farvels. They are of this world and now we are of this world. The Lord up there is not. He is a Nepptali from the Kingdoms of the Heavens."

"Stop this. Answer my question. The legends say—"

"Nonsense. Stories an old *sramana* told for amusement...for handouts if you want the truth. The bigger the tale the bigger the reward. *The more unbelievable the more believers*."

The wanderer rose stiffly to his feet. "I will still climb yon mountain."

"Go then," said the farvel, "and create the Legend of Suthralane."

The Books Of Marduk

BOOK OF RUNES
VERSE 5.6.2

Greater Wind began just as the wanderer came to Thrice-blessed Cathedral of White Mountain. *Kittim* filled the air. He gathered his cloak and, head down, crossed the wide piazza that formed a vast semi-circle fronting the great cathedral. The cathedral of a hundred blessings, of a hundred columns, the stairs of a hundred steps, but all was in ruin with not a single column standing. He did not bother to count the steps as he painfully mounted them, favoring his left leg.

Pilgrims no longer filled the cathedral. Queeti workshops were deserted and silent. The massive Nepptali turbines that powered the place had been sabotaged. The magnificent and holy interior, so vast and formidable, was dark and empty. Wood was splintered, artwork destroyed, oaken pews smashed and broken.

Death-like silence shouted blasphemies. An uncertain light, filtered through broken stain-glass, populated the interior with shifting shadows and dark, misshapen bodies. It reminded him of the Lordpool back in Nalanda. Even the High Altar had suffered wounds from axe, scythe and hoe.

Undeterred, the wanderer approached the High Altar. He smiled when he spied the glass case which contained an old yellow tooth. It was untouched as were the massive leather-bound papyrus books stacked nearby. He brushed his fingers lovingly over the engraved surfaces. Sandi letters worked into the thick leather spelled: *Runehayana*. Then he noticed that the Books had not gone completely untouched as he'd first thought. Tiny colorless worms crawled out from the papyrus sheets. The slow work of destruction had begun.

The tooth, as large as a man's fist, must have once belonged to one of the great leviathans from the Middle Sea. The wanderer laughed to himself. The archbishop said that the tooth was that of a man, and he had surely convinced himself of this fact.

(Believers it is so. You must not doubt.)

Another stood beside him.

A ponderous, shapeless mass detached itself from the enveloping darkness. Dressed in rich, crimson robes, jewel-encrusted and threaded with gold, the vaguely man-like form appeared to be King Ra' himself. Upon closer inspection in better light, the wanderer saw that it was indeed a man, grossly fat and very old, who seemed to walk by shifting from one hip to the other in a kind of pendulum-like gait that inched forward.

The Holy Father.

"Well, we never truly believed our son the archbishop. Although we are generally in the habit of believing *anything* when it's useful. And here you are, tooth intact we trust. We know thee, *sramana*, from our days in Nalanda."

The sudden appearance of the Holy Father didn't seem to startle the wanderer. He continued to gaze lovingly at the *Runehayana*.

The Holy Father followed his gaze and emitted a deep chuckle. "It's obsolete, you know."

"What is?"

"The *Runehayana*, the Lord's ancient babblings. Did you know that there're so many more, books upon books, upon books? Thousands upon thousands. The Nepptali preserved them. This copy belonged to them, and if you care to examine it you'll discover many differences—why, outright contradictions, between these and those of the priesthood. Foolish priests. Most of it's useless except for the technical stuff."

"Why is that, Duke Rudra?"

The Holy Father chocked his head and gave a clipped laugh. "Baiting me, huh? Well, because we got ourselves—or the queeti do—a new Almighty Lord. *You*, my boy. *Thou art Him.* Might as well grind that old tooth into dust. Thing is as big as a boulder anyways. We've got you. We'd guess the *kittim* had something to do with your resurrection."

"Very perceptive of you, Rudra. But I'd have preferred otherwise."

"Yes, well, of course... Hmm... the principle must be the same, *kittim* must work the same way as the Lord's self-assembled monolayers. Oh, forgive us the technical language. You've not read the Nepptali textbooks, have you?"

The wanderer turned and faced him. "Rudra, tell me, what lives on the summit of Elsseleron?"

"Nothing *lives* there," the Holy Father said with alacrity.

"Then, all this?" The wanderer waved a hand over the books.

"Why, we thought you smarter than that. The ancient priesthood, of course. They believed they perceived meaningful shadows beneath the surface of their green pool. But their pool was merely one of many in this world, just a deep and dark pool choked with weeds. The Nepptali possessed the original, we believe. Who can be certain of such things? Isn't belief wonderful, my boy? Really fills the gaps, hey?"

"And so you slaughtered them."

Rudra shrugged. "Not we. They. They slaughtered themselves. They were the first to know—"

"Know what?"

Rudra shrugged again. "*We* were coming to an end. But let us not concern ourselves with such things. The queeti believe in *you*. We must make good use of this opportunity."

"I see no opportunity."

"Oh but there is. We'll rule this world yet. Our son the archbishop's already laid the foundations. You, *sramana*, are their *savior*. You brought them out of their bondage to the White Lords. You'll be no invisible Lord-on-the-Mountain who is infinitely malleable because He is invisible. No, no, they'll *see* you, touch you, hear you. You are a *thou*. The archbishop worked out the details years ago. He's quite clever when it comes to lying."

"What sits on yon mountain's plateau, Rudra?"

"Nothing!" The Holy Father's bearded face twisted ever so slightly. "Forget that silly Suthralane nonsense... Yes, yes, we know all about your obsession. One would think that your resurrection would have canceled it."

The wanderer laughed softly as though at some interior joke. "It appears that many consider it their duty to educate me on my faults. Still, no one is able to explain *why* the *kittim* brought me back."

"They're mindless things, living machines without consciousness, without a purpose."

"Machines without a purpose?"

"We will provide the purpose."

"No, Rudra. I'm on the road to Elsseleron."

"Be careful, my son, you may die the true death this time."

The wanderer smiled.

The Holy Father's eyes narrowed and his brow wrinkled as if in concentration. Finally, seemingly making a profound decision, he said gravely: "You'll find wreckage and ruin, shattered dreams and designs, shattered remnants of great power, *and no Lord*."

"Ah Rudra, such a liar. You do it so well. I don't doubt what you say is literally true, though it is a lie."

The Holy Father drew a jeweled dagger from the vast folds of his shapeless robe. The wanderer was looking back to the books and appeared not to notice.

"I will put the Lord Almighty to the test."

The Holy Father scratched his beard and hid the dagger behind his back. His eyes shone in the dull light and his bloodless lips turned a sneer, revealing black and broken teeth. He studied the wanderer thoughtfully.

Minutes passed. Finally, he coughed and said: "You're correct, my son. We confess it. Just now, we did indeed spin a yarn. Such is called theology according to the archbishop. That's no excuse. *There is something on the mountain.* Something horrid, beyond hideous." His voice broke and he took a deep breath. "The Kingdoms of the Heavens did fall as the old legends say."

"You've seen it?"

The Holy Father gave a slight nod that could have been a shake of the head.

"Take me there."

"So be it. It's a long climb through the dug-out gorges and up ancient stairs. The winds and rains are dangerous."

The Holy Father backed into the shadows and sheathed his dagger. From a small table near the altar he took a loaf of moldy bread and a crude queeti gourde.

"Let's eat and drink to our success. Here's the archbishop's beer. Bread's been scarce since the rebellion and we've had to bake our own. Take it. You'll need your strength, and plenty of strong beer to face the Lord."

The wanderer accepted the bread which crumbled through his fingers. He ate a small morsel and then drank from the gourde.

The Holy Father ate and drank as well. He grinned. "We'd rather drink good ole Banalis wine," he remarked.

Exalted Father

BOOK OF RUNES
VERSE 5.6.3

Two pilgrims ascended the Mountain of the Lord and came to stand upon a great plateau. It was late afternoon of the third day of their pilgrimage.

The Lord's Mountain resembled a colossal cone that had been sliced diagonally across by a giant scythe sweeping down from the sky. On the north side of what was otherwise a sheer glass-like surface, a deep gorge had been cut into the rock—by wind, or water, or queeti or a combination of the three—the Holy Father knew not. A cold fog encircled the base of the mountain cone.

The Holy Father stumbled upon the rough stairs. He fell once and cursed many times. He uttered many profane words about the Lord-on-the-Mountain, especially having to do with the Lord's anatomy, which obviously had to be allegorical, although he sounded quite literal.

The wanderer appeared as light-footed and nimble as a mountain goat.

Five times during their ascent the mountain rains soaked them. Each rain transformed the gorge into a small river. That the Holy Father was not swept away surely counted as a sign from the Lord Almighty. At last the gorge opened wide and a series of massive stairs cut into the rock brought them to the slanted plateau.

A freezing mist covered the mountain top. Elsseleron's surface was a pockmarked mass of volcanic rock, sharp, crystalized spearpoints, and fantastic stone figures carved from living rock in the fearsome heat of creation, as the *Runehayana* described it and the wanderer remembered. He'd once recalculated those Runes, in a former life, but now he laughed to see the material forms that gave rise to his foolish calculations.

The Books Of Marduk

The Holy Father paused to catch his breath. He glared at the wanderer. "What's so funny?"

Rudra was used to being carried about seated in a sedan chair. Three days of physical exertion soured his mood, and his carefully contrived geniality faded and ran like the cheap queeti dyes of his gaudy robes.

"The Books. No matter how we read them, even adding passages liberally, devising as many doctrines as we wished, even then—"

"Farvel shit, eh?" the Holy Father growled. "And you believed you had all the Tribes fooled?"

The wanderer shrugged. "Why not? The more ridiculous we made it the more they believed. We believed even while we knew—"

"Don't fool yourself, fool. Despite what you knew you still believed."

"Who's the fool, Rudra? In the light you are brave and conceited. But when night comes and the winds howl, then the world becomes sinister and indistinct. Then you hear the Runes and do not laugh."

"Well, just you wait, my son." The Holy Father slid his hand inside his robes. The wanderer noticed but said no more.

They stood at the gateway to the plateau gazing east. The rays of the setting daystar seemed to bounce off something at the far end of the plateau. That *something* loomed at the boundary-edge of their horizon, a massive shadowy thing that soared above the broken surface and somehow reflected light. They began climbing towards it.

As they came closer, they saw a great pyramid-like mass of shiny metal resting at the far, elevated end of the plateau, its lofty point nearly piercing the clouds. The metal was as smooth as glass and perfectly reflected the daystar.

"There," said the Holy Father with difficulty. He gave the wanderer a strange look. "That is what you seek, though it is not what you believe."

Exalted Father

"What do I believe, Rudra?"

"That you're Suthra the Lame, and like him you'll put the Lord to the test. Poor fool."

"Then what is that thing? It looks like some kind of giant Nepptali fortress."

The Holy Father turned and faced him. "Tell us, my boy, how do you feel?"

The wanderer frowned. "Well, as long as you ask, I could use some more of that old bread we've been eating these past days. Did you bake it yourself?"

"All gone," said the Holy Father.

"And the beer?"

"Drank it all."

"No Banalis wine?"

"None."

"A shame. It would be nice to have a last meal before we visit the Lord."

"Yes. Especially you, my boy."

"Especially me...? Now tell me, Rudra, what is that damned thing?"

The Holy Father shrugged. "That's the whole secret. *We don't know.* But if we were to guess we'd say it is something the Nepptali engineered. Nepptali bastards ruled the Tribes of Men from the first day they settled Greenbottom. All else, the Unified Kingdom, even Nalanda, served their rule, consciously or not"

"The Nepptali?"

"We don't know exactly how they managed it. They're clever, especially in the art of number manipulation, you know, ciphering. The whole stupid Rune-scheme was their invention. They may have had a pact with the Ra'bim too. So-called medicinal somas made people gullible. Nepptali invented the Lord Almighty. Something like that."

"They came here? But when?"

"Don't know. Probably during the First Kalpa."

"But why?"

"Why not? Because they could."

"And the White Fathers? The King?"

The Holy Father hesitated. "Mountain demons," he said as though searching for the words. The archbishop has a theory, that the Nepptali woke them, aroused them from their slumber on these freezing peaks...that they were actually *of* cold and stone...or something....and the Nepptali gave them life, if only for a time. They're returning to the stone from which they came. Or something. The archbishop's imagination is endlessly fertile, unlike the daughters of men."

The wanderer laughed suddenly. "No, no, Rudra. There's more to it. Much more."

He paused and gazed across the rock-strewn plateau.

"Holy Father, know you my story?"

"The archbishop's version or the truth?"

"I am truly resurrected. The *kittim* are like your Nepptali—"

"Yes, yes," said the Holy Father impatiently, "we know that one too. Rudra was in the grave three days before his own resurrection. You hibernated for fifty years. A real feat, but not all that unusual for a *sramana*, especially one stuffed with Ra'bim somas. You should've seen old Vishnu. He turned black and bloated, and floated down the river like a log. Our canaries actually witnessed the event."

The wanderer smiled. "Why do you refuse to acknowledge what you really know?"

"We know... not," said the Holy Father, growing wary.

"You know it was not Ra'bim somas."

"We know not," said the Holy Father firmly.

"A *sramana* died. But no-thing was resurrected. *He was reconstructed*. He is a *ghoul,* but he is a ghoul who belongs to this world. The *kittim* saw to that. You are a ghoul but you do not belong, and you know. The queeti are right. We're ghouls. Marduk was a ghoul. Rudra was a ghoul, and a ghoul he remains even after his resurrection. We've come home. *This is the house of ghouls.*"

The Holy Father shook his head. "No, no, listen. Nepptali power can be ours. We are their true heirs. The power, its secret, is in the Runes."

"Ah, Rudra, go ahead and construct your new world and set it against this one. You still must use the very dirt and waste of this world. That's the catch…and the flaw."

The Holy Father ignored him. He was looking across the plateau. "It's all in the Nepptali Runes. The archbishop understands them perfectly. He calculates, he translates, he recalculates and retranslates, and all over again. The work drives him mad. He drinks and gives sermons. Oh how he gives sermons! He is a logic-machine, he is. Maybe you'll hear one someday."

The wanderer laughed. "Old Theophilus knew his Runes all right, and he could give sermons when the brandy was good. But he is no longer archbishop."

"What is this foolishness? You know we speak of the new one, our much-prized son."

"Father Leo?"

"Stop! Play the fool no longer. The archbishop understands. We fear for his sanity, though. He spouts crazy words 'bout the Kingdoms of the Heavens, some weird insects he calls nano-bugs. He speaks of other beings called mono-layers that secrete a Ra'bim soma he calls *deox-hee-rhino-newman-soma*, or some such nonsense. Nepptali and Ra'bim invented it together. It soaks into the soil and living things pop up like mushrooms. And that's us, and the Yakashas, and the Yellows, Grays, but not the queeti. So you see, friend wanderer, this is why we ought to rule. Congratulations, you've learned the secret from the lips of the Holy Father himself. *Thou hast heard.*"

The wanderer smiled but said nothing.

The Holy Father sighed. "You still don't believe, do you?"

The wanderer looked east. "You forget, Rudra, that I was once a scholar of the Runes."

"We speak of Nepptali Runes. The archbishop, formerly your old friend Jacob, was also a scholar, and he understands the technical parts."

"Ah, so that's him. I was wondering. Seems much happened while I slept. And just where is the humble ox? Sneaking up to slip a knife in my ribs?"

The Holy Father laughed. "Heavens no. He'll be along shortly. He had an important task to complete."

"My task is not yet completed."

"Go on then," said the Holy Father, his hand inside his robes, "thou art Suthralane."

EXALTED FATHER

BOOK OF RUNES
<u>VERSE 5.6.4</u>

The mountain winds formed a chorus of suffering voices moaning and crying in helpless agony. The winds blew from the east as if to push them away. They stumbled over ancient volcanic rock worked into eerie forms.

The formations resembled living beings. Some they recognized without much trouble, but others appeared strangely distorted. Not a few had to be of creatures long extinct, for these, though they were similar to living things, were still quite different. Some seemed utterly impossible, so grotesque that they could never have achieved life. It was as if a clumsy-fingered sculptor had tried to mold hot liquid rock into creatures taken from childhood nightmares. In fact, the artist seemed to be making a mockery of living things, perhaps from experiment, or playfulness, or downright wickedness.

Here was a wild boar with fins where there should have been legs. Here a water bird with a serpent's tail and a body covered by fish scales. Over there was a thing with a goat head stuck upon a confused torso of man-like arms and hands fused with a horse's body. It looked as if once upon a time a sea-creature existed on the mountain, but one that was a cross between a crocodile and a dog. Bodies that resembled the White Lords—white stone giants sprouting scaly tails— lay scattered haphazardly as if they'd been slain in battle. All were sickeningly distorted. Some had snakes for hair, eyes for genitals, heads on the ends of tails. Others looked reptilian, like giant lizards. One seemed to have grown colonies of tendril-like cilia in those places where there should have ears. Seemingly fashioned from volcanic rock, all of them remained eternally frozen in some artist's terrible mocking jest of nature.

As they came closer to the pyramid, the fossils became more chaotic and horrid. Here they noticed odd metal objects strewn about, massive metal eggs gathered in rocky nests, some silver, others black and gold. There were narrow cones of bright metal, thick cables and rope-like vines that might have been the entrails of monstrous beasts. Long transparent tubes filled with thick yellow fluid, like giant brown snakes from the Reed Sea marshes, led to the base of the pyramid.

The Holy Father, dagger in hand, picked his way through the debris. The wanderer followed.

Exalted Father

BOOK OF RUNES
VERSE 5.6.5

The daystar dropped below the rim of Elsseleron. Its last rays bounced off the upper tiers of the massive structure, which, as they came close, appeared to be constructed from some other-worldly metal, hard, smooth, seamless, reflecting images clearer than glass.

A jagged opening had been cut into the gleaming material at the base. Thick, transparent cables fell out of the ragged wound. Moist, coiled, and rubbery, the nest of cables resembled a heap of worms. Sinking into the rocky mountain floor, they carried a silver thick fluid that seemed to pump into the body of Elsseleron. Some were thicker than a man's thigh, others as thin and fragile as vines from the southern forest.

A putrid smell hung in the air, much like the odor of decaying vegetation. The foul gases seemed to resist the freezing winds of the high mountain. Here the climate was warm and moist.

The Holy Father peered into the opening. "Look here, my lord *sramana*," he said, pointing inside.

The wanderer gazed into the hole. It was dark, but not totally so. Inside were thousands of tiny lights. He moved closer. The cavity appeared huge and complex. It seemed to be filled with an intricate maze of honeycombs built from sheets, panels, of silver metal, thin as a page of papyrus and just as flexible. The panels were arranged in parallel, running vertically from the floor to the ceiling, or so he guessed, since they disappeared in the upper darkness. Many were cracked, some broken in half. They were separated from each other by less than a finger. And now, as his eyes adjusted, he saw other panels running horizontally, cutting through the verticals, forming millions of square cells that reached back into the interior and disappeared in the darkness. Irregular gaps broke the symmetry of the honeycomb.

Because of these random opennings, he saw that the entire interior was filled with what seemed to be an infinite series of cells in three dimensions. Each cell was so tiny that from a distance it appeared flat, like a two-dimensional square somehow carved into space.

Some of the cells contained tiny lights that glowed brightly. They resembled small diamonds set into the soft metal and were of different shapes. Many more cells were dark. Cells behind cells behind cells, lights behind lights, darkness behind darkness…all reaching into to a vanishing boundary of material existence, and perhaps beyond, with dimensionality itself going from two to three, and perhaps beyond, as complex as an infinite number of many-sided jewels perfectly reflecting one another endlessly.

"The Lord's brain," whispered the Holy Father. "Who but the Nepptali could have built such a thing? The White Lords call it the Ark, whatever that means. They were trying to build one in Tharas Major. But they failed. Queeti cannot decipher Nepptali diagrams." He laughed.

"Not Nepptali," the wanderer declared in a calm voice. "Not Nepptali—"

"Then who?"

"Ghouls."

"Still playing the fool, huh?"

"Ghouls of the Heavens."

The Holy Father spat. "Foolish priest. Look closely. See those engravings inside the lighted cells? *Runes*! Runes of the Tribes of Men."

The wanderer saw it. The lighted cells bore Runes, Runes stamped into the shinning metal. Runes, the Four Major Runes of the *Runehayana*.

EXALTED FATHER

And then he saw that some of the cells were flashing, very slowly, on and off in what seemed to be regular cycles. The transparent cables pumped silver blood into the rocks in rhythm with the oscillations of the flashing lights.

The Holy Father moved close, his massive bulk forcing the wanderer inside.

"It's difficult to see 'cause they're so small and there's so many, and the cycles are so slow. If you study them long enough you'll notice that each cell cycles with a different time. But taken together there appears to be a master cycle that governs the entire nest as far back as you can see. Given more time and patience, you'll see that the entire sequence of cycles forms a repeating pattern, a single cycle that never changes."

The wanderer seemed puzzled. "A pattern?"

"The *same pattern*...spelling out a series of Runes, and that pattern repeats itself, again and again."

Abruptly the wanderer laughed. "You're telling me that Lord *is* stuck?"

"Yeah. The Ark's stuck, frozen up. That's the secret."

"The Lord's suffered a breakdown?"

"Not the Lord. The Nepptali."

"How long, Rudra?"

"A Kalpa. Maybe more."

"Ah, Rudra, don't you see? The Lord began with a stutter, and finally passed into pronouncing gibberish, and the gibberish became flesh, like Yakashas, or White Lords, or maybe us. Then He just froze up, like you see now. *The Lord kept saying the same thing. And then He shut up and said nothing.*"

The Holy Father stared at him.

"The Nepptali are gone. The archbishop's a hopeless drunk. Only you, Lord Marduk. Only you, *priest* Marduk can heal this thing."

"I'm a wanderer, Rudra. Marduk died long ago."

"So did Rudra."

"No, Grand Duke. You're a ghoul. As I once was. The Yadish, the Akkadeans, Ra'bim, Banalis, Nepptali...all ghouls. This thing is the Lord of ghouls. That's the secret of Suthralane."

"Not so, not so—" The Holy Father's voice trembled and white froth wet his beard. "No one like you...*You were the only priest to ever write your own verses!*"

"Did Jacob tell you that?" The wanderer laughed. "A priest died. Then a *sramana* died. A wanderer rose. Two gazed up, the other down—"

"It is your destiny. You will heal the Ark. See that square of cells in the middle there—" He pointed. The center cells were all dark. Lights flashed on and off all around them, but a large central square of cells remained inert. There were sixteen such cells. The wanderer studied them and silently tried to work out the series of their Runes.

"A priest died, then a *sramana*..."

The Holy Father shook his head. "You do remember. We see it in your eyes. Resurrection does not abolish memory. We know thee, Marduk."

"The secret of Suthralane..."

"Yes, yes, that series of cells, the Runes etched into them. They contain a sequence all their own. Not the stupid fractions that connect them to Sandi. They connect to something else. Look. If you touch them they light. What is missing? The archbishop failed. He could find the missing Rune. We over-estimated him. Only *you*, you—*thou*."

"This thing does not belong here," the wanderer said softly. It sounded as if he were reciting a verse. "It's a product of madness, beyond madness. Let it die, as in the Kingdoms of the Heavens."

"Fool!" the Holy Father bellowed. "The Nepptali who built this thing were the Kings of the Heavens. Now they've gone and we've come. We are *King!*" His voice fell. "You know the truth. You who died like us. You've experienced the dread, the hollowness, the stony silence. There are no more children to come after us. We are the end and the conclusion. Restore this thing and you restore the meaning, the purpose of our existence. *You resurrect the fruit of our loins.* Our Kingdom shall have no end."

The wanderer shook his head sadly.

The Holy Father moved surprisingly fast. With a one powerful, claw-like hand, he seized the wanderer by the neck and with his other brought the dagger point to his jugular.

"Do it!" he hissed. "Complete the sequence."

The wanderer did not resist.

"Do it, damn you!"

"Release me," the wanderer croaked.

The Holy Father's eyes narrowed with suspicion. But he let go and stepped back.

The wanderer studied the panel. He reached into the folds of his cloak and brought forth three crumpled pages of Runes. The papyrus was old and torn and much of its writing had faded. The wanderer studied the pages and looked back to the panel. He felt great joy. Here the Runes were simply Runes. No fractions. Nothing was indeterminate. The old arbitrary rules were gone, for there was no transliteration into the Sandi. He had no need for meaning.

He reached out and touched the dead cells. His finger moved smoothly, tapping out a sequence. He did not pause.

Moving left to right, he began with the four Runes: X∧iV
Then: X
Followed by: ∧
And: i
V
X∧
Xi
XV
∧i

ᚱV
ᛁV
XᛁV
ᚱᛁV
XᛁV
Xᚱᛁ

He turned to the Holy Father and said: "On the Mountain of the Lord is the sacrifice accomplished." He tapped the sixteenth cell. *It lighted but it was empty.* No Rune disturbed its perfect emptiness.

Exalted Father

BOOK OF RUNES
VERSE 5.6.6

The queeti army halted its march just as Lesser Wind swept down from the north. They'd come to the eastern foothills of the Lord's Mountain, to the outer precincts of Thrice-blessed White Cathedral.

For many days—indeed, they'd lost count—the queeti had advanced unopposed. Some claimed that the last wisps had been killed at the Battle of Olive, where the slaughter was so great that the Redrain River turned to blood.

Every known road had passed into queeti paws. The great fortress-cities had fallen. Only White Cathedral remained, and finally the Mountain of the evil Exalted Father.

Six-fingered Augustii led the armies. The legions named him Augustii Magnus Victorious. The commoners knew him as *The Great Hetman*.

Kittim filled the air. The queeti paid them no heed. The butterfly creatures never touched a single bull, female or cub. They fluttered over their shaggy heads, moving south.

The queeti were setting camp when the ground began to quake. Suddenly, from the mountain came a blinding flash of light. The entire eastern horizon, fading into dusk, abruptly erupted with a blazing fire as if the daystar had instantaneously reversed course and fell upon the mountain. The flash was followed by a boom that penetrated to bone. A thousand times more deafening than the mightiest clap of thunder, it set them wailing and covering their ears.

The painful brilliance forced them to look away. Those who inadvertently gazed into the fireball would never see again.

The impossible light shone for many minutes. A fierce heat swept down upon them, followed by a curtain of black smoke and ash laced by lightning from the sky. Bolts flashed in every direction. Thunder rolled like a forest of drums. A giant black cloud swirled upwards, billowing out like an expanding balloon. The cloud met with Lesser Wind and strove against it. Like two giants, Lesser Wind and the black cloud traded blows.

Half an hour passed. Lesser Wind finally died away. The black cloud and its lightning bolts passed east of the mountain and out over the sea.

The queeti finally looked up. *Holy Elsseleron had exploded.*

EXALTED FATHER

THE BOOK OF RUNES

CHAPTER SEVEN – The Borderlands

VERSE 5.7.1

A peaceful morning fog hung suspended over the golden fields of the Redrain River valley. Flocks of *kittim* circled overhead, soaring high in the thin upper atmosphere, flying nowhere, for no purpose but to fly. Greater Wind gently brushed the tall wheat sending ripples over the fields. It gradually swept away the morning fog leaving the land fresh and clean.

Autumn had come to Starmirror. This morning's wind bore the chill of the north. Soon the daystar would break the jagged mountain horizon and warm the land, and the last wisps of fog that lingered in the lowlands would melt away like snow in the spring.

East of the valley, where Dewdrop Moon awaited the coming of the daystar, a thin spiral of smoke still rose from the blasted wreckage of Elsseleron. No more a mountain of mirror-like faces, Needleglass, as the old priests translated the Runes, it had become a smoldering black wreckage coughing with deep volcanic activity. Poisonous fumes issued from gaping crevices. No living creature dared approach the mountain. None could physically approach it even if they wanted to. Its base, and spreading many leagues beyond, was a field of sharp black rocks that created a landscape of knife-like serrated spires. Its atmosphere was poison to all living creatures.

(A poisonous, lingering heat bathed the blast area for thousands of years. Fallout, they labled it. The more superstitious among them believed that it was the entrance to the Underworld—*in those times.*)

EXALTED FATHER

BOOK OF RUNES
VERSE 5.7.2

On this glorious morning, two people, a man and a woman, sat beneath an old black elm overlooking a large green pond, almost the size of a lake and just as deep. On another day some might have argued that it was a lake.

They rested in sight of the ruined mountain. Everything about you is beautiful, the man had said. When I called to you, you did not answer, she'd replied. He kissed her lips. She traced his jawline with her finger, softly, like the wings of a *kittim,* her finger tips brushed his neck, his chest…

I still loved you, he'd said. She smiled and gently pushed him back, exploring further, and then mounting him. They each discovered a new experience that was an old memory. Their bodies *knew,* their cells, their molecules; the resurrection was full and complete.

Now they lay listening to the distant rush of the Topartz River and talking softly in broken sentences filled with long pauses. Across the pond-lake, farvels tended the ancient trees that grew about the banks of the pool and gave it shade. Upon occasion a rather old, gray-bearded, one-eyed farvel would lift its lion-head and gaze upon the mountain. Sometimes a dark-furred farvel, and a third all white and silver, would join it. The three stared at the blackened mountain for many minutes and then returned to their work. Silent Watchers.

The woman wore her black hair short and braided in the style of Akkad. Her skin was soft, wrinkle-free and very dark, a rich dark brown like a hazel nut. It had lost its former unhealthy pale hue. Her body was slender and strong, perfect of line and form, like a statue carved by the loving hands of a master artist. *Kittim* generative power, molecule by molecule, was flawless.

She laughed.

The man turned his head and looked at her. He wore his long black hair free-flowing in the style of the ancient priesthood during the First Kalpa. His skin was golden and his eyes bright green.

"Why do you laugh? Is it because I've forgotten my vows? Not that they would matter, even if I could recall them. I've forgotten so I could remember."

"I laugh at the winds, the trees, the pool, those farvels. The Lord's Mountain. And at you. *I remember my vow.*"

"To kill me?"

"Yes. But not a priest. Not a *sramana*. Not Marduk."

"What then?"

"A condition. A world—"

"Ah, poor girl, the *kittim* beat you to it."

"I laugh at the *kittim* too."

He looked up and saw the moth-like creatures dancing merrily in the wind. Abruptly a large flock of them, mostly green and yellow, separated itself from the main cloud and headed northeast towards the mountain.

"They are—the music of the world," he said. "Twice have they sung to me. I should think the second time was more difficult given the celestial fire that destroyed the mountain. It separates the very elements, you know."

"Still the priest," she chided him, "still the *sramana*."

He gazed at her with bright green eyes which were the color of grass after a summer's rain. "I am sorry for that," he said. "Vows are foolish things. Whatever they are meant to accomplish, these small, miserly conceits always turn out to be self-serving. They end up hurting those we love, even innocent bystanders. They try to avoid corruptions, temptations— they reject despair and melancholy, anger and hatred. But these things are existence. Cancel them and you cancel life. They reject the necessary intoxication of living. They put aside the pain of life. They are fit only for beings of stone, like the White Lords. I'm sorry. My new vow is to reject all vows—"

He picked up a smooth stone that looked like a crystal sphere. It bore the faded imprint of a tiny sea creature, a curled horn-like thing. He held it up in the growing light. "*Life,*" he said. "Not even the Nepptali for all their skill could achieve such a thing. Not even the Lord-on-the-Mountain."

He placed the crystal jewel in her hand. She leaned over and kissed him.

Once again they shed their orange robes and made love. Still patient, still as gentle as the *kittim*, they came together more fiercely, as if the daystar freed itself from the ruined horizon and burned the grasses.

And when they finished, the daystar had indeed reached its zenith, and the farvels had vanished.

Again she laughed. "Why *us*, oh vow-less priest?"

He shrugged. "They come to us, and others, as you can see. They took us, bit by bit. They replaced those bits, one at time, down to the very elements. See these orange robes they have made for us? It is as if they've replaced a thread at a time, one by one, with the same material, until it is a robe of completely new threads. Yet it retains an identical form and style. It is the same robe? Or different? A farvel told me."

"Not the same," she said solemnly. "They made improvements." Then she winked.

The man laughed. "I know."

"You know despite the vows? Your very cells know."

"Not merely that," the man laughed. "What the inept Lord-machine designed inside the *kittim* placed outside. It takes some getting used to— as you may have noticed." He laughed. "The *kittim*, I think, ended the curse of Suthralane. It was not the barrenness of women but the poor design of men, the sacks that hold seed of men should have been on the outside so that the seed does not burn up within the body. The Lord-on-the-Mountain did a poor job of reconstruction. A farvel told me."

"What else did the farvel tell?"

"The silver one compared the *kittim* to the finest Nepptali artisans, except to say that the Nepptali were like bungling amateurs, like the stupid Lord they emulated. Like Him, they could only reconstruct. They could copy but not create. The *kittim* resurrected—and created. They are the thoughts of this world, but their thoughts are the very seeds of all material things. He said that the Lord was an insane Nepptali who came from the *outside*. *We were His thoughts.* He was a bungler and we were not of this world. Now we are."

"This does not answer my original question. Why us?"

"Don't you know?"

She thought for a moment and then gently touched his face with a kiss.

"I know," she said.

EXALTED FATHER

BOOK OF RUNES
VERSE 5.7.3

A man and a woman, the woman and the man, went up from Starmirror and returned to the land of Greenbottom. They settled in Nalanda. It is also said that they visited Haran, Ai, Bethsham, journeying as far north as Emerald. They avoided Tholos for it had become an impossible bog of black water and choking fumes. But wherever else they went they discovered rich and fertile lands, and an overwhelming diversity of life.

In the springtime of the following year, the woman gave birth to a healthy baby girl. Others of their kind joined them, refuges from the Great Northern War. Many were Yads, a few were Akkadeans, and others came from the Banalis, Gad, Yasshur, Din and Symen Tribes. None were Zubs or Rabs, or Nepptali. Of the Min-Vena and Li'way no one knows, although queeti travelers from later times claim that the north has an over-abundance of farvels.

Every single refugee bore a *kittim* stain, it is said, and many were of extreme old age, although a significant number were young. Many bore the signs of resurrection. In time, there were children—as many as the stars in heaven, so the priestly saying goes. Every time a child was born the women laughed. A few women claimed that the Lord-on-the-Mountain opened their wombs. But the Lord-on-the-Mountain was no more, and the wombs of women had never been closed. It was the poor design of men. So said the vast majority of the women.

The men added that since the Lord-on-the-Mountain was no more, so too His curse of Suthralane was no more. When the Lord died so too did His sinners. Thus did fertility return to the Tribes of Men.

It is hard to say that anyone took such explanations seriously.

The *kittim* still came with the Winds, winter and summer, and it seemed that their numbers multiplied with the years.

Thus did the Third Kalpa complete its thousand years as recorded by queeti poet-historians.

EXALTED FATHER

BOOK OF RUNES
VERSE 5.7.4

Sometime during the following Kalpa the remnants of the Tribes of Men vanished from the world, which was quite surprising given their revival and sheer numbers. No queeti knows what became of them, or when, or how, or if they lived somewhere else—and nothing has ever been discovered of their burial places, if there even are burial places— and to this day.

And none know the fate of the wanderer, once priest, once *sramana*, or his wife, once warrior, Once-Queen. And so must we be content with the tradition that he wrote all this, and he struggled against the Lord face to face.

The Books Of Marduk

SUPPLEMENTAL 1

Quite unreliable as we know them to be, the queeti poet-historians of primitive times say that the War of Liberation dragged on for another twenty years. Even though the Augustii sacked and destroyed villages and towns of those traitorous queeti who remained loyal to the White Fathers, and subject these outcastes to wholesale slaughter, there still remained pockets of red and yellow wisps that resisted his authority. They fought hard and demonstrated a great deal of cunning. At last, they were driven north across the straits into the Edom desert where no queeti cared to follow. Their fate remains unknown to this day.[24]

It is also claimed that a smattering of gray wisps fled into the jungles of the Topartz where they suffered a long decline, ultimately dwindling into a stunted species of tree-dwellers. They lost the power of speech and became shrunken in body and mind.

The Augustii attempted to hunt them down but gave up the enterprise in a short time, proclaiming that a war against animals was ridiculous and beneath his dignity. A few wisps, as hairy as monkeys, were captured and placed in zoos. Things being what they were, this tiny population failed to reproduce and died off quickly. Again, not a trace of them has been discovered.

Over the centuries winds and storms gradually reduced the great fortress-cities to worn heaps of rock and sand. The winds howl through their rugged peaks, and some say they can still hear the voice

---

[24] Modern paleontologists have yet to discover a single Yakashas fossil. They must remain, therefore, creatures of myth and legend.

Exalted Father

of an entity they call the Old-Woman-of-the-Mountain thundering commands to vast invisible armies. In the mountains winds do make eerie sounds, it is true. Yet they are merely winds.

The son of Augustii Victorious, Augustii Imperious, sponsored the collection, transcription and translation into the queeti vernacular of the *Five Books of Marduk*, also labeled (in the vulgar parlance of the present times) *Exalted Father*.[25]

He also commissioned popular histories of the era, but these were no more than fabulous stories and national legends documenting the rise of the queeti. What follows in this Supplemental are a few samples from these popular texts. We include them mainly out of antiquarian curiosity and because, in some vague sense (we hope), they convey a feeling for those strange, long-lost eras.

---

[25] Unfortunately for scholars, this queeti version superseded all other collections of the Books, including those in ancient Sandi. Augustii Imperious ordered the destruction of Sandi collections, of which merely a few fragments have been recovered (excepting, of course, the recently discovered *Confessions*). Today, no complete uncorrupted version of *Exalted Father* exists. The fragments show signs of tampering, both in redactions and interpolations. Some scholars say that there are ancient scrolls buried in the ruins of Nalanda, yet archaeologists have failed to uncover a single scroll. The place has been thoroughly excavated.

THE BOOKS OF MARDUK

SUPPLEMENTAL 2

The Earliest Queeti Legend:

This early legend tells of how a terrible Demon-Lord inhabited the mountain Elsseleron. The Demon-Lord yoked the queeti with all sorts of impossible burdens. He made of the queeti a race of slaves. No queeti dared approach his mountain for the Demon-Lord would send forth clouds of poisonousness smoke and bolts of celestial fire. The Demon-Lord also called forth (formed) foul creatures who were dark minions of the netherworld. They fed upon queeti flesh.

In those dark times a mysterious being came to the queeti, a strange wandering creature they called *Liberator*. This being, also named *He-With-Us*, became their savior. They later came to call him *Exalted Father*.

Exalted Father, whose spirit guides the queeti to this day, journeyed to Elsseleron, climbed the mountain and did battle with the Demon-Lord in the name of the queeti. After a titanic struggle which shook the foundations of the world and destroyed the mountain utterly, Exalted Father threw the Demon-Lord down into ruin. He freed the queeti who then destroyed the lesser demonic beings that served the Demon-Lord.

The queeti disagreed over questions of the savior's kind, over what sort of being He was and where he came from. It was generally agreed that, after much debate and not a few minor wars, He came from the Kingdoms of the Heavens. A few heretics obstinately refused to accept this conclusion and were executed in the most fiendish ways. After several centuries, priests dropped the word "exalted" and simply named him *Father*. Theologians claimed that the Father descended from the Kingdoms of the Heavens in the humble form of a wandering monk to live among the queeti, and that He taught them the arts of civilization. Before He departed, he appointed the Augustii Victorious and the Priest Silver as His successors, for they had been His closest disciples and eyewitnesses to His many miracles, including His defeat of the Demon-Lord.

A Second Account:

Later priests came to reject this story, calling it infantile, naïve history that appealed to those simpletons who wallowed in the pleasure of their senses and sought frivolous fulfillments. The so-called Father, these critics argued, was pure spirit and had always been pure spirit. He was invisible, omniscient, omnipresent, immortal, and all-good—the thunder is His voice and the celestial fire His sword. Nothing was like Him, nothing could define Him.

In these sophisticated times, say deep-thinkers, the rebuttal of such humbug seems so obvious it barely needs mention. Back then it was a major discovery. Today the fallacy seems so blatant it is surprising any sane individual might believe it:

If nothing was like Him, and nothing could define Him, then how could any analogy or metaphor, or even a single word, signify anything remotely intelligible?

How could queeti priests of antiquity believe that any formula even came close to describing what could not be described?

A Third (Primitive) Account:

Priests say that the Father wrestled with the Demon-Lord on the summit of the mountain. Ancient veterans of that time—some claimed to have marched to the very foothills but had turned back because of the frightful choking darkness— told how they'd seen two giant figures trading blows. One was black as starless night, the other brighter than the daystar. The two titans battled on the very pinnacle of the mountain. The fires of their struggle took the forms of monstrous lightning bolts that resembled swords. Their battle blasted the mountain itself into liquid rock that smoldered for an age (a Kalpa).

The veterans say that the shining figure which was the Father struck His evil opponent with His great flaming sword, which was the celestial fire. He struck with the sword named *Protector of the Cosmos*, they said. And by the power of His irresistible mighty arm, He cut down the Demon-Lord and sliced him into pieces. The Demon-Lord's blood rained down, flooding the lands of the two continents, sizzling like poisonous acid. But the Father transformed the drops of blood into lovely flowers of many brilliant colors, which became butterflies.

In postdiluvian times following the great struggle, one might catch a glimpse of these divine flowers, gently borne aloft by the Great Winds of the world. Whence the flowers came and went no priest has ever said, except that they water the lands with the Father's blessings. Therefore they say that the entire world is the Father's garden, and the queeti are His gardeners. He is the Strong Protector of the Cosmos.

A Fourth (Late) Account:

Everyone knows that we grow and multiply, and that our numbers fill the two continents of the world. Our abilities, our stores of knowledge and our power are as great as our numbers. We are masters of the world. We rule over all others. All creatures bow before us. All are our servants.

We are the special ones, set apart from all other beings. The Father created the world specifically for our benefit and pleasure. In order to accomplish such a creation (for our sake), He banished the offending chaos. That is, He pronounced and established *laws* designed specifically to make the world habitable for such as us. Ancient, illiterate peasants personified the chaos, calling it Demon-Lord or something similar, as, say, the primitive word: *ghoul*.

EXALTED FATHER

Anathema on those who claim that the Father cannot be known! Anathema on those who say that the Father is the impersonal laws of the cosmos! For they worship the creation and not the creator.

In these times we have discarded the name "queeti", feeling that it is too diminutive for such extraordinary creatures as ourselves. We wear not the pelt of the beast, *nor did we ever*. We walk upright and adorn our bodies with the finest raiment. We call ourselves "the elect," or less popular and more awkward (and more ancient), "The Tribes of Men." According to some linguists the term originally meant something like "the noble ones," "the bright ones," or "the powerful." Many people have come to prefer the word *human*, another ancient word that some linguists claim was the original term for the Father's kind and those mythical sons of the Father.

These days, crowded cities grow along the banks of the Redrain and the Topartz. We have brought civilization to the valley of the Pearldew on the Northern Continent, once named Greenbottom (none know the name's origins).

Some archaeologists claim to have discovered evidence for an earlier civilization in the northern valley of the Pearldew, perhaps the mythical Tribe of Akkad, thus confirming at least a few parts of the *Books of Marduk*. Some even claim to have found rock formations that may be the ruins of the mythical Emerald.

Others scoff at such claims. Gullible people, even scholars—and especially scholars of antiquity—see in the rocks exactly what they're looking for, much as superstitious persons believe in the literal truth of the *Books of Marduk*.

We know that the story of *Exalted Father* is spiritually true, and we trust that some of it is literally accurate, though this may be hard to prove, especially to the hard-headed. Such people need to keep their dangerous poppy-chock to themselves lest they disturb and frighten normal people.

THE BOOKS OF MARDUK

A Modern Commentary

The Scholarly Consensus: We must not grant the far-past power over our freedom in the present. We must not allow the past to become yet another tyrant. These legends and myths—we ought to abandon the word "history"—come from hopeful (and nightmarish) imaginations of generations of queeti poet-historians. Who could have possibly witnessed all the events, or been privy to the very thoughts here narrated?

That said—we know the essential truth of these legends and myths. They speak of higher things than mere facts of profane history.

Some scholars say that the *Fourth Account* implies an animal-like coarseness, a kind of atavism, lurking within us. It is true that the so-called queeti are our primitive ancestors. They are something of an embarrassment. Alas, they still belong to the human species.

It has been well documented by modern science that there exists a tremendous amount of variation within a species. It may well be that the primitive queeti resembled these clownish caricatures in the *Books of Marduk*. But they were certainly not animals nor related to animals; they were created in the divine and glorious image of the Father. *And this Father must be a personal being.* How could the impersonal create the personal? How could something come from nothing? They (and we) are proof of the Father's magnificent guiding hand by which He governs all creation and from which meaning and purpose direct our lives. And some day we will join with Him in the Kingdoms of the Heavens, where we will live forever.

The Minority's Response: It must be admitted, however, that in these times there seems to be within us a certain restlessness, a rootlessness, which is like an inner yearning—perhaps it is, on the contrary, free-floating—a fear even, that time is moving too fast, that we are hurtling through the void, lost, and know not where we are or where we are going.

The problem, pitiful fools will say, is that the elect of the world, we humans, are still mortal, and in this we are the same as every other creature, no matter how lowly, and this is quite embarrassing. Somewhat paradoxically, reason tells us that we are unlike any creature. Reason proves that we are unique, special, apart, though in the dark of night, haunted by our mortality, we feel differently.

Priests, naturally, teach us that we will conquer mortality and continue on to live with the Father in the Kingdoms of the Heavens. This assertion is often made regardless of the fact that no priest has ever conceived a satisfactory and clear image of the Kingdoms of the Heavens (except for a vague gesture, a hand-waving, to the stars) and just how (and what) survives to go live there. Those that make an attempt encounter all sorts of absurdities and paradoxes (for example, do the elect defecate in the Heavens, have sex, eat, drink, play?). Either these writers sound ridiculous, or their compositions are far too abstract and airy to be meaningful in the service of life.

Perhaps there are other, deeper and more subtle meanings beneath the surface of these fantastic (yet logical) creations, but they tend to slip away like vague clouds that mimic vessels disappearing over a misty horizon, calling back in voices heard only in dreams.

So says the Minority.

And they add this:

Our restlessness, our illness too, is irritated and fed by rumors that drift through our cities like the Two Winds. It is said that in those few unsettled regions at the edges of civilization, especially those uncanny shadowed groves that encircle noxious green ponds, lives a race of strange beings. Usually at daybreak, or at dusk, when the light and darkness still dance together and the world refuses to click into place, an unwary traveler might by chance catch a glimmer of golden light. At times they claim to hear eerie, some say mocking, laughter. Perhaps they spy a white mist in the trees. Some have even claimed to have seen large, cat-like creatures silently watching their passage. They never hear these things laugh, but the phantom cats always appear to be smiling. Others say the beings are human-like in form and stature, but taller, noble, and infinitely more beautiful.

Many believe the laughter mocking, but others say that they hear bright, high voices, like children at play. No scholar can say for sure whether or not these ephemeral beings exist. They seem to slip in and out of the real world like brief but vivid dreams.

Critics, of course, regulate them to myth and legend, stories told to young ones in the dark of winter.

Having no other word for these beings except "watchers" or "spirits and ghosts," scholars have come to invent one. In actual fact, they themselves did not truly create the term. An archaeologist accidently discovered it while digging in ancient ruins at the base of an extinct volcanic mountain in the south. The site was extremely ancient. Deep in a cave she discovered papyrus sheaves, many thousands of years old. After nearly a century of study, scholars were finally able to decipher the script and language. As it turned out, the language predated the *Books of Marduk*, and yet was related to it. Some claim it is the root language, but this is by no means settled.

As to the word: given the majority opinion for the moment, it seems to be a term used by the ancients to mean "the weather," or "predicting the weather," or "the position of the stars at the beginning of spring." In this context the word simply means *to revolve*, or to *evolve. The Evolved Ones.*

However, there is a minority opinion, which is held by others including the discoverer of the texts. At one time, during those dark ages, the ancients used this word to describe our Father who defeated the Demon-lord upon the mountain. The name was later generalized to include all greater beings that haunted the imaginations of the primitive Tribes of Men. Such beings slid in and out of reality,

EXALTED FATHER

haunting dreams, populating the wilds of the unknown, responsible for both hope and fear.

The word invented to describe these wraiths is:

Gods.

THE END

CPSIA information can be obtained
at www.ICGtesting.com
Printed in the USA
LVHW11s1731190918
590669LV00005B/686/P